1975

This book may be kept

# FOURTEEN DAYS

A fine will be charged for each day the book is kept overtime.

| | | | |
|---|---|---|---|
| | | | |
| | | | |
| | | | |
| | | | |
| | | | |
| | | | |
| | | | |
| | | | |
| | | | |
| | | | |
| | | | |
| | | | |
| | | | |
| | | | |
| | | | |
| | | | |
| | | | |
| | | | |
| | | | |
| GAYLORD 142 | | | PRINTED IN U.S.A. |

# Utopian Literature

Advisory Editor:
*ARTHUR ORCUTT LEWIS, JR.*
*Professor of English*
The Pennsylvania State University

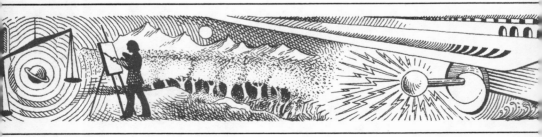

# American Utopias

SELECTED SHORT FICTION

*Edited, with an Introduction*
*by Arthur O. Lewis, Jr.*

ARNO PRESS & THE NEW YORK TIMES
NEW YORK · 1971

Reprint Edition 1971 by Arno Press Inc.
Introduction Copyright 1971 by Arno Press Inc.

Reprinted from a copy in The Pennsylvania State University Library

LC# 77-154448
ISBN 0-405-03530-6

Utopian Literature
ISBN for complete set: 0-405-03510-1

Manufactured in the United States of America

# TABLE OF CONTENTS

# INTRODUCTION

THE ELEVEN PIECES COLLECTED IN THIS VOLUME have little in common with each other except that they are short, fictional, utopian in intent, and have been relatively inaccessible to the ordinary reader. They offer a wide range of chronology, ideology, and literary technique and merit. Taken together they provide a reasonable view of many—though obviously not all—of the utopian ideas which have been prevalent in the United States since 1790. Because of their short length no one of these pieces presents a complete utopia, but among them they demonstrate something of the social, political, economic, and moral characteristics which have been of most interest to Americans. They serve as an introduction to the larger writings, or, for those who are already familiar with the genre, as a supplement to the major works.

The earliest and shortest of the selections, "An Allegorical Description of a Certain Island and Its Inhabitants," was published in the *Massachusetts Magazine* in 1790 and does not appear to have been reprinted previous to the present volume. The island is part of "the extensive dominions of the King of *Utopia*"; its inhabitants are "a sort of exiles [sic]; but not in a state of perpetual banishment, unless they continue incorrigibly rebellious." Clues to the intended allegory are not difficult to find. The unidentified author prefaces his work with slightly more than three lines of poetry from "Young" and follows it with four more lines. The poetry is actually seven lines drawn from Night Four, "The Christian Triumph," of Edward Young's *Night Thoughts* (1742-1744), divided in the middle of the fourth line by the Description itself. The section of Young's long poem from which these lines come deals with Young's belief that mankind can be reunited with God through the Christian faith. The "certain island," therefore, is simply this life, and the King of Utopia is God. The work is concerned less with what utopia may be than with how mankind may return from the island to Utopia and with the difficulties which have been placed in the way of this return. Utopia, then, is reunion with God, and this brief work presents one of the strongest of utopian ideals—the view that only through submission to God's will can utopia be reached. The location of this Christian-oriented land is "In the vast ocean of space."

Later proponents of this way to Utopia have been more specific and have placed it in Heaven (Elizabeth S. P. Ward, *Beyond the Gates,* 1884), in lost Eden (T. Wharton Collens, *Eden of Labor,* 1876), in Paradise regained (David Moore, *The Age of Progress,* 1856), on Mars (James Cowan, *Daybreak,* 1896), and, of course, in America (Sylvester Judd, *Margaret,* 1845; Edward Everett Hale, *How They Lived in Hampton,* 1888; and many others).

*Equality* is more substantial, the most completely described utopia in this volume, probably the earliest such work published in America, written by an American. Its author has been tentatively identified as Dr. James Reynolds of Philadelphia. The work was first published, in eight installments, in *The Temple of Reason* in 1802 and republished in book form in 1847 and 1947 and as a pamphlet in 1863. The first three appearances indicate something of its attraction. *The Temple of Reason* was a short-lived periodical advocating "a religion of benevolent theism, enlarged and generous popular instruction, and a political administration based upon, and guided by, those American Principles of which Paine was the expounder, the American nation in revolution, the proclaimer and vindicator, Jefferson the faithful and consistent administrator," (*Preface,* 1837). The first book edition was published by the Liberal Union of Philadelphia with a warning that it was full of errors and yet contained much to "encourage the best hopes of the true lover of Humankind." The pamphlet of 1863 was published by J. P. Mendum who was also the publisher of the *Boston Investigator,* "a weekly paper, devoted to the protection and development of Universal Mental Liberty, by means of those genuine Liberal Principles which are founded in Truth, Nature, Reason and Free Inquiry." All three of these publishers were concerned with reform of existing society. The last book publication was by the Prime Press, in 1947, as volume one of a proposed series of early utopian novels which appears to have petered out after publication of the second volume.

*Equality,* short as it is, contains many of the principles to be found in later utopian writings. Thus, on the island of Lithconia, money has been abandoned, each citizen's four hours of daily work being regarded as payment for anything he needs; those over fifty are not required to work. Emphasis is on useful articles; ornamentation of buildings and production of decorative objects, for example, are volunteer labor for fame or love of country. The island is devoid of towns and markets; all houses (built on identical plans) are placed along the roads, with public houses at the crossroads. Transportation, by a kind of railroad system, is fast and efficient. Food, clothing, and other needed items are distributed at regular intervals by the government, and farmers and manufacturers have nothing to do with the selling of their products. Family life has been abolished, as has marriage (as a result "women are transformed into angels"). Children leave their mothers at the age of five, and at fifteen receive their own private apartments. Education is universal, state controlled, and mostly of a practical nature. One may live wherever and with whomever he wishes.

As in many utopias, there is no need for lawyers, clergy, physicians, or professional soldiers (although universal military service is required). Personal crimes may be forgiven by the injured party, but for crimes against the public there is no pardon; jury duty is on an alphabetical, compulsory basis. Government is by district, with only those over fifty participating and those over sixty only if they choose to do so. There is no need for elections: in Lithconia's almost unique system the oldest person present automatically presides and the youngest serves as secretary at assemblies which decide all necessary matters. Variations of these characteristics are commonplace in numerous later utopias and need no special comment.

More important are the three chief principles which have produced Lithconia's success after much trial and error: The first step to every subsequent improvement was that "of getting the people into the habit of peaceably expressing their will, and of having it accurately known." The second step was the elimination of the basic evil of giving land to individuals; such practices had caused the separation of people into the rich and the poor and the development of institutions which served only to limit humanity. What made the difference was passage of a law which gave to the poor and to those without land the proceeds of those lands for which there was no direct heir; as more and more persons became members of the group protected by this common fund, those who held property separately found it to be a disadvantage, and eventually all land reverted to the government to be held for the benefit of all the people. The final step was adoption of the practice of making every possible use of machinery to save manual labor; inventors of labor-saving machinery were generously rewarded, with consequent development of better and better devices to reduce the effort required of human beings. Later examples of utopias using similar principles are numerous. Thus, for example, land reform is basic to Albert Chavannes' *The Future Commonwealth* (1892) and to Thomas McGrady's *Beyond the Black Ocean* (1901), peaceable expression of the will of the people is the means to development of utopia in Frederick Adams' *President John Smith* (1897), William Dean Howells' *A Traveler from Altruria* (1895), and especially William Child's *The Legal Revolution of 1902* (1898); and wise use of machinery is largely responsible for the good life in Alexander Craig's *Ionia* (1898), and Chauncy Thomas' *The Crystal Button* (1891).

"Three Hundred Years Hence" was first published in 1836, the longest piece in the anonymous volume, *Camperdown, or, News from Our Neighbourhood,* and again, separately, in 1950, as Number Two in the abortive series of which *Equality* was the first. The author has been identified as Mrs. Mary Griffith. As in many utopian works, the hero dreams of the future, in this case a Jeffersonian, agrarian democracy. Mrs. Griffith's utopia offers no drastic changes but rather shows a world 300 years into her own future which is the logical—though technologically much advanced—development of the society she herself knew. As might be expected, she places emphasis on the role of women in society and on the need for a greater concern with religion, but there are no surprises. Thus, college education stresses both the practical and the liberal arts, each student being required to learn a trade or handicraft as well as a profession. New kinds of machinery have made the world better: fast moving vehicles, balloons, mechanical plows and agricultural combines, huge road building and construction machinery are commonplace. Cities have become more fireproof; water supplies are pure and more abundant; markets are clean and convenient. The only tax is a direct tax on the value of a man's labor, property, or business, and this tax is sufficient to conduct the government. Railroads are under joint control of the national and state governments, and highways have been much improved. The slavery question has been solved by moving all slaves to Liberia and "other healthy colonies," with compensation for their owners. It is a clean, well-regulated world in which the arts play an important role, where disease is uncommon, where international trade is important, and where the moral influence of women has abolished war. Children are better treated; women have extensive property rights and have taken their place in the business world. For the author, an important characteristic of this society is that clergymen and professors are not only well paid but also never lured away from their positions by offers of higher pay. As is so often the case in utopia, liquor and tobacco have been banned as part of the moral reformation. Although it is doubtful that later utopian writers were much aware of Mrs. Griffith's work, there are similarities. Among the more noteworthy are Edward Bellamy's method of presentation in *Looking Backward* (1888), John Macnie's view of practical education in *The Diothas* (1883), Milan C. Edson's concern with agriculture in *Solaris Farm* (1900), and H. Pereira Mendes' emphasis on the role of the clergy in *Looking Ahead* (1899).

Although a statistical survey could never be completed with any degree of accuracy, it would appear that one of the characteristics of American utopian writers is the frequency with which they choose their native land as the place where utopia will someday come to be. Where European utopians have tended to find the perfect world in some yet-undiscovered realm (as, of course, have some Americans), the American mode has been based on the belief that this land will indeed become that best of all possible worlds which has been so much a part of the American dream. Such is the case in the two selections published in *Voices from the Kenduskeag*.

Placed only a century ahead in time from that of publication, the "Vision of Bangor" and its "Sequel" are excellent illustrations of that civic pride which has been so great a moving force in the development of the United States, as well as of the intellectual ferment of mid-nineteenth century small-town society—even one on the edge of the wilderness like the Bangor of 1848. Even the impulse to publication of the "Bangor Book" is typical of small-town enterprise. In the comparatively lengthy introduction to the "Vision," it becomes clear that, under the influence of feminine civic leaders, a number of persons have been persuaded to contribute to a book which is to be sold by subscription "for the cause of the fatherless and the destitute." The interplay between Governor Edward Kent, who has been identified as author of the "Vision," and Mrs. Jane Sophia Appleton, editor of the book as a whole, who has also been identified as author of the "Sequel," sets the tone. There are unifying observations in the two works and a quiet, often witty, criticism of each other that adds to the charm of the two pieces. Both use the dream technique as entrance to the world of 1978, and, since they are complementary to each other, can profitably be examined together in some detail.

Kent, following the gentle but persuasive demand of the editor that he finally write his contribution, dreams of his own city of Bangor in 1978, a time close enough to his own so that he feels reasonably at home. Characteristics of the new world are splendid buildings, rapid transportation, abolition of slavery, a much increased population, and, as reading one of several available daily papers demonstrates, a nation now extended through all of South America. The dollar remains representative of value, but lumbering, the chief industry of the city in Kent's day, has given way to trading and manufacturing in cotton, woolens, and mixed goods. Of great interest to Kent, presumably because of his discussion with the fair editor, is the status of the family and of women. His inquiry in regard to the community system (obviously much talked of in Bangor in his day) produces the information that "that nonsense died a natural death, and with it the kindred absurdities of women's rights to participate in government and to direct affairs out doors as well as in." Apparently, there had been some attempt to set up community bakeries, laundries, and restaurants, and to put women into governmental positions. But all this ended, as Kent's informer points out, because women could not be kept in party lines (they cast their votes for all the wrong reasons), the legislature was unable to accomplish its business (female members insisted on keeping hairdressing appointments, but not legislative secrets). Thus, "after a considerable struggle between the sexes, they both became satisfied that it was best to compromise, and let the *women* rule indoors, and the *men* out." Kent's twentieth-century Bangor is thus more beautiful and somewhat more prosperous but really little changed from his own day. Before awakening he notes without comment his discovery that alcohol has been banned and that the orphan asylum for which the book had been commissioned is thriving.

Following her reading of Kent's vision, Mrs. Appleton dreams that she is the same dreamer. Somewhat longer, the "Sequel" deals with more matters than the "Vision," but "corrects," from the feminine point of view, some of the things Kent had learned earlier. His first discovery is a building in which the weapons of war have been kept "both as curiosities, and as affecting memorials of the atrocities" now banned forever. Next, he learns that churches have agreed not "to *set themselves in antagonism with each other*" and that all go along quietly worshipping in their own way, bothering the others not at all. A long description of the demise of secret societies as represented by the Odd Fellows is followed by the dreamer's attempt to speak gallantly, as in his own time, to a fair lady, and this leads to a discussion of the role of women in the new Bangor. As the dreamer's informant puts it, "Your age *fondled* woman. *Ours* honors her. You gave her *compliments*. We give her *rights.*" Men and women work together to produce a better society. Both men and women are educated in the broadest possible way: "to fit them for their entrance into the cares and toils of life." At this point, Mrs. Appleton's Bangor differs from that of Kent, for the community system has been continued. Although, as Kent had been informed, people continue to live in families, the influence of Fourier has brought about development of cooperative restaurants, laundries, bakeries, and other public conveniences. Because women no longer work so hard merely to keep house, they are able to take active roles in any business they may desire and, as a result, marriage and the family have been strengthened. Appleton and Kent agree on one matter—women are not involved in government—but for very different reasons. In Kent's "Vision" women were regarded as incapable of taking part in the government. In Appleton's "Sequel," they have chosen not to be part of it. At one time "men became completely eaten up with the love of money" and had little interest in anything else, including government. "If their attention was called to any other matters than those which touched their pockets," they would say, "I'll—go home and ask my wife." The result was that women were really running the country whether they wanted to or not. "At last, things got to such a pass that the female part of the community concluded it would not do." Their ensuing, but undescribed actions were effective: "Once more order and beauty were restored to society, and men became men again."

Incomplete as they are, the two Bangor visions give an indication of the kind of talk which must have been going on in the intellectual and cultural circles of towns all over the United States in the middle of the nineteenth century. Their concern for the end of slavery, for beautification of cities, for helping orphaned children, for expansion of women's horizons, for an end to religious bickering, for better education, for expansion of trade, for the end of hypocrisy in social life are all part of what might be a better world. If they paid little attention to the techniques of producing this better world (thus, Kent describes only briefly the transportation system and Appleton barely mentions means for laying dust in the streets), at least their concerns were for those things which would make life more human and livable. One likes to think that this gently satiric but pleasant description of the future (which attains only its second printing in the present collection) had some real effect on the people of Bangor in the years following its publication.

Cyrus Elder's dream (not previously reprinted) is a slight piece and of comparatively little literary merit. Although the word *utopia* never appears in this story, the selection has a place in the present collection because it describes, albeit satirically, a world in which the principle of *laissez faire* has been carried to its "logical" extreme. To those who objected to the difficulties of life in nineteenth-century America, a frequent reply was that of the free traders to the effect that laws got in the way of production. Greater production would lead to cheaper goods which, in turn, would lead to a better life in which people might do what they wished rather than the difficult things required by society. The professor-narrator of this story dreams of "the happy country of *Laissez Faire,* where the laws interfere in no way with the employments of the people, and everybody does what is easiest to him." His brief visit demonstrates the harm resulting from literal application of the principle: there are no taxes, no schools, no farms, no business, no houses, no transportation. Even children are no more and, as we discover to our amazement, there is in fact only one remaining inhabitant, and a scrawny one at that. This is heavy-handed satire, but it criticizes some of the same aspects of society as do Bellamy's famous parable of the stagecoach and Satterlee's less well known dream of Working Man's Pond. That the *Laissez Faire* solution has not totally disappeared is made evident in even so recent a utopian work as Ayn Rand's *Atlas Shrugged* (1957).

Unquestionably the most important literary figure represented in this volume is Mark Twain, and short as this description of "The Curious Republic of Gondour" is, there is enough in it to make one wish he had written more. And it is strange that he did not, for surely he was that right combination of idealist and skeptic which has been responsible for some of the best utopian writing. His lifelong dissatisfaction with society is clear, as even the most cursory reading of such works as *Pudd'nhead Wilson, The Mysterious Stranger,* "The Man That Corrupted Hadleyburg," "To The Person Sitting in Darkness," and even the irate letter to the gas company will demonstrate. That Mark Twain believed life could be improved is made evident by his continued devotion of time, energy, and literary talent to good causes, as well as by such literary examples as Huck Finn's decision to protect Nigger Jim and the present seldom-noticed but worthy utopian piece. Although it was published anonymously, Twain was encouraged by his good friend, William Dean Howells (who was himself later to produce some of the most important utopian writing of the century), to continue the work, and there is some evidence that Twain intended to do so. However, like so many of his projects, this too was never completed and was, in fact, not published in book form until 1919, nine years after his death.

There is nothing new in the basic premise, which is simply to improve society by having the intellectuals take charge. As far back as Plato's Guardians, such had been a goal of utopian writers, and most utopias have been designed to achieve this kind of government. It is the method which sets this one apart; as always Twain is not only idealistic but also practical in his proposal. In this multiple-vote society two roads to additional votes are recognized:

The first is the practical road of allowing accumulation of wealth to determine some votes. This is, of course, the way it is in the real world. Even in a one-man-one-vote society, men of property may cast only one vote but they have always had greater influence than their single vote would insure. Granting of multiple votes for accumulation of property simply brings this fact into proper perspective. But more important is the second, more idealistic road, that of "immortal votes" produced through education. Since the ordinary multiple vote can be lost if the property is lost, it soon becomes obvious that the immortal votes are the only ones worth having, and in Gondour, rather than accumulate property, men begin to work toward greater education. The result is that the best educated men are those who are most honored, and they are the men who establish the directions society is to take. In showing the effects of this much-to-be-desired end, Twain, satirist that he was, could not resist criticism of some of the things he disliked in his own world, such as the spoils system, the ability to buy justice, the selfish drive for more wealth, the ride to the top of those least suited to be at the top, and, above all, the lack of patriotism among his contemporaries. The multiple vote idea did not attract much attention; the most recent and almost the only book to propose the system is Nevil Shute's *In the Wet* (1953). Still, one may regret that Twain did not continue Gondour; with his great humanity and enormous talent, his might well have been the definitive American utopia.

In terms of public response, the most successful utopian writer of all times was Edward Bellamy. *Looking Backward* (1888), and its sequel, *Equality* (1897), inspired hundreds of other utopian works, some concerned with forwarding Bellamy's views and some with attacking them as unworkable. Nationalist clubs were formed to attempt to implement some of Bellamy's proposals, and at least in the United States, the impact of these clubs on politics was considerable.

Bellamy also wrote a number of other, shorter utopian works of which perhaps the best is "To Whom This May Come." This well-written story makes no attempt to describe a complete utopia as do the novels. Most of the emphasis is placed on what can only be labeled a gimmick. But it is this gimmick that produces the perfect society, which, whether it is so-named or not, is really Utopia. On the small island where the narrator is shipwrecked, development of the ability to understand each other through telepathy has led these happy people to a high state of perfection. The narrator "discovers the delightful exhilaration of moral health and cleanness, the breezy oxygenated mental condition, which resulted from the consciousness that I had absolutely nothing concealed!" Such self-knowledge leads to perfect marriage, perfect families, perfect society, for since nothing can be concealed, each person becomes more aware of others and wishes only to do good for them. In some ways, this easy more-than-human solution avoids the true problem of achieving utopia, but its existence adds to our understanding of Bellamy's longer works. The impulse to utopia in Bellamy was in his deep conviction that human beings are better than they seem to be and that it is only necessary to remove the obstacles of mistrust and physical ill to create men near to the angels. Such a condition was Bellamy's real goal. The importance of this short story in his own mind is demonstrated by the fact that its first periodical publication was in the year immediately following *Looking Backward* and its first book publication, as part of a collection including several similar stories, in the year following *Equality*.

*The Milltillionaire* is a short but eclectic piece which incorporates many widely varying utopian ideas; it has not been previously reprinted. The actual date of publication is not known although internal evidence suggests the middle of the 1890's. Nor is it clear why the author, who has been identified as Albert Waldo Howard, chose so unusual a pseudonym. There is no plot, and the style of writing is, to say the least, peculiar. Even the structure, which is in three parts, is unusual; Part First is made up of one paragraph plus one sentence; Part Second is something less than three pages and simply stops for no apparent reason except to make way for Part Third; Part Third, subtitled "The Earth in the Inaugural Century of the Millenium," comes to an abrupt unprepared-for end on page 30.

The utopia described springs forth fully developed on the first page. Little indication is given of the manner in which the Grand Bardic State came to be beyond the bare statement that the Milltillionaire "with his unlimited wealth" purchased "the land and its attachments incognito through his agents, within a period of a few years" and came to own the entire planet. He is obviously a benevolent despot, for the only revenue he "requires from any individual after attaining the age of twenty-five years is that he allot a minim portion of his time daily, weekly, or annually to the continuance of the Universal Welfare of the Planet." In return for this every individual lives very well indeed.

In this "true millennium" are "laws which recognize no class of criminals of any description, but recognize all individuals as either well, or ill, physically or intellectually." Everything anyone needs is given him for the asking in return for the 15 years of work he renders. There are no private residences; everyone lives in "State Residences (that is Hotels)." All cities are "gradually transformed into immense palaces nicely intermingled with fragrant gardens and luxuriant parks— there being no dirty streets or unsightly habitations of any description."

The most interesting idea presented in this utopia is that of the Triple Canopied Highway. Two hundred feet in width, with 400 feet of lawn (used for recreation) on each side, and providing two levels for one-way traffic for electric vehicles and a third, or upper, level for pedestrians and cyclists, as well as the canopy itself for these latter in fair weather, these structures are "as secure from all storms and dust and heat as the marbled hall of any palace." The huge freight and utilities subways beneath the highways solve the problem of air and noise pollution. Structurally, these highways are not as impressive as the Viaduct Railway 15,000 feet in the air "built upon the principle of a gigantic suspension bridge" from city to city or the buildings which "tower several thousand feet in the air, the smallest of which is capable of housing comfortably and luxuriously one million citizens." There are only about twenty cities "the smallest of which possesses a population of one hundred trillion inhabitants," circular in form with a diameter of about 200 miles. (The chief city of the world, BARDO-CITO-UNO, was once Boston and has a population of one quadrillion souls; other cities named were, in order of size, once Paris, Chicago, San Francisco, Berlin, London, Venice, New York, St. Petersburg and Canton.)

Among other wonders of this world is the educational system, described in some detail, which begins at age seven and concludes with a five-year stay at the university with graduation at the age of 17, following which are three years of vacation, a four-year post-graduate course of travel and research, and a year in which to choose a vocation; the Socratic method of teaching is used throughout. There is some discussion of science, including the fantastic power source called Omni-Magnetism and its corollary Psycho-omni-magnetism, control of the weather and air conditioning by means of the Calorifico-Electric

Element, government (by a group called the Alphabeta made up of twenty-six Bards, half men, half women), abandonment of tobacco and liquor, telepathic communication, hospitals, and vegetarianism (a two-page sample menu is provided). Most impressive is a description of the "Bardic Capito-Temple of the Planet," 25,000 feet high with an observatory from which one can watch the exploration of "the Planets, the Sun, or the Stars!" The work ends abruptly in the conservatory of music where five million people are listening to a new opera with "the latest and most improved musical instruments, among which is the grand Universo-Piano which renders the sounds of all kinds of musical instruments a la solo, or a l'orchestra, being played electrically or manipulated by hand at option. Anon, combining in a grand chorus the power of five thousand pianos and one thousand pipe-organs in the most Subline [sic] Harmonies and Entrancing Rhapsodies." In fact as the author concludes "What . . . a most grand, lovely and sublime Future!"

It is easy to dismiss *The Milltillionaire* as mere fantasy, the daydream of one who found his own world wanting, but had no real ability to change it. Thus, although Howard presents a grand vision of utopia, his explanations of its marvels are superficial. The most cursory reading will show the impossibility—in the absence of hard evidence—of some of the things he describes. For example, suspension bridges thousands of feet in the air and spanning hundreds of miles do not seem feasible even today. Neither do buildings five miles in height, nor an earth population of "several hundred quadrillions." The most important basic assumption of the work, that one man could accumulate enough wealth to buy all the government, all the land, and all the property on earth and turn it to his own uses, seems even farther fetched. However benevolent his intentions, it is unlikely that any man would be permitted to do so.

On the other hand, some proposals which would have seemed equally impossible in Howard's day are not unusual in ours. Social security numbers differ little from the Bardic State's "life-numbers" and they are used for much the same purposes. Satellites circumnavigate the globe well under the two hours of Howard's "Air Line"; men have walked on the moon if not on the planets; earth's population expands with ever increasing speed; buildings grow taller, bridges longer, and cities larger; freeways, double-decker highways, shopping plazas, and all-weather sports stadiums are part of our daily life.

To list Howard's sources or indicate other works in which similar ideas may be found would require a very long bibliography of utopian writings. However, a few resemblances are worth noting. Mysterious devices draw energy from the air in William Alexander Taylor's *Intermere* (1901); vegetarianism is practiced in Henry Olerich's *A Cityless and Countryless World* (1893) and in Herman Hine Brinsmade's *Utopia Achieved* (1912); spectacular engineering feats are at the heart of Charles William Wooldridge's *Perfecting the Earth* (1902) and Alvarado M. Fuller's *A.D. 2000* (1890). Creation of the new society through the power of gold is the subject of both Ignatius Donnelly's *The Golden Bottle* (1892) and H. R. Chamberlain's *6,000 Tons of Gold* (1894).

In some ways "The Coup d'Etat of 1961" is also a demonstration of the power of one man's wealth to change the world. In this case the new society is not worldwide but simply a new American empire, created through one man's use of his enormous wealth to manipulate the political structure to his own ends. This short pseudo-history describes the chief events of a ten-year period, 1950 to 1960, "Now that a generation has passed since the disturbed events of which I write." The change occurs with surprising ease and little bloodshed. Robert Campbell's rapid acquisition of a fortune through application of a technique for improving the fertility of arid regions of the southwestern part of the country, his subsequent control of seven states, his appointment as governor-general of the Chinese provinces ceded to the United States by England as a prize of war, his success in buying up most of the business of the country following the panic of 1960, the decision against his rival, Hugo Schmidt, by the United States Circuit Court of Arizona, and his seizure of power at Schmidt's inauguration with help from several regiments of the Arizona militia and the private forces of powerful corporations owned by his faction have the ring of possibility about them. It comes as no surprise to learn that Campbell gains complete control and that by the time of the writing he had been re-elected president every four years till his death, with his son then succeeding to the titles of "Lord Suzerain of South America, High Protector of China, Chief Ruler of the Pacific Archipelago." Nor is it surprising to learn that the sole business of Congress is to authorize stock transactions. It is, we quickly come to feel, all too possible, an example of still another way to the better society, to accept, as have so many, the belief that those of great wealth are best qualified to govern, and that if they choose to do so in dictatorial fashion, one need not complain if he has enough to eat. Sedgwick claims "impartiality" without "political bias," and he is reasonably successful. However, there is something tongue-in-cheek about the statement near the end that "This elasticity of the Constitution is mainly due, not to the forefathers who framed it, but to those greater interpreters of the last century who have realized that law is founded on policy. . . ." It is not unreasonable to assume that, like Sinclair Lewis in *It Can't Happen Here* (1935) and David Karp in *One* (1953), to name two among many, Sedgwick wrote to warn against any dictatorship, however benevolent. Similar uses of pseudo-history to describe the coming of the better world are found in Arthur Bird's *Looking Forward* (1899) and H. Pereira Mendes' *Looking Ahead* (1899).

From its beginnings Utopia has meant a land of plenty, a material well-being for humanity. Achievement of this goal has meant increased production and better distribution of goods, and many of the best utopian writers have devoted much of their attention to these matters. Some—for example, Frank Rosewater in *'96: A Romance of Utopia* (1884)—have taken the view that limitation of production for any reason is the chief cause of poverty for the individual and evil in society.

Frederick Pohl's "The Midas Plague" starts from the premise that this utopian goal has been achieved. Production is not only maximum but out of control and the cause of social difficulty. This satiric, well written, and perhaps prophetic short story deals with a society in which the need to consume is overwhelming and the duty to consume is the individual's most important social responsibility. Status is achieved by using up more and more of the national product; success means classification at a higher level where less consumption is expected. Thus, the poor are those required to consume most, and the story's poor hero, Morey Fry with his "twenty-six rooms, five cars, nine robots," envies his wife's wealthy parents, their five-room cottage, tiny runabout, and "severely simple and probably rented garments."

Robots have made the difference, for they turn out whatever is needed—and much more—ceaselessly: "The pipeline of production spewed out riches that no king in the time of Malthus could have known. But a pipeline has two ends. The invention and power and labor pouring in at one end must somehow be drained out at the other." Our hero thus finds himself forced to eat and drink more than he can hold, to attend circuses, operas, and nightclubs, to wear out athletic equipment he has no time to use, even to undergo group therapy in which he is the sole patient of eleven assorted medical men—all under pain of demotion to a still poorer class if he fails in his duty.

In the end, Morey solves the problem by creating "A real closed cycle," robots with built-in "satisfaction circuits" who will use up the various products that human beings cannot. For this feat he is "thanked, complimented, rewarded, given a ticker-tape parade through the city." Man's ingenuity has conquered again, and he now has the best of two worlds, that of conspicuous consumption and that of doing as he pleases. Neither inadequate supply nor overproduction can henceforth affect him. What is needed is there; what is not needed is re-cycled. Pohl's satire appears to be founded on the solid ground of faith in man's progress. What appeared at first to be anti-utopian has, in its own way, become as pro-utopian as any selection in the volume, and only the title with its reminder of the fate of Midas provides the possibility that the final solution has not been attained. Later publication in a collection of similar stories, *The Case Against Tomorrow,* would seem to support this view.

It would be foolish to attempt to draw profound conclusions about so diversified a collection as this one. The most that can be said is that these eleven short pieces are honest reflections of the times and places in which they first appeared. Taken together they show American aspirations to a better world over a period of nearly two centuries. If most of the goals they set have not yet been attained, history shows that, on the whole, the nation has not done badly, and, as the author of "An Allegorical Description" put it: "all have reasonable grounds to believe, that if they will but accommodate their minds to their situation, it will be comfortable; that if they will exert themselves to retrieve their circumstances and character, they shall not exert themselves in vain." Such accommodation and such exertion are the stuff of which these works have been made.

ARTHUR O. LEWIS
MAY 1971

# AN ALLEGORICAL DESCRIPTION
## OF A
## CERTAIN ISLAND AND ITS INHABITANTS

FOR THE MASSACHUSETTS MAGAZINE.

# The PHILANTHROPIST. No. XVI.

An allegorical DESCRIPTION of a certain ISLAND and its INHABITANTS.

> " From Nature's *Continent*, immensely wide,
> " Immensely blest, this little *Isle of life*,
> " This dark, incarcerating *Colony*,
> " Divides us." —————————— YOUNG.

IN the vast ocean of space, which is continually traversed by myriads of active beings, for the various purposes of negotiation and benevolence, there is a certain island belonging to the extensive dominions of the King of *Utopia*. This island, though remote and small, compared with the whole territory of this monarch, may be seen from several of the other islands with which this ocean is interspersed. When viewed at a distance by transnavigators, it appears uniform and beautiful, and as a fit habitation for innocence and indefectibility. But upon a nearer approach, it looks less inviting. The shores and surface are, for the most part, broken and inhospitable, and the atmosphere frequently obscured by fogs and clouds, agitated by tempestuous winds, and rendered insalubrious by noxious exhalations. Yet it is inhabited by a race of beings, who, though almost universally uneasy and dissatisfied with their situation, are so much attached to the island, as to be exceeding loth to quit it, even at the invitation or summons of their prince. There have been various opinions with respect to the nature and qualities both of the island and its inhabitants. But all in general, are agreed, that the people, by some misdemeanor, have, at some time or other, incurred the displeasure of their sovereign, and were destined to this island as a suitable place in which they might do penance, and receive those meliorating corrections which they have merited, and which are fitted to restore them to a temper of obedience, and thereby to the favour of their prince. They are a sort of ex-

iles; but not in a state of perpetual banishment, unless they continue incorrigibly rebellious. They have no right to quit the island without special permission : Yet here and there one is daring enough to make the attempt, by plunging, uncalled, into the ocean. But these are considered, by their fellow delinquents, as cowardly and sneaking, and by their sovereign, as putting a finishing hand to their incurable rebellion. It is observed that these islanders are recalled promiscuously, without any regular order, and often without warning or notice. And the herald who is sent to summon them, generally appears, and is considered, more like an executioner than a friendly messenger.

But every disadvantage they labour under, has, whether they notice it or not, its counterbalance. During their residence on this island, they receive all their supplies from their king ; and he condescends to send them many tokens and messages to convince them that he is not unpropitious ; that though they wear the marks of degradation and disgrace, and are at a humbling distance from the imperial city, yet he is ready to hearken to any decent petition they may send, however imperfectly conceived or expressed, provided it bears the marks of sincerity and humility.

It is in their power to render the place of their exile agreeable or painful, a place of punishment or enjoyment, according to the sentiments and dispositions which they cherish. None are ignorant to whose jurisdiction they belong, nor of the allegiance they owe. And all have reasonable grounds to believe, that if they will but accommodate their minds to their situation, it will be comfortable; that if they will exert themselves to retrieve their circumstances and character, they shall not exert themselves in vain; that if they will endeavour, in earnest, to regain the favour of their prince, they will regain it; that allowance will be made for the disadvantages they lie under, if they do not plead those disadvantages as an excuse for perverseness and negligence.

The degrees of information among these islanders, respecting the will of their sovereign, and their own duty and destination, are various. Some have no more than can be contained on a small piece of parchment on their breasts, inscribed in a character scarcely legible; yet there is a sentence or two which every one may read and understand, particularly this, *of him, to whom little is given, little will be required*. Others have a large volume of instructions, and a sufficient number of monitors, both to direct and excite them, together with their sovereign's proclamations infixed upon the posts of their doors, and at the corners of their streets. But unhappily, these monitors, who are also the interpreters of the royal orders, agree not among themselves. According to their different turns of mind and complexions of temper, they conceive differently of their sovereign's character and intentions. Some, who are mild and gentle in themselves, give such an amiable representation of their king, as to work upon the benevolent affections and generous principles of the faulty subjects, and, by animating their hopes, call forth their gratitude and obedience. Others, though perhaps as faithful as the former, yet being of a more gloomy and austere disposition, lead those who are of a similar cast, or timid in their make, to entertain an awful idea of their generous prince, as one who is arbitrary and inexorable, and who capriciously bestows upon some of his subjects, and withholds from others, certain peculiar endowments which must come from him, and which he requires in all, upon pain of his perpetual displeasure. From these representations, and also, from the various humiliating circum-

stances and vexations, to which this colony is subjected, some have been ready to admit an unfavourable opinion of their sovereign, as if his government was bordering on the tyrannical. But this is owing to misconception. For they who are best acquainted with his character, who are admitted to the most familiar intercourse with him, and who take an impartial view of his administration, are convinced, that though he is an absolute prince, yet he governs his subjects with benignity and equity; that lenity, forbearance and placability continually beam from his throne, even upon those presumptuous subjects who have reared the standard of rebellion.

Distant and beclouded as this island is, the peaceful shores of the Utopian continent may be discerned from it. Some of the inhabitants have a more clear and distinct view of those delightful abodes than others; but none are wholly precluded. By ascending certain eminences and temples sacred to contemplation, which all are instructed to do, they find the medium so clear, and the organs of vision so strengthened, that they can descry many of the beauties of that inviting region, the glittering spires of the imperial city, and the magnificent palace of their king. All have an intimation that this is their native country, and that they shall be favoured with a return to it, if during their stay on this island, they manifest a fixed allegiance to their sovereign, a fidelity in executing their task, a patient acquiescence in the discipline they are under, and a cherished gratitude for the supplies, the invitations, and the visits they have received. If these intimations are regarded, if these prospects are suffered to have their influence, their views of Utopian splendour and magnificence will be more and more clear and transporting; and they will feel more sensibly the attractive force of that happy country, and perceive their attachments to their imprisoning isle to grow weaker and weaker.

" Happy day! that breaks their chain;
" That manumits; that calls from exile
     home;
" That leads to nature's great *metropolis*,
" And readmits them to their father's
     throne."

# SEQUEL TO THE VISION OF BANGOR IN THE TWENTIETH CENTURY

[ Jane Sophia Appleton ]

## ERRATA.

Page 247, line 10th, read "*elongation* of a point," for "*elongature* of a point."
Page 259, line 18th, read "good puddings; *and* as in," for "good puddings, as in."
Page 260, line 5th, read "actually *enacting*," for "actually *enacted*."
Page 260, line 28th, read "would not out," for "would not *rub* out."

# SEQUEL TO THE "VISION OF BANGOR IN THE TWENTIETH CENTURY."

*"Your young men shall see visions, and your old men shall dream dreams."*

ONE day happening by chance to peep into a gentleman's escritoire, I discovered a " Vision of Bangor in the twentieth century." To my shame be it spoken, I did not resist the temptation thus spread before me, but allowed my curiosity the gratification of reading it from beginning to end. The same night having supped on oysters, *I*, too, had a dream, and what was very singular, it appeared to *join on* most remarkably to the one which had amused me so much in the morning. I seemed even to have entered into the person of the quondam dreamer, and to be actually the same individual. I shall plead therefore the extravagance of a dream, as my apology for merging my identity in his, as I relate the scenes which passed before me.

I stood by a building of very singular and imposing architecture, constructed of hewn stone, and adorned with magnificent paintings from the top to the bottom, which on nearer examination, I found to be emblematic and exquisitely beautiful representations of the triumph of the spirit of peace over that of strife and conquest, among the nations of the earth. I turned to ask the name of this building of the individual who had hitherto acted as my guide, but to my surprise he had disappeared, and in his place stood a hale, hearty old gentleman, with a right honest countenance, and an eye wherein a spice of roguery was bewitchingly blended with a deep, manly earnestness. He seemed to be aware of my situation as a stranger, and as one who had long been absent from these sublunary scenes, and answered me with the utmost good nature.

"That," said he, "is a building wherein are kept the weapons of war, (so far as they could be obtained,) which have been used in all ages of the world.

"They are preserved both as curiosities, and as affecting memorials of the atrocities which the indulgence of evil passions, and the imagined necessity of maintaining what was falsely called 'national honor,' once led the human race to commit."

I had scarcely expressed my congratulations upon the great moral advance of society which the existence of such an edifice for such a purpose argued, when I espied in a neighboring street, in the midst of magnificent piles of stone and marble, a ruined structure, which looked as if it might have been a church, but was so fallen into decay and covered with the "moss of ages," that one could hardly distinguish its original form.

"And what ruin have we here?" I asked. "That was once, I believe, an Episcopal church, although the Episcopalians hardly acknowledge it now. Their present structures are all so splendid, they are unwilling to believe that there was ever an Episcopal church built of wood in this great city. There is an old organ in this building, which report says sometimes sends forth strange sounds at the 'witching hour of night.' The rumor may perhaps be founded upon a tradition, representing it as a most wonderful organ in its day, — being determined to 'go,' with or without hands, unless it was constantly watched! What strange power the eyes of the 'three watchers,' who, the legend says, sat by it day and night, were endowed with, that they could 'hold' the heavenly harmonies, I

know not; but that they had some such power, the fact
that whenever they were careless enough to fall asleep,
the ' troublesome thing *would* go,' strongly intimates."

" What is the present state of religious sects here?"
I asked. " Have they, as some prophesied in my day,
been merged in one universal church?"

" No, they have not, but they have done what I think
is quite as well, ' agreed to disagree.' Each still maintains some distinctive doctrines, but with so much Christian harmony, that a stranger might think them one
united body, divided for convenience into distinct congregations. There has been a great change in the specific items of faith held by some sects since your time,
and others have disappeared entirely. But the greatest
change has been in the *spirit* which pervades the religious community. Where once all was rancor, misrep-
resentation, and hostility, now all is forbearance and
love. The great secret of this change has been, and is,
that sects have ceased to *set themselves in antagonism
with each other*. They go on quietly in their own course,
teach, preach, and live the truths which they think the
gospel inculcates, and *let each other alone*. The hate-
ful voice of religious controversy is now scarcely heard
in our land. Sects do not, even by implication, or by
the application of exclusive titles to themselves, con-
demn each other. Calvinists no longer proclaim their
' *evangelical*' distinctions, nor do Unitarians plume themselves on their ' *liberal*' tendencies. The word ' Orthodox' is obsolete as applied to a sect, and a Unitarian
would stare in astonishment if you should call him a
' liberal Christian.' Baptists have opened their arms
wide to welcome the Christian world to the communion
of their Lord, and, what is the greatest triumph of all,
Episcopalians have done talking about ' *the church*,' and
Swedenborgians have conceded that somebody besides

Swedenborg *can* have a new idea! Thank God, the times of religious *cant* are over!

" So soon as sects ceased to place themselves in a controversial attitude, so soon they began to see that really there was ' some light' in their neighbors.

" Trinitarians found it possible to believe that Unitarians ' *might* be saved upon a pinch,' and Unitarians that Trinitarians were ' not such fools after all,' (as, in spite of their ' *liberality*,' even the most intelligent of their body were apt to think a hundred years ago). The next step in reform, after they had come to *see* clearly the good and truth existing in their neighbors, was, in all Christian humility to adopt it, which they have done, and are daily doing. Thus renouncing their own errors, and receiving others' truths, they are becoming constantly more similar, although whether some great points will ever be harmonized so as to merge the various sects in one church, remains a matter of doubt."

I mused awhile on the delightful state of things I had heard described, and then my thoughts turned to an institution which had always ranked in my estimation next to the church.

" Can you tell me, sir, how many lodges of Odd Fellows there are here?" He put his hand to his head with a bewildered expression — " Odd Fellows," said he, " Odd Fellows — I am sure I have heard the name, and yet I cannot imagine where. Ah! I have it! I have read of them in a volume in the Antiquarian library. I had forgotten the *name* only, for the history of the decline of the institution I remember well. I think they disappeared about the year 1868. The circumstances were not a little peculiar.

" A parcel of wags, bent on finding sport for themselves, having bored a convenient number of holes in the ceiling of the Odd Fellows' assembly room, resolved to look in upon them, and what is more, to *break* in upon them, should they not be discovered before the 'fulness of time' in the execution of their project had arrived. Accordingly, being disguised in grotesque costumes, and armed with the various utensils suited to their purpose, they repaired to their observatory. The scene that was exposed to their view was quite worth describing.

"The chief officer, (his round and sleek proportions would forbid that *he* ever should be accused of being the 'elongature of a point,') who had patiently gone through all the grades of office, until he had reached the highest, was standing upon a rostrum, slowly bowing, until his head touched the ground, waving his arms majestically to and fro, and swaying his body from side to side, with a graceful undulatory motion, while he slowly pronounced a Greek oration. This exercise was intended to promote ease and dignity of manner! Another 'brother' was lying on his back, with his mouth extended to its utmost dimensions, while a third was pouring water down his throat! If he could bear a certain quantity of the fluid, he was to be advanced a degree in the honors of the lodge! A fourth was swinging upon a rope suspended from the ceiling, and at every backward swing receiving from a staging above him, the contents of an immense tub of iced water upon his shoulders! This was a punishment for betraying some of the secrets to his wife! It was such an 'unheard of thing for a *man* to reveal a secret,' as the chief officer remarked, 'that the punishment was rendered more severe than it would otherwise have been.' They did not wish to be cruel, however, and had appointed an officer to read a poem in praise of Odd-Fellowship to him, as an alleviation of his sufferings! A group of six or seven young men, (as yet uninitiated), were standing huddled together in a corner, making wry faces at each other. The fortunate one who

could make the worst face, was to be exempted from the
ceremony of 'riding the goat' in the coming initiation!
A portion of the 'brethren,' (*Odd Fellows* indisputably),
were squatting on the ground in a circle, with bare feet,
while one stood in the centre with a red-hot iron, which
he cautiously approached towards the pedal extremities
of one and another of the company.   It seemed that
whoever bore this test of courage without shrinking or
winking, was allowed to leave the circle, and thencefor-
ward to be a candidate for the highest office ; while those
poor devils whose flesh winced at hot iron, were condemned to be branded with it in the centre of the left
foot, and to endure other tests, until they attained the
requisite degree of firmness.   Another group were lying
prostrate, with their faces downward, drinking sweetened
water from *thimbles !* (which were filled by an attendant
as fast as they were emptied).   This was an exercise
calculated to increase the holy virtue of patience !   And
as they were condemned to drink a *gallon each* of the
liquid before relaxing their exertions, it was certainly
most admirably adapted for its purpose !   One member,
who was often a speaker in the meetings of the Lodge,
was seated in a sort of prisoner's box, while another was
*pulling his hair* with great violence , causing a series of
short, piercing shrieks to proceed from his mouth !   To
this he was condemned in order to obtain *command of
voice*, the operation upon the hair having a tendency to
increase the volume of the tones !

   " A curious circumstance now caught the attention of
our observers, which was, that the walls of the room
were lined with men, lying one upon another, neatly
packed, from the floor to the ceiling !   These were in the
process of being 'cured' of a disposition to worry and
torment each other in matters of business, which had
been reported to the Lodge, and as, by the least motion

of hand, foot or muscle, they would inevitably incommode their neighbors, and unquestionably be incommoded in return, they were fast learning to 'forbear one another in love.'    This last scene threatened to be quite too much for the fast-failing gravity of the conspirators.   Deciding therefore that they had 'seen enough,' they shouldered their tools, and repaired to the doors, which, assailing with all their strength, and with accompaniments of howls, groans, hollow noises, and ghostly vociferations, they soon removed from their hinges, and rushed into the midst of the frightened assembly; when, suddenly coming to order, one of their number, accoutred as a ghost, exclaimed in sepulchral tones, ' There is nothing covered that shall not be revealed ; and hid, that shall not be known.'

"Such a tumbling and sprawling from the walls as followed this announcement, such a scattering of gathered up limbs, such a scrambling for the door, is not easily imagined.   Suffice it to say, that in a much shorter space of time than the enunciation of the fearful sentence had occupied, the hall was deserted by all but the intruders.

"After this, there was not such a thing heard of throughout the country, as an 'Odd Fellow.'   If any who had been *supposed* to be members of the institution were interrogated about the order, they were entirely innocent of any knowledge of it whatever, 'having never been an Odd Fellow,' — oh no !

"After a while, however, some of the old members began to recollect the good deeds that had proceeded from the institution, (and, notwithstanding the laugh raised against it, no one could deny that they were numberless as well as noble,) and formed themselves into a benevolent society, under a new name, which still exists, and exemplifies as beautifully as did the 'Odd Fellows' of old, the quality of that mercy which 'droppeth as the

gentle dew from heaven,' without the drawbacks of secrecy and ceremony."

Just as my companion paused in his discourse, I observed a lady approaching us, on whom my eyes were
immediately riveted.   Grace and dignity were blended
in her mien with a noble simplicity ; and the expression
of command enthroned upon her brow, was chastened
by the winning sweetness which distinguished the lower
part of her expressive face.

" Do you know her? " I eagerly asked.   " Oh yes, very
well; and if she enters the gallery of paintings, whither
I think she is bending her steps, we will go in, and you
shall know her also."

Our hopes were realized, and in the space of a few
moments, we all found ourselves together in the gallery.
After an introduction, some cursory discussion of the
pictures, and going through some of the commonplaces
with which I was familiar in my day, I began, as my contemporaries were much in the habit of doing, to express
the admiration I really felt for her, but in a style respectful and delicate.   She appeared surprised and embarrassed, but spoke not.   Presuming she did not understand me, I endeavored to make my language more un-
equivocal, and thinking it might seem in better taste than
the more personal adulation I had commenced with, I
included her whole sex in my expressions of admiration.

She turned her large earnest eyes full upon me, and
remained lost in astonishment.   Determined that I *would*
make an impression upon her by my gallantry, I returned
to the attack with increased vigor, and begged that she
" would not be offended or imagine that I was flattering
her, for upon my honor I was truly sincere in every word
I had uttered.   That woman had been all I had described
her, to *me*, during my pilgrimage on earth, and that even
if I had had no experience in the matter until now, I

should be equally sure of the truth of what I had said, for who could look upon the incomparable being before me, and doubt that woman was to man the 'morning star' that shone through his youthful dreams, the 'day-star' that gilded his manly prime, the 'evening-star' that shed a halo over his declining years, and — and —"

"You might add the 'dog-star,'" quietly remarked the lady, with an expression about the mouth which plainly revealed the struggle that was going on in her mind, between politeness and mirth. The struggle was but for an instant. The beautiful lips parted, and out came a peal of uncontrollable laughter. Again it was checked, — the "eloquent blood spoke" in her cheek, and pleading "shopping," while she gracefully apologized for her rudeness, she left us. (So the women "shop" yet, thought I.)

"Now in the name of wonder, tell me what is the meaning of all this," I ejaculated, turning to my friend. To my great vexation, I found him laughing as heartily as she had done. As soon as he had recovered himself a little, he replied, "I was in as much of a maze as the lady, to hear your style of conversation, until I remembered having read in worm-eaten volumes of something similar. But talking to ladies after that fashion was obsolete many years ago."

"What? Obsolete, do you say?" "Yes, truly so. Woman is no longer considered as a mere object for caresses and pretty words. Men might as well attempt to cut away the Andes with a penknife, as to carve themselves a place in her esteem by flattery. She is not now petted and pacified with adulation, while her true dignity is forgotten, nor does she obtain 'sugar-plums' when she only asks for *justice*. *Your* age *fondled* woman. *Ours* honors her. You gave her *compliments*. *We* give her *rights*.

"Your contemporaries, if I have read rightly, looked

upon woman as a mere *adjunct* to man.   As merely the
'companion to cheer *his* pathway,' the 'angel to soothe *his*
sorrows,' the 'wife to adorn *his* fireside,' etc. etc.   With
you, all things in woman had a reference to *man*.   We
think not so, but regard her as *complete in herself.*   (Not
indeed independent of man, nor man of her, but both, in
a high and noble sense, created for each other.)   Not
needing man to *eke her out into an individual,* but in *herself* the 'image of God.' Not ' God's last, best gift to *man,*'
but *with* man, not *next* to him, or *before* him, ' God's last,
best gift' to creation.   Man is not thought of as the solid
masonry of life, and woman as the *gingerbread-work,* but
both together, as the solemn and beautiful architectural
pile of humanity; which, without either, or with either
subordinate to the other, would lose half its majesty and
harmony.

   " Admired, woman may be, and *is,* in these latter times,
but not for the fair hair, or the azure eye, nor yet for the
graceful manner, or elegant accomplishment alone, but
for the *soul* that burns within her, and now only has freedom to show itself.   Nor, much as we elevate and reverence her, do we aim to abolish the difference in the intellect and constitution of man and woman.   On the contrary, we acknowledge and cherish it, only waiving the
worn-out question of the intellectual *rank* of the sexes.

   " The old-fashioned notions about woman that prevailed in your day, are now scarcely remembered as having
existed, except by the antiquarian and the scholar.   Some
ancient books, with whose lore *they* alone are conversant,
still preserve the recollection of them.   'T is well that
my memory has been recently refreshed by one of these
very books, as well as by a ' History of the manners, customs and opinions of the past,' or I should be lost in astonishment at the light in which you contemplate the
sex.   There is one book, however, whose almost inspired

pages are open not alone to the scholar, — I refer to Milton's 'Paradise Lost,' in which there is an allusion to some such ideas as your contemporaries had. It is in this remarkable address from Eve to Adam: 'God thy law, thou, mine.' There has been an immense amount of controversy upon this passage, but I believe commentators at length agree in considering it a false reading. Although of course aware of the condition of woman, at the time in which Milton lived, they believe him to have been incapable of putting a sentiment into the mouth of his ideal of womanly perfection, which makes God a God to *her*, only *through her husband*. They are the more confirmed in this, as in another immortal poem, ' Comus,' he makes his heroine a model of all that is free and noble, and as a still more ancient and world famed poet, Shakspeare, represents woman in quite a different way."

" What is the standard of intellectual cultivation among women now."

" Culture of the broadest kind is considered necessary to both men and women, to fit them for their entrance into the cares and toils of life."

" But how do women find time for this? They could not do so in my day."

" You know the old adage, ' where there's a will, there's a way.' Since woman has awoke to the importance of self-culture, the means are found quite practicable. And besides, there are the increased facilities for domestic labor, to be considered in this matter. The household arrangements of this age are somewhat different from those of yours, I imagine. At this moment, you may see an exemplification of it, in the gay groups of people which you notice yonder, just filling the streets, as they go to their eating houses."

" Eating houses ! Ah, it seems to me that looks a little like Fourierism, but the tall individual whom I met in

12

the morning, told me that the community system 'died out' long ago, and that people lived in families, and women cooked and scrubbed, baked and patched, as of old."

" And so people do live in families, and always will, I reckon; Ah! your tall friend! I know him like a book! A cross-grained, conservative old creature, who cannot endure the modern improvements which leave woman freedom to pursue her individual tastes. He spoke of things as he wished them to be, rather than as they are. Never believe a word he tells you on this subject. Poor fellow! he was once of goodly proportions, fully rounded out, sleek and fair; one of the most popular men in society. In early life he possessed a wife, a most exemplary woman, who devoted herself unusually to the promotion of his comfort; but having had the misfortune to lose her, he could find no other so docile and obedient, and he has really become the melancholy, attenuated being you saw, by venting his indignant ire against the progress of the sex in these days. ' Woman's rights,' as he sneeringly terms them, are the constant theme of his discourse, and the rich old fellow having been refused by at least a dozen ladies, revenges himself by slurs upon the whole woman part of creation."

" Rich! is he? and will not his long purse procure him a wife ? "

" Riches procure him a wife here! You forget, my dear sir, that women are not bought and sold now, as in your day."

" Oh, they were not exactly that, in my day, but then, as now, I suppose, they found it necessary to be clothed and fed, and to move in genteel society, and what would you have them do, if they had no money of their own, the father bankrupt, perhaps, and a homeless old age before them ? What better *could* they do, than marry a rich husband, and so provide for themselves, and destitute sisters perhaps? For my part, I always pitied, more than blamed, when I saw them doing so."

"'Pitied!' 'blamed!' Let me tell you, my good friend, that things have indeed changed with woman. As to 'clothing and food,' she provides them, (when necessity or inclination prompts) by her own hands or head, and what is more, can follow the impulses of her heart, in maintaining a feeble brother or sister, or an aged parent. She is therefore not obliged to enter the marriage state, as a harbor against poverty. And as for 'genteel society,' riches neither admit nor exclude from that, but man and woman both mingle in the circle for which talent or cultivation fit them, and take their places as easily as flowers turn to the light, or fold their leaves in the shade And for this progress, we are mainly indebted to the genius of Charles Fourier, who, by his profound insight into the evils of society, induced such changes as gave due compensation to all industry, whether in man, woman or child. Coöperation substituted for competition, has in a great measure removed indigence from society, and division of labor in domestic art has increased the facilities of housekeeping as much as electricity has that of conveying news. Yet the labor of woman was lightened more reluctantly than other improvements, and the natural patience of that sex, and the selfishness of ours, might have made the eternal track of household labor go on as of old, but for the impossibility of getting female domestics for an occupation which brought so much social degradation and wear and tear of body and clothes! The factory, the shop, and the field even, came to be preferred before it, and men found that they must either starve, or contrive some better way of being fed.

"True, there are no 'Associations' properly, and many things that the genius of Fourier dreamed of, have never been realized.   The reformer's plans seldom *are* fulfilled, as he foresees them, but much that that great man taught has been heeded, and men now bless his labor, and respect his name.

" Taking the hint from him, the poor first combined to purchase their supplies at shops established expressly for them, that their small parcels might come to them at wholesale prices.   Rich men built comfortable, cheap dwellings, with the privilege for each tenant of a certain right in a common bakery, school, etc.   Other changes followed.   Philanthropists guided legislation in the poor man's behalf, till he gradually lost sight of his poverty, while the *hoarder* became unable to heap up wealth from the sweat of his less prosperous brother.

" True, we do not live in the ' phalanx,' but you have noticed the various houses for eating which accommodate the city.   Covered passages in some of the streets, the arcade style of building generally adopted in others, and carriages for the more isolated and wealthy residences, make this a perfectly convenient custom, even in our climate, and 't is so generally adopted by our people, that only now and then a fidgetty man, or a *peremptory woman*, attempts anything like the system of housekeeping in your day.   Nothing but extraordinary wages enables a man now to have a little tea, a little cake, a little meat, a little potato, cooked under his own roof, served all by itself, on a little table for him especially.   But the recluse and monk will be found in all ages.

" You would hardly recognize the process of cooking in one of our large establishments.   Quiet, order, prudence, certainty of success, govern the process of turning out a ton of bread, or roasting an ox ! — as much as the weaving a yard of cloth in one of our factories.   No fuming, no fretting over the cooking stove, as of old !   No ' roasted lady' at the head of the dinner table !   Steam, machinery, division of labor, economy of material, make the whole as agreeable as any other toil, while the expense to pocket is as much less to man, as the wear of patience, time, bone and muscle, to woman.

"Look at that laundry establishment on the other side of the old Penobscot! See the busy boys and girls bearing to and fro the baskets of snowy linen, in exchange for the rolled and soiled bundle of clothes. There is a little fellow, now, just tumbling his load into this end of the building; — by the time he fairly walks round to the other side, it will be ready to place on his shoulders, clean, starched, and pressed with mirror-like polish! Ah, you did not *begin to live* in your benighted nineteenth century! Just think of the absurdity of one hundred housekeepers, every Saturday morning, striving to enlighten one hundred girls in the process of making pies for one hundred little ovens! (Some of these ovens remain to this day, to the great glee of antiquarians.) What fatigue! What vexation! Why, ten of our cooks, in the turning of a few cranks, and an hour or so of placing materials, produce pies enough to supply the whole of this city; — rather more than all your ladies together could do, I fancy. Window cleansing, carpet shaking, moving, sweeping, and dusting, too, are processes you would never know now, though, by the way, there is much less of this to do than there used to be, owing to a capital system of laying the dust by artificial showers which has long been used. Indeed, this was hinted at in your day I think, by a very acute observer of nature, laughed at then, as a dreamer. 'Professor Espy' was his name."

"I asked a while ago, how women could find *time* for the culture you were speaking of, but I am constrained to change my question now, and ask, what, for mercy's sake, is there left for them to do?" said I, indignantly, thinking of the unceasing turmoil of "washing-day," baking and ironing day, which my poor wife had always been obliged to submit to. "How lazy your women must be!"

"Lazy! why they take part in all these very processes. Labor no longer makes them fear to lose caste, and they join in hand or head work as they please, and from having greater variety of employments, those which were deemed more exclusively theirs, such as sewing or teaching, not being crowded, command as high remuneration as any. No, woman is not made lazy by this social progress. She finds abundance of work and freedom to do it. In every station, pecuniary independence is her own. Her duties as mother and daughter are now more faithfully fulfilled than ever, as freedom is more favorable to the growth of the affections than coercion, while in the marriage relation the change is too great to describe. No longer induced to enter it as a refuge from the ennui of unoccupied faculties, free also from the injurious public opinion which makes it necessary to respectability to wed, woman as well as man may go to her grave single if she pleases, without being pitied for having failed of the great end of her existence. Marriage is therefore seldom entered, except from mutual choice and strong affection. True, mistakes are made now, as in your day, by the young with vivid imaginations, but the prevailing habit of useful occupation makes such mistakes far rarer now than then. The family and the home are indeed sacred, and the bond only broken by death. Children are reared under holy influences, and the generations grow and increase in the love and wisdom of God and man."

"But your women do not take part in the affairs of state, do they? At least, so the 'cross-grained, conservative old creature,' as you called him, who answered my question this morning, told me."

"Oh no, they have no wish to do so."

"But that individual told me they had made the attempt;" and here I recapitulated the description he had given me of women in the halls of legislation.

"Oh, that was all a joke! And a capital one it was too."

"A joke! How can that be?"

"Why, men were strangely sore and sensitive upon that subject, always imagining that women wanted to rule. If a word of fault was found with woman's condition, they would immediately take fire, and reply, 'Oh, you want a share in government do you? Better stay at home and darn your stockings.' If a sigh was breathed over woman's want of freedom, intellectual and social, 'Ah! you'd like to go to the polls would you? Better learn to make a good pudding!' To which women answered in effect, that 'they had n't any particular objection to 'darning their hose,' and that they liked of all things to *eat 'good* puddings,' as in the then condition of 'help' they could n't reasonably expect to eat unless they made them, and as they were really quite indifferent to taking a share in government, they thought they should accept the advice offered them, and go on, for a while at least, 'darning their stockings and making good puddings.'

"But men were not so easily satisfied. Still, when the lovers of progress expressed a wish for a broader female culture, they shrugged their shoulders and ejaculated, 'Oh! a share in government!' and if some unlucky dog chanced to stumble on the word 'woman,' — 'Humph! Good pudding.' Still went on the deep, silent current of reform, and still men pricked up their ears and looked fearfully about them, scared lest woman was beginning to 'rule.' Still woman cried 'onward,' and still man groaned, 'darn stockings!' They bore this patiently for some time. At last some mischievous ones declared 'they would bear it no longer. It was too good a subject for fun to be longer treated seriously. It was quite too bad that men had for so many years cried "wolf" in vain. Now the wolf should really come!' And so, indeed, he did; these female wags actually enacted the very scenes you have described to me, in their zeal to 'quiz' their male tormentors. How well they succeeded in quizzing them, you can judge from the story you heard.

"But women were at one time obliged to take part in government, which was '*no* joke.'"

"Ah! how happened it?"

"Men became completely eaten up with the love of money. This frightful disease had begun to show itself in your day, but it afterward made much more rapid and terrible advances. It became a raging pestilence, destroying everything within its reach. It prevailed over our whole country, but more fatally than anywhere else, in this our good city. All other things became subordinate to this burning fever. Social intercourse was abandoned. Amusement was ridiculed as absurd. The church was deserted. The Sabbath habitually desecrated. And even the master-passion, *love*, was forgotten. The effect of this money-leprosy (for I think of no more appropriate name) upon the body, was truly terrific; withering the skin, and changing it to a lurid copper color, with large livid spots upon it, seeming like the ghosts of dollars, (which, like the Lady Macbeth's spots of blood, 'would not rub out'); giving the eyes the appearance of burning cents, sunk deep in the head; impregnating the breath with a fœtid metallic odor, and, as some declared, even imparting to the blood a dull coppery tinge; causing the hands to grope and fumble in vacancy, as if in search of bank bills, while the tongue muttered continually, 'dollars,' 'interest,' 'stock,' 'dividends,' and other words of pecuniary import.

" Of course, with this fearful disease upon them men neglected their duties in the Legislature, in Congress, in courts of law, etc., except those which related directly to their pecuniary interests.

" If their attention was called to any other matters than those which touched their pockets, they would look as bewildered as an owl in the day time, — blushing, stammering, and finally ejaculating, ' Well — I — do n't know, but — I 'll — I 'll — go home and ask my wife ! ' And so ' go home and ask their wives' they did, and their wives, poor things ! having never turned their attention to these matters, and not feeling that they knew much about them, actually had to go to work and make themselves acquainted with all sorts of statistics, political economy, and even law, to help their money-crazed husbands out of their difficulties; so that for a long time women had as much, and even more, to do with the affairs of state than men.

" At last, things got to such a pass that the female part of the community concluded it would not do. That something must be done to stop the progress of the disease which was desolating their homes, and turning society topsy-turvy. And something *was* done. I will not stop to relate all the details of their mode of operations, but will be satisfied with saying, that a system was immediately commenced, which, after sundry discouragements and years of laborious effort, was at length crowned with success. (This much I will say, however, that with the exception of establishing hospitals for the treatment of the infected, their methods of restoration were altogether of the domestic kind.) Once more order and beauty were restored to society, and men became men again."

The scene changed. I was in the midst of a large and brilliant assembly. Thousands of lights gleamed from

12*

the ceiling upon the festive throng. Music was heard in the alcoves. The merry laugh sounded from group to group, as the sparkling witticism flashed along the circle; and "many-twinkling feet" were heard in the distance, "wreathing the fantastic dance."

My faithful friend was at my elbow. "Where are we?" I asked in some surprise. "At a levee at Mrs. ——'s. You must open your eyes wide and see all there is to be seen, for you will not have a better opportunity of learning the social peculiarities of our age." I took his hint, and wandered from circle to circle, to discover, if possible, the bent of the social tastes which I was to see exhibited. My first impression had been, that the assembly I found myself in the midst of was very similar to the festive gatherings of my own age; but I was soon convinced of my error. Externally, it is true, it was so. There were the same graceful exteriors, the same courtly manners, the same beaming faces. There was man in his pride and woman in her beauty. But under all these there was a *soul*.* The courtly manners, the graceful exteriors, and the beaming faces, veiled a *spirit*. Man was there in his manly sincerity, as well as pride, and woman in her majesty, as well as beauty. The assembly went not there to pass an idle hour in mere frivolity, or to obey the demands of ceremony or fashion. They went for the pure interchange of social joys. Friend greeted friend, and heart met heart. Man went not to flatter and cajole, and then boast of his victory over poor ensnared woman. Woman went not to be admired and caressed for a thoughtless hour, and then flung lightly away as a plaything to the winds. But both to meet

* God forbid I should intimate that those who frequented social assemblies in my day had no souls. Only that they usually left them at home when they "went into company."

each other as friends and companions, as spirits bound to the same haven, and created for the same objects.

I have spoken of the sparkling witticism, — and truly it was abundant. Fresh and clear it gushed from the well of thought, and gladdened all within its reach. But it was not, as in my day, *all* the evidence of mind allowed to appear in the festive circle. *Freedom* was there as well as wit, and the guests were not forbidden by the voice of imperious fashion to be serious or gay, as their humor moved them.

I found myself a listener to many circles where subjects which my contemporaries would have thought quite shocking in the social assembly, from their seriousness or profoundness, were chaining a delighted group in closer and closer interest. *Woman*, too, joined in them, and no fear of the world's smile cramped the vigorous intellect, and no visions of "blue stockings" repressed the soul that *would* be free.

To other circles, where the grave and gay, the profound and brilliant, were elegantly blended, I lent a willing ear, and joined with a whole heart, and lungs most glad to do their office, in the "laugh" which varied and vivified the entertainment. (They did laugh, those girls, as if they were afraid of no mortal. — And God bless them! why should they be?)

I observed that some of the assembly were quietly reading, as if they had been in their own parlors, others, in secluded corners or curtained alcoves, were reciting or reading aloud to a neighbor, others were engaged in playing chess and kindred games, and others still were seen tête-à-tête for a great length of time with one individual. I was much surprised at this, and asked an explanation of my companion, remarking that "anything of the kind would not have been allowed in my day, and that indeed *I* could not consider it quite polite, as one would think

the guests might find time at home for such purposes."
" Oh, that," said he, " is a matter of opinion. *We* think
it the truest politeness to allow our guests to find amusement for themselves, provided their way of doing so does
not annoy others. Freedom is with us the highest enjoyment."

At this moment my eye was caught by a strange looking object in a corner, examining a picture through a quizzing glass, with most grotesque contortions. His hair
was brushed perfectly upright on the crown of his head,
and trimmed very precisely in *points*, while from the
crown to the neck it fell in elaborate ringlets, powdered
and perfumed with all the art of the friseur. His whiskers were abundant, and finished in points like his hair.
(Points were " all the rage," as I afterwards learned )
An immense moustache "cultivated" into ringlets at the
ends, adorned his upper lip, and a delicate goatee his under.

The rest of his toilet was in keeping. Loads of gold
and silver lace decorated his green velvet coat, and the
richest of thread lace his crimped shirt-bosom ! Immense gold and pearl pendants hung from his ears, and
his watch, set in pearl, dangled in full relief against his
black velvet pantaloons. On his diminutive hands were
squeezed gloves of the most dazzling whiteness, over
which sparkled numerous rings of various value and
beauty. Apertures in the fingers of these admitted to
the light nails a full half inch in length, gracefully curled
upward, and ending in the usual finishing of points ! His
pantaloons were short enough to display an exquisitely
turned ancle ; and shoes of white satin, embroidered with
flosses of the richest hues, and ornamented with gold
and pearl buckles, completed the toilet of this singular
being.

My companion had been observing my minute scrutiny of the grotesque object before me, and at length asked me " what I thought of him." " I cannot decide. Is he a man ? and if not, to what title *can* he lay claim ? "

" I suppose he must *pass* for a man," he said, laughing. " He is one of the *exquisites* of the day."

" What ! In the high state of social progress where I find you is it possible you have ' exquisites ? ' Has woman made so great an advance as you have represented, and does man still remain so far behind her as to allow such a thing as a dandy to exist ? "

" It is even so, although to do ourselves justice I must say that such creatures are very rare, and hardly tolerated in society. He was not invited here to-night I understand, but got in by some trick of his remarkable assurance."

I looked again at the " exquisite," attracted by a strange sound, which seemed to come from his vicinity. He was laughing, as near as I could judge by the singular contortions of his phiz and the nervous agitation of his body, although the sound I never should have recognized as that of mirth, it being part squeal, part cackle, and part a suppression of both. It is said laughing is infectious. However this may be usually, *his* most assuredly was, and accordingly my friend and I began to *shake* in unison, then to laugh audibly, and finally to roar. Our unearthly noises seemed strangely to agitate our " surroundings." The walls began to totter. The flame of the lamps waved hither and thither. The furniture rocked. The floor rose and fell like the sea in a storm. A hapless Falstaff, overturned and set rolling by the " swell," came tumbling over my unlucky " corns," and bawling, I awoke.

70721

*THE*

*MILLTILLIONAIRE.*

BY

M. AUBURRÉ HOVORRÈ.

# THE

# MILLTILLIONAIRE.

## PART FIRST.

At last, one morn, late in the Age of the Planet Earth, there came a Dawn which scintillated with resplendent, lurid ray—heralding forth a Grand Day—in which I descried a speck on the rim of the fiery horizon, now fairly ablaze with the splendor of the approaching orb of day, which with my lorgeette I discovered to be a unique specimen of the genus homo, gazing far out into the orient hemisphere below,—when lo! I beheld the great Sun roll upon the Earth, producing the effect of the man being thereon, who, as the glorious luminary glided on, appeared to turn and step therefrom to the earth.

And well may have this man hailed from the Sun — he was a MILLTILLIONAIRE.

## PART SECOND

Ah, the Milltillionaire! What is he?—a being of such colossal and illimitable wealth and power, one might say he was a very god—or God. Indeed, we may recognize in him the True Bard, or POSITIVE POET. With his Milltillions does he dethrone all nations or governments and unite them in one universal Bardic State at his pleasure. Everyone being at his service we may perceive the Milltillionaire to be the Absolute and True Monarch of the Planet. Specie or money to him is nothing but gewgaws, or fragments of rock,—for all time he converts into illimitable wealth.   The only revenue the Bardic State requires from any individual after attaining the age of twenty-five years is that he allot a minim portion of his time daily, weekly, or annually to the continuance of the Universal Welfare of the Planet.   Thus, relatively speaking, no slaves can exist, all persons being bound by this one simple law to render equal service to the Bardic State.   Absolutely, all beings, as an inevitable necessity are slaves to Life, whatever their form of existence.   Hence, the wise will observe that the Grand Bardic State is only a relative Paradise,—as an Absolute Heaven implies the entire Universe with life as it is—or Absolute Knowledge of the Universe or Life—which is incompatible with any form of existence, since if any individual could obtain Absolute Knowledge, he would no longer exist, as all beings exist in virtue of their unconsciousness of Absolute Existence. Could we comprehend Absolute Being, life would not only be no longer desirable, but there would be nothing left of it   For in truth Life consists in an eternal aspiration for some beloved purpose.   Could this purpose be absolutely discovered or removed, there would be nothing left to life.   Life would then not be merely undesirable but impossible.   We continue to live by our undying efforts to fathom the secret of Life ;— happily, all is in vain, for did we but probe deep enough to discover the secret, life would instantly dissipate itself as an empty bubble.   Though we seem to be men, relatively, yet we are always children in regard to Absolute Knowledge of Life.

The life of every individual, regarded from a poetic standpoint, is a fairy tale.   The personal history of certain persons is marked, and that of a Milltillionaire would be especially so, reading more like a romance than real life.   Yet " truth is stranger than fiction " in every private history, and would be so perceived if the inner history of all beings were revealed to the world.   All the silent struggles, defeats and victories one undergoes are never known, except to one's self.—even in the autobiographies of great men.   Every one has an interesting history if he were able to portray it in adequate language.

Now, behold the Milltillionaire not only King to the Millionaire (an indigent being in comparison) but Lord o'er the Earth, having with his unlimited wealth possessed himself of all landed property of all civil countries, purchasing the land and its attachments incognito through his agents, within the period of a few years. The Milltillionaire thus virtually owning the Earth, controls or sways the nations at his pleasure, or could annihilate or transform them at his option.

First, however, the Milltillionaire proceeds to establish throughout all the States of the world laws which recognize no class of criminals of any description, but recognize all individuals as either well, or ill, physically or intellectually. Accordingly in all the principal cities and towns of the Planet are to found both the Physical Hospital and the Mental Hospital where persons respectively afflicted are cared for to the best knowledge of the Science of Health. Ensuing this it were easy for the Milltillionaire with his bardic disposition to secure the erection of immense caravanseries, or Bardic Hotels, where all people are to be equally and luxuriously provided for, and thereafter the State allows no private or individual residences—only State Residences (that is Hotels) where all are provided for very sumptuously at the expense of the State. The virtue of this law exists in the fact that all persons are compelled to receive a complete education both physically and intellectually. The only revenue the State derives then resolves itself to the sole Tax on Time, required from all well denizens after the age of twenty-five years until forty years of age, they rendering to the Universal Welfare a few hours per day, a few days per week, seven months per year, the rest of the time not so required being at their own disposal Thus money having become useless, everything required to be had for the asking, it is eventually relegated to the earth whence it came as so much rock or dust and nothing more.

Under such a bardic regime all cities become gradually transformed into immense palaces nicely intermingled with fragrant gardens and luxuriant parks — there being no dirty streets or unsightly habitations of any description, the cities being interlined with Triple Highways, canopied and as secure from all storms and dust and heat as the marbled hall of any palace.

The virtue of such an ideal or millenial city exists through the law which obliges all individuals to keep themselves scrupulously clean, well-dressed and well-deported, under the penalty of being confined to a hospital if found incapacitated for properly caring for themselves.

A palace is very expensive.    A palatial city is still more expensive.    A palatial planet is far more expensive.

Nevertheless, the Milltillionaire, or TRUE BARD, with his unlimited milltillions, will solve the problem of expense once and forever, for the Planet Earth.

As long as people are unable to meet the expense of a want, they are to that degree barbaric.    Thus the millenial man is seen to possess the ability to command the full realization of an ideal existence—and thuswise only through the omni-magnetic genius of a Milltillionaire transpires the Inauguration of the TRUE MILLENIUM.

---

## PART THIRD.

### THE EARTH IN THE INAUGURAL CENTURY OF THE MILLENIUM.

Lo! behold the Planet Earth
Ensconced in the Magnificent Glory of a Millenial Dawn.

The sky is clear and azure.    The birds sing and all the people rejoice in unspeakable happiness throughout the realm of the Bardic State, which now embodies all the civilized peoples of the world—there only remaining a few remnants of savages and barbarians who still adhere to their native swamps, but who are fast becoming extinct like other wild animals.

Thus, all the great intellectual races of people are seen to march gloriously forward in increasing power and prosperity. All cities are fast becoming palaces of colossal caravanseries gracefully interblended with grand and beautiful conservatories of Art, Literature, Music, Opera and Science.

All Emporiums and Manufacturing Establishments are situate by themselves, as is proper, without the environs of the City,—but which are readily accessible by virtue of our Millenial Transit, travelling by our exquisite electric vehicles which glide over the rails of the electric viaduct, spanning the tall buildings several thousand feet in the air, at the enormous velocity of one thousand miles an honr.

All avenues or boulevards are required to be one thousand feet in width and interlined by a Tripled Canopied Highway two hundred feet in width, with four hundred feet of lawned avenue on each side of the thoroughfare proper, with no flower-plots, shubberry or trees to mar the beauty of the open green, or open space intervening between the towering cliffs of granite and marble, which embank as cannons the stately and sublimely beautiful avenues. It is, however, to be noted that these exquisitely turfed lawns are not designed as a superfluous ornament : far from that. Accordingly you do not see the lawn disfigured with multitudinous signs : "KEEP OFF THE GRASS" staring you in the face at every step, as did our poor ancestors in their vanity and greed despoil the true beauty of their lawns and parkways. Indeed, on every fair day you will observe the lawns flowering with the beauty of childhood and youth, lovingly swaying to and fro amid the zephyrs, and growing in the artistic aud rapturous games and sports of nature.

The Triple Canopied Highway is directly connected with all buildings on each side thereof as one continuous Hall or Public passage of three levels : the First, or Lower Level, being allotted exclusively to electric vehicles travelling in one direction; the Second, or middle Level, to electric vehicles traveling in the opposite direction ; the Third, or Upper Level, for the service of pedestrians and cyclists, one-hundred feet in the centre being reserved entirely to the use of cycles with fifty feet in each direction, as likewise fifty feet on the sides for the Promenades. The Canopy of the Third Level is so constructed as to serve as a fourth level for promenaders and cyclists in fair weather who desire to enjoy the sunshine and magnifieent prospect afforded from thi altitude. Directly beneath the Triple Highway runs a Subway one-thousand feet wide and exclusively for the transportation of all freight traffic and conveyance of electric wiring and all sewerage. In addition it is to be observed that no Horse or Steam-power is allowed, electric and magnetic forces now supplying all powers of locomotion other than human. In point of fact, horses, cattle, dogs, cats and so forth are only to be seen in the Zoological Parks as curiosities or pets.

With the event of the Canopied Highway, all people are able to enjoy travel in any part of the city under the protection of this spacious hallway, beautifully and smoothly floored with granite and marble, as warm and comfortable as any of the Bardic Hotels, and as perfectly secure from all storms of dust, rain or snow, the sides being enclosed in heavy plate glass, which may be opened when desired.

The Viaduct Railway answers for express travel from city to city together with the Aerial Ships which span the seas and glance from continent to continent at so prodigious a velocity that the best of the ships of the Air Line in a straight line actually circumnavigate the planet in about two hours, flying through space at the tremendous rate of ten thousand miles per hour.

The Viaduct Railway starting from ten thonsand to fifteen thousand feet in the air, and thus having no barriers in the way of hills or mountains to surmount or wind around, enjoys a level stretch of steel from city to city, over which the trains speed so swiftly that the rails scarce support any weight, acting rather as guides merely to the coaches over which they fly Thus the construction of the Viaduct is found very economical, being built upon the principle of a gigantic suspension bridge, with spans of cable vaulting through space, one hundred miles at a stretch. Again, it is wonderful how suddenly our trains can be brought to a full stop, so powerfully are they controlled, yet without the slightest jar. Indeed, our forefathers would have turned a somersault if they could have seen one of our electric flyers in a moment of time become a mere standing point at a station. But in our Age, happily, even the passengers possess sufficient force of mind to retain their firm but luxurious seats, however abrupt may be the cessation of the train's flight. Truly, it is a spectacle to behold the passengers rise immediately but gracefully the moment that the train pauses in its aeriel passage.

All cities are now circular in form the radii of which is one hundred miles, with an approximate circumference of seven hundred miles. The largest city, BARDO–CITO–UNO (called by the ancients Athens or Boston)—possessing a population of one quadrillion souls. To our ancestors very likely this would have seemed an impossibility, but it is to be accounted for by the fact that our immense caravanseries tower several thousand feet in the air, the smallest of which is capable of housing comfortably and luxuriously one million citizens. The second city in size, BARDO–CITO–DUO (Paris); the third, BARDO–CITO – TRIO (Chicago); the fourth, BARDO – CITO – QUARTO, (San Francisco), the fifth, BARDO–CITO–CINQUO, (Berlin); the sixth, BARDO–CITO–SEXTO, (London); the seventh, BARDO–CITO–SEPTO, (Venice); the eighth, BARDO–CITO–HUITO, (New York); the ninth, BARDO – CITO – NONO, (Saint Petersburg); the tenth, BARDO–CITO–DIXIO, (Canton), and so on to the end of the list.

In all there are about twenty cities, the smallest of which possesses a population of one hundred trillion inhabitants, and thus it will be seen the total census of our Planet comprises several hundred quadrillions of denizens.

All people now reside in the cities, the country being devoted exclusively to State Agriculture and Horticulture Gardens and Parks. Reviewing the vast quadrangular Gardens of Agriculture and Horticulture, one hundred miles square, in contradistinction to the circular form of cities, we perceive them to be artistically and substantially enclosed by acres of glass, and the plants and fruit grown by electricity at night,—gardens which know no night, nor winter. Indeed, by the all potent power of electricity, man is now able to convert an entire continent into a tropical garden at his pleasure. The gardens are manipulated by vast automatic machines, but requiring the pressure of a knob to translale their immobility into instantaneous and incessant action—thus to speak.

Thuswise is the soil tilled and drilled automatically in a moment of time ; thus all vegetable produce is harvested ; thus all fruits are delicately gathered into receivers and by electric transmittors directly despatched to their destination to be consumed immediately, while fresh, ere they have time for decay. Today we have no waste, and no opportunity for it allowed. In verity all our departmental affairs of State, thus essentially embody, and are regulated by the beautiful Economy and Harmony of a Bardic State.

We too, rightly pride ourselves upon our Infant Schools, Academies of Art, Music and Science, and Universities of Knowledge, all of which together form a most excellent and consummated System of Education. All children on attaining the age of seven years commence their technical education at the Infant Schools where they continue for a period of three years, when they are prepared to enter upon a two years' course at the Academies, which finished, they graduate after pursuing a five years' curriculum at the Universities. Then all alike are allowed three years of vacation and rest from their studies ; after which they take a four years' post-graduate course of travels and researches or explorations of the Planet. Following this they enjoy one year's choice of a vocation or of several professions (any number of prosessions being allowed for the sake of variety and change to those who desire them) upon which they enter their career at the end of twenty-five years. It is, too, an important fact, our superior method of instruction, compared with that in vogue as late as the Nineteenth Century, it being no more or less than the simple and true principle which nature employs, which is now employed in all our schools. Thus no longer are children fatigued and over-worked with torturing " examinations" and "catechisms." Rather now pupils ask questions, the questions of their tutor concerning topics, problems or sciences which they do not comprehend and he is expected to answer all such inquiries satisfactorily. In fact, we may say each student fills out a list of a limited number of questions per lesson on a certain subject which he does not understand, and which it concerns him to know, Allowing ten questions per student, in a class of twenty, we

will say there is an average of one hundred different inquiries
on the subject called for, from which very much is learned that
would not be thought of by one individual alone, while it is ex-
haustively treated by being considered from all the various
views or standpoints of the different members of the class.
Secondly, by this method of oral instruction, the minds of the
young are more deeply impressed than they would be by merely
scanning the same information in a book.

Sequentially, today, such a thing is impossible as boring,
fatiguing and punishing a pupil for his ignorance on matters of
which as a child he has not yet learned.    Parenthetically, we
may add that no private or exclusive schools of any description
are allowed.    All schools, academies, and universities are public
and open to all alike at their respective age.    Nor do we pharisaically establish separate eleemosynary schools for the incarce-
ration of the deaf and blind, and imposing upon them a prison
diet, et cetera, while ostentatiously pretending to afford the
half-starved inmates an education, consisting in the accomplishment of a few digitarial feats (the most absurd of all tricks of
legerdemain) and the acquirement of a parrot erudition, as,
alas ! ignominiously and nefariously did the people in the last
Century preceding our Age.    All deaf and blind pupils,
and all others who require special instruction, receive the
same at the Public Schools in Individual Recitation Halls.
Thus no longer are any pupils inhumanly torn asunder from
their parents in order to attend school, but all may reside with
their parents until their graduation from the universities
at the age of seventeen, when they are qualified to take care of
themselves.    Neither are we annoyed with petty charges and
tuition fees and other trifles of a like nature, since all the
schools are entirely free to all as indeed is everything throughout the State, as free as air, to be had for the asking.    Likewise, the mottoes of our Temples of Knowledge are, "ASK,
AND YE SHALL KNOW."

On graduation the old class apothegm, "Know Thyself, is
superfluous to us, for WE KNOW OURSELVES.    For indeed we
are taught everything respecting ourselves, and especially is no

false modesty allowed to injure us by any ignorance of our physical and sexual requirements. The prudishness and religio- istic modesty of our forefathers of yore no longer obtains, and their supposed virtue, "modesty," is now rightly considered a vice. No such modesty exists with us in any shape, as any one can easily verify by visiting our public baths, where men and women, boys and girls, mingle together in their natural state, entirely disencumbered of all vesture of clothing what- ever, enjoying their baths, while no one is shocked or abashed, or shy, but every one delights him or herself by frolicking in in the watery element as it pleases them, in a manner perfectly free and natural. From virtue of such naturalness, young people when they now fall in love with each other, are not bashful and shy, nor do they cut a ludicrous figure or commit some horrible blunder owing to sexual ignorance or prudish modesty, but they fully understand each other and enjoy their love naturally, as is right ; they are not shocked at each other, and rendered miserable and wretched and thereby driven to suicide by those horrible VICES of our ancestors.

The school year consists of eight months, with two terms of four months each, with two months' vacation intervening be- tween each term ; the week comprises five days out of seven, with two hours per day allotted to study. Thus our pupils and students are not allowed to over-work themselves, and such a thing never occurs in this Age, as it did in the past, stranding the intellect of many a student, and leaving him a poor mental wreck upon the craggy shore of the Sea of Knowledge.

With respect to our Religion, we are happily now able to say, that, visibly, Religion is a thing of the Past : For we have learned that True Religion is invisible, and should pervade all of our institutions through our hearts at all times universally, and not ridiculously and hypocritically be relegated to ONE day in a week, and to ONE particular institution. Pure Religion we know to be Pure Love—which we realize in all our actions, which are invariably deeds of Love. We no longer mock the Universal Deity of Love or Being with superficial and idola- trous symbols, rites and ceremonies. We have no churches, or any so-called " charitable " institutions, for we have need of none; no longer do we prostrate ourselves with lugubrious prayers, hymns, etc., but ever walk erect and upright as becomes the love of a true man, who respects himself and loves his fellow belngs. With us "charity" has long since been discovered to be a vulgar misnomer, and an obsolete word in our lexicons. The charity (?) of the Church Societies and Municipal Organizations of the Past, a mockery of true love, which employed itself with vain, empty words and abominable dispensations of watery soup. coffee and stale bread, or of some dirty, ragged clothes to the poor, with these mottoes staring you in the face from over their portals; "Half-a-loaf is better than no bread," or rather, as they verified it, "A smell of soup is better than no soup," or. "Rotten meat is better than no food," "or "Garbage is better than nothing," or, more truly, "Slow-poison is better than food"—an empathic manner of preparing them to meet death—fortunately, this exists no more. All individuals now enjoy opportunity for employment, and thus have no need to beg for even food or clothing, everyone having abundance of which to eat and wherewith to clothe themselves. Indeed, no one can say that he has more to eat than another, or dresses better For all are supplied equally with the best that the Earth yields.

In dress, too, both men and women array themselves in uniform styles, with the option of choosing the color of cloth they prefer to wear. With the exception this pleasing variety of color, it has been found that this simplicity and comfortableness of dress giving full freedom to the body in all manner of exercise is the most becoming and therefore the most artistic, as well as being the best adapted to one's health—in contrast with the old styles of vanity, with their vulgar ruffles, frills, and starched linen, always the source of some annoyance or nuisance to the wearer. As a sensible and a reasonable people we have thus disposed of all these vain dress encumbrances, and instead enjoy a perfect naturalness of costume. Neither do we barbarously deck our person with vulgar trinkets, or cord our fingers, or puncture our ear or nose with jewelric rings. Oh, the vain stuff! but of this we have no more. In point of fact we have no more jewelry of any description, not even a watch, we have no need for it, all buildings and vehicles in in which we travel containing a timepiece, we thus always have the time before us wherever we are, without the trouble of burdening our person with it.    For scientific purposes we of course have astronomical iustruments by which we can ascertain the time at any moment directly, and hence we can never be at loss for the time.

Futher we have no occasion for loading our pockets down with other trash as did our ancestors, since any necessary tool or material is always at hand in its proper place.    Indeed we have use for one pocket in which we carry our handkerchief.

We being thus lightly armed, are ever free to dance or run as the moment may require.

In resumé we may note that all the Religion we have is invisible—is felt but not seen—A Religion of warm love prevading all our hearts and emanating in natural actions of love, enriching our souls with the happiness of True Love !   No longer is Religion a mockery of that which it should be, and which we now realize by our Millenniel Society ! !—A Society of Universal love ! ! !

Let us now review the amazing and perfectly astounding progress of Science compared with that existing in the XIX Century which was thought extremely wonderful.    To-day Magnetism supersedes Electricity and PSYCHO-OMNI-MAGNETISM transcends Hypnotism.    All of our artificial illumination is effected by a magnetic current so powerful that one lamp will illumine an area ten miles square slmost as brilliantly as sunlight.    By Psycho-omni-magnetism a man who has omni-magnetieally qualified himself is not only able to magnetise a few individuals, but is able to omni magnetise his entire environment of whatever persons it may be composed so that they will be impelled to harmoniously co-operate with him in the prosecution of any enterprise.    Thus great designs intended to promote the Advancement of the Public Weal are now achieved with a celerity that would have astonished our ancestors who fretted and fumed for years over " rapid transit " and other public projects.

Omni-Magnetism we have found is the element of  elements,

and by virtue of which we exist. The greater the degree of Omni-Magnetism which we possess, the more deeply and powerfully do we exist. The predominating quality of Omni-Magnotism is True Love or True Friendship to our fellow-beings, absolutely. Though, as a matter of fact, we are not able to exercise this quality intimately, with but a limited number of our friends, who are most in harmony with us by virtue of the mutual sympathy of our respective natures. Yet we can and should omni-magnetically harmonize our entire euvironment of whatever beings it may consist, so that they all will love us and be impelled to arrange themselves in sympathy with our being to the utmost extent of their nature. This is indeed to rightly grandly and beautifully live. Verily a Millennial Existence.

The Science of Calorificrtion and Refrigeration has also finally reached the acme of its existence. By Calorification of a Calorifico-Electric Ether, which we are now able to coutrol fully. all our buildings are heated, all our locomotors empowered for their work and frigid climes rendered temperate or tropical ad libitum. In operation there is no steam, smoke or other noxious vapors emanating therefrom, but in lieu thereof you behold in action one of the finest and neatest elments imaginable. Another admirable property about this Calorifico-Electric Element is that it may be condensed and pocketed in small cases with a small lever button, by the pressure of which the bottled heat may be disengaged when desired, radiating through the atmosphere around one for ten or twenty feet, and transforming the most frigid climate into as mild and temperate a state as one would desire. This is a great convenience which all tourists and explorers know how to appreciate. By its use we have long since visited the most frigid regions of the Planet and the North and South Poles, as the axial extremities of our spheroid were formealy appelated, is now a dissipated illusion. In point of fact, the frigid zones are now the realms of our "summer resorts," where we may dine luxuriously and comfortably upon a plateau of ice. In brief, this admirable Calorifico-Electric Ether, may well be compared in its beautiful effect to the sunlight, with this difference that by virtue of our absolute control of it we are able to avoid excessive heat of the Sun

Planet    The greatest amazement that this marvellous Calorifico-Electric Ether excited is when we observe how intense a
degree of heat it is capable of attaining—so very intense and
potent that it dissolves the most refractory substances, as rocks
and diamonds, into liquids and gases—which can again be solidified at our option.    Today, therefore, we are able to produce
our marble blocks artificially, in any size or shape desired, and
thus rendering unnecessary the arduous labor of quarrying, et
cetera, of our past generations.    By the very intensity of the
heat of this element its nature is different from the combustion
that consumes wood and other fibrous materials—hence it does
not develop like the combustion of paper and straw, and therefore we happily incur no danger of burning up the entire Earth
as the ignorant formerly feared we would.

By Refrigeration of a Refrigerifico-Electric Ether, we are also
able to cool all our buildings, congeal our ices, and convert
tropic zones into temperate or frigid climes ad libitum.    In
brief, the hottest and coldest regions of the planet are now
Mutually transferable (so to speak) as the occasion requires.
By this Refrigerifico Element we are able to produce a most
intense degree of frigidity, so extreme that many substances
hitherto thought uncongealable are now readily solidified at our
option.    Even the tropic seas may be frozen at our pleasure
by permeating the waters with this irresistible Element.

Like the Calorifico-Ether, similarly may this Refrigerifico-
Electric Ether be compressed and transportable in small cases
for the conveniency of tourists and scientists.

By a combination of the two above Ethers, we have obtained
a most marvellous compound element, known as a Calorifico.
Electrico, Refrigerifico Ether by which all undesirable combustions and conflagrations may be instantaneously subdued-
Though all our buildings are positively fire-proof, yet fires, or
rather spontaneous combustions. will at times arise in our forests or outlying regions, and would greatly ravage the beauty
of our realms but for this serviceable, all-potent fire subduing
Element, which we always have at hand ready for instant use.
Besides this the Calorifico–Electrico–Refrigerifico Element,
possesses great value for many scientific purposes and dealing

with other elements, through virtue of its power to maintain a neutrallty between the contending elements, heat and cold.

We are not only able to produce rain, as the incipient rain-makers of yore anticipated, but what is more, to prevent showers deluging us when their advent is undesired.

We, however, do not induce the clouds to shed their tears for us by exploding our lungs at them, the manner in which our ancestors ludicrously attempted to obtain the condescension of their Highness. In fact, we have simply to diffuse a Magnetie-Ether which, permeating the atmosphere, instantly induces a condensation of the suspended vapors.

When showers are imminent. by the simple application of the Calorifico--Electrico--Refrigerifico Ether, which maintains a neutrality between the heat and cold of the atmosphere, thereby preventing premature condensation of the clouds, and allowing them to pass over to the country where they are needed or to the seas where they belong. Indeed, no showers ever obtain in the cities now, because they are not necessary to the growth of our architectural plants, and our city parks are more satisfactorily watered by machines, and hence, very properly all rain is relegated to the country where it is desired. In truth, we have absolute control of the weather. and may evolve any special weather from the elements that are at any moment to embellish the occasion either warm or cold, fair or cloudy, rain or shine. Today no fog, mist, steam, smoke or other noxious vapors and gases obtain in our atmospheres. which ever show forth unto us the most serene and pellucid skies.

Reviewing the system of government of our Bardic State we pereeive it to consist in the utmost simplicity of adminis-tration, thereby rendering utteily impossible the political in-trigues which obtained through the complicity ot governmental affairs in the past, did any motive longer exist for such intrigues.

The Bardic State embraces the entire Earth and all its people. This Universal State is advised by The Alphabeta. The Alphabeta is composed of twenty-six Bards, answering to each letter of the English Language, ( now the universal writ-

ten language) or rather, thirteen men and thirteen women who
are bardically qualified.  All of the Alphabeta, however must
be Absolute Bards, philosophically and scientifically educated,
possessing profound discretion in intellectual matters, and thus
able to exercise the greatest insight in the execution of State
affairs.  The first of the Alphabeta, Bardo "A" (or our masculine term for Bard) is known as the Bard Regent.  The Bard
Regent is the otherwise Administrator–in–Chief of the Universal Bardic State.  The remaining twenty-five of the Alphabeta
are the counsellors and successors of the Bard Regent.  The
Bard Regent is authorized to appoint the Alphabeta, (also in
case of their death and retirement from service on attaining
the age of forty years, when all of the Alphabeta, including the
Bard Regent, retire), and also to appoint a Municipal Bard
for each city.  The Municipal Bards in turn appoint Man-
ging Bards of the Caravanseries and Conservatories of
the municipality.  The Managing Bards in turn appoint
Poets, formerly called clerks or laborers, for service in
their respective buildings.  The Poets are in every respect
equal to the highest Administrator, except possibly in intellectual merit which is a matter of personal culture.  All
individuals, whether of the Poets, Managing Bards, Municipal
Bards, or Alphabeta receive the same emolument which is an
equal share in the Universal Wealth of the World.  All people
dine at the same table—so to speak—eat the same food, and
enjoy equally all fhe luxuries of the table that the earth yields.
We no longer have any first, second, or third tables, as the
people of the past pharasaically ordained, esteeming themselves
better than their neighbor.  All tables are the best so there is
no chance for jealousy or envy to ruminate upon.  We all now
love our neighbors as ourselves, and in this lies the greater
part of the secret of our Millennial State.

The Alphabeta are empowered to appoint Managing Bards
of the Agriculture, Horticulture, and Park Departments,
Manufactories and Emporiums.  In brief, to them is allotted
the supervision of the Rural Affairs of the World.  After the
Bard Regent, comes his successor, a female Bard of the Alphabeta. known as Barda " B " (our feminine term for Bard).  Then

follows Bardo " C," Barda " D," Bardo " E " and so on, altern-
ately to the end of the Alphabeta. The Bard Regent, together
with the Alphabeta, is also empowered to issue such Universal
Rules of Instruction as are deemed essential to the Peace and
Welfare of the State, and to determine any difficulties that may
arise All incentives and motives to crime now being removed,
very little strife ever obtains among our people, so that the
Alphabeta seldom have occasion to exercise the latter preroga-
tive. Thus, assuredly, we have no need of the service of the
ancient "lawyers," a profession only concomitant with warring
factors and elements of ignorance, and the existence of which
is virtually impossible in a Millennial State—since, did they exist,
it would not be a MILLENNIAL State.

We will now visit the great Caravanseries, the sublime and
beautiful residences of our people. These immense buildings,
towering from ten thousand to fifteen thousand feet in the air,
and averaging about one hundred stories, the deeper stories of
which range from 300 to 500 feet in depth, no story being less
than 100 feet from floor to ceiling,—are erected in all conceive-
able styles, Trianglar, Quadrangular, Hexagonal, Septagonal,
Octagonal, Circular, et eetera, producing a pleasing and artistic
diversity, that relieves the eye from the monotony of the ancient
brick structures constructed in uniform siyles and on a tow line
with the street. (Be it observed with have no "brick" buildings
of any kind. that all our structures are built with solid granite
or marble,—marble predominating. Though no building may
approach within the 1000 feet street limit, yet any building
may recede more or less from this line as desired.)

We will enter Caravansery ONE (Number ONE. the
Caravnseries of each city being distinguished by consecutive
numerals.) where resides the Bard Regent. (the Inagural Bard
of the Millennium.) The Bard Regent, however, does not alone
inhabit this colossal building, but many of his friends domicile
here, besides thonsands of tourists who reside transiently at the
Caravansery. Each family has allotted to itself a superb suite
of rooms, which they may occupy permanently, if they so desire,
and every individual on attaining student age has reserved to his
own exclusive use rooms for solitary sturdy or repose.

The Caravansery is in itself a grand Block of Marble and Diamond Embellishment, erected in the unique composite style of an Octagon — Septagon — Hexagon — Quadrangle — Triangle — Circle — Globe! The foundation being an Octagon of ten stories, upon which grows a Septagon of ten stories, from which shoots a Hexagon of as many stories from which evolves a Heptagon, and thence a Quadrangle, Triangle and the Circle from which blossoms the most dreamably beautiful, brilliant, and all-resplendent diamond-blue Globe,—a Globe illumed by a powerful, magnetic light which is seen far, far, far out at sea,—the great Caravansery being erected upon a lofty prominence of the Massachusetts sea coast, a site within Bardo–Cito–Uno, (formerly Boston).

Now stand back and behold the grandeur and sublimity of this vast and lofty pile of White Marble, scintillating with diamond light, and capped with a lovely globule flower poised fifteen thousand feet in space.

In circumference the building is about four miles for a pedestrian, though scarce a mile to an electric vehicle, and diametrically a mile. But ere we tire of further distance let us hie away to the Delectable Dining Salon, where we may repast upon the most artistic and ideal Menu — a Menu fit for a feast of the Gods.

## La MENU De CARAVANSERY.

POTATIONS.

Water.          Chocola.          Orangeade.
Lemonade.          Milk.          Cocca.

FRUITS.
All Kinds.

CEREALS.
All Kinds.

VEGETABLES.
All Kinds.

BREAD.
All Kinds.

CAKES.
All Kinds.

DESSERT.
Chemico—Fruito—Pudding.
Nuts.    Cream.

GRAND FINALE.

MINERAL WATERS.
Eau de Jupiter—from Planet Jupiter.
Eau de Neptune—from Planet Neptune.
Eau de Venus—from Planet Venus.

Indeed a most godly Menu. Yet, doubtless, a Nineteenth Century pagan, with his beastly appetite, would gape in wonder, and fancy something lacking, when he perceived the absence of all meat dishes, fish, et cetera. Happily our science and experience have discovered to us not only the superfluity of such meat dishes, but the utter beastliness and barbarism of indulgence in a meat or fish diet. We would as soon think of swallowing a live snake, as gorging our stomachs with birds, cattle and fish, which is, indeed a species of cannibalism, Man (himself an animal) devouring another animal. Further, we know that such beastly foods tend to lower the intellect, and cause brutal passions similar to those of the animals devoured, while vegetable and fruit foods conduce to higher refinement of the faculties to deeper culture, peace of mind and intellectual Wisdom.

In the primal days, or ages of man, during famines, he may have been justificd in living upon a meat diet, but we, in our Intellectual Age, who have an abundance of Cereals, Fruit Foods and Vegetables, have not the least necessity for indulgence in such beastly, barbaric diet.

Neither do we slaughter birds or animals for sport (?)

We see no sport in the torture and slaughter of harmless birds and animals. Therefore, no "angling" or "hunting," or the indulgence of any similar sports of barbarians or beasts is now allowed. All of our pastimes and games are intellectual and refined. We are no longer a barbaric people in any respect, and do not crave for murderous sports. We are a Bardic People and enjoy Bardic diversions.

Neither do we indulge in tobacco, wine or other poisonous luxuries. We find luxuries enough without indulging in *poison* for a luxury.

During the progress of the Dinner we find ourselves enchanted by the most soul-enrapturing harmonies, tuning our hearts to love sublime, as the delectable melodies issue fragrantly from colossal pillars of music artistically placed here and there throughout the Grand Salon,— an Octagonal Salon five hundred feet in depth and two thousand feet in diameter, whose spacious capacity admits one million people at one seating.

We no longer have human waiters but electric waiters, which ascend from the cuisine beneath the floor in the centre of a circular table within the reach of all, who can help themselves to their dishes from the tray or waiter, their orders being sent by the pressure of an electric signal by the side of each chair.

Having sated our appetites we ascend by the grand elevators to the Roof - Garden to inhale the mountainous air while we enjoy our after-dinner repose.

All our Caravanseries have roof-gardens of the most exquisite beauty of flowers and umbrage.

Later we make a business trip by our Aerial Ship to the great Emporiums to secure some articles of wear, arriving at our destination in a few seconds, though the Emporiums are situated over three hundred miles from the City limits. Having descended to the roof of the vast Emporium, we enter a grand electric vehicle which conveys us slowly through the immense building, allowing us time to examine any of the articles that we wish, which are displayed beside the route of our open electric. Here we or any one can select all the articles they need, and obtain them for the mere asking, free of all charge—nor are we first obliged to produce a check-card or certificate in order to procure anything that we want. Very probably our suspicious ancestors would have fancied this a great opportunity for persons to get their clothes and other goods for nothing, or without having earned them. But this is utterly impossible, even if the people today were so ignorant as to condescend to such Pharasaic folly, by virtue of our Universal Register of the Planet in which individual is registered by a specific number at his respective Caravansery—thuswise, we can know at any time the Census of the Planet, the highest number on register always being the total population, (all vacant numbers caused by death being first re-assigned to new persons before any higher numbers are added). Each individual is thus known to the world by his specific number, which is stamped upon all of his clothes and hats, and corresponds with the number of his resident domicile in his respective Caravansery. Though thus known by a number of which there is no duplicate ever registered every one among his intimate friends may be known by a given name, as Albert, Charles, Fred, et cetera, or Alice, Dora, Julia, et cetera. Also, in case of anyone's attaining great distinction in Music, Literature or any Art, for convenience he may take an assumed name (in addition to his life-number) as, for instance, BARDO HONORE (for a man), or BARDA ZOVA (for a woman), and by which name they may be known posthumously to history, as all numbers cease to be to the individual at his death, and are reissued. All mail or packages are sent by the number of the person which is invariably stamped thereon (not written) and instantly arrives at its true destinatson,—no error being possible as only one person can answer to that number. For communication by letter or telegram, we no longer have any use, since all messages are transmitted telepathically from Soul to Soul, throughout the Solar System. Indeed, the laws of the telepathic current—as also the laws of dreams—are now fully comprehended as scientifically taught in all our Universities, and every one uuderstands the operation of these Psychic Elements. We now know that

the one Law of Thought and Dream is this.—
  IF YOU  THINK  OR DREAM OF A PERSON, THAT
PERSON SIMULTANEOUSLY OR INSTANTANEOUS-
LY THINKS OR DREAMS OF YOU IN PROPROTION-
ATE DEGREE.

  This is found to be  invariably true, though, as  a  matter  of
course the deeper be the Thought or the Dream, the more vivid
and intimate is the communication established between the two
friends thus conversing.    In operation the Telepathic current
is similar to the Electric current, which  glances from  pole  to
pole illuming  the different lamps instantaneously, thus does the
Telepathic  current, only more  rapidly,  glance  from  mind  to
mind, illuming the two minds (which are en  rapport, or thrown
into circuit), simultaneously, as it were, with the same Psychic
Phenomena.    Formerly, all  such  communication occurred un-
consciously or involuntarily, but  now that we understand  the
laws of  the mind, we are  able  to control the  psychic element,
and communicate with any friend  that we desire, though he be
a million miles distant, by simply  placing ourselves  en  rapport
with him.    Further, we are not  only able to communicate telepathically with persons living in the  Present Body, but we can
also converse psychically with Souls who have passed the portal
Death, and re-incarnated themselves in  a  new costume, whenever we throw ourselves into the  Psychic  current with  them.
In the Nineteenth Century people speculated  much regarding
Psychical Phenomena. but very few seemed  to  have  divined
anything approximating to the truth of the laws  of  Psychical
Phenomena,  and  failed  to  perceive  that they are realities as
much  as  are  Physical Phenomena,  although of a  finer  and
more subtle nature.  Our Science has, however, disposed of the
'' Future Problems of Religion '' by establishing the certainty
of a future existence of all egos or Souls.    We moreover know
that life beyond Death is a continuation of our  Present  Life,
according  to  our  merit  or  qualification of entering  a  more
advanced sphere of life through re-incarnation in a new form.
En passant, the true hypothesis of the existence of the Universe
is, that it has being in virtue of an Eternal Universality.    That
this Universality has  for ever  existed  in  some  one  form  or

multitudinous forms. Were it admissible or conceivable that
the Universe could be resolved into an Absolute "Nothing," it
would follow that this "Nothing" from which the Universe
evolves itself, must be "Something." Indeed, we may thus
perceive that there is absolutely no such thing as "Nothing,"
—for after all it proves to be ' Something," if SOME THING
is evolved from it. Truly SOMETHING HAS ALWAYS
EXISTED and SOMETHING ALWAYS WILL EXIST.
HENCE, we see the utter folly of the "Nothing Theories."
In resume, "Nothing" is a misnomer applied by ignorance in
absence of its Knowledge of the Cause of a Specific Event.
Accordingly, the Universe can only be rightly predicated as,
SOMETHING WHICH IS UNIVERSALLY ETERNAL.

This Something, we know to be Pure Soul — eternally
metamorphosing from form to form, and ever evolving itself
into a higher form. The soul never retrogrades, though the
"body" or "form" vanishes, but steadily advances Forever,—
since there is no limit to the Advancement of the Soul, any
more than there can be a limit to the extension of the Universe.

Returning from our digression, to the subject of the Universal State Register, which is jointly supervised by the Managing
Bards of their respective Caravanseries; it is also to be observed
that the prolixity of our numbers if enumerated by the Roman
numerals is greatly abridged by an abbreviated system of
numerals by which we can condense an otherwise large number
into a very small space, as for instance, two billion, four million,
five hundred thousand and four, may be written thus :

$$B-M-HT$$
$$2-4-\ 5-4$$

being less than half the longitudinal space that would be
occupied by the Old System of Numeration.

People in travelling are known by their Life–Numbers, and
in taking rooms at a foreign Caravansery, the rooms are temporarily designated by their Numbers, thus enabling anyone to
readily find them, in whatever part of the world they might
happen to be. After having ordered our goods shipped by
Number to our abode, we take our departure from the
Emporium, which is open at all hours Day and Night, though

no one performs more than two hours, (and is not obliged to work more than one hour) in twenty–four hours, the service being conducted by relays of Poets, who gladly devote thus an hour's service per diem to the UNIVERSAL WEAL,—and on our arrival at the Caravansery receive our goods with our Number stamped thereon, which were directly dispatched. by the Electric Subway, after being numbered. as are all clothes and goods first indelibly stamped with the owner's number to avoid change by mistake, or the disposal of them to others as second class, when discarded. In fact, we have no "second class" goods, all clothing and other articles when discarded being sent to the Chemical Manufactories, where the material is re-utilized, as Nature utilizes ashes.

In case of illness or accident, one is immediately admitted to the Physical Hospital or the Mental Hospital according to the nature of his case, where he is as sumptuously and luxuriously ensconced as he would be at the Caravansery, and receives every attention the occasion requires.

All the Hospitals both Physical and Mental are situate sanitarily either in the montains, or on some elevated sea-coast, without the environs of the City and thus sequestered. Here all our physicians reside, we having no need of itinerant doctors, all persons being hygienically and medically educated in all that pertains to their health and thus able to cure themselves in the greater number of instances that are liable to occur among a people of our intelligence and cleanliness. Indeed, we have learned that the vast number of the diseases of our ancestors resulted from their uncleanliness, their filthy habits of indulging in .tobacco and rum and other poisonous and nasty luxuries. In brief, they wallowed in the hot-bed of all ignorance and uncleanliness, so that we do not wonder they suffered from the most horrible and obnoxious diseases. Happily Science has now long since dispelled this nauseating fog of the past, so that we now very seldom require the service of a physician, and indeed have but few hospitals.

Our methods of treatment and remedies, also, vastly differ from those of the Past. The market is no longer surfeited and overflowing with numberless quack nostrums and drugs for every little ailment, and the thousand and o ie ailments which no longer have any existence.

Our simplest and most Universal Remedy is the application of Psycho-Ether to the part or parts of the body affected, being applied, omni magnetically by oneself, by our friend, or by a physician, which application usually effects the desideratum in a very brief period.

En passant, we are happy to say that we have also disposed of all Prisons and Insane Asylums, and all similar paganistic and pharisaic institutions of the Past. We no longer thrust people into wretched cells or horrible dungeons for so-called "criminal" cases, a method of treatment which, far from remedying the case, invariably aggravates it, and often translating the poor incarcerated individual into a hardened wretch of the most despicable conception. Instead of thus inhumanly and pharisaically regarding such individuals, though we have but few cases of the kind to attend, we perceive that the so—termed " criminal " is rather mentally diseased, and labors under a temporary illusion which leads him to commit an abnormality, and accordingly we place him in the Mental Hospital where he receives philanthropic treatment, being omni—magnetized by his physician, until brought back into his normal condition of being, when the patient naturally feels very grateful for the service rendered him (in lieu of being disposed to revenge himself upon the physician or the institution as soon as he escapes from it as he would be were it a Prison) and leaves the Hospital a truly reformed man.

The mulitudinous "crimes" of " theft," "robbery" et cetera, obtain no longer, there being absolutely no cause for them, any thing needed being obtained for the asking. Neither do the many " crimes " arising from rum, intoxication, ignorance, etc., longer obtain, all these causes now being removed. Thus, hardly any incentives to ''crimes'' ever arise today, and as previously averred they are few and far between. Also, thereby, have been removed the many causes of Insanity and Suicide, consequently we have no suicides and a very small number of our people succumb to Insanity. The number of our insane is further greatly reduced by the fact that, we no longer incarcerate individuals who differ from the majority in being original, or incipient geniuses, who were thus formerly pharisaically regarded and persecuted.

Ensuing death we have our bodies cremated, and the ashes of the same deposited in the sea from an Aerial Ship. Dead bodies are no longer superstitiously and insanitarily inhumed in the earth to the pollution of the waters of the land.   Thus we have no cemeteries, nor does a vestige of the cemeteries of the Past remain, but all ere this have been completely obliterated, and thereon, where once they are supposed to have been, now stand some of our most immense buildings and Temples of Art and Science

In respect to the Pharasaic Institution of Marriage which caused so much trouble to our forefathers, and rendered " marriage" a confessed failure, we are very happy to say that that institution has succumbed to dissolution We have no institution of the kind.   People have now sufficient intelligence to unite themselves where union is desired.   Consequently we have no divorce cases as resulted from the forced and artificial marriages of yore.  Neither is man superstitiously limited to union with but one woman, or, vice versa, is woman abridged of her liberty to one man, but either may seek union with as many persons, succeesively as their natures may require. Nonetheless, every man aud woman is expected to look after their entire family, however large, until their children attain the age of independence on their graduation from the Universities. It is observable, however, that these self–unions verv rarely occur ere both contracting parties are above thirty years old or more, when they find themselves matured both physically and intellectually and fully qualified to undertake the duties of paternity and maternity.

We will now take a flying trip to the great Bardic Capito– Temple of the Planet, the largest and greatest building ever erected upon our Planet.   Here are the presiding offices of the Bard Regent. the Alphabeta, and the headquarters of Art, Music and Science.  Ere entering the building let us first enjoy a consummate view of its beautiful and sublime exterior. Lo! behold situate upon a rocky promontory (Cape Ann) of the

Atlantic Sea, an immense Triangle ten miles in length, with equal sides of five miles, the apex of which pointing sea-ward ascends to an altitude of five thousand feet, from which lofty Triangle shoots an Octagonal Column five thousand feet higher, from thence a quadrangle Tower five thousand feet higher. And thence, lastly shoots up a beautiful brilliant blue-green Circular Tower of Marble five thousand feet higher, culminating in a sublime Diamond Cone five hundred feet higher, and upon which is poised four magnificent Globes of Ether Light—a light so powerful that from their altitude of twenty five thousand feet it is actually descried from the Planet Mars. Venus, Jupiter and other Planets.

The entire building is constructed of white marble, with the exception of the Circular Tower and Diamond Cone. In this Tower and Cone are situate our immense and powerful astronomic instruments, by which we are able to perceive all that is transpiring on the nearer planets of our Solar System. However, we have now less occasion to use our astronomical observatories, being able, with our Aerial ships which are transported by ether and controlled by an Electric—lever, to suspend ourselves in mid air at any altitude like a planet, and thus entirely overcoming the force of gravitation, we may travel hither we would and explore the Planets, the Sun or the Stars !

En passant, a recent exploring party to the Planet Jupiter, returning bringing with them a specimen Jupiterian for Exhibition. We regret to observe however that he does not seem to thrive very well upon our Air and Diet—and thus we are obliged to keep him in a Glass Case and manufacture a special "Air" and "Diet" for him. Accordingly, we do not fancy the experiment will be repeated as they can be observed and studied to better advantage upon their native Planet. The Jupiterians as a people do not seem to be so far advanced intellectually as we are, but they are a fine race physically and musically. In form they are very similar to our people, but rather larger, more atheletic, and they do not wear any dress at all, their atmosphere being warm and mild at all times of the year. The acoustic properties of their atmosphere are very rare and fine and thus they are able to become the accomplished singers and musicians. Their language is a most beautiful one, but quite different from any language of our Earth and thus peculiar to us. Its greatest resemblance is to a compound Latin–Persian language, only far more poetical and musical. Instead of calling their Planet "Jupiter", as we do, they have named it "O Rooluu." Thoug' e have not learned their language, we are able to communicate with them telepathically, and fully comprehend their mind

Let us now enter the Temple and secure a seat in the grand and vast Conservatory of Music and enjoy the latest Opera with 5,000.000 souls. The seating capacity of our Conservatory being thus immense, erected around a colossal Musical Tower, with five circular levels (or floors) each level seating 1,000,000 people, simultaueously. Here we have the latest and most improved musical instruments, among whlch is the grand Universo-Piano, which renders the sounds of all kinds of musical instruments a la solo, or a l'orchestra, being played electrically or manipulated by hand at option. Anon, combining in a grand chorus the power of five thousand pianos aud one thousand pipe-organs in the most Subline Harmonies and Entrancing Rhapsodies,

Again, you hear the most wonderful instrument reproducing exactly all the sounds and noises of Nature, the roaring of the cataract, the singing of the brooklet, the noises of insects, animals, birds, and the awful and sublime Thunder of the very Heavens! Hark!—Ah!—What entracing solo melody of bliss is that! portraying our future—a most grand, lovely and sublime Future ! ! !

M. Auburre Hoverre.

Finis.

# TO WHOM THIS MAY COME

Edward Bellamy

# TO WHOM THIS MAY COME

IT is now about a year since I took passage at Calcutta in the ship *Adelaide* for New York. We had baffling weather till New Amsterdam Island was sighted, where we took a new point of departure. Three days later a terrible gale struck us. Four days we flew before it, whither, no one knew, for neither sun, moon, nor stars were at any time visible, and we could take no observation. Toward midnight of the fourth day the glare of lightning revealed the *Adelaide* in a hopeless position, close in upon a low-lying shore, and driving straight toward it. All around and astern far out to sea was such a maze of rocks and shoals that it was a miracle we had come so far. Presently the ship struck, and almost instantly went to pieces, so great was the violence of the sea. I gave myself up for lost, and was indeed already past the worst of drowning when I was recalled to consciousness by being thrown with a tremendous shock upon the beach. I had just strength enough to drag myself above the reach of the waves, and then I fell down and knew no more.

When I awoke, the storm was over. The sun, already half-way up the sky, had dried my clothing and renewed the vigor of my bruised and aching limbs. On sea or shore I saw no vestige of my ship or my companions, of whom I appeared the sole survivor. I was not, however, alone. A group of persons, apparently the inhabitants of the country, stood near, observing me with looks of friendliness which at once freed me from apprehension as to my treatment at their hands. They were a white and handsome people, evidently of a high order of civilization, though I recognized in them the traits of no race with which I was familiar.

Seeing that it was evidently their idea of etiquette to leave it to strangers to open conversation, I addressed them in English, but failed to elicit any response beyond deprecating smiles. I then accosted them successively in the French, German, Italian, Spanish, Dutch, and Portuguese tongues, but with no better results. I began to be very much puzzled as to what could possibly be the nationality of a white and evidently civilized race to which no one of the tongues of the great seafaring nations was intelligible. The oddest thing of all was the unbroken silence with which they contemplated my efforts to open communication with them. It was as if they were agreed not to give me a clew to their language by even a whisper, for while they regarded one another with looks of smiling intelligence, they did not once open their lips. But if this behavior suggested that they were amusing themselves at my expense, that presumption was negatived by the unmistakable friendliness and sympathy which their whole bearing expressed.

A most extraordinary conjecture occurred to me. Could it be that these strange people were dumb? Such a freak of nature as an entire race thus afflicted had never indeed been heard of, but who could say what wonders the unexplored vasts of the great Southern Ocean might thus far have hid from human ken? Now among the scraps of useless information which lumbered my mind was an acquaintance with the deaf-and-dumb alphabet, and forthwith I began to spell out with my fingers some of the phrases I had already uttered to so little effect. My resort to the sign language overcame the last remnant of gravity in the already profusely smiling group. The small boys now rolled on the ground in convulsions of mirth, while the grave and reverend seniors, who had hitherto kept them in check, were fain momentarily to avert their faces, and I could see their bodies shaking with laughter. The greatest clown in the world never received a more flattering tribute to his powers to amuse than had been called forth by mine to make myself understood. Naturally, however, I was not flattered, but, on the contrary, entirely discomfited. Angry I could not well be, for the deprecating manner in which all, excepting of course the boys, yielded to their perception of the ridiculous, and the distress they showed at their failure in self-control, made me seem the aggressor. It was as if they were very sorry for me, and ready to put themselves wholly at my service if I would only refrain from reducing them to a state of disability by being so exquisitely absurd. Certainly this evidently amiable race had a very embarrassing way of receiving strangers.

Just at this moment, when my bewilderment was fast verging on exasperation, relief came. The circle opened, and a little elderly man, who had evidently come in haste, confronted me, and bowing very politely, addressed me in English. His voice was the most pitiable abortion of a voice I had ever heard. While having all the defects in articulation of a child's who is just beginning to talk, it was not even a child's in strength of tone, being in fact a mere alternation of squeaks and whispers inaudible a rod away. With some difficulty I was, however, able to follow him pretty nearly.

"As the official interpreter," he said, "I extend you a cordial welcome to these islands. I was sent for as soon as you were discovered, but being at some distance, I was unable to arrive until this moment. I regret this, as my presence would have saved you embarrassment. My countrymen desire me to intercede with you to pardon the wholly involuntary and uncontrollable mirth provoked by your attempts to communicate with them. You see, they understood you perfectly well, but could not answer you."

"Merciful heavens!" I exclaimed, horrified to find my surmise correct; "can it be that they are all thus afflicted? Is it possible that you are the only man among them who has the power of speech?"

Again it appeared that, quite unintentionally, I had said something excruciatingly funny, for at my speech there arose a sound of gentle laughter from the group, now augmented to quite an assemblage, which drowned the plashing of the waves on the beach at our feet. Even the interpreter smiled.

"Do they think it so amusing to be dumb?" I asked.

"They find it very amusing," replied the interpreter, "that their inability to speak should be regarded by any one as an affliction, for it is by the voluntary disuse of the organs of articulation that they have lost the power of speech, and as a consequence the ability even to understand speech."

"But," said I, somewhat puzzled by this statement, "didn't you just tell me that they understood me, though they could not reply, and are they not laughing now at what I just said?"

"It is you they understood, not your words," answered the interpreter. "Our speech now is gibberish to them, as unintelligible in itself as the growling of animals; but they know what we are saying because they know our thoughts. You must know that these are the islands of the mind-readers."

Such were the circumstances of my introduction to this extraordinary people. The official interpreter being charged by virtue of his office with the first entertainment of shipwrecked members of the talking nations, I became his guest, and passed a number of days under his roof before going out to any considerable extent among the people. My first impression had been the somewhat oppressive one that the power to read the thoughts of others could only be possessed by beings of a superior order to man. It was the first effort of the interpreter to disabuse me of this notion. It appeared from his account that the experience of the mind-readers was a case simply of a slight acceleration from special causes of the course of universal human evolution, which in time was destined to lead to the disuse of speech and the substitution of direct mental vision on the part of all races. This rapid evolution of these islanders was accounted for by their peculiar origin and circumstances.

Some three centuries before Christ one of the Parthian kings of Persia, of the dynasty of the Arsacidæ, undertook a persecution of the soothsayers and magicians in his realms. These people were credited with supernatural powers by popular prejudice, but in fact were merely persons of especial gifts in the way of hypnotizing, mind-reading, thought-transference, and such arts, which they exercised for their own gain.

Too much in awe of the soothsayers to do them outright violence, the king resolved to banish them, and to this end put them, with their families, on ships and sent them to Ceylon. When, however, the fleet was in the neighborhood of that island, a great storm scattered it, and one of the ships, after being driven for many days before the tempest, was wrecked upon one of an archipelago of uninhabited islands far to the south, where the survivors settled. Naturally the posterity of parents possessed of such peculiar gifts had developed extraordinary psychical powers.

Having set before them the end of evolving a new and advanced order of humanity, they had aided the development of these powers by a rigid system of stirpiculture. The result was that after a few centuries mind-reading became so general that language fell into disuse as a means of communicating ideas. For many generations the power of speech still remained voluntary, but gradually the vocal organs had become atrophied, and for several hundred years the power of articulation had been wholly lost. Infants for a few months after birth did, indeed, still emit inarticulate cries, but at an age when in less advanced races these cries began to be articulate, the children of the mind-readers developed the power of direct mental vision, and ceased to attempt to use the voice.

The fact that the existence of the mind-readers had never been found out by the rest of the world was explained by two considerations. In the first place, the group of islands was small, and occupied a corner of the Indian Ocean quite out of the ordinary track of ships. In the second place, the approach to the islands was rendered so desperately perilous by terrible currents and the maze of outlying rocks and shoals that it was next to impossible for any ship to touch their shores save as a wreck. No ship at least had ever done so in the two thousand years since the mind-readers' own arrival, and the *Adelaide* had made the one hundred and twenty-third such wreck.

Apart from motives of humanity, the mind-readers made strenuous efforts to rescue shipwrecked persons, for from them alone through the interpreters could they obtain information of the outside world. Little enough this proved when, as often happened, the sole survivor of a shipwreck was some ignorant sailor, who had no news to communicate beyond the latest varieties of forecastle blasphemy. My hosts gratefully assured me that as a person of some little education they considered me a veritable godsend. No less a task was mine than to relate to them the history of the world for the past two centuries, and often did I wish, for their sakes, that I had made a more exact study of it.

It is solely for the purpose of communicating with shipwrecked strangers of the talking nations that the office of the interpreters exists. When, as from time to time happens, a child is born with some powers of articulation, he is set apart and trained to talk in the interpreters' college. Of course the partial atrophy of the vocal organs, from which even the best interpreters suffer, renders many of the sounds-of language impossible for them. None, for instance, can pronounce *v*, *f*, or *s*, and as to the sound represented by *th*, it is five generations since the last interpreter lived who could utter it. But for the occasional intermarriage of shipwrecked strangers with the islanders it is probable that the supply of interpreters would have long ere this quite failed.

I imagine that the very unpleasant sensations which followed the realization that I was among people who, while inscrutable to me, knew my every thought, were very much what any one would have experienced in the same case. They were very comparable to the panic which accidental nudity causes a person among races whose custom it is to conceal the figure with drapery. I wanted to run away and hide myself. If I analyzed my feeling, it did not seem to arise so much from the consciousness of any particularly heinous secrets, as from the knowledge of a swarm of fatuous, ill-natured, and unseemly thoughts and half-thoughts concerning those around me and concerning myself, which it was insufferable that any person should peruse in however benevolent a spirit. But while my chagrin and distress on this account were at first intense, they were also very short-lived, for almost immediately I discovered that the very knowledge that my mind was overlooked by others operated to check thoughts that might be painful to them, and that, too, without more effort of the will than a kindly person exerts to check the utterance of disagreeable remarks. As a very few lessons in the elements of courtesy cures a decent person of inconsiderate speaking, so a brief experience among the mind-readers went far in my case to check inconsiderate thinking. It must not be supposed, however, that courtesy among the mind-readers prevents them from thinking pointedly and freely concerning one another upon serious occasions, any more than the finest courtesy among the talking races restrains them from speaking to one another with entire plainness when it is desirable to do so. Indeed, among the mind-readers, politeness never can extend to the point of insincerity, as among talking nations, seeing that it is always one another's real and inmost thought that they read. I may fitly mention here, though it was not till later that I fully understood why it must necessarily be so, that one need feel far less chagrin

at the complete revelation of his weaknesses to a mind-reader than at the slightest betrayal of them to one of another race. For the very reason that the mind-reader reads all your thoughts, particular thoughts are judged with reference to the general tenor of thought. Your characteristic and habitual frame of mind is what he takes account of. No one need fear being misjudged by a mind-reader on account of sentiments or emotions which are not representative of the real character or general attitude. Justice may indeed be said to be a necessary consequence of mind-reading.

As regards the interpreter himself, the instinct of courtesy was not long needed to check wanton or offensive thoughts. In all my life before I had been very slow to form friendships, but before I had been three days in the company of this stranger of a strange race I had become enthusiastically devoted to him. It was impossible not to be. The peculiar joy of friendship is the sense of being understood by our friend as we are not by others, and yet of being loved in spite of the understanding. Now here was one whose every word testified to a knowledge of my secret thoughts and motives which the oldest and nearest of my former friends had never, and could never, have approximated. Had such a knowledge bred in him contempt of me, I should neither have blamed him nor been at all surprised. Judge, then, whether the cordial friendliness which he showed was likely to leave me indifferent.

Imagine my incredulity when he informed me that our friendship was not based upon more than ordinary mutual suitability of temperaments. The faculty of mind-reading, he explained, brought minds so close together, and so heightened sympathy, that the lowest order of friendship between mind-readers implied a mutual delight such as only rare friends enjoyed among other races. He assured me that later on, when I came to know others of his race, I should find, by the far greater intensity of sympathy and affection I should conceive for some of them, how true this saying was.

It may be inquired how, on beginning to mingle with the mind-readers in general, I managed to communicate with them, seeing that while they could read my thoughts, they could not, like the interpreter, respond to them by speech. I must here explain that while these people have no use for a spoken language, a written language is needful for purposes of record. They consequently all know how to write. Do they, then, write Persian? Luckily for me, no. It appears that for a long period after mind-reading was fully developed, not only was spoken language disused, but also written, no records whatever having been kept during this period. The delight of the people in the newly found power of direct mind-to-mind vision, whereby pictures of the total mental state were communicated, instead of the imperfect descriptions of single thoughts which words at best could give, induced an invincible distaste for the laborious impotence of language.

When, however, the first intellectual intoxication had, after several generations, somewhat sobered down, it was recognized that records of the past were desirable, and that the despised medium of words was needful to preserve it. Persian had meantime been wholly forgotten. In order to avoid the prodigious task of inventing a complete new language, the institution of the interpreters was now set up, with the idea of acquiring through them a knowledge of some of the languages of the outside world from the mariners wrecked on the islands.

Owing to the fact that most of the castaway ships were English, a better knowledge of that tongue was acquired than of any other, and it was adopted as the written language of the people. As a rule, my acquaintances wrote slowly and laboriously, and yet the fact that they knew exactly what was in my mind rendered their responses so apt that, in my conversations with the slowest speller of them all, the interchange of thought was as rapid and incomparably more accurate and satisfactory than the fastest of talkers attain to.

It was but a very short time after I had begun to extend my acquaintance among the mind-readers before I discovered how truly the interpreter had told me that I should find others to whom, on account of greater natural congeniality, I should become more strongly attached than I had been to him. This was in no wise, however, because I loved him less, but them more. I would fain write particularly of some of these beloved friends, comrades of my heart, from whom I first learned the undreamed-of possibilities of human friendship, and how ravishing the satisfac-

tions of sympathy may be. Who among those who read this has not known that sense of a gulf fixed between soul and soul which mocks love! Who has not felt that loneliness which oppresses the heart when strained to the heart that loves it best! Think no longer that this gulf is eternally fixed, or is any necessity of human nature. It has no existence for the race of our fellow-men which I describe, and by that fact we may be assured that eventually it will be bridged also for us. Like the touch of shoulder to shoulder, like the clasping of hands, is the contact of their minds and their sensation of sympathy.

I say that I would fain speak more particularly of some of my friends, but waning strength forbids, and moreover, now that I think of it, another consideration would render any comparison of their characters rather confusing than instructive to a reader. This is the fact that, in common with the rest of the 'mind-readers, they had no names. Every one has, indeed, an arbitrary sign for his designation in records, but it has no sound value. A register of these names is kept, so that they can at any time be ascertained, but it is very common to meet persons who have forgotten titles which are used solely for biographical and official purposes. For social intercourse names are of course superfluous, for these people accost one another merely by a mental act of attention, and refer to third persons by transferring their mental pictures—something as dumb persons might by means of photographs. Something so, I say, for in the pictures of one another's personalities which the mind-readers conceive, the physical aspect, as might be expected with people who directly contemplate each other's minds and hearts, is a subordinate element.

I have already told how my first qualms of morbid self-consciousness at knowing that my mind was an open book to all around me disappeared as I learned that the very completeness of the disclosure of my thoughts and motives was a guarantee that I would be judged with a fairness and a sympathy such as even self-judgment cannot pretend to, affected as that is by so many subtle reactions. The assurance of being so judged by every one might well seem an inestimable privilege to one accustomed to a world in which not even the tenderest love is any pledge of comprehension, and yet I soon discovered that open-mindedness had a still greater profit than this. How shall I describe the delightful exhilaration of moral health and cleanness, the breezy oxygenated mental condition, which resulted from the consciousness that I had absolutely nothing concealed! Truly I may say that I enjoyed myself. I think surely that no one needs to have had my marvellous experience to sympathize with this portion of it. Are we not all ready to agree that this having a curtained chamber where we may go to grovel, out of sight of our fellows, troubled only by a vague apprehension that God may look over the top, is the most demoralizing incident in the human condition? It is the existence within the soul of this secure refuge of lies which has always been the despair of the saint and the exultation of the knave. It is the foul cellar which taints the whole house above, be it never so fine.

What stronger testimony could there be to the instinctive consciousness that concealment is debauching, and openness our only cure, than the world-old conviction of the virtue of confession for the soul, and that the uttermost exposing of one's worst and foulest is the first step toward moral health? The wickedest man, if he could but somehow attain to writhe himself inside out as to his soul, so that its full sickness could be seen, would feel ready for a new life. Nevertheless, owing to the utter impotence of words to convey mental conditions in their totality, or to give other than mere distortions of them, confession is, we must needs admit, but a mockery of that longing for self-revelation to which it testifies. But think what health and soundness there must be for souls among a people who see in every face a conscience which, unlike their own, they cannot sophisticate, who confess one another with a glance, and shrive with a smile! Ah, friends, let me now predict, though ages may elapse before the slow event shall justify me, that in no way will the mutual vision of minds, when at last it shall be perfected, so enhance the blessedness of mankind as by rending the veil of self, and leaving no spot of darkness in the mind for lies to hide in. Then shall the soul no longer be a coal smoking among ashes, but a star set in a crystal sphere.

From what I have said of the delights which friendship among the mind-readers derives from the perfection of the mental rapport, it may be imagined how intoxicating must be the experience when one of the friends is a woman, and the subtle attractions and correspondences of sex touch with passion the intellectual sympathy. With my first venturing into society I had begun, to their extreme amusement, to fall in love with the women right and left. In the perfect frankness which is the condition of all intercourse among this people, these adorable women told me that what I felt was only friendship, which was a very good thing, but wholly different from love, as I should well know if I were beloved. It was difficult to believe that the melting emotions which I had experienced in their company were the result merely of the friendly and kindly attitude of their minds toward mine, but when I found that I was affected in the same way by every gracious woman I met, I had to make up my mind that they must be right about it, and that I should have to adapt myself to a world in which friendship being a passion, love must needs be nothing less than a rapture.

The homely proverb, "Every Jack has his Gill," may, I suppose, be taken to mean that for all men there are certain women expressly suited by mental and moral as by physical constitution. It is a thought painful, rather than cheering, that this may be the truth, so altogether do the chances preponderate against the ability of these elect ones to recognize each other even if they meet, seeing that speech is so inadequate and so misleading a medium of self-revelation. But among the mind-readers the search for one's ideal mate is a quest reasonably sure of being crowned with success, and no one dreams of wedding unless it be, for so to do, they consider, would be to throw away the choicest blessing of life, and not alone to wrong themselves and their unfound mates, but likewise those whom they themselves and those undiscovered mates might wed. Therefore, passionate pilgrims, they go from isle to isle till they find each other, and as the population of the islands is but small, the pilgrimage is not often long.

When I met her first we were in company, and I was struck by the sudden stir and the looks of touched and smiling interest with which all around turned and regarded us, the women with moistened eyes. They had read her thought when she saw me, but this I did not know, neither what the custom was in these matters, till afterward. But I knew from the moment she first fixed her eyes on me, and I felt her mind brooding upon mine, how truly I had been told by those other women that the feeling with which they had inspired me was not love.

With people who become acquainted at a glance, and old friends in an hour, wooing is naturally not a long process. Indeed it may be said that between lovers among the mind-readers there is no wooing, but merely recognition. The day after we met she became mine.

Perhaps I cannot better illustrate how subordinate the merely physical element is in the impression which mind-readers form of their friends than by mentioning an incident that occurred some months after our union. This was my discovery, wholly by accident, that my love, in whose society I had almost constantly been, had not the least idea what was the color of my eyes, or whether my hair and complexion were light or dark. Of course, as soon as I asked her the question, she read the answer in my mind, but she admitted that she had previously had no distinct impression on those points. On the other hand, if in the blackest midnight I should come to her, she would not need to ask who the comer was. It is by the mind, not the eye, that these people know one another. It is really only in their relations to soulless and inanimate things that they need eyes at all. It must not be supposed that their disregard of one another's bodily aspect grows out of any ascetic sentiment. It is merely a necessary consequence of their power of directly apprehending mind, that whenever mind is closely associated with matter the latter is comparatively neglected on account of the greater interest of the former, suffering as lesser things always do when placed in immediate contrast with greater. Art is with them confined to the inanimate, the human form having, for the reason mentioned, ceased to inspire the artist. It will be naturally and quite correctly inferred that among such a race physical beauty is not the important factor in human fortune and felicity that it elsewhere is. The absolute openness of their minds and hearts to one another makes their happiness far more dependent on the moral and mental qualities of their companions than upon their physical. A genial temperament, a wide-grasping, godlike intellect, a poet soul, are incomparably more fascinating to them than the most dazzling combination conceivable of mere bodily graces.

A woman of mind and heart has no more need of beauty to win love in these islands than a beauty elsewhere, of mind or heart. I should mention here perhaps that this race which makes so little account of physical beauty is itself a singularly handsome one. This is owing doubtless in part to the absolute compatibility of temperaments in all the marriages, and partly also to the reaction upon the body of a state of ideal mental and moral health and placidity.

Not being myself a mind-reader, the fact that my love was rarely beautiful in form and face had doubtless no little part in attracting my devotion. This, of course, she knew, as she knew all my thoughts, and knowing my limitations, tolerated and forgave the element of sensuousness in my passion. But if it must have seemed to her so little worthy in comparison with the high spiritual communion which her race know as love, to me it became, by virtue of her almost superhuman relation to me, an ecstasy more ravishing surely than any lover of my race tasted before. The ache at the heart of the intensest love is the impotence of words to make it perfectly understood to its object. But my passion was without this pang, for my heart was absolutely open to her I loved. Lovers may imagine, but I cannot describe, the ecstatic thrill of communion into which this consciousness transformed every tender emotion. As I considered what mutual love must be where both parties are mind-readers, I realized the high communion which my sweet companion had sacrificed for me. She might indeed comprehend her lover and his love for her, but the yet higher satisfaction of knowing that she was comprehended by him and her love understood she had foregone. For that I should ever attain the power of mind-reading was out of the question, the faculty never having been developed in a single lifetime. Why my inability should move my dear companion to such depths of pity I was not able fully to understand until I learned that mind-reading is chiefly held desirable, not for the knowledge of others which it gives its possessors, but for the self-knowledge which is its reflex effect. Of all they see in the minds of others, that which concerns them most is the reflection of themselves, the photographs of their own characters. The most obvious consequence of the self-knowledge thus forced upon them is to render them alike incapable of self-conceit or self-deprecation. Every one must needs always think of himself as he is, being no more able to do otherwise than is a man in a hall of mirrors to cherish delusions as to his personal appearance.

But self-knowledge means to the mind-readers much more than this: nothing less, indeed, than a shifting of the sense of the identity. When a man sees himself in a mirror he is compelled to distinguish between the bodily self he sees and his real self, the mental and moral self, which is within and unseen. When in turn the mind-reader comes to see the mental and moral self reflected in other minds as in mirrors, the same thing happens. He is compelled to distinguish between this mental and moral self which has been made objective to him, and can be contemplated by him as impartially as if it were another's, from the inner ego which still remains subjective, unseen, and indefinable. In this inner ego the mind-readers recognize the essential identity and being, the noumenal self, the core of the soul, and the true hiding of its eternal life, to which the mind as well as the body is but the garment of a day.

The effect of such a philosophy as this —which indeed with the mind-readers is rather an instinctive consciousness than a philosophy—must obviously be to impart a sense of wonderful superiority to the vicissitudes of this earthly state, and a singular serenity in the midst of the haps and mishaps which threaten or befall the personality. They did indeed appear to me, as I never dreamed men could attain to be, lords of themselves.

It was because I might not hope to attain this enfranchisement from the false ego of the apparent self, without which life seemed to her race scarcely worth living, that my love so pitied me.

But I must hasten on, leaving a thousand things unsaid, to relate the lamentable catastrophe to which it is owing that instead of being still a resident of those blessed islands, in the full enjoyment of that intimate and ravishing companion-ship which by contrast would forever dim the pleasures of all other human society, I recall the bright picture as a memory under other skies.

Among a people who are compelled by the very constitution of their minds to put themselves in the places of others, the sympathy which is the inevitable consequence of perfect comprehension renders envy, hatred, and uncharitableness impossible. But of course there are people less genially constituted than others, and these are necessarily the objects of a certain distaste on the part of associates. Now, owing to the unhindered impact of minds upon one another, the anguish of persons so regarded, despite the tenderest consideration of those about them, is so great that they beg the grace of exile, that, being out of the way, people may think less frequently upon them. There are numerous small islets, scarcely more than rocks, lying to the north of the archipelago, and on these the unfortunates are permitted to live. Only one lives on each islet, as they cannot endure each other even as well as the more happily constituted can endure them. From time to time supplies of food are taken to them, and of course, at any time they wish to take the risk, they are permitted to return to society.

Now, as I have said, the fact which, even more than their out-of-the-way location, makes the islands of the mind-readers unapproachable, is the violence with which the great antarctic current, owing probably to some peculiar configuration of the ocean bed, together with the innumerable rocks and shoals, flows through and about the archipelago.

Ships making the islands from the southward are caught by this current and drawn among the rocks, to their almost certain destruction, while, owing to the violence with which the current sets to the north, it is not possible to approach at all from that direction, or at least it has never been accomplished. Indeed, so powerful are the currents that even the boats which cross the narrow straits between the main islands and the islets of the unfortunate to carry the latter their supplies are ferried over by cables, not trusting to oar or sail.

The brother of my love had charge of one of the boats engaged in this transportation, and being desirous of visiting the islets, I accepted an invitation to accompany him on one of his trips.

know nothing of how the accident happened, but in the fiercest part of the current of one of the straits we parted from the cable, and were swept out to sea. There was no question of stemming the boiling current, our utmost endeavors barely sufficing to avoid being dashed to pieces on the rocks. From the first there was no hope of our winning back to the land, and so swiftly did we drift that by noon—the accident having befallen in the morning—the islands, which are low-lying, had sunk beneath the southeastern horizon.

Among these mind-readers distance is not an insuperable obstacle to the transfer of thought. My companion was in communication with our friends, and from time to time conveyed to me messages of anguish from my dear love; for being well aware of the nature of the currents and the unapproachableness of the islands, those we had left behind as well as we ourselves knew well we should see each other's faces no more. For five days we continued to drift to the northwest, in no danger of starvation, owing to our lading of provisions, but constrained to unintermitting watch and ward by the roughness of the weather. On the fifth day my companion died from exposure and exhaustion. He died very quietly—indeed, with great appearance of relief. The life of the mind-readers while yet they are in the body is so largely spiritual that the idea of an existence wholly so, which seems vague and chill to us, suggests to them a state only slightly more refined than they already know on earth.

After that I suppose I must have fallen into an unconscious state, from which I roused to find myself on an American ship bound for New York, surrounded by people whose only means of communicating with one another is to keep up while together a constant clatter of hissing, guttural, and explosive noises, eked out by all manner of facial contortions and bodily gestures. I frequently find myself staring open-mouthed at those who address me, too much struck by their grotesque appearance to bethink myself of replying.

I find that I shall not live out the voyage, and I do not care to. From my experience of the people on the ship I can judge how I should fare on land amid the stunning Babel of a nation of talkers. And my friends—God bless them! —how lonely I should feel in their very presence! Nay, what satisfaction or consolation, what but bitter mockery, could I ever more find in such human sympathy and companionship as suffice others and once sufficed me—I who have seen and known what I have seen and known! Ah, yes, doubtless it is far better I should die; but the knowledge of the things that I have seen I feel should not perish with me. For hope's sake men should not miss this glimpse of the higher, sun-bathed reaches of the upward path they plod. So thinking, I have written out some account of my wonderful experience, though briefer far, by reason of my weakness, than fits the greatness of the matter. The captain seems an honest, well-meaning man, and to him I shall confide the narrative, charging him, on touching shore, to see it safely in the hands of some one who will bring it to the world's ear.

Note.—The extent of my own connection with the foregoing document is sufficiently indicated by the author himself in the final paragraph.—E. B.

# DREAM

OF A

# FREE-TRADE PARADISE

CYRUS ELDER.

DREAM OF A FREE-TRADE PARADISE.

# DREAM

OF A

# FREE-TRADE PARADISE,

BY

## CYRUS ELDER.

———•◦•———

PHILADELPHIA:
PUBLISHED FOR THE INDUSTRIAL LEAGUE.
BY
HENRY CAREY BAIRD,
INDUSTRIAL PUBLISHER,
406 WALNUT STREET.
1872.

# DREAM OF A FREE-TRADE PARADISE.

## A Laissez Faire Tale.

NOTE.—"*Laissez faire*" is a French phrase nearly equivalent to "let alone"—much used by Free-Traders to express their doctrine, that things should be allowed to take their own course without protection or restraint by law.

I AM a hard-worked professor in a Western college, and, among other things, I teach political economy. Wayland's is our text-book; and having committed it to memory years ago, and made a good many boys memorize and recite it, I am a Free-Trader, of course. I used to have no trouble, but of late there is a good deal of bother with it. The boys read the newspapers out of school, and General Schenck's speeches, and Senator Scott's speeches, and other publications, give them ideas not in the book, and they ask questions sometimes that are hard to answer.

I thought it would be well to study up a little during vacation, so I got several speeches on the free-trade side, and I read one of them in the cars the other day. After I finished it, I undertook to read the platform of principles of the Free-Trade League, but I found in it much food for thought, and made but slow progress. Every proposition tended to one thing—cheapness; and though I believe, of course, that to "buy where you can buy cheapest" is the first maxim of political economy, I was not just then so much concerned about where or how I would buy, as about the sale of my labor for the coming year. I had expected to be re-engaged at the college, of course, but a down-east professor had offered his services at a good deal less per year than I was receiving. Self-respect would not allow me to bid against him, and I believed the trustees would prefer home industry to foreign industry that was untried; but I could not help thinking, suppose they should conclude to "buy where they could buy cheapest?" What, in that case, would become of me?

One proposition, however, pleased me greatly. It was this: " Every country has its peculiar natural advantages, and to

---

**Where all must shovel and hoe, wages must be low.**

11

**Diversified industry is a defence against famine.**

THE PROFESSOR IN THE CAR.

produce what can be most easily produced in it, and to exchange such products for what is more easily produced elsewhere, is the most profitable exertion of industry."

Here, I thought, is an idea that admits of indefinite extension. "Every country"—that means the people, of course; and as the rule should apply to every man, for the nation is composed of individuals, it follows that instead of trying to coerce nature, every person should respect the bent of his genius by pursuing his natural advantages, that is, do whatever comes easiest for him. There are my school boys, for instance; why should they be hammering away at the hardest tasks; and men—why should they consider it meritorious to overcome great obstacles? Why shouldn't they all do the easiest things?

Just here we went through a tunnel, and I asked an intelligent stranger beside me how long it was.

"Nearly a mile," said he.

"Couldn't they get around this place?" I asked.

"Yes," said he, "but it took four miles to do it."

**Where men compete with cheap foreign labor, women will find no work.**

**The rewards of labor increase as occupations become diversified.**

"Well, but it seems to me, that it would have been easier and cheaper to go around than to make such an enormous work as this?"

"You are right, sir; it would have been easier and cheaper to do it the first time, or for a year, or perhaps ten years; but when you consider the saving of that three miles of distance to all the trains that travel over this road in twenty, thirty, or forty years, the tunnel is the best investment the company have made, for it overcomes the difficulty once for all. It's like the tariff that makes us pay something for a few years to build up manufactories, which then give us a more plentiful supply of cheaper goods than we could ever get in any other way."

Ah, thought I, here is one of those Pennsylvania monopolists that I have so often heard about. Of course I did not answer him, but looked out of the car window, where I saw a man grubbing away on a very rough piece of land; and while I was wondering if he intended to sow wheat, and how stupid it was of him, and why he didn't buy his wheat, or go somewhere else where it was easier to raise it, I fell fast asleep.

On awaking I found myself lying on the grass in a little grove, and near me was sitting a venerable man, clad in a closely-fitting suit of fur, and engaged in reading a newspaper, from which he glanced occasionally to regard me with kindly interest.

Surprised, but in no way alarmed, I gathered myself up, and my companion also arising with a friendly nod, I took it upon myself to open a conversation.

"Will you be kind enough to tell me where I am?" said I.

"Sir," said the venerable being, "you are now in the happy country of *Laissez Faire*, where the laws interfere in no way with the employments of the people, and everybody does what is easiest to him. The present government was established by free-trade philosophers, and is now in the hands of Special Commissioners, of whom I am highest in authority."

"Judging from your literary appearance," said I, "you must also be at the head of some institution of learning; and being a teacher myself, I would be glad to know on what principle your schools are conducted."

"On the principle of doing what is easiest," said he. "A boy, for instance, finds it difficult to learn arithmetic, but quite easy to go fishing. He therefore goes fishing. Of course he is a poor scholar, but he probably becomes a good fisherman."

"How are the schools supported?" I asked; "is there a school tax?"

**The introduction of manufactures diversifies agriculture.**

Free-traders say we must not attempt labors in which other nations excel.

THE PROFESSOR AWAKING.

" Oh, no," he replied, " that is one of the heresies of the doctrine of Protection, long since discarded here.   It wont do to tax
one class for the benefit of another; and besides, government has
nothing to do with education.   The let-alone policy is the best.
Every man pays for his own schooling, and the schools are not
crowded, for we recognize the folly of wasting time and trouble
with the mass of children who can never become as clever as the
few who have natural genius for some branch of study.   We
attend to the latter, and let the others pursue some employment
for which they possess natural advantages."

" Might not the dull pupils, however," I asked, " if labored
with and encouraged, eventually develop powers which would
enable them to excel; or, if not, is not the discipline of study of
value to all?"

" That is another heresy of the doctrine of Protection," he
replied.   " There is more profit in doing what comes easiest, and
such experiments are costly.   In this country, cheapness is the

True Americans say we must equal other nations in all good works.

The Earth is a machine given to man to be fashioned for his purposes.

principal consideration, and cheapness and easiness are convertible terms."

" I presume you have no regular course of study, then, for all pupils?" said I.

" No, sir," said he; " and we have discarded several branches which were in vogue in early days. Geography, for instance, is not taught. How absurd it was for a child to spend several years of labor, and a teacher as much of toil, at great expense to the parent, for the purpose of memorizing the facts of this science, when a few pence will purchase a book containing them fully. The child would never be able to remember all the facts in the book, at any rate. To go to memory for such things is a costly and laborious way : to go to the book is easy and cheap, and we prefer it, of course."

Passing from the grove, we entered upon an exceedingly rough, and, indeed, almost impassable road, which conducted us into a small valley, watered by a considerable stream. Observing on the way that the land seemed to have been at one time cultivated, but was now abandoned and grown up with weeds and a young forest, I asked my conductor what it meant.

" Before our Board of Commissioners came in power," said he, " the policy of doing the easiest thing was not understood, and some foolish people had made farms around here; but the soil is naturally poor, and the commissioners obliged them to quit and go over to the other side of the country, which possesses natural advantages for agricultural pursuits."

" Might not this soil, by cultivation, have been made fertile?" I asked.

" Some stupid people maintained this," he replied, " and it was asserted that if the farmers would dig down a number of feet to the limestone, quarry it out, burn it, and spread it on the land, great crops might be produced; but such absurdity could not be encouraged. It would cost too much; and, besides, the business of a farmer is to farm, not to quarry stone or turn lime-burner."

" How did they take the matter?" said I; " did they object to removing?"

" Some did," said he; " but after the stupid business in the valley below us was stopped, all were glad to go. Most of them went over to the other side on the rich lands, but they are a grumbling set, and complain that the rich lands are worked out, and are poorer than these hill-sides."

Passing along, we presently came to a bend in the stream,

Our Mother, the Earth, gives nothing, but is willing to lend everything.

where the valley opened out, and here I saw some ancient ruins which looked like the remains of a furnace, dwelling-houses, and other buildings.

"What is this place?" said I.

"Another triumph of our commissioners," said my companion. "In the former reign of which I spoke, it had been usual to send a fleet of boats twice a year to a large island across the sea, to obtain iron and a variety of implements of the chase and of war, for which were traded the gold and silver in which this country is so very rich. But some curious fellows discovered in these hills veins of rough stone, out of which they declared iron could be made; and they engaged to furnish all that would be needed, and a great deal more than was usually consumed, if the Government would ensure them a sale for it at a fair price. The authorities knew no better than to give such a guarantee, and the work went on. Hundreds of workmen were employed in digging ore and smelting it, and the manufacture of various implements out of the native iron was begun, and the work was progressing on a large scale when the Special Commissioners came into power. Of course they soon found out that iron-making was one of the hardest things to do; and, besides, the iron cost too much, and the Government guarantee was annulled."

"Well, could not the works go on without that?" I asked.

"Oh, no," said he; "it was tried for a while, but the boats brought in a lot of cheaper iron, and the business was abandoned, as was right, and the workers resorted to more productive industries."

"What were they, for instance, if I may ask?"

"Farming the rich land on the other side of the country," he replied. "Of course the grumbling farmers over there complained about so many more coming into the business, and said that it made food so cheap nobody wanted to buy it, which was absurd, of course. The first duty of Government is to see that everything is made cheap, and cheap food is the most important of all. There were other factories, but when the iron went down, they went down also, as was right, of course. The country has no natural advantages for manufacturing, and it is easier and cheaper to get goods from over the sea, where they know how to make everything."

"I should think," said I, "that such remarkable changes could not be made without some trouble, and a great deal of suffering."

"It was all in accordance with nature," said he. "We hold

Labor is the original purchase-money for all things having exchangeable value.

THE GREAT PEANUT SPEECH.

that any industry that cannot sustain itself ought to perish. One man ought not to be taxed to sustain the business of another. There was a pestilent party that argued strongly to us, that we should encourage the making of iron, but the peanut argument shut them up."

"The peanut argument," said I; "what is that?"

"Did you never read my great speech entitled, 'A plea for the peanut, or principles of ·protective political economy?'" he inquired.

"Never," said I.

"You have lost something, then," said he. "I showed how many acres of land in the country would grow peanuts, and how many tons could be produced to the acre, if the Government would only give a bounty for every bushel raised, and what amount of tax it would be on every man, woman, and child in the country; and when the iron-makers came forward with their claims, I put in my plea for the protection of peanuts, and, of

**Labor is the most perishable of commodities.**

course, the absurdity of the whole business was seen by everybody."

"Did no one suggest," I asked, "that in a national point of view, the production of pig-iron and of peanuts might not be equally important?"

"Well, yes, that suggestion was made, but we laughed it down," said he.

As we passed further along into the valley, I was surprised to find no signs of habitation, and observed to my companion that as yet I had seen no dwelling-houses.

"Certainly not," said he. "We long ago gave over building them, for we found out that it was much easier to live in caves in the ground, than to employ a variety of workmen in getting together materials and erecting houses. It is more in accordance with the natural advantages of the country. Besides being costly, buildings are not really necessary, for people are not as plentiful as they used to be."

"Oh, indeed; and what is the reason of that?" I asked.

"There are a number of causes for it," he replied. "There were at one time too many of them, but a large number left the country, which was a good thing, of course. Then, as the farmers had discovered that it was easier to grow peanuts than any other crop, they quit raising everything else, which was all right. It happened, however, that there came a bad peanut year, and a good many people died, which was fortunate, as it was not nearly so easy for the commissioners to find food for them as to bury them."

I had been so much interested in my companion's discourse, that I had not noted the lapse of time, and now suggested to him that I might be detaining him from his duties.

"O, no," said he, "I am not much employed just now, for there is no school."

"Indeed," said I, "and why not?"

"It is, in point of fact," said he, "because there are no children."

"No children," I exclaimed, "and why not?"

"The commissioners discovered that men were about the most costly product of the country," he replied. "During long years of infancy they had to be fed and cared for, yet could do nothing; and to clothe and teach them was also a tremendous labor and expense; while, on the other hand, a cow, ox, or horse was serviceable or fit for food in a few years. So the commissioners determined that it was easier to produce other animals, and

There is no monopoly of home industry.

" NO CHILDREN."

cheaper to get men already full grown from over the seas. The birth of children had already fallen off greatly, for the commissioners had been long opposed to encouraging a surplus of population, and by judiciously strangling or drowning such children as appeared, the product soon ceased. The scheme worked admirably, with the exception that the stupid people over the seas cannot now be induced to come here."

"Then," said I, in amazement, "you have no grown people, either?"

"No," said he, "none whatever. The commissioners survived everybody else, and I survived them, and you see in me all the theoretical beauties of free-trade philosophy reduced to practice, and perfectly illustrated."

More amazed than ever, I scrutinized my companion more closely, and now observed that what I had taken for a neat dress of animal fur, was really his own skin, covered with a growth of hair, and discolored in places by exposure to the weather. I noticed, too, for the first time, that the papers which had helped

Protection is the only defence against monopoly.

---

Protection benefits the State by giving employment to the people.

---

to impress me with his literary character were a copy of the New York *Evening Post*, and the last Report of Hon. D. A. Wells, United States Special Commissioner of Revenue.

" Dear professor," said I, " I observe that the country of *Laissez Faire* still maintains some trade with the outer world ; yet, as you at this time seem to produce nothing, I am at a loss to know what you give in exchange for your favorite literature."

" It is sent to me gratis by the Free-Trade League," he replied.

At this moment I heard a distant noise, which grew in intensity until I recognized a sound which belongs not to the country of *Laissez Faire*—it was a steam whistle. While puzzling over this incongruity, with a sudden jerk the cars stopped, and I awoke from my dream.

# THREE HUNDRED YEARS HENCE

Mary Griffith

# THREE HUNDRED YEARS HENCE.

## CHAPTER I.

It is seldom that men begin to muse and sit alone in the twilight until they arrive at the age of fifty, for until that period the cares of the world and the education of their young children engross all their thoughts. Edgar Hastings, our hero, at thirty years of age was still unmarried, but he had gone through a vast deal of excitement, and the age of musing had been anticipated by twenty years. He was left an orphan at fourteen, with a large income, and the gentleman who had the management of his estates proved faithful, so that when a person of talents and character was wanted to travel with the young man, a liberal recompense was at hand to secure his services. From the age of fourteen to twenty-one he was therefore travelling over Europe; but his education, instead of receiving a check, went on much more advantageously than if he had remained at home, and he became master of all the modern languages in the very countries where they were spoken. The last twelve months of his seven years' tour was spent in England, being stationary in London only during the sitting of Parliament.

B

His talents thus cultivated, and his mind enlarged by liberal travel, he returned to America well worthy the friendship and attention of those who admire and appreciate a character of his stamp. He had not therefore been back more than a year, before his society was courted by some of the best men in the country; but previous to his settling himself into *a home*, he thought it but proper to travel through his own country also. His old friend, still at his elbow, accompanied him; but at the close of the excursion, which lasted nearly two years, he was taken ill of a fever caught from an exposure near the Lakes, and died after a few days' illness.

Edgar Hastings was now entirely alone in the world, and he would have fallen into a deep melancholy, had he not engaged in politics. This occupied him incessantly; and, as his purse was ample and his heart liberally disposed, he found the demands on his time gradually increasing. He had occupations heaped upon him—for rich, disengaged, and willing, every body demanded his aid; and such were the enthusiasm and generosity of his nature, that no one applied in vain.

His first intention, on returning from his tour through his own country, was to improve an estate he had purchased in Pennsylvania, promising himself an amiable and beautiful wife to share his happiness; but politics interfered, and left him no time even for the luxury of musing in the evening. But a man can get weary of politics as well as of any other hard up-hill work; so, at the end of seven years, seeing that the young trees which he had planted were giving shade, and that the house that they were to overshadow was not yet begun, he fell to musing. He wanted something, likewise, to love and protect—so he fell to musing about that. He wished to convert a brisk stream, that fell down the side of a hill opposite to the south end of his grounds, into a waterfall—so he fell to musing about that. He wanted to make an opening through a noble piece of woods that bounded the north side, that he might catch a view of the village steeple— so he fell to musing about that. A beautiful winding river lay in front of his estate, the bank of which sloped down to the water's edge; this tranquillizing scene likewise operated on his feelings, so that politics faded away, and his mind became calm and serene. Thus it was, that at thirty years of age he had these fits of abstraction, and he became a muser.

Men of his age—sensible men—are not so easily pleased as those who are younger. He admired graceful, easy manners, and a polished mind, far before beauty or wealth; and thus fastidious, he doubted whether he should marry at all. Every now and then, too, an old bachelor feeling came over him, and he feared that when his beloved twilight found him sitting under the noble porticos which he intended to build, his wife would drag him away to some far distant route in the city; or that she would, untimely, fill the house with visiters. So, with all the dispositions in the world, he lived alone, though every fit of musing ended by finding a wife at his side, gazing on the dim and fading landscape with him.

While his house was building, he occupied a small stone farm house, at the extremity of the estate. Here he brought his valuable books and prints, well secured from damp and insects by aromatic oils; here did he draw his plans during the day, and here, under a small piazza, did he meditate in the evening, transferring his musings to the little parlour as soon as the damp evenings of autumn compelled him to sit within doors.

Adjoining his estate lived a quaker, by the name of Harley, a steady, upright man, loving his ease, as all quakers do, but having no objection to see his neighbours finer or wiser than himself. He took a fancy to our hero, and the beloved evening hour often found him sitting on the settee with Hastings, when, after enjoying together an animated conversation, he also would fall into the deep feeling which fading scenery, and the energy of such a character as his young friend's, would naturally excite in a mind so tranquil as his own.

At length, the quiet quaker spoke of his daughter, but it was not with a view to draw Edgar's attention; he mentioned her incidentally, and the young man was delighted. In a moment, his imagination depicted her as a beautiful, graceful, accomplished creature; and there could be no doubt that she was amiable and gentle; so he strolled over to his friend's house, ànd was regularly introduced to her. She *was* beautiful, and amiable, and gentle—all this he saw at a glance; but, alas! she had no accomplishment farther than that she wrote an exquisitely clear, neat hand, and was an excellent botanist and florist. But "propinquity" softened down all objections. Every time he strayed away to Pine Grove the eligibilities of the match became more apparent, and his love of grace and polish of mind seemed to be of comparatively littl importance, when he listened to the breathings of the innocent quaker, who thought all of beauty was in a flower, and who infinitely preferred the perfume of a rose or a lilac, to the smell of a dozen lamps in a crowded room. Her name was Ophelia, too.

Mr. Harley, or friend Harley as he was called, was nowise rigid in his creed; for the recent lawsuits between the Orthodox and Hicksite quakers had very much weakened his attachments to the forms of quakerism. He found that the irritable portion of his society had great difficulty in keeping *hands off*, and in preserving the decorum of their order. Peaceful feelings, equable temperaments, being the foundation—the cement, which, for so many years, had bound the fraternity together, were now displaced for the anger and turbulence so often displayed by other sects of Christians.

Litigations amongst themselves—the law—had done that which neither fine nor imprisonment, the derision nor impositions of other sects, could accomplish. The strong cement had cracked along the edge of the bulwarks, where strength was the most necessary, and the waters of discord and disunion were insinuating themselves into every opening. The superstructure was fast crumbling away, and friend Harley looked to the no very distant period when his posterity should cast off the quaker dress, and naturally follow the customs and obey the general laws which govern the whole body of Americans.

This was sensible Valentine Harley's opinion and feeling; in rules of faith he had never been inducted—are there any quakers, apart from a few of their leaders, who can define what their religious faith is? So, although he loved the forms in which he had been educated—although he wore the quaker dress, and made his son and daughter do the same —yet when Edgar Hastings left off musing in the twilight, and was seen at that hour walking slowly down the glen, with Ophelia hanging on his arm, he only heaved a sigh, and wished that the young man said *thee* and *thou*. But this sigh was far from being a painful one; he felt that when the obscure grave, which shuts out all trace of the quaker's place of rest, should close over him, his memory would live fresh and green in the heart of his daughter. Far more should he be reverenced, if he gave her gentle spirit to the strong arm, the highly gifted mind of such a man as Edgar Hastings, than if he compelled her to marry a man of

their own order—to the one who was now prefer-
ing his suit, friend Hezekiah Connerthwaite, a rich,
respectable, yet narrow minded and uneducated
man.

That he consented to his daughter's marriage
willingly, and without an inward struggle, was a
thing not to be expected; but he was too manly,
too virtuous, to use a mean subterfuge with his sect
that he might escape the odium which falls on the
parent who allows his daughter to marry out of the
pale.  He would not suffer his child to wed clan-
destinely, when in reality his heart and reason approved of her choice; when her lover's merits and
claims, and her own happiness, strongly over-
balanced his scruples.  She might have married
privately, and her father, thus rid of the blame of
consenting to her apostacy, could, as usual, take
his seat in their place of worship, without the fear
of excommunication. But Valentine Harley scorned
such duplicity and foolishness; Ophelia was therefore married under her father's roof, and received
her father's blessing; and here, in this well regulated house, Edgar Hastings spent the first year of
his·wedded life.  Here, too, his son was born; and
now no longer a being without kindred or a home,
he found how much happier were the feelings of a
husband and father than those of a selfish, isolated
being.

As he was building a spacious, elegant, and durable mansion, one that should last for many years,
he went slowly to work.  It was begun a year before his marriage, and it was not until his young
son was three months old that he could remove his
family, of which Mr. Harley now made a part, to
their permanent home.  The younger Harley, who
had married and settled at a distance, being induced
to come among them, again to take the property at
Pine Grove, thus adding another link to the bond

of friendship which this happy marriage had created. In the month of May the younger Harley was expected to take possession of his father's house.

It was now February. The new house was completely furnished, and every thing ready for their removal as soon as Mr. Hastings returned from New York, where he had some business of importance to transact. As it called for immediate attention, he deferred unpacking his books, or indeed taking them from the farm house, until his return. It was with great reluctance that he left his wife, who grieved as if the separation was to last for years instead of a fortnight; but he was compelled to go, so after a thousand charges to take care of her health, and imploring her father to watch over her and his little boy, he once more embraced them and tore himself away. His wife followed him with her eyes until she saw him pass their new habitation, cross over the stile and turn the angle; here he stopped to take one more look at the spot where all he loved dwelt, and seeing the group still looking towards him, he waved his handkerchief, and a few steps farther hid him from their sight.

The farm house was at the extremity of the estate, and as it lay on the road leading to the ferry, he thought he would look at the fire which had been burning in the grate all the morning. Mr. Harley said he would extinguish it in the afternoon, and lock up the house, but still he felt a curiosity to see whether all was safe. His servant, with the baggage, had preceded him, and was now waiting for him at the boat; so he hurried in, and passed from the hall to the middle room, where the books were. Here he found an old man sitting, apparently warming himself by the still glowing coals, who made an apology for the intrusion, by saying

that he was very cold, and seeing a fire burning,
for he had looked in at the window, he made bold
to enter.

Mr. Hastings bade him sit still, but the man said
he was about to cross the ferry and must hurry
on, observing that he thought there would be a
great thaw before morning, "and in that case,"
said he, pointing up to the hill, at the foot of which
the house stood, "that great bank of snow will
come down and crush the roof of this house."
Hastings looked up and saw the dangerous position
of the snow bank, and likewise apprehending a
thaw, he begged the man to hurry on and tell his
servant to go over with his baggage, and get all
things in readiness for him on the other side, and
that he would wait for the next boat, which crossed
in fifteen minutes after the other. He gave the
poor man a small piece of money, and after he left
the house Hastings wrote a note about the snow
bank to Mr. Harley, which he knew that gentleman
would see, as he was to be there in the afternoon.
Knowing that he should hear the steam boat bell,
and feeling cold, he drew an old fashioned chair,
something in the form of an easy chair, and fell into
one of his old fits of musing. He thought it would
not be prudent to return to his family merely to say
farewell again, even if there were time, but a melancholy *would* creep over him, as if a final separation
were about to take place. In vain he tried to rouse
himself and shake it off; he closed his eyes, as if by
doing so he could shut out thought, and it did, for
in less than five minutes he was fast asleep.

## CHAPTER II.

HEARING a noise, he suddenly started up. It was dusk, and having lain long in one position, he felt so stiff as to move with difficulty; on turning his head, he saw two strangers looking at him with wonder and pity. "Is the steamboat ready?" exclaimed he, still confused with his long sleep. "Has the bell rung, gentlemen? Bless me, I have overslept myself—what o'clock is it? Why, it is almost dark—I am ashamed of myself."

Finding, after one or two attempts, that he could not get up easily, the two strangers hastened forward and assisted him to rise. They led him to the door, but here the confusion of his mind seemed rather to increase than diminish, for he found himself in a strange place. To be sure, there lay the river, and the hills on the opposite shore still rose in grandeur; but that which was a wide river, now appeared to be a narrow stream; and where his beautiful estate lay, stretching far to the south, was covered by a populous city, the steeples and towers of which were still illuminated by the last rays of the sun.

"Gentlemen," said the bewildered man, "I am in a strange perplexity. I fell asleep at noon in this house, which belongs to me, and after remaining in this deep repose for six hours I awoke, and find myself utterly at a loss to comprehend where I am. Surely I am in a dream, or my senses are leaving me."

"You are not dreaming, neither is your mind wandering; a strange fate is yours," said the elder of the two young men. When you are a little more composed we will tell you how all this has happened; meantime, you must come with me; I shall

take you where you will find a home and a welcome."

"What is your name," said the astonished Hastings, "and how have I been transported hither."

"My name is Edgar Hastings," said the young
man; "and I feel assured that yours is the same.
If I thought you had sufficient fortitude to hear the
strange events which have occurred, I would tell
you at once; but you had better come with me,
and during the evening you shall know all."

Hastings suffered himself to be led by the two
strangers, as he felt cramped and chilly; but every
step he took revived some singular train of thought.
As he proceeded, he saw what appeared to be his
own house, for the shape, dimensions and situation
were like the one he built, and the distance and
direction from his farm house was the same. What
astonished him most was the trees; when he saw
them last they were silver pines, chestnuts, catal-
pas, locusts and sycamores—now the few that remained were only oak and willow; they were of
enormous size, and appeared aged.

"I must wait, I see," said poor Hastings, "for an
explanation of all this; my hope is, that I am dreaming. Here lie trees newly felled, immense trees
they are, and they grew on a spot where I formerly
had a range of offices. I shall awake to-morrow,
no doubt," said he, faintly smiling, "and find myself recompensed for this miserable dream. Pray
what is your name?"—turning to the younger of
the two men.

"My name is Valentine Harley, and I am related
to this gentleman; our family have, at intervals,
intermarried, for upwards of three hundred years."

"Valentine Harley!" exclaimed Hastings, "that
is the name of my wife's father. There never was
any of the name of Valentine, to my knowledge,
but his; and I did not know that there was another

Edgar Hastings in existence, excepting myself and my young son."

They were now in front of the house—the massive north portico had been replaced by another of different shape; the windows were altered; the vestibule, the main hall, the staircase, no longer the same—yet the general plan was familiar, and when they opened the door of a small room in the north wing, he found it exactly to correspond with what he had intended for his laboratory.

After persuading him to take some refreshments, they conducted him to his chamber, and the two young men related to the astonished Hastings what follows. We shall not stop to speak of his surprise, his sufferings, his mortal agony—nor of the interruptions which naturally took place; but the group sat up till midnight. It is needless to say that not one of the three closed his eyes the remainder of the night.

"Early this morning," began the younger Edgar Hastings—"and be not dismayed when I tell you, that instead of the 15th of February, 1835, it is now the 15th of April, 2135—several of us stood looking at some labourers who were at work cutting a street through the adjoining hill. Our engines had succeeded in removing the trees, rocks and stones, which lay embedded in the large mounds of earth, and about ten o'clock the street, with the exception of the great mass which covered your farm house, was entirely cut through to the river. This portion of it would have been also removed, but both from papers in my possession and tradition, a stone building, containing many valuable articles, was supposed to be buried there, by the fall of the hill near which it stood.

"To extend the city, which is called Hamilton, my property, or rather, I should say, your property, was from time to time sold, till at length nothing remains in our possession but this house and a few acres of ground; the last we sold was that strip on which your farm house stands. It was with great reluctance that I parted with this portion, as I could not but consider it as your sepulchre, which in fact it has proved to be.

"When they commenced cutting through the hill the top was covered with large oaks, some of which, when sawed through, showed that they were upwards of a century old; and one in particular, which stood on the boundary line, had been designated as a landmark in all the old title deeds of two hundred years' standing.

"About three hours before you were liberated the workmen came to a solid stratum of ice, a phenomenon so extraordinary, that all the people in the vicinity gathered to the spot to talk and ponder over it. An aged man, upwards of ninety, but with his faculties unimpaired, was among the number present. He said, that in his youth his great grandfather had often spoken of a tradition respecting this hill. It was reported to have been much higher, and that a ravine, or rather a precipitous slope, a little below the road, was quite filled up by the overthrow of the hill. That the fall had been occasioned by an earthquake, and the peak of the hill, after dislodging a huge rock, had entirely covered up a stone building which contained a large treasure. He very well remembered hearing his aged relative say, that the hill was covered with immense pines and chestnuts.

"The truth of part of this story was corroborated by ancient documents in my possession, and I hastened to my library to search for some old family papers, which had been transmitted to me with great care. I soon found what I wanted, and with a map of the estate, in which, from father to son, all the alterations of time had been carefully marked down, I was able to point out the exact spot on which the old stone farm house stood. In a letter from a gentleman named Valentine Harley, which, with several from the same hand, accompanied the different maps, an account was given of the avalanche which buried the house and filled up the ravine and gap below. As the originals were likely to be destroyed by time, they had been copied in a large book, containing all the records of the family, which, from period to period, receive the attestation of the proper recording officer, so that you may look upon these documents as a faithful transcript of every thing of moment that has occurred within the last three hundred years. It was only last November that I entered an account of the sale of this very strip of land in which the stone house lay.

" Here is the first thing on record—a letter, as I observed, from the father-in-law of Edgar Hastings, my great ancestor—but I forget that it is of you he speaks. Believe me, dear sir, that most deeply do we sympathize with you; but your case is so singular, and the period in which all this suffering occurred is so very remote, that your strong sense will teach you to bear your extraordinary fate like a man. Allow me to read the letter; it is directed to James Harley, son to the above mentioned Valentine Harley.

" 'Second month, 17th, 1834. My dear son— Stay where thou art, for thy presence will but aggravate our grief. I will give thee all the particulars of the dreadful calamity which has befallen us. I have not yet recovered from the shock, and thy sister is in the deepest wo; but it is proper that thou shouldst know the truth, and there is no one to tell thee but myself. On Monday the 15th, my dear son Edgar Hastings took a tender fare-

c

well of thy sister and his babe, shaking hands with me in so earnest and solemn a manner, that one prone to superstition would have said it was prophetic of evil. We saw him walk briskly along the road until the angle, which thou knowest is made by the great hill, shut him from our sight; but just before he turned the angle he cast a look towards the house wherein all his treasure lay, and seeing that we were watching his steps, he waved his handkerchief and disappeared. His intention, thou knowest, was to proceed to New York; Samuel, his faithful servant, was to accompany him, and had gone forward in the carriage with the baggage, as Edgar preferred to walk to the boat. Thy poor sister and myself stood on the old piazza waiting until the little steamboat—it was the Black Hawk—should turn the great bend and appear in sight, for it was natural, thou knowest, to linger and look at the vessel which held one so dear to us both. It was the first time that thy sister had been separated from Edgar, and she stood weeping silently, leaning on my arm, as the little steamboat shot briskly round the bend and appeared full in sight. Thou must recollect that the channel brings the boat nearly opposite the stone farm house, and even at that distance, although we could not distinguish features or person, yet we fancied we saw the waving of a handkerchief. At that instant the Black Hawk blew up, every thing went asunder, and to my affrighted soul the boat appeared to rise many feet out of the water. I cannot paint to thee our agony, or speak of the profound grief, the unextinguishable grief, of thy dear sister; she lies still in silent wo, and who is there, save her Maker, who dares to comfort her.

"'I told thee in a previous letter, written I believe on the 12th, that I apprehended a sudden thaw. I mentioned my fears to our dear Edgar, and with his usual prudence he gave orders to strengthen some of the embankments below the ravine. Among other things I thought of his valuable books and instruments, which still remained in the stone farm house, and that very afternoon I intended to have them removed to Elmwood. At the instant the dreadful explosion took place, the great snow bank, which thou recollectest lay above the house in the hollow of the hill, slid down and entirely covered the building; and, in another second, the high peak of the hill, heavily covered with large pines, fell down and buried itself in the ravine and gap below. The building and all its valuable contents lie buried deep below the immense mass of earth, but we stop not in our grief to care for it, as he who delighted in them is gone from us for ever.

" 'Thy sister, thy poor sister, when the first horrible shock was over, would cling to the hope that Edgar might be spared, and it was with the greatest difficulty that I could prevent her from flying to the spot where the crowd had collected. Alas! no one lived to tell how death had overtaken them. Of the five persons engaged on board, three of their bodies have since been found; this was in dragging the water. It seems there were but few passengers, perhaps only our beloved Edgar, his poor servant Samuel, and one or two others. An old man was seen to enter the boat just as she was moving off; *his* body was found on the bank, and on searching his pockets a small piece of silver, a quarter of a dollar, was taken out, which I knew in a moment; it was mine only an hour before, and had three little crosses deeply indented on the rim, with a hole in the centre of the coin; I made these marks on it the day before, for a particular purpose; I could therefore identify the money at once. About an hour before Edgar left us, thinking he might want small silver, I gave him a handful, and this piece was among the number.  He must have given it to the man as soon as he got on board, perhaps for charity, as the man was poor, and probably had begged of him.  This at once convinced me that our dear Edgar was in the fatal boat.  We have made every exertion to recover the body, but are still unsuccessful; nor can we find that of our poor faithful Samuel.  The body of the horse was seen floating down the river yesterday; and the large trunk, valueless thing now, was found but this morning near the stone fence on the opposite shore.

" ' There were some valuable parchments, title deeds, in a small leather valise, which our dear Edgar carried himself—but what do we care for such things now, or for the gold pieces which he also had in the same case.  Alas! we think of nothing but of the loss of him, thy much valued brother. Edgar Hastings has been taken from us, and although thy poor sister is the greatest sufferer, yet *all* mourn.

" ' Offer up thy prayers, my son, that God will please to spare thy sister's reason; if that can be preserved, time will soften this bitter grief, and some little comfort will remain, for she has Edgar's boy to nourish and protect.  As to me, tranquil as I am compelled to be before her, I find that my chief pleasure, my happiness, is for ever gone.  Edgar was superior to most men, ay, to any man living, and so excellent was he in heart, and so virtuous and upright in all his ways, that I trust his pure spirit has ascended to the Great Being who gave it.

" ' Do not come to us just now, unless it be necessary to thy peace of mind; but if thou shouldst come, ask not to see thy sister, for the sight of any one, save me and her child, is most painful to her.

" ' Kiss thy babe, and bid him not forget his afflicted grandfather.  God bless thee and thy kind wife.—Adieu, my son.    VALENTINE HARLEY.' "

It need not be said that Edgar Hastings was plunged in profound grief at hearing this epistle read; his excellent father, his beloved wife, his darling child, were brought before him, fresh as when he last saw them; and now the withering thought came over him that he was to see them no more! After a few moments spent in bitter anguish, he raised his head, and motioned the young man to proceed.

"Meantime the workmen proceeded in their labours, and so great was the anxiety of all, that upwards of fifty more hands were employed to assist in removing the thick layer of ice which apparently covered the whole building. When the ice was removed, we came immediately to the crushed roof of the house, into which several of the labourers would have worked their way had we not withheld them. After placing the engines in front they soon cleared a road to the entrance, and by sundown Valentine Harley and myself stood before the doorway of the low stone farm house.

"It was not without great emotion that we came thus suddenly in view of a building which had lain under such a mass of earth for three centuries. We are both, I trust, men of strong and tender feelings, and we could not but sigh over the disastrous fate of our great ancestor, distant as was the period of his existence. We had often thought of it, for it was the story of our childhood, and every document had been religiously preserved. We stood for a few moments looking at the entrance in silence, for among other letters there were two or three, written late in life by your faithful and excellent wife—was not her name Ophelia?"

"It was, it was," said the afflicted man; "go on, and ask me no questions, for my reason is unsteady."

"In one of these letters she suggested the possi-

c 2

bility that her beloved husband might have been buried under the ruins; that the thought had sometimes struck her; but her father believed otherwise. That within a few years an old sailor had returned to his native place, and as it was near Elmwood, he called on her to state that it was his firm belief that Mr. Hastings did not perish in the Black Hawk. His reason for this belief was, that on the way to the ship he encountered an old friend, just at that moment leaving the low stone building. 'I wanted him,' said the old sailor, 'to jump in the wagon and go with me to the wharf, but he refused, as he had business on the other side of the river. Besides, said my friend, the gentleman within, pointing to the door, has given me a quarter of a dollar to go forward and tell the captain of the Black Hawk that he cannot cross this trip. This gentleman, he said, was Mr. Hastings.'

"Another letter stated—I think it was written by the wife of James Harley, your brother-in-law—that, in addition to the above, the old sailor stated, that the ship in which he sailed had not raised anchor yet, when they heard the explosion of the Black Hawk, of which fact they became acquainted by means of a little fishing boat that came alongside, and which saw her blow up. He observed to some one near, that if that was the case, an old shipmate of his had lost his life. The sailor added likewise, that he had been beating about the world for many years, but at length growing tired, and finding old age creeping on him, he determined to end his days in his native village. Among the recitals of early days was the bursting of the Black Hawk and the death of Mr. Hastings, which latter fact he contradicted, stating his reasons for believing that you were not in the boat. The idea of your being buried under the ruins, and the dread that you might have perished with hunger, so afflicted the poor Lady Ophelia that she fell into a nervous fever, of which she died."

"Say no more—tell me nothing farther," said the poor sufferer; "I can listen no longer—good night—good night—leave me alone."

The young men renewed the fire, and were about to depart, when he called them back.

"Excuse this emotion—but my son—tell me of him; did he perish?"

"No—he lived to see his great grandchildren all married: I think he was upwards of ninety when he died."

"And what relation are you to him?"

"I am the great grandson of your great grandson," said Edgar Hastings the younger; "and this young man is the eighth in descent from your brother, James Harley. We both feel respect and tenderness for you, and it shall be the business of our lives to make you forget your griefs. Be comforted, therefore, for we are your children. In the morning you shall see my wife and children. Meantime, as we have not much more to say, let us finish our account of meeting you, and then we trust you will be able to get a few hours' rest."

"Rest!" said the man who had slept three hundred years, "I think I have had enough of sleep; but proceed."

"When the thought struck us that your bones might lie under the ruins, we did not wish any common eye to see them; we therefore dismissed the workmen, and entered the door by ourselves. We came immediately into a square hall, at the end of which was the opening to what is called in all the papers the middle room; the door had crumbled away. The only light in the room proceeded from a hole which had been recently made by the removal of the ice on the roof, but it was sufficient to show the contents of the room. We saw the boxes, so often mentioned in all the letters, nine in number, and four large cases, which we supposed to be instruments. The table and four chairs were in good preservation, and on the table lay the very note which you must have written but a few minutes before the ice covered you. On walking to the other side of the room, the light fell on the large chair in which you were reclining.

" ' This is the body of our great ancestor,' said Valentine Harley, ' and now that the air has been admitted it will crumble to-dust. Let us have the entrance nailed up, and make arrangements for giving the bones an honourable grave.'

" ' Unfortunate man,' said I; ' he must have perished with hunger—and yet his flesh does not appear to have wasted. It is no doubt the first owner of our estate, and he was buried in the fall of the ice and hill. The old sailor was right. His cap of seal-skin lies at the back of his head, his gloves are on his lap, and there is the cameo on his little finger, the very one described in the paper which offered that large reward for the recovery of his body. The little valise lies at his feet—how natural—how like a living being he looks; one could almost fancy he breathes.'

" ' My fancy is playing the fool with me,' said Valentine; ' he not only appears to breathe, but he moves his hand. If we stay much longer our senses will become affected, and we shall imagine that he can rise and walk.'

" We stepped back, therefore, a few paces; but you may imagine our surprise, when you opened your eyes and made an attempt to get up. At length you spoke, and we hastened to you; our humanity and pity, for one so singularly circumstanced, being stronger than our fears. You know the rest. I picked up the valise, and there it lies."

We shall draw a veil over the next two months of our hero's existence. His mind was in distress and confusion, and he refused to be comforted; but the young men devoted themselves to him, and they had their reward in seeing him at length assume a tranquil manner—yet the sad expression of his countenance never left him. His greatest pleasure—a melancholy one it was, which often made him shed tears—was to caress the youngest child; it was about the age of his own, and he fancied he saw a resemblance. In fact, he saw a strong likeness to his wife in the lady who now occupied Elmwood, and her name being Ophelia rendered the likeness more pleasing. She had been told of the strange relationship which existed between her guest and themselves; but, at our hero's request, no other human being was to know who he was, save Edgar Hastings the younger and his wife, and Valentine Harley. It was thought most prudent to keep it a secret from the wife of the latter, as her health was exceedingly delicate, and her husband feared that the strangeness of the affair might disturb her mind.

Behold our hero, then, in full health and vigour, at the ripe age of thirty-two, returning to the earth after an absence of three hundred years! Had it not been for the loss of his wife and son, and his excellent father, he surely was quite as happily circumstanced, as when, at twenty-one, he returned from Europe, unknowing and unknown. He soon made friends *then*, and but for the canker at his heart he could make friends again. He thought of nothing less than to appear before the public, or of engaging in any pursuit. His fortune, and that part of his father-in-law's which naturally would have fallen to him, was now in the possession of this remote descendent. He was willing to let it so remain, retaining only sufficient for his wants; and his amiable relation took care that his means were ample.

To divert his mind, and keep him from brooding

over his sorrows, his young relative proposed that
they should travel through the different states.
"Surely," said he, "you must feel a desire to see
what changes three hundred years have made. Are
not the people altered? Do those around you talk,
and dress, and live as you were accustomed to do?"

"I see a difference certainly," said Hastings,
"but less than I should have imagined. But my
mind has been in such confusion, and my grief has
pressed so heavily on my heart, that I can observe
nothing. I will travel with you, perhaps it may be
of service; let us set out on the first of May. Shall
we go northward first, or where?"

"I think we had better go to New York," said
Edgar, "and then to Boston; we can spend the
months of May, June and July very pleasantly in
travelling from one watering place to another. We
now go in locomotive cars, without either gas or
steam."

"Is that the way you travel now?" exclaimed
Hastings.

"Yes, certainly; how should we travel? Oh, I
recollect, you had balloons and air cars in your
time."

"We had balloons, but they were not used as
carriages; now and then some adventurous man
went up in one, but it was merely to amuse the people. Have you discovered the mode of navigating
balloons?"

"Oh yes; we guide them as easily through the
air, as you used to do horses on land."

"Do you never use horses to travel with now?"

"No, never. It is upwards of a hundred years
since horses were used either for the saddle or carriage; and full two hundred years since they were
used for ploughing, or other farming or domestic
purposes."

"You astonish me; but in field sports, or horse
racing, there you must have horses."

The young man smiled. "My dear sir," said he, "there is no such thing as field sports or horse racing now. Those brutal pastimes, thank heaven, have been entirely abandoned. In fact, you will be surprised to learn, that the races of horses, asses and mules are almost extinct. I can assure you, that they are so great a curiosity now to the rising generation, that they are carried about with wild beasts as part of the show."

"Then there is no travelling on horseback? I think that is a great loss, as the exercise was very healthy and pleasant."

"Oh, we have a much more agreeable mode of getting exercise now. Will you take a ride on the land or a sail on the water?"

"I think I should feel a reluctance in getting into one of your new fashioned cars. Do the steam-boats cross at what was called the Little Ferry, where the Black Hawk went from when her boiler exploded?"

"Steamboats indeed! they have been out of use since the year 1950. But suspend your curiosity until we commence our journey; you will find many things altered for the better."

"One thing surprises me," said Hastings. "You wear the quaker dress; indeed, it is of that fashion which the gravest of the sect of my time wore; but you do not use the mode of speech—is that abolished among you?"

The young man, whom we shall in future call Edgar, laughed out. "Quaker!" said he; "why, my dear sir, the quakers have been extinct for upwards of two centuries. My dress is the fashion of the present moment; all the young men of my age and standing dress in this style now. Does it appear odd to you?"

"No," said Hastings, "because this precise dress was worn by the people called Friends or Quakers, in my day—strange that I should have to use this curious mode of speech—my day! yes, like the wandering Jew, I seem to exist to the end of time. I see one alteration or difference, however; you wear heavy gold buckles in your shoes, the quakers wore strings; you have long ruffles on your hands, they had none; you wear a cocked hat, and they wore one with a large round rim."

"But the women—did they dress as my wife does?"

"No.—Your wife wears what the old ladies before my time called a *frisk* and petticoat; it is the fashion of the year 1780. Her hair is cropped and curled closely to her head, with small clusters of curls in the hollow of each temple. In 1835 the hair was dressed in the Grecian style—but you can see the fashion. You have preserved the picture of my dear Ophelia; she sat to two of the best painters of the day, Sully and Ingham; the one *you* have was painted by Ingham, and is in the gay dress of the time. The other, which her brother had in his possession, was in a quaker dress, and was painted by Sully."

"We have it still, and it is invaluable for the sweetness of expression and the grace of attitude. The one in your room is admirable likewise; it abounds in beauties. No one since has ever been able to paint in that style; it bears examination closely. Was he admired as an artist in your day?"

"Yes; he was a distinguished painter, but he deserved his reputation, for he bestowed immense labour on his portraits, and sent nothing unfinished from his hands."

"But portrait painting is quite out of date now; it began to decline about the year 1870. It was a strange taste, that of covering the walls with paintings, which your grandchildren had to burn up as useless lumber. Where character, beauty and grace were combined, and a good artist to embody them, it was well enough; a number of these beautiful fancy pieces are still preserved. Landscape and historical painting is on the decline also. There are no good artists now, but you had a delightful painter in your day—Leslie. His pictures are still considered as very great treasures, and they bring the very highest prices."

"How is it with sculpture? That art was beginning to improve in my day."

"Yes; and has continued to improve. We now rival the proudest days of Greece. But you must see all these things. The Academy of Fine Arts in Philadelphia will delight you; it is now the largest in the world. In reading an old work I find that in your time it was contemptible enough, for in the month of April of 1833, the Academy of Fine Arts in that city was so much in debt, as to be unable to sustain itself. It was with the greatest difficulty that the trustees could beg a sum sufficient to pay the debts. The strong appeal that was made to the public enabled them to continue it a little longer in its impoverished condition, but it seems that it crumbled to pieces, and was not resuscitated until the year 1850, at which time a taste for the art of sculpture began to appear in this country."

On the first of May the two gentlemen commenced their tour—not in locomotive engines, nor in steamboats, but in curious vehicles that moved by some internal machinery. They were regulated every hour at the different stopping places, and could be made to move faster or slower, to suit the pleasure of those within. The roads were beautifully smooth and perfectly level; and Hastings observed that there were no dangerous passes, for a strong railing stretched along the whole extent of every elevation. How different from the roads

D

of 1834! Then men were reckless or prodigal of life; stages were overturned, or pitched down some steep hill—rail cars bounded off the rails, or set the vehicles on fire—steamboats exploded and destroyed many lives—horses ran away and broke their riders' necks—carts, heavily laden, passed over children and animals—boats upset in squalls of wind—in short, if human ingenuity had been exerted to its fullest extent, there could not be contrivances better suited to shorten life, or render travelling more unsafe and disagreeable.

Instead of going directly to New York, as they at first contemplated, they visited every part of Pennsylvania. Railroads intersected one another in every direction; every thing was a source of amazement and amusement to Hastings. The fields were no longer cultivated by the horse or the ox, nor by small steam engines, as was projected in the nineteenth century, but by a self-moving plough, having the same machinery to propel it as that of the travelling cars. Instead of rough, unequal grounds, gullied, and with old tree stumps in some of the most valuable parts of the field, the whole was one beautiful level; and, where inclinations were unavoidable, there were suitable drains. The same power mowed the grass, raked it up, spread it out, gathered it, and brought it to the barn—the same power scattered seeds, ploughed, hoed, harrowed, cut, gathered, threshed, stored and ground the grain—and the same power distributed it to the merchants and small consumers.

"Wonderful, most wonderful," said the astonished Hastings. "I well remember this very farm; those fields, the soil of which was washed away by the precipitous fall of rain from high parts, are now all levelled smooth. The hand of time has done nothing better for the husbandman than in perfecting such operations as these. Now, every inch of ground is valuable; and this very farm, once only capable of supporting a man, his wife and five children in the mere necessaries of life, must now give to four times that number every luxury."

"Yes, you are right; and instead of requiring the assistance of four labourers, two horses and two oxen, it is all managed by four men alone! The machines have done every thing—they fill up gullies, dig out the roots of trees, plough down hills, turn water courses—in short, they have entirely superseded the use of cattle of any kind."

"But I see no fences," said Hastings; "how is this? In my day, every man's estate was enclosed by a fence or wall of some kind; now, for boundary lines I see nothing but a low hedge, and a moveable wire fence for pasturage for cows."

"Why should there be the uncouth and expensive fences, which I find by the old books were in use in 1834, when we have no horses; there is no fear of injury now from their trespassing. All our carriages move on rails, and cannot turn aside to injure a neighbouring grain field. Cows, under no pretence whatever, are allowed to roam at large; and it would be most disgraceful to the corporate bodies of city or county to allow hogs or sheep to run loose in the streets or on the road. The rich, therefore, need no enclosure but for ornament, which, as it embellishes the prospect, is always made of some pleasant looking evergreen or flowering shrub. In fact, it is now a state affair, and when a poor man is unable to enclose the land himself, it is done by money lawfully appropriated to the purpose."

"And dogs—I see no dogs," said Hastings. In my day every farmer had one or more dogs; in little villages there were often three and four in each house; the cities were full of them, notwithstanding the dog laws—but I see none now."

" No—it is many years since dogs were domesticated; it is a rarity to see one now. Once in awhile some odd, eccentric old fellow will bring a dog with him from some foreign port, but he dare not let him run loose. I presume that in your time hydrophobia was common; at least, on looking over a file of newspapers of the year 1930, called the Recorder of Self-Inflicted Miseries, I saw several accounts of that dreadful disease. Men, women, children, animals, were frequently bitten by mad dogs in those early days. It is strange, that so useless an animal was caressed, and allowed to come near your persons, when the malady to which they were so frequently liable, and from which there was no guarding, no cure, could be imparted to human beings."

" Well, what caused the final expulsion of dogs?"

" You will find the whole account in that old paper called the Recorder of Self-Inflicted Miseries; there, from time to time, all the accidents that happened to what were called steamboats, locomotive engines, stages, &c. were registered. You will see that in the year 1860, during the months of August and September, more than ten thousand dogs were seized with that horrible disease, and that upward of one hundred thousand people fell victims to it. It raged with the greatest fury in New York, Philadelphia, and Baltimore; and but for the timely destruction of every dog in the South, ten times the number of human beings would have perished. The death from hydrophobia is as disgraceful to a corporate body, as if the inhabitants had died of thirst, when good water was near them."

" This was horrible; the consternation of the people must have been very great—equal to what was felt during the cholera. Did you ever read of that terrible disease?"

" No, I do not recollect it——Oh, yes, now I re-

member to have read something of it—but that came
in a shape that was not easy to foresee. But dogs
were always known to be subject to this awful disease, and therefore encouraging their increase was
shameful. Posterity had cause enough to curse the
memory of their ancestors, for having entailed such
a dreadful scourge upon them. The panic, it seems,
was so great, that to this day children are more
afraid of looking at a dog, for they are kept among
wild beasts as a curiosity, than at a Bengal tiger."

"I confess I never could discover in what their
usefulness consisted. They were capable of feeling
a strong attachment to their master, and had a show
of reason and intelligence, but it amounted to very
little in its effects. It was very singular, but I used
frequently to observe, that men were oftentimes
more gentle and kind to their dogs than to their
wives and children; and much better citizens would
these children have made, if their fathers had bestowed half the pains in *breaking them in*, and in
training them, that they did on their dogs. It was a
very rare circumstance if a theft was prevented by
the presence of a dog; when such a thing *did* occur, every paper spoke of it, and the anecdote was
never forgotten. But had they been ever so useful,
so necessary to man's comfort, nothing could com-
pensate or overbalance the evil to which he was
liable from this disease. Were the dogs all destroyed at once?"

"Yes; the papers say, that by the first of October
there was but one dog to be seen, and the owner of
that had to pay a fine of three thousand dollars, and
be imprisoned for one year at hard labour. When
you consider the horrible sufferings of so many
people, and all to gratify a pernicious as well as
foolish fondness for an animal, we cannot wonder
at the severity of the punishment."

"I very well remember how frequently I was

D 2

annoyed by dogs when riding along the road. A
yelping cur has followed at my horse's heels for five
or six minutes, cunningly keeping beyond the reach
of my whip—some dogs do this all their lives.
Have the shepherd's dogs perished likewise—all,
did you say ?"

"Yes ; every dog—pointers, setters, hounds—all
were exterminated ; and I sincerely hope that the
breed will never be encouraged again. In fact, the
laws are so severe that there is no fear of it, for no
man can bring them in the country without incur-
ring a heavy fine, and in particular cases imprisonment at hard labour. We should as soon expect to
see a wolf or a tiger running loose in the streets as
a dog."

Every step they took excited fresh remarks from
Hastings, and his mind naturally turned to the
friends he had lost. How perfect would have been
his happiness if it had been permitted that his wife
and his father could be with him to see the improved
state of the country. When he looked forward to
what his life might be—unknown, alone—he re-
gretted that he had been awakened : but his kind
relative, who never left him for a moment, as soon
as these melancholy reveries came over him hurried him to some new scene.

They were now in Philadelphia, the Athens of
America, as it was called three centuries back.
Great changes had taken place here. Very few
of the public edifices had escaped the all-devouring
hand of time. In fact, Hastings recognised but
five—that beautiful building called originally the
United States Bank, the Mint, the Asylum for the
Deaf and Dumb, and the Girard College. The
latter continued to flourish, notwithstanding its
downfall was early predicted, in consequence of the
prohibition of clergymen in the direction of its affairs. The dispute, too, about the true signification

of the term "orphan" had been settled; it was at length, after a term of years, twenty, I think, decided, that the true meaning and intent of Stephen Girard, the wise founder of the institution, was to make it a charity for those children who had lost *both* parents.

"I should not think," said Hastings, on hearing this from Edgar, "that any one could fancy, for a moment, that Girard meant any thing else."

"Why no, neither you nor I, nor ninety-nine out of a hundred, would decide otherwise; but it seems a question was raised, and all the books of reference were appealed to, as well as the poets. In almost every case, an *orphan* was said to be a child deprived of one or both parents; and, what is very singular, the term orphan occurs but *once* throughout the Old and New Testaments. In Lamentations it says, 'We are *orphans*, and fatherless, and our mothers are as widows.' Now, in the opinion of many, the *orphan* and *fatherless*, and those whose mothers are as widows, here mentioned, are three distinct sets of children—that is, as the lament says, *some* of us are orphans, meaning children without father and mother, *some* of us are fatherless; and the third set says, 'our mothers are as widows.' This means, that in consequence of their fathers' absence, their mothers were as desolate and helpless as if in reality they were widows by the *death* of their husbands. This text, therefore, settles nothing. Girard, like all the unlettered men of the age, by the term *orphan*, understood it to mean a child without parents."

"I very well remember," said Hastings, "that on another occasion when the term came in question, I asked every man and woman that worked on and lived near the great canal, what they meant by orphan, and they *invariably*, without a *single* exception, said it meant a child without parents."

" Well, the good sense of the trustees, at the end of the time I mentioned, decided after the manner of the multitude—for it was from this mass that their objects of charity were taken. And there is no instance on the records, of a widow begging admittance for her fatherless boys. They knew very well what being an orphan meant, but to their praise be it said, if *fatherless* children had been included in the term, there were very few who would not have struggled as long as it was in their power, before their boys should be taken to a charitable institution."

" I recollect, too," said Hastings, " that great umbrage was taken by many persons because the clergy were debarred from any interference in the management of the college. No evil, you say, has arisen from this prohibition ?"

" None at all," replied Edgar. " The clergy were not offended by it; they found they had enough to do with church affairs. It has been ever since in the hands of a succession of wise, humane, and honest men. The funds have gone on increasing, and as they became more than sufficient for the purposes of the college, the overplus has been lawfully spent in improving the city."

" In the year 1835—alas, it seems to me that but a few days ago I existed at that period—was there not an Orphan Asylum here ?"

" Yes, my dear sir, the old books speak of a small establishment of that kind, founded by several sensible and benevolent women ; but it was attended with very great personal sacrifices—for there was in that century a very singular, and, we must say, disgusting practice among all classes, to obtain money for the establishment of any charitable, benevolent, or literary institution. Both men and women—women for the most part, because men used then to shove off from themselves all that was irk-

some or disagreeable—women, I say, used to go
from door to door, and in the most humble manner
beg a few dollars from each individual. Sometimes,
the Recorder of Self-Inflicted Miseries says, that
men and women of coarse minds and mean education were in the habit of insulting the committee
who thus turned beggars. They did not make their
refusal in decent terms even, but added insult to it.
In the course of time the Recorder goes on to say,
men felt ashamed of all this, and their first step was
to relieve women from the drudgery and disgrace
of begging. After that, but it was by degrees, the
different corporate bodies of each state took the
matter up, and finally every state had its own humane and charitable institutions, so that there are
now no longer any private ones, excepting such as
men volunteer to maintain with their own money."

"Did the old Orphan Asylum of Philadelphia, begun by private individuals, merge into the one now
established?"

"No," replied Edgar; "the original asylum
only existed a certain number of years, for people
got tired of keeping up a charity by funds gathered
in this loose way. At length, another man of immense wealth died, and bequeathed all his property
to the erection and support of a college for orphan
girls—and this time the world was not in doubt as
to the testator's meaning. From this moment a new
era took place with regard to women, and we owe
the improved condition of our people entirely to the
improvement in the education of the female poor;
blessed be the name of that man."

"Well, from time to time you must tell me the
rise and progress of all these things; at present I
must try and find my way in this now truly beautiful city. This is Market street, but so altered that
I should scarcely know it."

"Yes, I presume that three hundred years would

improve the markets likewise. But wherein is it altered ?"

" In my day the market was of one story, or rather had a roof supported by brick pillars, with a neat stone pavement running the whole length of the building. Market women not only sat under each arch and outside of the pillars, but likewise in the open spaces where the streets intersected the market. Butchers and fish sellers had their appropriate stalls; and clerks of the market, as they were called, took care that no imposition was practised. Besides this, the women used to bawl through the streets, and carry their fish and vegetables on their heads."

" All that sounds very well ; but our old friend, the Recorder of Self-Inflicted Miseries, mentions this very market as a detestable nuisance, and the manner of selling things through the streets shameful. Come with me, and let us see wherein this is superior to the one you describe."

The two friends entered the range above at the Schuylkill, for to that point had the famous Philadelphia market reached. The building was of two stories, built of hewn stone, and entirely fire-proof, as there was not a particle of wood-work or other ignitable matter in it. The upper story was appropriated to wooden, tin, basket, crockery, and other domestic wares, such as stockings, gloves, seeds, and garden utensils, all neatly arranged and kept perpetually clean. On the ground floor, in cool niches, under which ran a stream of cold, clear water, were all the variety of vegetables; and there, at this early season, were strawberries and green peas, all of which were raised in the neighbourhood. The finest of the strawberries were those that three centuries before went by the name, as it now did, of the *dark hautbois*, rich in flavour and delicate in perfume. Women, dressed in close caps and snow white aprons, stood or sat modestly by their baskets—not, as formerly, bawling out to the passers-by and entreating them to purchase of them, but waiting for their turn with patience and good humour. Their hair was all hidden, save a few plain braids or plaits in front, and their neck was entirely covered. Their dress was appropriate to their condition, and their bearing had both dignity and grace.

"Well, this surpasses belief," said Hastings. " Are these the descendants of that coarse, vulgar, noisy, ill dressed tribe, one half of whom appeared before their dirty baskets and crazy fixtures with tawdry finery, and the other half in sluttish, uncouth clothes, with their hair hanging about their face, or stuck up behind with a greasy horn comb? What has done all this?"

" Why, the improvement which took place in the education of women. While women were degraded as they were in your time"——

"In my time, my dear Edgar," said Hastings, quickly—" in my time! I can tell you that women were not in a degraded state then. Go back to the days of Elizabeth, if you please; but I assure you that in 1835 women enjoyed perfect equality of rights."

" Did they! then our old friend, the Recorder of Self-Inflicted Miseries, has been imposing on us— but we will discuss this theme more at our leisure. Let us ask that neat pretty young woman for some strawberries and cream."

They were ripe and delicious, and Hastings found, that however much all other things had changed, the fine perfume, the grateful flavour, the rich consistency of the fruit and cream were the same— nature never changes.

There were no unpleasant sights—no rotten vegetables or leaves, no mud, no spitting, no——in short, the whole looked like a painting, and the women all seemed as if they were dressed for the purpose of sitting for their portraits, to let other times have a peep at what was going on in a former world.

"If I am in my senses," said Hastings, "which I very much doubt, this is the most pleasing change which time has wrought; I cannot but believe that I shall wake up in the morning and find this all a dream. This is no market—it is a picture."

"We shall see," said Edgar. "Come, let us proceed to the butchers' market."

So they walked on, and still the rippling stream followed them; and here no sights of blood, or stained hands, or greasy knives, or slaughter-house smells, were present. The meats were not hung up to view in the open air, as in times of old; but you had only to ask for a particular joint, and lo! a small door, two feet square, opened in the wall, and there hung the identical part.

"This gentleman is a stranger," said Edgar, to a neatly dressed man, having on a snow white apron; "show him a hind quarter of veal; we do not want to buy any, but merely to look at what you have to sell."

The little door opened, and there hung one of the fattest and finest quarters Hastings had ever seen.

"And the price," asked he.

"It is four cents a pound," replied the man.

A purchaser soon came; the meat was weighed within; the man received the money, and gave a ticket with the weight written on it; the servant departed, and the two friends moved on.

"Our regulations are excellent," said Edgar; "formerly, as the old Recorder of Self-Inflicted Miseries says, the butchers weighed their meats in the most careless manner, and many a man went home with a suspicion that he was cheated of half or three quarters of a pound. Now, nothing of this kind can take place, for the clerks of the market stand at every corner. See! those men use the graduated balance; the meat is laid, basket and all, on that little table; the pressure acts on a wheel —a clicking is heard—it strikes the number of pounds and quarters, and thus the weight is ascertained. The basket you saw, all those you now see in the meat market, are of equal weight, and they are marked 1, 2, 3, 4 or more pounds, as the size may be. Do you not see how much of labour and confusion this saves. I suppose, in your day, you would have scorned to legislate on such trifling objects; but I assure you we find our account in it."

"I must confess that this simplifies things wonderfully; but the cleanliness, order and cheerfulness that are seen throughout this market—these are things worthy of legislation. I suppose all this took place gradually?"

"Yes, I presume so; but it had arrived to this point before my time; the water which flows under and through the market was conveyed there upward of a century ago. But here is beef, mutton, all kinds of meat—and this is the poultry market— all sold by weight, as it should be; and here is the fish market—see what large marble basins; each fishmonger has one of his own, so that all kinds are separate; and see how dexterously they scoop up the very fish that a customer wants."

"What is this?" said Hastings, looking through one of the arches of the fish market; "can this be the Delaware?"

"Yes," replied Edgar; "the market on which we are now, is over the Delaware. Look over this railing, we are on a wide bridge—but let us proceed to the extremity; this bridge extends to the

E

Jersey shore, and thus connects the two large cities Philadelphia and Camden."

" In my day, it was in contemplation to build a bridge over the Delaware; but there was great opposition to it, as in that case there would be a very great delay, if not hinderance, to the free passage of ships."

New wonders sprung up at every step—vessels, light as gossamer, of curious construction, were passing and repassing under the arches of the bridge, some of three and four hundred tons burden, others for the convenience of market people, and many for the pleasure of the idle. While yet they looked, a beautiful vessel hove in sight, and in a moment she moved gracefully and swiftly under the arches, and by the time that Hastings had crossed to the other side of the bridge she was fastened to the pier.

" Is this a steamboat from Baltimore?" said Hastings. " Yet it cannot be, for I see neither steam nor smoke."

" Steamboat!" answered his companion—"don't speak so loud, the people will think you crazy. Why, steamboats have been out of date for more than two hundred years. I forget the name of the one who introduced them into our waters, but they did not continue in use more than fifty years, perhaps not so long; but so many accidents occurred through the extreme carelessness, ignorance and avarice of many who were engaged in them, that a very great prejudice existed against their use. No laws were found sufficiently strong to prevent frequent occurrences of the bursting of the boilers, notwithstanding that sometimes as many as nine or ten lives were destroyed by the explosion. That those accidents were not the consequence of using steam power—I mean a *necessary* consequence— all sensible men knew; for on this river, the Delaware, the bursting of the boiler of a steam engine was never known, nor did such dreadful accidents ever occur in Europe. But, as I was saying, after one of the most awful catastrophes that ever took place, the bursting of a boiler which scalded to death forty-one members of Congress, (on their way home,) besides upwards of thirty women and children, and nine of the crew, the people of this country began to arouse themselves, and very severe laws were enacted. Before, however, any farther loss of lives occurred, a stop was put to the use of steamboats altogether. The dreadful accident of which I spoke occurred in the year 1850, and in that eventful year a new power was brought into use, by which steamboats were laid aside for ever."

"What is the new principle, and who first brought it to light?"

"Why, a lady. The world owes this blessed invention to a female! I will take you into one of our small boats presently, where you can handle the machinery yourself. No steam, nor heat, nor animal power—but one of sufficient energy to move the largest ship."

"Condensed air, is it?—that was tried in my time."

"No, nor condensed air; that was almost as dangerous a power as steam; for the bursting of an air vessel was always destructive of life. The Recorder of Self-Inflicted Miseries mentions several instances of loss of life by the bursting of one of the air machines used by the manufacturers of mineral waters. If that lady had lived in *this* century, her memory would be honoured and cherished; but if no memorial was erected by the English to Lady Mary Wortley Montagu, a reproach could not rest upon us for not having paid suitable honours to the American lady."

"Why, what did lady Mary Wortley Montagu do?" said Hastings; "I recollect nothing but that

she wrote several volumes of very agreeable letters
—Oh, yes, how could I forget—the small-pox!
Yes, indeed, she did deserve to have a monument;
but surely the English erected one to her memory?"

"Did they?—yes—that old defamer of women,
Horace Walpole, took good care to keep the public feeling from flowing in the right channel. He
made people laugh at her dirty hands and painted
cheeks, but he never urged them to heap honours
on her head for introducing into England the practice of innoculation for the small-pox. If this American lady deserved the thanks and gratitude of her
country for thus, for ever, preventing the loss of
lives from steam, and I may say, too, from shipwreck—still farther was Lady Mary Wortley Montagu entitled to distinction, for the very great benefit she bestowed on England. She saved thousands
of lives, and prevented, what sometimes amounted
to hideous deformity, deeply scarred faces, from
being universal.—Yes, the benefit was incalculable
and beyond price—quite equal, I think, to that which
the world owes to Dr. Jenner, who introduced a
new form of small-pox, or rather the small-pox pure
and unadulterated by any affinitive virus. This
modified the disease to such a degree, that the
small-pox, in its mixed and complicated state, almost
disappeared. The Recorder of Self-Inflicted Miseries states, that after a time a new variety of the
small-pox made its appearance, which was called
*varioloid*; but it was quite under the control of medical skill."

"Well, you live in an age so much in advance of
mine, and so many facts and curious phenomena
came to light during the nineteenth century, that
you can tell me what the settled opinion is now respecting small-pox, kine-pox, and varioloid."

"The settled opinion now is, that they are one
and the same disease. Thus—the original disease,

transferable from an ulcer of the cow's udder to the broken skin of a human being, produced what is called the kine or cow-pox. This virus of the kine-pox, in its original state, was only capable of being communicated by contact, and only when the skin was broken or cut; but, when *combined* with the other poison, infected the system by means of breathing in the same atmosphere. The poison from the ulcer called cow-pox was never communicated to or by the lungs, neither was the poison which had so strong an affinity for it communicated in that way; but when the two poisons united, and met in the same system, a third poison was generated, and the *small-pox was the result.* But here we are discussing a deep subject in this busy place —what gave rise to it?—oh, steamboats, the new power now used, Lady Mary Wortley, and Dr. Jenner."

"I presume," said the attentive Hastings, "that Dr. Jenner fared no better than your American lady and Lady Mary Wortley."

"You are much mistaken," said Edgar. "Dr. Jenner was a *man*, which in your day was a very different circumstance. I verily believe if it had been a woman who brought that happy event about, although the whole world would have availed itself of the discovery, her name would scarcely be known at this day."

Hastings laughed at his friend's angry defence of women's rights, but he could not help acknowledging the truth of what was said—there was always a great unwillingness in men to admit the claims of women. But it was not a time, nor was this the place, to discuss so important a subject; he intended, however, to resume it the first leisure moment. He turned his eye to the river, and saw vessels innumerable coming and going; and on the arrival of one a little larger than that which he first saw,

E 2

the crowd pressed forward to get on board as soon as she should land.

"Where is that vessel from?" said Hastings; "she looks more weather-beaten than the rest—she has been at sea."

"Yes; that is one of our Indiamen. Let us go to her, I see a friend of mine on board—he went out as supercargo."

They went on board of the Indiaman, and although it had encountered several storms, and had met with several accidents, yet the crew was all well and the cargo safe. The vessel was propelled by the same machinery—there was neither masts nor sails!

"How many months have they been on their return?" said Hastings.

"Hush!" said his friend Edgar; "do not let any one hear you. Why, this passage has been a very tedious one, and yet it has only occupied four weeks. In general twenty days are sufficient."

"Well," said Hastings, "after this I shall not be surprised at any thing. Why, in my time we considered it as a very agreeable thing if we made a voyage to England in that time. Have you many India ships?"

"Yes; the trade has been opened to the very walls of China: the number of our vessels has greatly increased. But you will be astonished to hear that the emperor of China gets his porcelain from France."

"No, I am not, now that I hear foreigners have access to that mysterious city, for I never considered the Indian china as at all equal to the French, either in texture or workmanship. But I presume I have wonders to learn about the Chinese?"

"Yes, much more than you imagine. It is not more than a century since the change in their system has been effected; before that, no foreigner was allowed to enter their gates. But quarrels and dissensions among themselves effected what neither external violence nor manœuvring could do. The consequence of this intercourse with foreign nations is, that the feet of their women are allowed to grow, and they dress now in the European style. They import their fashions from France; and I see by the papers that the emperor's second son intends to pay this country a visit. They have English and French, as well as German and Spanish schools; and a great improvement in the condition of the lower classes of the Chinese has taken place; but it was first by humanizing the women that these great changes were effected. Their form of government is fast approaching that of ours, but they held out long and obstinately."

"Their climate is very much against them," observed Hastings; "mental culture must proceed slowly, where the heat is so constant and excessive."

"Yes; but, my dear sir, you must recollect that they have ice in abundance now. We carry on a great trade in that article. In fact, some of our richest men owe their wealth to the exportation of this luxury alone. Boston set the example—she first sent cargoes of ice to China; but it was not until our fast sailing vessels were invented that the thing could be accomplished."

"I should think it almost impossible to transport ice to such a distance, even were the time lessened to a month or six weeks, as it now is."

"You must recollect, that half of this difficulty of transporting ice was lessened by the knowledge that was obtained, even in your day, of saving ice. According to the Recorder, who sneered at the *times* for remaining so long ignorant of the fact, ice houses could be built above ground, with the certainty that they would preserve ice. It was the expense of building those deep ice houses which

prevented the poor from enjoying this luxury—
nay, necessary article. Now, every landlord builds
a stack of ice in the yard, and thatches it well with
oat straw; and the corporation have an immense
number of these stacks of ice distributed about the
several wards."

"I have awakened in delightful times, my friend.
Oh, that my family could have been with me when
I was buried under the mountain."

Young Hastings, seeing the melancholy which
was creeping over the unfortunate man, hurried
him away from the wharf, and hastened to Chestnut street. Our hero looked anxiously to the right
and to the left, but all was altered—all was strange.
Arcades now took precedence of the ancient, inconvenient shops, there being one between every
square, extending from Chestnut to Market on one
side, and to Walnut on the other, intersecting the
smaller streets and alleys in their way. Here alone
were goods sold—no where else was there a shop
seen; and what made it delightful was, that a fine
stream of water ran through pipes under the centre
of the pavement, bursting up every twenty feet in
little jets, cooling the air, and contributing to health
and cleanliness. The arcades for the grocers were
as well arranged as those for different merchandize,
and the fountains of water, which flowed perpetually
in and under their shops, dispersed all impure smells
and all decayed substances.

"All this is beautiful," said Hastings; "but where
is the old Arcade—the original one?"

"Oh, I know what you mean," said Edgar;
"our old Recorder states that it fell into disuse,
and was then removed, solely from the circumstance that the first floor was raised from the level
of the street; even in our time people dislike to
mount steps when they have to go from shop to
shop to purchase goods."

"And what building is that?—the antiquated one,
I mean, that stands in the little court. The masons
are repairing it I perceive."

"That small, brick building—oh, that is the house
in which William Penn lived," said Edgar. "It
was very much neglected, and was suffered to go
to ruin almost, till the year 1840, when a lady of
great wealth purchased a number of the old houses
adjoining and opened an area around it, putting the
whole house in thorough repair. She collected all
the relics that remained of this great man, and
placed them as fixtures there, and she left ample
funds for repairs, so that there is a hope that this
venerable and venerated building will endure for
many centuries to come."

"And what is this heap of ruins?" said Hastings,
"it appears to have tumbled down through age; it
was a large pile, if one may judge from the rub-
bish."

"Yes, it was an immense building, and was called
at first the National Bank. It was built in the year
1842, during the presidency of Daniel Webster."

"What," said Hastings, "was he really president
of the United States? This is truly an interesting
piece of news."

"News, my dear sir," said Edgar, smiling—"yes,
it was news three hundred years ago, but Daniel
Webster now sleeps with his fathers. He was
really the chief magistrate for eight years, and
excepting for the project of a national bank, which
did not, however, exist long, he made an able president, and, what was very extraordinary, as the old
Recorder of Self-Inflicted Miseries states, he gained
the good will even of those who were violently
opposed to him. He was the first president after
Washington who had independence of mind enough
to retain in office all those who had been favoured

by his predecessor. There was not a single removal."

"But his friends—did not they complain?" said Hastings.

"It is not stated that they did; perhaps he did not promise an office to any one: at any rate the old 'Recorder' treats him respectfully. It was during his term that copyrights were placed on a more liberal footing here. An Englishman now can get his works secured to him as well as if he were a citizen of the country."

"How long is the copy right secured! it used to be, in my time," sighed poor Hastings, "only fourteen years."

"Fourteen years!" exclaimed Edgar—"you joke. Why, was not a man entitled to his own property for ever? I assure you that an author *now* has as much control over his own labours after a lapse of fifty years as he had at the moment he wrote it. Nay, it belongs to his family as long as they choose to keep it, just the same as if it were a house or a tract of land. I wonder what right the legislature had to meddle with property in that way. We should think a man deranged who proposed such a thing."

"But how is it when a man invents a piece of machinery? surely the term is limited then."

"Oh, yes, that is a different affair. If a man invent a new mode of printing, or of propelling boats, then a patent is secured to him for that particular invention, but it does not prevent another man from making use of the same power and improving on the machinery. But there is this benefit accruing to the original patentee, the one who makes the improvement after him is compelled to purchase a right of him. Our laws now, allow of no monopolies; that is, no monopolies of soil, or air, or water.  On these three elements, one person has as good a right as another; he that makes the greatest improvements is entitled to the greatest share of public favour, and, in consequence, the arts have been brought to their present state of perfection."

"But rail-roads—surely *these* it was necessary to guarantee to a company on exclusive privilege for a term of years, even if a better one could be made."

"And I say, surely not.  Why should all the people of a great nation be compelled to pass over an unsafe road, in miserably constructed cars, which made such a noise that for six hours a man had to be mute, and where there was perpetual fear of explosion from the steam engine—why should this be, when another company could give them a better road, more commodious cars, and a safer propelling power?  On consulting the Recorder of Self-Inflicted Miseries, you will find that in the year 1846, the monopolies of roads, that is public roads, were broken up, and these roads came under the cognizance of the state governments, and in the year 1900 all merged under one head.  There was then, and has continued ever since, a national road—the grand route from one extreme of the country to the other.  Cross roads, leading from town to town and village to village, are under the control of the state governments.  Here, let us get in this car which is going to Princeton; it is only an hour's ride.  Well, here we are seated in nice rocking chairs, and we can talk at our ease; for the fine springs and neat workmanship make the cars run without noise, as there is but little friction, the rails of the road and the tires of the wheels being of wood.  In your time this could not be the case, for as steam and manual labour were expensive, you were forced to club all together—there were, therefore, large cars that held from eight to

fourteen persons; consequently, there had to be
heavy iron work to keep these large machines
together. Now, you perceive, the cars are made
of different sizes, to accommodate either two or
four persons, and they run of themselves. We have
only to turn this little crank, and the machine stops.
This is Bristol. It was a very small town in your
day, but by connecting it to Burlington, which lies
slantingly opposite, the town soon rose to its present
eminence. Burlington, too, is a large city—look
at the green bank yonder; it is a paradise: and
look at that large tree—it is a buttonwood or
sycamore; we cannot see it very distinctly; take
this pocket glass. Well, you see it now at the foot
of the beautiful green slope in front of the largest
marble building on this bank. That tree is upwards
of four hundred years old, but the house was built
within the last century."

"What a change," said Hastings, as they returned
to their car,—"all is altered. New Jersey, the
meanest and the poorest state in the union, is now
in appearance equal to the other inland states. It
was in my time a mere thoroughfare. What has
thus changed the whole face of nature."

"Why canals and rail roads in the first place,
and rail roads now; for in a few years canals were
entirely abandoned. That is, as soon as the new
propelling power came into use, it was found far
more economical to travel on rail roads. The
track of canals through four of the principal states
is no longer to be seen."

At Princeton, the first thing to be seen was
the college; not the same that existed in Hastings's
day, but a long, deep range of stone buildings,
six in number, with work shops attached to them,
after the mode so happily begun by Fellenberg. In
these work shops the young men worked during
leisure hours, every one learning some trade or

some handicraft, by which he could earn a living if necessity required it. Large gardens lay in the rear, cultivated entirely by the labour of the students, particularly by those who were intended for clergymen, as many of this class were destined to live in the country. The college was well endowed, and the salaries of the professors were ample. It was able to maintain and educate three hundred boys—the children of the rich and the poor.

"How do they select professors?" said Hastings; "in my day a very scandalous practice prevailed. I hope there is a change in this particular."

"Oh, I know to what you refer," said Edgar; "I read an account of it in the Recorder. It seems that when a college wanted a professor, or a president, they either wrote a letter, or sent a committee of gentlemen to the professor of another college, and told him that if he would quit the people who had with so much difficulty made up a salary for him, they would give him a hundred dollars a year more. They made it appear very plausible and profitable, and the idea of being thought of so much consequence quite unsettled his notions of right and wrong, so that, without scruple, he gave notice to his patrons that they must get another man in his place. I believe this is the true state of the case. Is it not?"

"Yes, that is the *English* of it, as we say. The funds for the support of a professor were gathered together with great difficulty, for there were very few who gave liberally and for the pure love of the advancement of learning. When by the mere force of entreaty, by appealing to the feelings, to reason, to—in short, each man's pulse was felt, and the ruling passion was consulted and made subservient to the plan of beguiling him of his money. Well, the money thus wrung from the majority,— for you must suppose that a few gave from right

F

motives,—was appropriated to the salary of a professor, and then the question arose as to the man to be selected. They run their eye over the whole country, and, finally, the fame of some one individual induced them to consider him as a suitable candidate. This man was doing great service where he was; the college, almost gone to decay, was resuscitated by his exertions; students came from all parts on the faith of his remaining there; in fact, he had given an impulse to the whole district. What a pity to remove such a man from a place where the benefits of his labour and his energies were so great, and where his removal would produce such regrets and such a deteriorating change! But our new professor, being established in the new college, instead of going to work with the same alacrity, and with the same views, which views were to spend his life in promoting the interests of the college which he had helped to raise, now began to look '*a-head*,' as the term is, and he waited impatiently for the rise of another establishment, in the city perhaps, where every thing was more congenial to his newly awakened tastes. Thus it went on—change, change, for ever; and in the end he found himself much worse off than if he had remained in the place which first patronised him. It is certainly a man's duty to do the best he can for the advancement of his own interest, and if he can get five hundred dollars a year more in one place than in another, he has a right to do it; but the advantage of change is always problematical. The complaint is not so much against him, however, as against those who so indelicately inveigle him away."

"Yes. I can easily imagine how hurtful in its effects such a policy would be, for instance, to a merchant, although it is pernicious in every case. But here is a merchant—he has regularly inducted a clerk in all the perplexities and mysteries of his business; the young man becomes acquainted with his private affairs, and by his acuteness and industry he relieves his employer of one half of his anxieties and cares. The time is coming when he might think it proper to raise the salary of the young man, but his neighbours envy the merchant's prosperity, and they want to take advantage of the talent which has grown up under his vigilance and superintending care. 'If he does so well for a man who gives him but five hundred dollars a year, he will do as well, or better, for ten.' So they go underhandedly to work, and the young man gives the merchant notice that his neighbour has offered him a larger salary. The old Recorder is quite indignant at this mean and base mode of bettering the condition of one man or one institution at the expense of another. But was it the case also with house servants?—did the women of your day send a committee or write a letter to the servant of one of their friends, offering higher wages—for the cases are exactly similar; it is only talent of another form, but equally useful."

"Oh, no, indeed," said Hastings—" then the sex showed their superior delicacy and refinement. It was thought most disgraceful and unlady-like conduct to enveigle away the servant of a neighbour, or, in fact, of a stranger ; I have heard it frequently canvassed. A servant, a clerk, a professor, or a clergyman, nine times out of ten, would be contented in his situation if offers of this kind were not forced upon him. A servant cannot feel an attachment to a mistress when she contemplates leaving her at the first offer ; no tender feeling can subsist between them, and in the case of a clergyman, the consequence is very bad both to himself and his parish. In the good old times"—

"And in the good new times, if you please," said

Edgar; "for I know what you are going to say. In our times there is no such thing as changing a clergyman. Why, we should as soon think of changing our father! A clergyman is selected with great care for his piety and learning—but principally for his piety; and, in consequence of there being no old clergymen out of place, he is a young man, who comes amongst us in early life, and sees our children grow up around him, he becomes acquainted with their character, and he has a paternal eye over their eternal welfare. They love and reverence him, and it is their delight to do him honour. His salary is a mere trifle perhaps, for in some country towns a clergyman does not get more than five or six hundred dollars a year, but his wants are all supplied with the most affectionate care. He receives their delightful gifts as a father receives the gifts of his children; he is sure of being amply provided for, and he takes no thought of what he is to eat or what he is to wear. He pays neither house rent, for there is always a parsonage; nor taxes; he pays neither physician nor teacher; his library is as good as the means of his congregation can afford; and there he is with a mind free from worldly solicitude, doing good to the souls of those who so abundantly supply him with worldly comforts. In your day, as the Recorder states"—

"Yes," said Hastings, "in my day, things were bad enough, for a clergyman was more imposed upon than any other professional man. He was expected to subscribe to every charity that was set on foot—to every mission that was sent out—to every church that was to be built—to every paper that related to church offices; *he had to give up all his time to his people*—literally all his time, for they expected him to visit at their houses, not when ill, or when wanting spiritual consolation, for that he would delight to do, but in the ordinary chit-chat, gossiping way, that he might hear them talk of their neighbours' backslidings, of this one who gave expensive supper parties, and of another who gave balls and went to theatres. Never was there a man from whom so much was exacted, and to whom so little was given. There were clergymen, in New York and Philadelphia, belonging to wealthy congregations, who never so much as received a plum cake for the new year's table, or a minced pie at christmas, or a basket of fruit in summer; yet he was expected to entertain company at all times. His congregation never seemed to recollect that, with his limited means, he could not lay up a cent for his children. Other salaried men could increase their means by speculation, or by a variety of methods, but a clergyman had to live on with the melancholy feelings that when he died his children must be dependent on charity. Women *did* do their best to aid their pastors, but they could not do much, and even in the way that some of them assisted their clergymen there was a want of judgment; for they took the bread out of the mouths of poor women, who would otherwise have got the money for the very articles which the rich of their congregation made and sold for the benefit of this very man. Feeling the shame and disgrace of his being obliged to subscribe to a charity, they earned among themselves, *by sewing*, a sum sufficient to constitute him a 'life member!' What a hoax upon charity! What a poor, pitiful compliment,—and at whose expense? The twenty-five dollars thus necessary to be raised, which was to constitute their beloved pastor a life member of a charitable society, would be applied to a better purpose, if they had bought him some rare and valuable book, such as his small means could not allow him to buy."

F 2

"I am glad to hear that one so much respected by us had those sentiments," said Edgar, "for the old Recorder, even in the year 1850, speaks of the little reverence that the people felt for their clergy. Now, we vie with each other in making him comfortable; he is not looked upon as a man from whom we are to get our pennyworth, as we do from those of other professions—he is our pastor, a dear and endearing word, and we should never think of dismissing him because he had not the gift of eloquence, or because he was wanting in grace of action, or because he did not come amongst us every day to listen to our fiddle-faddle. When we want spiritual consolement, or require his services in marriage, baptism, or burial, then he is at his post, and no severity of weather withholds him from coming amongst us. In turn we call on him at some stated period, when he can be seen at his ease and enjoy the sight of our loving faces, and happy is the child who has been patted on the head by him. When he grows old we indulge him in preaching his old sermons, or in reading others that have stood the test of time, and when the infirmities of age disable him from attending to his duties, we draw him gently away and give him a competence for the remainder of his life. What we should do for our father, we do for our spiritual father."

"I am truly rejoiced at this," said Hastings, "for in my day a clergyman never felt secure of the affections of his people. If he was deficient in that external polish, which certainly is a charm in an orator, or was wanting in vehemence of action, or in enthusiasm, the way to displace him was simple and easy: dissatisfaction showed itself in every action of theirs—to sum up all, they 'held him uneasy,' and many a respectable, godly man was forced to relinquish his hold on his cure to give place to a younger and a more popular one."

"Do you send a committee to a popular clergyman, and cajole him away from his congregation, by offering him a larger salary or greater perquisites?"

"Oh no—never, never; the very question shocks me. Our professors and our clergymen are taken from the colleges and seminaries where they are educated. They are young, generally, and are the better able to adapt themselves to the feelings and capacities of their students and their congregation. Parents give up the idle desire which they had in your time, of hearing fine preaching at the expense of honour and delicacy. When a congregation became very much attached to their pastor, and he was doing good amongst them, it was cruel to break in upon their peace and happiness merely because it was in a person's power to do this. We are certainly much better pleased to have a clergyman with fine talents and a graceful exterior, but we value him more for goodness of heart and honest principles. But, however gifted he may be, we never break the tenth commandment, we never desire to take him away from our neighbour, nor even in your time do I think a clergyman would ever seek to leave his charge, unless strongly importuned."

"Pray can you tell me," said Hastings, "what has become of that vast amount of property which belonged to the —— in New York?"

"Oh, it did a vast deal of good; after a time it was discovered that the trustees had the power of being more liberal with it; other churches, or rather all the Episcopal churches in the state, were assisted, and, finally, each church received a yearly sum, sufficient to maintain a clergyman. Every village, therefore, had a church and a clergyman; and in due time, from this very circumstance, the Episcopalians came to be more numerous in New

York than any other sect. It is not now as it was in your time, in the year 1835; then a poor clergyman, that he might have the means to live, was compelled to travel through two, three, and sometimes four parishes: all these clubbing together to make up the sum of six hundred dollars in a year. Now this was scandalous, when that large trust had such ample means in its power to give liberally to every church in the state."

"Why, yes," said Hastings, "the true intent of accumulating wealth in churches, is to advance religion; for what other purposes are the funds created? I used to smile when I saw the *amazing* liberality of the trustees of this immense fund; they would, in the most freezing and pompous manner, dole out a thousand dollars to this church, and a thousand to that, making them all understand that nothing more could be done, as they were fearful, even in doing this, that they had gone beyond their charter."

"Just as if they did not know," said Edgar, "that any set of men, in any legislature, would give them full powers to expend the whole income in the cause of their own peculiar religion. Why I cannot tell how many years were suffered to elapse before they raised what was called a Bishop's Fund, and you know better than I do, how it was raised, or rather, how it commenced. And the old Recorder of Self-Inflicted Miseries, states, that the fund for the support of decayed clergymen and their families, was raised by the poor clergymen themselves. Never were people so hardly used as these ministers of the Gospel. You were an irreverend, exacting race in your day; you expected more from a preacher than from any other person to whom they gave salaries—*they* were screwed down to the last thread of the screw; people would have their pennyworth out of them. It is no wonder that you had such poor preachers in your day; why few men of liberal education, aware of all the exactions and disabilities under which the sacred cloth laboured, would ever encounter them. But, now, every village has its own pastor; and some of them are highly gifted men, commanding the attention of the most intelligent people. The little churches are filled, throughout the summer, with such of the gentry of the cities who can afford to spend a few months in the country during the warm weather. No one, however, has the indecency or the unfeelingness to covet this preacher for their own church in the city. They do not attempt to bribe him away, but leave him there, satisfied that the poor people who take such delight in administering to his wants and his comforts, should have the benefit of his piety, his learning and his example. Why, the clergymen, now, are our best horticulturists too. It is to them that we owe the great advancement in this useful art. They even taught, themselves, while at college, and now they encourage their parishioners to cultivate gardens and orchards. Every village, as well as town and city, has a large garden attached to it, in which the children of the poor are taught to work, so that to till the earth and to 'make two blades of grass grow where only one grew before,' is now the chief aim of every individual; and we owe this, principally, to our pastors. I can tell you that it is something now to be a country clergyman."

"But how were funds raised for the purchase of these garden and orchard spots?"

"Why, through the means of the *general tax*, that which, in your day, would have been called direct tax."

"Direct tax! Why my dear Edgar, such a thing could never have been tolerated in my time; people would have burnt the man in effigy for only proposing such a thing. It was once or twice attempted, indirectly, and in a very cautious way, but it would not do."

" Yes—direct tax—I knew you would be startled, for the old Recorder of Self-Inflicted Miseries states that at the close of Daniel Webster's administration something of the kind was suggested, but even then, so late as the year 1850, it was violently opposed. But a new state of things gradually paved the way for it, and now we cannot but pity the times when all the poor inhabitants of this free country were taxed so unequally. There is now, but one tax, and each man is made to pay according to the value of his property, or his business, or his labour. A land-holder, a stock-holder and the one who has houses and bonds and mortgages, pays so much per cent. on the advance of his property, and for his annual receipts—the merchant, with a fluctuating capital, pays so much on his book account of sales—the mechanic and labourer, so much on their yearly receipts, for we have no sales on credit now—that demoralizing practice has been abolished for upwards of a century."

" The merchants, then," said Hastings, " pay more than any other class of men, for there are the customhouse bonds."

" Yes," said Edgar, " I recollect reading in the Recorder of Self-Inflicted Miseries,—you must run your eye over that celebrated newspaper—that all goods imported from foreign ports had to pay *duties*, as it was called. But every thing now is free to come and go, and as the custom prevails all over the world, there is no hardship to any one. What a demoralizing effect that duty or tariff system produced ; why honesty was but a loose term then, and did not apply to every act as it now does. The Recorder was full of the exposures that were yearly occurring, of *defrauding the revenue*, as it was called. Some of these frauds were to a large amount; and then it was considered as a crime; but when a man smuggled in hats, shoes, coats and other articles of the like nature, he was suffered to go free; such small offences were winked at as if defrauding the revenue of a dollar were not a crime *per se* as well as defrauding it of a thousand dollars—just as if murdering an infant were not as much murder as if the life had been taken from a man—just as if killing a man in private, because his enemy had paid you to do it, was not as much murder in the first degree as if the government had paid you for killing a dozen men in battle in open day—just as if"—

" Just as if what?" said the astonished Hastings, " has the time come when killing men by wholesale, in war, is accounted a crime?"

" Yes, thank Heaven," said Edgar, " that blessed time has at length arrived; it is upwards of one hundred and twenty years since men were ordered to kill one another in that barbarous manner. Why the recital of such cruel and barbarous deeds fills our young children with horror. The ancient policy of referring the disputes of nations to single combat, was far more humanizing than the referring such disputes to ten thousand men on each side; for, after all, it was ' might that made right.' Because a strong party beats a weaker one, that is not a proof that the *right* was in the strong one; yet, still, if men had no other way of settling their disputes but by spilling blood, then that plan was the most humane which only sacrificed two or one man. As to national honour! why not let the few settle it? why drag the poor sailors and soldiers to be butchered like cattle to gratify the fine feelings of a few morbidly constructed minds?"

" Oh, that my good father, Valentine Harley, could have seen this day," said Hastings. " But this bloodthirsty, savage propensity—this murdering our fellow creatures in cold blood, as it were, was cured by degrees I presume. What gave the first impulse to such a blessed change?"

"The old Recorder states that it was brought about by the *influence of women;* it was they who gave the first impulse. As soon as they themselves were considered as of equal importance with their husbands—as soon as they were on an equality in *money matters*, for after all, people are respected in proportion to their wealth, that moment all the barbarisms of the age disappeared. Why, in your day, a strange perverted system had taken deep root; *then,* it was the *man that was struck* by another who was disgraced in public opinion, and not the one who struck him. It was that system which fermented and promoted bloodthirstiness, and it was encouraged and fostered by men and by women both.

"But as soon as women had more power in their hands, their energies were directed another way: they became more enlightened as they rose higher in the scale, and instead of encroaching on our privileges, of which we stood in such fear, women shrunk farther and farther from all approach to men's pursuits and occupations. Instead of congregating, as they did in your time, to beg for alms to establish and sustain a charity, that they might have some independent power of their own—for this craving after distinction was almost always blended with their desire to do good—they united for the purpose of exterminating that *war seed* above mentioned—that system which fastened the *disgrace* of a blow on the one who received it. This was their first effort; they then taught their children likewise, that to kill a man in battle, or men in battle, when mere national honour was the war cry, or when we had been robbed of our money on the high seas, was a crime of the blackest die, and contrary to the divine precepts of our Saviour. They taught them to abstain from shedding human blood, *excepting in self defence*—excepting in case of invasion.

"They next taught them to reverence religion; for until bloodthirstiness was cured, how could a child reverence our Saviour's precepts? How could we recommend a wholesome, simple diet to a man who had been accustomed to riot in rich sauces and condiments? They had first to wean them from the savage propensities that they had received through the maddening influence of unreflecting men, before a reverence for holy things could be excited. Then it was that clergymen became the exalted beings in our eyes that they now are—then it was that children began to love and respect them. As soon as their fathers did their mothers the poor justice of trusting them with all their property, the children began to respect her as they ought, and then her words were the words of wisdom. It was then, and not till then, that war and duelling ceased. We are amazed at what we read. What! take away a man's life because he has robbed us of money! Hang a man because he has forged our name for a few dollars! No: go to our prisons, there you will see the murderer's fate—solitary confinement, at hard labour, for life! that is his punishment; but murders are very rare now in this country. A man stands in greater dread of solitary confinement at hard labour than he does of hanging. In fact, according to our way of thinking, now, we have no right, by the Divine law, to take that away from a human being for which we can give no equivalent. It is right to prevent a murderer from committing still farther crime; and this we do by confining him for life at hard labour, *and alone.*"

G

"Women, you say, produced a reform in that miserable code called *the law of honour.*"

"Yes, thanks be to them for it. Why, as the old Recorder states, if a man did not challenge the fellow who struck him, he was obliged to quit the army or the navy, and be for ever banished as a coward, and it was considered as disgraceful in a private citizen to receive a blow without challenging the ruffian that struck him. But the moment that women took the office in hand, that moment the thing was reversed. They entered into a compact not to receive a man into their society who had struck another, unless he made such ample apology to the injured person as to be forgiven by him; and not only that, but his restoration to favour was to be sued for by the injured party himself. A man soon became cautious how he incurred the risk."

"It often occurred to me," said Hastings, "that women had much of the means of moral reform in their power ; but they always appeared to be pursuing objects tending rather to weaken than to strengthen morals. They acted with good intentions, but really wanted judgment to select the proper method of pursuing their benevolent schemes. Only look at their toiling as they did to collect funds towards educating poor young men for the ministry."

"Oh, those young men," replied Edgar, "were, no doubt, their sons or brothers, and even then they must have been working at some trade to assist their parents or some poor relation, and thus had to neglect themselves."

"No, indeed," said Hastings, "I assure you these young men were entire strangers, persons that they never saw in their lives, nor ever expected to see."

"Then, all I can say is, that the women were to be pitied for their mistaken zeal, and the men ought to have scorned such aid—but the times are altered; no man, no poor man stands in need of women's help now, as they have trades or employments that enable them to educate themselves. Only propose such a thing *now*, and see how it would be received; why a young man would think you intended to insult him. We pursue the plan so admirably begun in your day by the celebrated Fellenberg. When we return this way again, I will show you the work-shops attached to the college—the one we saw in Princeton."

" While we are thus far on the road, suppose that we go to New York," said Hastings, " I was bound thither when that calamity befell me. I wonder if I shall see a single house remaining that I saw three hundred years ago."

Edgar laughed—" You will see but very few, I can tell you," said he, " houses, in your day, were built too slightly to stand the test of *one* century. At one time, the corporation of the city had to inspect the mortar, lest it should not be strong enough to cement the bricks! And it frequently happened that houses tumbled down, not having been built strong enough to bear their own weight. A few of the public buildings remain, but they have undergone such changes that you will hardly recognize them. The City Hall, indeed, stands in the same place, but if you approach it, in the rear, you will find that it is of marble, and not freestone as the old Recorder says it was in your time. But since the two great fires at the close of the years 1835 and 1842 the city underwent great alterations."

" Great fires; in what quarter of the city were they? They must have been disasters, indeed, to be remembered for three hundred years."

" Yes, the first destroyed nearly seven hundred houses, and about fifteen millions of property; and the second, upwards of a thousand houses, and

about three millions of property; but excepting that
it reduced a number of very respectable females to
absolute want, the merchants, and the city itself,
were greatly benefited by it. There were salutary
laws enacted in consequence of it, that is, after the
second fire; for instance, the streets in the burnt
districts were made wider; the houses were better
and stronger built; the fire engines were drawn by
horses, and afterwards by a new power: firemen
were not only exempt from jury and militia duty,
but they had a regular salary while they served
out their seven years' labour; and if any fireman
lost his life, or was disabled, his family received the
salary for a term of years. The old Recorder
says that there was not a merchant of any enterprise who did not recover from his losses in three
years."

"But what became of the poor women who lost
all their property? did they lose insurance stock?
for I presume the insurance companies became in-
solvent."

"The poor women?—oh, they remained poor—
nothing in *your* day ever happened to better their
condition when a calamity like that overtook *them*.
Men had enough to do to pity and help themselves.
Yes, their loss was in the insolvency of the insurance companies; but stock is safe enough now,
for the last tremendous fire (they did not let the
first make the impression it ought to have done,)
roused the energies and *sense* of the people, and insurance is managed very different. Every house,
now, whether of the rich or the poor man, is in-
sured. It has to pay so much additional tax, and
the corporation are the insurers. But the tax is so
trifling that no one feels it a burden; our houses
are almost all fire-proof since the discovery of a
substance which renders wood almost proof against
fire. But I have a file of the Recorder of Self-In-

flicted Miseries, and you will see the regular gradation from the barbarisms of your day to the enlightened times it has been permitted you to see."

"But the water, in my day,"—poor Hastings never repeated this without a sigh—"in my day the city was supplied by water from a brackish stream, but there was a plan in contemplation to bring good water to the city from the distance of forty miles."

"Where, when was that? I do not remember to have read any thing about it.—Oh, yes, there was such a scheme, and it appears to me they did attempt it, but whatever was the cause of failure I now forget; at present they have a plentiful supply by means of boring. Some of these bored wells are upwards of a thousand feet deep."

"Why the Manhattan Company made an attempt of this kind in my time, but they gave it up as hopeless after going down to the depth of six or seven hundred feet."

"Yes, I recollect; but only look at the difficulties they had to encounter. In the first place, the chisel that they bored with was not more than three or four inches wide; of course, as the hole made by this instrument could be no larger, there was no possibility of getting the chisel up if it were broken off below, neither could they break or cut it into fragments. If such an accident were to occur at the depth of six hundred feet, this bored hole would have to be abandoned. We go differently to work now; with our great engines we cut down through the earth and rock, as if it were cheese, and the wells are of four feet diameter. As they are lined throughout with an impervious cement, the overflowing water does not escape. Every house is now supplied from this neverfailing source—the rich, and the poor likewise, use this water, and it is excellent. All the expense comes within the one yearly general tax: when a man builds he

G 2

knows that pipes are to be conveyed through his house, and he knows also that his one tax comprehends the use of water. He pays so much per centum for water, for all the municipal arrangement, for defence of harbour, for the support of government, &c., and as there is such a wide door open, such a competition, his food and clothing do not cost half as much as they did in your day."

"You spoke of wells a thousand feet deep and four feet wide; what became of all the earth taken from them—stones I should say."

"Oh, they were used for the extension of the Battery. Do you remember, in your day, an ill constructed thing called Fort William, or Castle Garden? Well, the Battery was filled up on each side from that point, so that at present there are at least five acres of ground more attached to it than when you saw it, and as we are now levelling a part of Brooklyn heights, we intend to fill it out much farther. The Battery is a noble promenade now."

They reached New York by the slow line at two o'clock, having travelled at the rate of thirty miles an hour; and after walking up Broadway to amuse themselves with looking at the improvements that had taken place since Hastings last saw it—three hundred years previous—they stopped at the Astor Hotel. This venerable building, the City Hall, the Public Mart, the St. Paul's Church, and a stone house at the lower end of the street, built by governor Jay, were all that had stood the test of ages. The St. Paul was a fine old church, but the steeple had been taken down and a dome substituted, as was the fashion of all the churches in the city—the burial yards of all were gone—houses were built on them:—vaults, tombs, graves, monuments—what had become of them?

The Astor Hotel, a noble building, of simple and

chaste architecture, stood just as firm, and looked just as well, as it did when Hastings saw it. Why should it not? stone is stone, and three hundred years more would pass over it without impairing it. This shows the advantage of stone over brick. Mr. Astor built for posterity, and he has thus perpetuated his name. He was very near living as long as this building; the planning and completing of it seemed to renovate him, for his life was extended to his ninety-ninth year. This building proves him to have been a man of fine taste and excellent judgment, for it still continues to be admired.

"But how is this?" said Hastings, "I see no houses but this one built by Mr. Astor that are higher than three stories; it is the case throughout the city, stores and all."

"Since the two great fires of 1835 and 1842, the corporation forbid the building of any house or store above a certain height. Those tremendous fires, as I observed, brought people to their senses, and they now see the folly of it.

"The ceilings are not so high as formerly; more regard is shown to comfort. Why the old Recorder of Self-Inflicted Miseries states, that men were so indifferent about the conveniences and comforts of life, that they would sometimes raise the ceilings to the great height of fourteen and fifteen feet! Nay, that they did so in despite of their wives' health, never considering how hard it bore on the lungs of those who were affected with asthma or other visceral complaints. Heavens and earth! how little the ease and pleasure of women were consulted in your day."

"Yes, that appears all very true," said Hastings, "but you must likewise recollect that these very women were quite as eager as their husbands to live in houses having such high flights of stairs."

" Poor things," exclaimed Edgar, " to think of their being trained to like and desire a thing that bore so hard on them. Only consider what a loss of time and breath it must be to go up and down forty or fifty times a day, for your nurseries were, it seems, generally in the third story. We love our wives too well now to pitch our houses so high up in the air. The Philadelphians had far more humanity, more consideration; they always built a range of rooms in the rear of the main building, and this was a great saving of time and health."

" Where, at length, did they build the custom house?" said Hastings; " I think there was a difficulty in choosing a suitable spot for it."

" Oh, I recollect," said Edgar. " Why they did at length decide, and one was built in Pine street; but that has crumbled away long since. You know that we have no necessity for a custom house now, as all foreign goods come free of duty. This direct tax includes all the expenses of the general and state governments, and it operates so beautifully that the rich man now bears his full proportion towards the support of the whole as the poor man does. This was not the case in your day. Only think how unequally it bore on the labourer who had to buy foreign articles, such as tea, and sugar, and coffee, for a wife and six or eight children, and to do all this with his wealth, which was the labour of his hands. The rich man did not contribute the thousandth part of his proportion towards paying for foreign goods, nor was he taxed according to his revenue for the support of government. The direct tax includes the poor man's wealth, which is his labour, and the rich man's wealth, which is his property."

" But have the merchants no mart—no exchange? According to the map you showed me of the two great fires, the first exchange was burnt."

"Yes, the merchants have a noble exchange. Did you not see that immense building on State street, surrounded by an area? After the first great fire they purchased—that is, a company purchased—the whole block that included State street in front, Pearl street in the rear, and Whitehall street at the lower end. All mercantile business is transacted there, the principal post office and the exchange are there now; the whole go under the general name of Mart—the City Mart."

"Is it not inconvenient to have the post office so far from the centre of business?—it was a vexed question in my day," said Hastings.

"You must recollect that even then, central as the post office was, there were many sub-post offices. If men in your day were regardless of the many unnecessary steps that their wives were obliged to take, they were very careful of sparing themselves. We adopt the plan now of having two sets of post men or letter carriers; one set pass through the streets at a certain hour to receive letters, their coming being announced by the chiming of a few bells at their cars, and the other set delivering letters. They both ride in cars, for now that no letter, far or near, pays more than two cents postage—which money is to pay the letter carriers themselves—the number of letters is so great that cars are really necessary. All the expense of the post office department is defrayed from the income or revenue of the direct tax—and hence the man of business pays his just proportion too. It was a wise thing, therefore, to establish all the mercantile offices near the Battery; they knew that the time was coming when New York and Brooklyn would be as one city."

"One city!" exclaimed Hastings; "how can that be? If connected by bridges, how can the ships pass up the East river?"

" You forget that our vessels have no masts;
they pass under the bridges here as they do in the
Delaware."

" Oh, true, I had forgotten; but my head is so
confused with all the wonders that I see and hear,
that you must excuse my mistakes. The old theatre stood there, but it has disappeared, I suppose. It
was called the Park Theatre. How are the play
houses conducted now? is there only one or two
good actors now among a whole company?"

" Well, that question really does amuse me. I
dare say that the people of your day were as much
astonished at reading the accounts handed down to
them of the fight of gladiators before an audience,
as we are at your setting out evening after evening
to hear the great poets travestied. If we could be
transported back to your time, how disgusted we
should be to spend four hours in listening to rant
and ignorance. All our actors now, are men and
women of education, such as the Placides, the
Wallacks, the Kembles, the Keans, of your day. I
assure you, we would not put up with inferior
talent in our cities. It is a rich treat now to listen
to one of Shakspeare's plays, for every man and
woman is perfect in the part. The whole theatrical
corps is held in as much esteem, and make a part
of our society, as those of any other profession do.
The worthless and the dissolute are more scrupulously rejected by that body than they are from
the body of lawyers or doctors; in fact it is no
more extraordinary now, than it was in your day
to see a worthless lawyer, or merchant, or physician, and to see him tolerated in society too, if he
happen to be rich. But there is no set of people
more worthy of our friendship and esteem than
the players. A great change, to be sure, took
place in their character, as soon as they had reaped
the benefit of a college education. I presume you

know that there is a college now for the education of public actors?"

"Is it possible?" said Hastings; "then I can easily imagine the improvements you speak of; for with the exception of the few—the stars, as they were called—there was but little education among them."

"Here it is that elocution is taught, and here all public speakers take lessons," said Edgar; "you may readily imagine what an effect such an institution would have on those who intended to become actors. In your day, out of the whole theatrical corps of one city, not more than six or seven, perhaps, could tell the meaning of the *words* they used in speaking, to say nothing of the *sense* of the author. There is no more prejudice now against play-acting than there is against farming. The old Recorder states, that, before our revolution, the farmers were of a more inferior race, and went as little into polite society as the mechanics did. Even so far back as your time a farmer was something of a gentleman, and why an actor should not be a gentleman is to us incomprehensible. One of the principal causes of this change of personal feeling towards actors has arisen from our having expunged all the low and indelicate passages from the early plays. Shakspeare wrote as the times then were, but his works did not depend on a few coarse and vulgar passages for their popularity and immortality; they could bear to be taken out, as you will perceive, for the space they occupied is not now known; the adjoining sentence closed over them, as it were, and they are forgotten. There were but few erasures to be made in the writings of Sir Walter Scott; the times were beginning to loathe coarse and indelicate allusions in your day, and, indeed, we may thank the other sex for this great improvement. They never disgraced their pages with sentences and expressions which would excite a blush. Look at the purity of such writers as Miss Burney, Mrs. Radcliffe, Miss Edgeworth, Miss Austin, Madame Cotton, and others of their day in Europe,—it is to woman's influence that we owe so much. See what is done by them now; why they have fairly routed and scouted out that vile, disgraceful, barbarous practice which was even prevalent in your time—that of beating and bruising the tender flesh of their children."

" I am truly rejoiced at that," said Hastings, "but I hope they extended their influence to the schools likewise—I mean the common schools; for, in my day in the grammar school of a college, a man who should bruise a child's flesh by beating or whipping him would have been kicked out of society."

" Why, I thought that boys were whipped in the grammar schools also. In the year 1836, it appears to me, that I remember to have read of the dismissal of some professor for injuring one of the boys by flogging him severely."

" I do not recollect it; but you say 1836—alas! I was unconscious then. It was the remains of barbarism ; how a teacher could get roused to such height of passion as to make him desire to bruise a child's flesh, I cannot conceive—when the only crime of the poor little sufferer was either an unwillingness or an inability to recite his lessons. I can imagine that a man, when drunk, might bruise a child's flesh in such a shocking manner as that the blood would settle under the skin, because liquor always brutalizes. Is drunkenness as prevalent now as formerly ?"

" Oh no, none but the lowest of the people drink to excess now, and they have to get drunk on cider and wine, for spirituous liquors have been prohibited by law for upwards of two hundred years. A law was passed in the year 1901, granting a divorce to any woman whose husband was proved to be a drunkard. This had a good effect, for a drunkard knew that if he was abandoned by his wife he must perish; so it actually reclaimed many drunkards at the time, and had a salutary effect afterwards. Besides this punishment, if a single man, or a bachelor, as he is called, was found drunk three times, he was put in the workhouse and obliged to have his head shaved, and to work at some trade. It is a very rare thing to see a drunkard now. But what are you looking for?"

"I thought I might see a cigar box about—not that I ever smoke"—

"A what?—a cigar? Oh yes, I know—little things made of tobacco leaves; but you have to learn that there is not a tobacco plantation in the world now. That is one of the most extraordinary parts of your history: that well educated men could keep a pungent and bitter mass of leaves in their mouth for the pleasure of seeing a stream of yellow water running out of it, is the most incomprehensible mystery to me; and then, to push the dust of these leaves up their nostrils, which I find by the old Recorder that they did, for the mere pleasure of hearing the noise that was made by their noses! The old Recorder called their pocket handkerchiefs flags of abomination."

Hastings thought it was not worth while to convince the young man that the disgusting practice was not adopted for such purposes as he mentioned. In fact his melancholy had greatly increased since their arrival in this city, and he determined to beg his young friend to return the next day to their home, and to remain quiet for another year, to see if time could reconcile him to his strange fate. He

H

took pleasure in rambling through the city hall, and the park, which remained still of the same shape, and he was pleased likewise to see that many of the streets at right angles with Broadway were more than twice the width that they were in 1835. For instance, all the streets from Wall street up to the Park were as wide as Broadway, and they were opened on the other side quite down to the Hudson.

"Yes," said Edgar, "it was the great fire of 1842 which made this salutary change; but here is a neat building—you had nothing of this kind in your time. This is a house where the daughters of the poor are taught to sew and cut out wearing apparel. I suppose you know that there are no men tailors now."

"What, do women take measure?"

"Oh no, men are the measurers, but women cut out and sew. It is of great advantage to poor women that they can cut out and make their husbands' and children's clothes. The old Recorder states that women—poor women—in the year 1836, were scarcely able to cut out their own clothes. But just about that date, a lady of this city suggested the plan of establishing an institution of this kind, and it was adopted. Some benevolent men built the house and left ample funds for the maintenance of a certain number of poor girls, with a good salary for those who superintend it. And here is another house: this is for the education of those girls whose parents have seen better days. Here they are taught accounts and book-keeping—which, however, in our day is not so complicated as it was, for there is no credit given for any thing. In short these girls are instructed in all that relates to the disposal of money; our women now comprehend what is meant by stocks, and dividends, and loans, and tracts, and bonds, and mortgages."

"Do women still get the third of their husband's estate after their husband's death?"

"Their thirds? I don't know what you mean— Oh, I recollect; yes, in your day it was the practice to curtail a woman's income after her husband's death. A man never then considered a woman as equal to himself; but, while he lived, he let her enjoy the whole of his income equally with himself, because he could not do otherwise and enjoy his money; but when he died, or rather, when about making his will, he found out that she was but a poor creature after all, and that a very little of what he had to leave would suffice for her. Nay, the old Recorder says that there have been rich men who ordered the very house in which they lived, and which had been built for their wives' comfort, during their life time, to be sold, and who thus compelled their wives to live in mean, pitiful houses, or go to lodgings."

"Yes," said Hastings,—quite ashamed of his own times,—"but then you know the husband was fearful that his wife would marry again, and all their property would go to strangers."

"Well, why should not women have the same privileges as men? Do you not think that a woman had the same fears? A man married again and gave his money to strangers—did he not? The fact is, we consider that a woman has the same feelings as we have ourselves—a thing you never once thought of—and now the property that is made during marriage is as much the woman's as the man's; they are partners in health and in sickness, in joy and in sorrow—they enjoy every thing in common while they live together, and why a woman, merely on account of her being more helpless, should be cut off from affluence because she survives her husband, is more

than we of this century can tell. Why should not
children wait for the property till after her death,
as they would for their father's death? It was a
relic of barbarism, but it has passed away with
wars and bloodshed. We educate our women
now, and they are as capable of taking care of
property as we are ourselves. They are our trustees, far better than the trustees you had amongst
you in your day—they seldom could find it in their
hearts to allow a widow even her poor income. I
suppose they thought that a creature so pitifully
used by her husband was not worth bestowing their
honesty upon."

"But the women in my day," said Hastings,
"seemed to approve of this treatment; in fact, I
have known many very sensible women who
thought it right that a man should not leave his
wife the whole of his income after his death.
But they were beginning to have their eyes
opened, for I recollect that the subject was being
discussed in 1835."

"Yes, you can train a mind to acquiesce in any
absurd doctrine, and the truth is, that as women
were then educated, they were, for the most part,
unfit to have the command of a large estate. But
I cannot find that the children were eventually benefited by it; for young men and women, coming
into possession of their father's estate at the early
age of twenty-one, possessed no more business talent than their mother; nor had they even as much
prudence and judgment in the management of money matters, as she had. Men seldom thought of
this, but generally directed their executors to divide
the property among the children as soon as they
became of age—utterly regardless of the injustice
they were doing their wives, and of the oath which
they took when they married—that is, if they mar-

ried according to the forms of the Episcopal church. In that service, a man binds himself by a solemn oath ' to endow his wife with *all* his worldly goods.' If he swears to endow her with all, how can he in safety to his soul, *will* these worldly goods away from her. We consider the practice of depriving a woman of the right to the whole of her husband's property after his death, as a monstrous act of injustice, and the laws are now peremptory on this subject."

"I am certain you are right," said Hastings, "and you have improved more rapidly in this particular, during a period of three hundred years, than was done by my ancestors in two thousand years before. I can understand now, how it happens, that children have the same respect for their mother, that they only felt for their father in my time. The custom, or laws, being altogether in favour of equality of rights between the parents, the children do not repine when they find that they stand in the same relation of dependence to their mother, that they did to their father; and why this should not be, is incomprehensible to me now, but I never reflected on it before."

"Yes, there are fewer estates squandered away in consequence of this, and society is all the better for it. Then to this is added the great improvement in the business education of women. All the retail and detail of mercantile operations are conducted by them. You had some notion of this in your time; for, in Philadelphia, although women were generally only employed to make sales behind the counter, yet some were now and then seen at the head of the establishment. Before our separation from Great Britain, the business of farming was also at a low ebb, and a farmer was but a mean person in public estimation. He ranks now amongst the highest of our business men; and in fact, he is equal to any man whether in business or not, and this is the case with female merchants. Even in 1836, a woman who undertook the business of a retail shop, managing the whole concern herself, although greatly respected, she never took her rank amongst the first classes of society. This arose, first, from want of education, and, secondly, from her having lived amongst an inferior set of people. But when women were trained to the comprehension of mercantile operations, and were taught how to dispose of money, their whole character underwent a change, and with this accession of business talent, came the respect from men for those who had a capacity for the conducting of business affairs. Only think what an advantage this is to our children; why our mothers and wives are the first teachers, they give us sound views from the very commencement, and our clerkship begins from the time we can comprehend the distinction of right and wrong."

"Did not our infant schools give a great impulse to this improvement in the condition of women, and to the improvement in morals, and were not women mainly instrumental in fostering these schools?"

"Yes, that they were; it was chiefly through the influence of their pen and active benevolence, that the scheme arrived at perfection. In these infant schools a child was early taught the mystery of its relation to society; all its good dispositions and propensities were encouraged and developed, and its vicious ones were repressed. The world owes much to the blessed influence of infant schools, and the lower orders were the first to be humanized by them. But I need not dwell on this particular. I shall only point to the improvement in the morals of our people at this day, to convince you that it is owing altogether to the benign influence of women.

As soon as they took their rank as an equal to man, equal as to property I mean, for they had no other right to *desire;* there was no longer any struggle, it became their ambition to show how long the world had been benighted by thus keeping them in a degraded state. I say degraded state, for surely it argued in them imbecility or incapacity of some kind, and to great extent, too, when a man appointed executors and trustees to his estate whilst his wife was living. It showed one of three things—that he never considered her as having equal rights with himself; or, that he thought her incompetent to take charge of his property—or, that the customs and laws of the land had so warped his judgment, that he only did as he saw others do, without considering whether these laws and customs were right or wrong. But if you only look back you will perceive, that in every benevolent scheme, in every plan for meliorating the condition of the poor, and improving their morals, it was women's influence that promoted and fostered it. It is to that healthy influence, that we owe our present prosperity and happiness—and it is an influence which I hope may forever continue."

It was not to such a man as Hastings that Edgar need have spoken so earnestly; he only wanted to have a subject fairly before him to comprehend it in all its bearings. He rejoiced that women were now equal to men in all that they ever considered as their rights; and he rejoiced likewise that the proper distinction was rigidly observed between the sexes—that as men no longer encroached on their rights, they, in return, kept within the limits assigned them by the Creator. As a man and a christian, he was glad that this change had taken place; and it was a melancholy satisfaction to feel that with these views, if it had been permitted him to continue with his wife, he should have put her on an equality with himself.

The moment his wife and child appeared to his mental vision, he became indifferent to what was passing around him; Edgar, perceiving that he was buried in his own thoughts, proposed that they should return home immediately, and they accordingly passed down Broadway to the Battery, from which place they intended to take a boat. They reached the wharf—a ship had just arrived from the Cape of Good Hope, with a fine cargo. The captain and crew of which were black.

——— " That is true," said Hastings, " I have seen very few negroes; what has become of them. The question of slavery was a very painful one in my time, and much of evil was apprehended in consequence of a premature attempt to hasten their emancipation. I dread to hear how it eventuated."

" You have nothing to fear on that score," said Edgar, " for the whole thing was arranged most satisfactorily to all parties. The government was rich in resources, and rich in land; they sold the land, and with the money thus obtained, and a certain portion of the surplus revenue in the course of ten years, they not only indemnified the slaveholders for their loss of property, but actually transplanted the whole of the negro population to Liberia, and to other healthy colonies. The southern planters soon found that their lands could be as easily cultivated by the labour of white men, as by the negroes."

" But a great number remained, I presume, for it would not have been humane to force those to go who preferred to stay."

" All that chose to settle in this country were at liberty to do so, and their rights and privileges were respected; but in the course of twenty or thirty years, their descendants gradually went over to their own people, who by this time, had firmly established themselves."

" Did those that remained, ever intermarry with the white population, and were they ever admitted into society ?"

" As soon as they became free, as soon as their bodies were unshackled, their minds became enlightened, and as their education advanced, they learned to appreciate themselves properly. They saw no advantage in intermarrying with the whites; on the contrary, they learned, by close investigation, that the negro race becomes extinct in the fourth remove, when marriages took place between the two colours. It seemed to be their pride to keep themselves a distinct people, and to show the world that their organization allowed of the highest grade of mental culture. They seemed utterly indifferent likewise about mixing in the society of white men, for their object and sole aim was to become independent. Many of their descendants left the United States with handsome fortunes. You could not insult a black man more highly than to talk of their intermarrying with the whites—they scorn it much more than the whites did in your time."

" How do they treat the white people that trade with them in their own country ?"

" How ? why as Christians—to their praise be it said, they never retaliated. The few excesses they committed whilst they were degraded by slavery, was entirely owing to a misdirection of their energies; but the moment the white man gave up his right over them, that moment all malignant and hostile feelings disappeared. The name of negro is no longer a term of reproach, he is proud of it; and he smiles when he reads in the history of their servitude, how indignant the blacks were at being called by that title. They are a prosperous and happy people, respected by all nations, for their trade extends over the whole world. They would never have arrived at their present happy condition if they had sought to obtain their freedom by force; but by waiting a few years—for the best men of their colour saw that the spirit of the times indicated that their day of freedom was near—they were released from bondage with the aid and good wishes of the whole country. It showed their strong good sense in waiting for the turn of the tide in their favour; it proved that they had forethought, and deserved our sympathies."

" I am glad of all this," said Hastings—" and the Indians—what has become of them, are they still a distinct people ?"

" I am sorry you ask that question,—for it is one on which I do not like to converse—but

> ' The Indians have departed—gone is their hunting ground,
> And the twanging of their bow-string is a forgotten sound.
> Where dwelleth yesterday—and where is echo's cell?
> Where hath the rainbow vanished—there doth the Indian
>      dwell!'

" When our own minds were sufficiently enlightened, when our hearts were sufficiently inspired by the humane principles of the Christian religion, we emancipated the blacks. What demon closed up the springs of tender mercy when Indian rights were in question I know not ?—but I must not speak of it!"

They now proceeded homewards, and in three hours—for they travelled slowly, that they might the better converse,—they came in sight of the low, stone farm-house, in which poor Hastings had taken his nap of three hundred years. They alighted from the car, and as he wished to indulge himself in taking one more look at the interior—for the building was soon to be removed—his young relative left him to apprize his family of their arrival. After casting a glance at Edgar, he entered the house, and seating himself mechanically in the old arm chair, he leaned his head back in mournful reverie. Thoughts innumerable, and of every variety chased each other through his troubled brain; his early youth, his political career, his wife and child, all that they had ever been to him, his excellent father, Valentine Harley, and all their tender relationship, mingled confusedly with the events that had occurred since his long sleep—copy-rights—mad dogs—bursting of steam boilers—the two great fires in New-York—direct tax—no duties—post-offices—the improved condition of clergymen—no more wars—no bruising of children's flesh—women's rights—Astor's hotel—New-York Mart in State-street—Negro emancipation—all passed in rapid review, whilst his perplexities to know what became of the Indians were mixed with the rest, and ran through the whole scene. At the same time that all this was galloping through his feverish brain, he caught a glance of his young relative, and in his troubled imagination, it appeared that it was not the Edgar Hastings who had of late been his kind companion, but his own son. He was conscious that this was only a trick of the fancy, and arose from his looking so earnestly at the young man as he left him at the door of the house; but it was a pleasant fancy, and he indulged in it, till a sudden crash or noise of some kind jarred the windows and aroused him. He was sensible that footsteps approached, and he concluded it was his young friend who had returned to conduct him home.

"Edgar—Edgar Hastings—my son is it thou—didst thou not hear the cannon of the Black Hawk—hast thou been sleeping?"

" Amazement! Was that the voice of his father —was this the good Valentine Harley that now assisted him to rise—and who were those approaching him—was it his darling wife, and was that smiling boy his own son, his little Edgar!"

"You have been asleep, I find, my dear husband," said the gentle Ophelia, "and a happy sleep it has been for me, for us all. See, here is a letter which makes it unnecessary for you to leave home."

" And is this reality ?—do I indeed hold thee to my heart once more, my Ophelia—oh, my father, what a dream !"

# A VISION OF BANGOR
# IN THE TWENTIETH CENTURY

[ Edward Kent ]

## ERRATA.

Page 62, line 22d, read *cause of humanity*, for "*curse* of humanity."
Page 65, line 21st, and page 73, line 2d, read *Baskahegan*, for "Buskahegian."
Page 66, line 20th, read "State of Peru, *and* a paragraph" for "State of Peru, *a* paragraph."
Page 71, line 21st, read "there *were*." for "there *was*,"

# A VISION OF BANGOR, IN THE TWENTIETH CENTURY.

I AM not a nervous man, or one addicted to seeing visions and dreaming dreams, but once, as I journeyed through the wilderness of this world, I had a dream, "which was not all a dream," but partly a vision of the future, like those vouchsafed to the clairvoyant in his magnetic state. I do not know that I had been magnetized, and yet, I half suspect that distant passes had been made at me, or some charmed tooth-pick or pencil-case had been charged with the subtle essence, and put under my pillow to work the wondrous devilment. I would charge no one rashly, and yet truth compels me to state facts, and then, as the newspapers say, a candid public will judge, whether or no I have been fairly dealt with. I am one of the unfortunate victims, selected, I know not on what principle, who were months since pencilled down on gilt-edged note-paper in a fair Italian hand, as the masculine contributors to the "Bangor Book," to "do" the rough and solid work in this superstructure of the wit and wisdom of Down East. The list was soon exhibited, by an inexorable woman, and the fatal cross stood thereon, like the marks on the death roll of the Roman triumvirate. At first, I laughed outright, and snapped my fingers in defiance, and indignant resistance. I write in a book!! A Bangor book! I, of all men!

"The dog star rages."

For a wonder, like the wonder in heaven, the woman
4

said nothing, but looked calm, confident and secure, and I began to feel like the entwined fly in the web of the spider. I was left alone, after a significant nod, and the single words, — " prepare, the time is short." I mused awhile, and then rushed into business. In its vortex I actually drove, at times, from my mind the injunction and the warning. But time passed, and I felt a gentle pull, and " is it ready ?" in a low, soft, musical voice, fell upon my ear. " What ?" said I. " The contribution in prose or verse," said she. " Ready, my dear woman, — no, and never will be." " Yes, it will be. The paper is made on which it will be written; the pen and ink are waiting. Beware of the third time of asking." And she turned away to speak to another of the unfortunate *listed* men. I only heard her say the printers will reach your page next week — and there can be no delay — the boy will call for copy — " I defy the *devil* and all his works," said the incipient author. I could not resist whispering in his ear, " So you may, but who can stand against the determined purpose of a woman ?" (His article appears in the volume, and stands the voluntary offering of an unpractised author, to the great curse of humanity.) I turned again to my fair dictator, determined to break away from the strange enchantment, for I began actually to feel a sort of itching in my fingers, and to look with unwonted interest towards the ink-standish and the writing-desk. I found myself parting my hair, and smoothing it down and opening my vest and turning down my collar *à la Byron.* I saw myself in the mirror, and there was a new and most ludicrously grotesque, sentimental, half-poetic and half-transcendental, and altogether lackadaisical stare of the eyes, and dropping of the eyebrows. The case began to look alarming. Everything about me looked " *blue.*" The " *cacoethes scribendi*" was developing its symptoms, and whether taken in the natural way or by inoculation, it threatened a fatal result.

I roused myself for an impressive appeal. I knew that woman was ever ready to succor and relieve distressed humanity. "My good friend," said I, "listen to reason." "Listen to a fiddle-stick!" (She did not say a "fool," but she did look a little contemptuous, and more impatient.) "Why do you resist? Are you not 'listed,' and booked, and have we not devoted ten pages to you?" "But how can I write? I never wrote a line for a book in my life; and the idea of having my words, written by my hands, actually printed, and hot-pressed, and screwed and bound in real hard covers, is entirely overwhelming." "Now does not this pass all endurance?" said she; "that you, and others like you, self-styled 'lords of the creation,' with fierce whiskers, and broad shoulders, and the assumed air of independence, and with the roughness of bears, should not have the heart of a hen-partridge — whilst we women, timid, delicate and retiring, as is our nature and destiny, are ready to go boldly forth to the public, and to write our prettiest and our best, and have it printed, too, *solely* from our love for the cause of the fatherless and the destitute." "But think of the Bangor public, and the cynical and severe critics in their midst, who, not being willing to write, are yet over-willing to carp, and ridicule and disparage." "Think of the orphans," said she! "Think of the reviewers," said I! "What *reviewers*," said she, " would ever think our down east book worthy of notice. "That's true again," said I. "Then write your article, not having the fear of the reviewers before your eyes."

I went home, feeling like one spell-bound. "Seven women shall take hold of one man," was the text of scripture for this night's meditation. Must I write! and if so, what shall I write? I was in a fix, and as a last resort I went to bed.

I did not search for witch-hazel or magnetized implements, as I before said, but I soon fell asleep, and my last thoughts were of steel pens, paper manufactories and printers' ink. I have an indistinct remembrance of a half-sleeping and half-waking vision of a ragged and suffering orphan, who held up to me a ream of foolscap, and asked me, in plaintive tones, to write, and then she strangely vanished, repeating the line of the children's play, " He can do little that can't do this." I turned, but my destiny was before me. Methought I arose, determined to escape in the open air, from the sight of objects calculated to remind me of the unperformed task, and with the lurking thought that perchance I might gather materials or suggestions to be brain-woven into the fatal " article." In a moment I was in " the square," but it was strangely altered. I could not recognize a single tenement. I gazed upward and saw on one granite front the letters — " Erected 1938." There was an appearance of age about the building. It looked discolored and gray. As far as the eye could reach were ranges of high and splendid stores. What does all this mean? I involuntarily asked ; and as I spoke, I saw a man the exact image of T——, and felt relieved. He was a tall, lank, long-sided Yankee, six feet and two inches in height. I addressed him familiarly. He gave me a keen and independent look, such as a Yankee only can give, and replied, " You have the advantage of me." " How so?" " You seem to know me, but I do not know you." In the sauciness of a dream I thought, I am not sure that it is for the advantage of any one to know you. But I was polite and said nothing of the kind. " Why, certainly, your name is T——." " O yes." " You know me, A——?" " Never heard the name in these parts." " Why, did we not board together at the old Hatch house, in the times of Thomas?" "Never heard of such a house." "Pray," said I, utterly confounded, "who was your great grandfather?" "I don't know," but like an American, always looking ahead, he added, "I know who my son is, and there he stands." "Who were your relations?" "I don't know as I ever had any relations nearer than uncles." "Do you live in Bangor?" "Yes, I was born and grew up here, man and boy, sixty odd years." "Where is Taylor's corner?" "There," said he, pointing to a splendid block, covered with signs of Banks, Insurance offices and brokers. "It has been so named for more than a hundred years — and is still owned by descendants of the original possessor." "I am glad of it," said I, "if the successors are as honest men as he was." "Can you show me the mark of high water in the great freshet of 1846." "No," said he, "I have heard of that great rise, and there have been a great many attempts to find some stone or mark to show the height, but strange to say, the antiquarians of that day were so busy in hunting up antediluvian relics, and taking the measure of the Buskahegian giant, that they forgot that they, and their days, would ever become antiquity." "But where," said I, "is the Kenduskeag stream?" "Under those buildings and bridges," said he; "if you will go up above the 'Lovers Leap,' you can see it — and you can get a glimpse of it near the market." As we passed along, I saw Jerome's X press office in large letters, and then I at once felt at home. "And there," said he, "is the man himself — a little stiff in the joints, for he is our oldest inhabitant, and nobody knows how old he is. But he is as good as new, and ready always *expressly* for the occasion. He says he hopes to live until he discovers something a little quicker than lightning, and then he shall be ready to be gathered in."

A familiar nod and ready smile from my old friend, assured me that in him there was "no mistake."

The market, a long and commodious building, extending up the middle of the stream, reminded me of the plan I saw in 1836. It was well filled with fat carcasses, and fatter men. "Oleaginous" was written on every side — man and beast. "How many people have you in this city?" "About one hundred thousand," said he, "according to the last census in 1970."

I began to be wearied, and stept into an office to rest. I took up the paper of the day, Sept. 10, 1978, and called "the Bangor Daily News." It was one of twelve dailies and numerous able weeklies, as I was told. I read, as I could, the news column, but I found many new words, and many old ones strangely altered. I gathered from the paragraphs, that the Southern portion of the South American continent, including Cape Horn, had yielded to the inevitable destiny of the Saxon race, and had been conquered and annexed, because they would not give up without fighting. "Later news from the State of Peru," a paragraph headed, "Presidential election," attracted my attention. It contained a column of States, fifty-six in number, and at the bottom, "We have partial returns by telegraph, of the voting yesterday at Oregon city. One of the candidates residing in that region, gives great interest to the votes of the Pacific States." The editor, who was evidently a little of an antiquarian, had hunted up an old file of newspapers, and had copied as curiosities some of the notices of the year 1848, of the "Whig, Democratic and Liberty" parties, and their stirring appeals — and the editor adds, "Can it be believed, that in 1848, men were actually held as chattels, and sold at auction like oxen. We yesterday saw a shipmaster, who told us that he had seen and talked with black men in the south, who were once slaves, and they and their children had been sold by an auctioneer. Thank heaven, we have seen the last of that horrid system." I took up another paper, in phonographic words. The editor complained, that, although the reformers had worked diligently more than a century, yet the mass of men would persist in rejecting their improvements. As far as I could judge, the parties in politics were divided mainly on the question of the union of the States.

In an adjoining building was the telegraph office. I looked and saw that instead of wires, they had, near the ground, rails of a small size. I asked why this change, and was told that they sent passengers on them, driven by electricity to Boston in four minutes. " But how can the human system stand such velocity." " O, we ' *stun* ' them," the fellow said, " with the Letheon, and then tie them in boxes on little wheels, and they go safely, and come out bright. There are rival lines," he continued, " and great efforts are being made to bring the passage within three minutes. We have to put on rather a large dose of the Letheon when we attempt this, but the passengers all say they will run the risk of never waking again, rather than be beat. We have had to bury a few, but what is that to saving a minute, and beating the rascally opposition line ? The people all say ' go ahead.' "

By a sudden transition, I remember not how, I found myself at Mount Hope, the final resting-place of the dead. The avenue was shaded delightfully. At the base of the conical hill were two beautiful ponds, surrounded by the weeping willow — that long cherished emblem of sadness and mourning. The garden in front was full of beautiful and fragrant plants. And the grounds sacred to sepulture were filled with all the varied monuments which affectionate love could devise, from the uprising shaft and costly sculpture, to the single rose tree, or the modest violet. I gazed around on the forest, natural and transplanted, which covered all the public and private grounds, and the solid masonry of the stone wall which enclosed the whole area. I sought for familiar names, but long in vain. I found old tombstones at last, some lying on the ground, and others all but illegible. I traced names once familiar and dear, and many, that, had it not been the confusion of a dream, I should have known were now young and full of life and promise. On the tombstone of one who was daily in my sight, the beautiful, the admired in the midst of the years of young existence, I read — " Sacred to the memory of —— ——, who died aged 85 years : bowed down with the weight of years, she was ready to depart." I saw a funeral procession enter the grounds, and the tears of heartfelt anguish which fell fast and freely from those parents' eyes as they saw the child of their affections consigned to the silent tomb, testified to me, that as of yore " man was made to mourn," and that the same hearts yet beat in human bosoms. I saw my *own* name on a marble headstone, but the tall rank grass hid the date from my vision ; but I read such a long list of unremembered virtues, that a smile which covered my face was very near being turned into a hearty laugh at this, to me, tangible evidence of the *value* of monumental epitaphs.

Anon the scene changed, and I was on the shore of the Kenduskeag, looking upward to that firm pile of the everlasting rocks, rising perpendicularly from the shore. Man had not changed this, and *here* I was on my own ground. I saw two lovers in their quiet, slow, and absorbed walk — as they talked in low and touching tones — and watched the eyes which spoke more effective language than the tongue, and heard them utter vows and build airy castles of future happiness, and I felt that, although art had wrought such mighty revolutions all around me, there was the same interchange of the soft affections of the heart as in my own youthful days, the same undoubting trust and unclouded hopes for the future, which no experience of others could ever calm or conquer.

Again I was in the busy haunts of men. I heard them conversing at the corners, — " *Dollars,* — thousands ! — great bargain ! — worth his hundred thousand," were the emphatic words. This sounded as familiar talk to my ears. The dollar still remained the representative of value, and the idol of men.

And now I seemed to feel and know that I was in the midst of the twentieth century, and that I was but a spectator, looking at posterity. I was not awed, but curious. The man I had before seen was at my side. "My friend!" said I, "do boards sell readily at 21 — 14 — 8." He opened wide his eyes, but said nothing. "What is the price of stumpage? Does the lumber hold out of a good quality, or is it shaky and concosy? Is Veazie's boom large enough to hold all that comes down? How does the wood scale hold out?" I poured these questions upon him, but he shook his head in despair. " I don't know what you mean — your terms are all Greek or Indian to me." " You can at least tell me how many million feet of boards are sawed and shipped yearly on the rivers?" " Million feet!" said he, " I never heard of such a quantity!" " Is not lumber your great staple for export?" " Lumber! why, we have not shipped a cargo for fifty years. We have to search closely to get hemlock enough to use here, and as to good pine, we have to depend on Oregon." " And how do you get it?" " O," said he, "by the Oregon railroad, and the lakes, and the St. Lawrence railroad. You see the depot over there." " And what *is* your business here?" " All kinds of trading, and great manufacturing establishments of cotton, woollen and mixed goods, to supply the markets

4*

of the world. Do you think we could have built up such a city as this, by chipping up logs with a saw. That might have helped our great-grandfathers, when they lived along side of the Indians. But the vast factories at Treat's Falls, on the costly dam, and these long rows of warehouses — these extended streets — were never built by the lumber trade. See, yonder, the Cathedral, and near to it the spire of the Stone church, and all around you the evidences of thrift, and industry, and improvement. See that splended granite front; within those walls is the Bangor Public Library, open to all, and free to the poor and the rich alike, containing seventy thousand volumes, founded in 1848 — and ever honored be the name of Vattemare, who first started the plan — and thanks to those, our predecessors, who followed his suggestions." "Permit me," said I, "to inquire as to social arrangements; do men and women yet live in families, or did the reformers of my day succeed in introducing the community system." "O," said he, "that nonsense died a natural death, and with it the kindred absurdities of women's rights to participate in government and to direct affairs out doors as well as in — all this was given up long ago, except, that now and then some old, cross-grained or disappointed maid, sets up a sort of snarl, but nobody minds her, our women bake and darn stockings and tend the babies, and mend their husbands' clothes, teach their children the way they should go, and walk with them in it, and read their bibles and as many books as they can find time to. They tried those schemes to which you allude, a great while ago — but nature was too strong for abstract theories, and after a considerable struggle between the sexes, they both became satisfied that it was best to compromise, and let the *women* rule indoors, and the *men* out." "Not much of a compromise," said I, "for the women always did that." "Well," said he,

" they were satisfied to give up the new schemes, (the man somehow seemed now to be aware of my actual condition) for they tried their hands a little at government." "Pray, tell me about it." "Why, they fretted and teased until in several of the states the people, for the sake of quiet, admitted them to a participation on equal footing with the men. The first difficulty was in voting at the polls. It was impossible to keep the women within party lines. They would vote for the youngest and handsomest and most agreeable man; and they would see and hear all the candidates, and insisted upon good looks and genteel clothes; and when their own sex were candidates, it was almost impossible to make one woman vote for another. They all liked the men best. But when the legislature met it was impossible to get along at all. One lady had her hair to dress, and could not be in that day. Another was shopping — there were such *dear* beauties of silks just imported. Another must have leave of absence, for her baby must be looked after. Another would not attend because there was no looking-glasses in committee rooms. And yet another because her milliner had made a horrid fit. And those that were there would not observe any rules, but each insisted on talking without stint or limit. And then on committees, the reports were not forthcoming, for the bachelors had been making love to the maids.

" The members of both sexes were all good looking, but the public business needed some rougher outsides and some better heads than those which belonged to the Adonises of the halls.

" They once held a private session on matters which required the most profound secrecy. The doors were closed, windows barred; but the next day, before the morning papers were out, the whole matter was the town talk. Upon investigation, it was found that each of the female members had told it, but in strict confidence, as they all declared, to a female friend."

I found myself strolling in Broadway, and stood beneath the shade of aged and venerable and wide spreading elms, "still wearing proudly their panoply of green," extending as far as the eye could reach on each side of the spacious central walk. I saw the children at their sports beneath the arching canopy, and heard the same animated cries and joyous shouts, and earnest vociferations, which had always been the characteristics of childhood. I saw the marbles and the hoops, and the bat and ball — all familiar and unaltered. A bevy of girls and boys were engaged in reading books. I looked over their shoulders and saw " Mother Goose's Melodies," with the old pictures, " Robinson Crusoe," in his hairy skin suit, and one sober miss intent on the " Pilgrim's Progress." It seemed there were some books that would *never* be consigned to oblivion.

I passed into a bookstore, but I remember only that I saw the old Saxon Bible in King James's translation, Shakspeare, and Milton, and Robert Burns, and Don Quixote. I asked if they had a copy of the Bangor Book? " O yes," said the shopman, and handed me a thick octavo. It was the Bangor Directory for 1978. " I mean," said I, " the work published in 1847; surely that must have survived, for it was preserved by Attic salt in *blue* covers, and contained the best efforts of the Penobscot mind in prose and verse; we all looked to posterity for our reward." " Never heard of it," said the man. A little dried-up specimen of a man who was poring over a book in a corner, addressing me, said, " I have seen that book, I am quite sure, at least the outside of it, in one of the alcoves of the rooms of the Antiquarian Society, labelled 'the day of small things,' where are kept the relics and curiosities of the first settlements on the river, and also Indian gouges, axes and hatchets, miniature birch canoes, and the portrait of the Buskahegian Giant, so called." "Is there not also one of the striped pig?" "I never saw any," quoth he. "Speaking of the striped pig," said I, "have you any licensed grog-shops?" "O no, we have conquered King Alcohol, and are all temperance men now; and the ladies of the present time look with wonder and dismay in their countenances, when they are informed that their sex did once even *here* by their example countenance the use of wine as a beverage in their evening levees!"

Once more in the street I moved towards my home as I remembered it. As I passed onward, I was attracted by a beautiful arch at the entrance of a substantial, elegant, and commodious building, bearing this inscription: "The Bangor Female Orphan Asylum, founded in 1839, and sustained by the benevolence of its citizens." I looked with interest on the groups of healthy, happy, and well conditioned children, but alas! I was reminded of the dreaded "article," and the faces before so pleasant seemed to change into looks of reproach and regret. I involuntarily exclaimed — "When shall I find a subject, and finish the task appointed me?" I looked up and recognized the same orphan face that appeared at my bedside, tranquil and satisfied; and the little urchin with a triumphant smile replied, — "It is completed."

# THE MIDAS PLAGUE


Frederik Pohl

# The Midas Plague

AND SO THEY WERE MARRIED.

The bride and groom made a beautiful couple, she in her twenty-yard frill of immaculate white, he in his formal gray ruffled blouse and pleated pantaloons.

It was a small wedding—the best he could afford. For guests, they had only the immediate family and a few close friends. And when the minister had performed the ceremony, Morey Fry kissed his bride and they drove off to the reception. There were twenty-eight limousines in all (though it is true that twenty of them contained only the caterer's robots) and three flower cars.

"Bless you both," said old man Elon sentimentally. "You've got a fine girl in our Cherry, Morey." He blew his nose on a ragged square of cambric.

The old folks behaved very well, Morey thought. At the reception, surrounded by the enormous stacks of wedding gifts, they drank the champagne and ate a great many of the tiny, delicious canapés. They listened politely to the fifteen-piece orchestra, and Cherry's mother even danced one dance with Morey for sentiment's sake, though it was clear that dancing was far from the usual pattern of her life. They tried as hard as they could to blend into the gathering, but all the same, the two elderly figures in severely simple and probably rented garments were dismayingly conspicuous in the quarter-acre of tapestries and tinkling fountains that was the main ballroom of Morey's country home.

When it was time for the guests to go home and let the newlyweds begin their life together Cherry's father shook Morey by the hand and Cherry's mother kissed him. But as they drove away in their tiny runabout their faces were full of foreboding.

It was nothing against Morey as a person, of course. But poor people should not marry wealth.

Morey and Cherry loved each other, certainly. That helped. They told each other so, a dozen times an hour, all of the long hours they were together, for all of the first months of their marriage. Morey even took time off to go shopping with his bride, which endeared him to her enormously. They drove their shopping carts through the immense vaulted corridors of the supermarket, Morey checking off the items on the shopping list as Cherry picked out the goods. It was fun.

For a while.

Their first fight started in the supermarket, between Breakfast Foods and Floor Furnishings, just where the new Precious Stones department was being opened.

Morey called off from the list, "Diamond lavaliere, costume rings, earbobs."

Cherry said rebelliously, "Morey, I *have* a lavaliere. Please, dear!"

Morey folded back the pages of the list uncertainly. The lavaliere was on there, all right, and no alternative selection was shown.

"How about a bracelet?" he coaxed. "Look, they have some nice ruby ones there. See how beautifully they go with your hair, darling!" He beckoned a robot clerk, who bustled up and handed Cherry the bracelet tray. "Lovely," Morey exclaimed as Cherry slipped the largest of the lot on her wrist.

"And I don't have to have a lavaliere?" Cherry asked.

"Of course not." He peeked at the tag. "Same number of ration points exactly!" Since Cherry looked only dubious, not convinced, he said briskly, "And now we'd better be getting along to the shoe department. I've got to pick up some dancing pumps."

Cherry made no objection, neither then nor throughout the rest of their shopping tour. At the end, while they were sitting in the supermarket's ground-floor lounge waiting for the robot accountants to tote up their bill and the robot cashiers to stamp their ration books, Morey remembered to have the shipping department save out the bracelet.

"I don't want that sent with the other stuff, darling," he explained. "I want you to wear it right now. Honestly, I don't think I ever saw anything looking so *right* for you."

Cherry looked flustered and pleased. Morey was delighted with himself; it wasn't everybody who knew how to handle these little domestic problems just right!

He stayed self-satisfied all the way home, while Henry, their companion-robot, regaled them with funny stories of the factory in which it had been built and trained. Cherry wasn't used to Henry by a long shot, but it was hard not to like the robot. Jokes and funny stories when you needed amusement, sympathy when you were depressed, a never-failing supply of news and information on any subject you cared to name—Henry was easy enough to take. Cherry even made a special point of asking Henry to keep them company through dinner, and she laughed as thoroughly as Morey himself at its droll anecdotes.

But later, in the conservatory, when Henry had considerately left them alone, the laughter dried up.

Morey didn't notice. He was very conscientiously making the rounds: turning on the tri-D, selecting their after-dinner liqueurs, scanning the evening newspapers.

Cherry cleared her throat self-consciously, and Morey stopped what he was doing. "Dear," she said tentatively, "I'm feeling kind of restless tonight. Could we—I mean do you think we could just sort of stay home and—well, relax?"

Morey looked at her with a touch of concern. She lay back wearily, eyes half closed. "Are you feeling all right?" he asked.

"Perfectly. I just don't want to go out tonight, dear. I don't feel up to it."

He sat down and automatically lit a cigarette. "I see," he said. The tri-D was beginning a comedy show; he got up to turn it off, snapping on the tape-player. Muted strings filled the room.

"We had reservations at the club tonight," he reminded her.

Cherry shifted uncomfortably. "I know."

"And we have the opera tickets that I turned last week's in for. I hate to nag, darling, but we haven't used *any* of our opera tickets."

"We can see them right here on the tri-D," she said in a small voice.

"That has nothing to do with it, sweetheart. I—I didn't want to tell you about it, but Wainwright, down at the office, said something to me yesterday. He told me he would be at the circus last night and as much as said he'd be looking to see if we were there, too. Well, we weren't there. Heaven knows what I'll tell him next week."

He waited for Cherry to answer, but she was silent.

He went on reasonably, "So if you *could* see your way clear to going out tonight—"

He stopped, slack-jawed. Cherry was crying, silently and in quantity.

"Darling!" he said inarticulately.

He hurried to her, but she fended him off. He stood helpless over her, watching her cry.

"Dear, what's the matter?" he asked.

She turned her head away.

Morey rocked back on his heels. It wasn't exactly the first time he'd seen Cherry cry—there had been that poignant scene when they Gave Each Other Up, realizing that their backgrounds were too far apart for happiness, before the realization that they *had* to have each other, no matter what. . . . But it was the first time her tears had made him feel guilty.

And he did feel guilty. He stood there staring at her.

Then he turned his back on her and walked over to the bar. He ignored the ready liqueurs and poured two stiff highballs, brought them back to her. He set one down beside her, took a long drink from the other.

In quite a different tone, he said, "Dear, what's the *matter?*"

No answer.

"Come on. What is it?"

She looked up at him and rubbed at her eyes. Almost sullenly, she said, "Sorry."

"I know you're sorry. Look, we love each other. Let's talk this thing out."

She picked up her drink and held it for a moment, before setting it down untasted. "What's the use, Morey?"

"Please. Let's try."

She shrugged.

He went on remorselessly, "You aren't happy, are you?

And it's because of—well, all this." His gesture took in the richly furnished conservatory, the thick-piled carpet, the host of machines and contrivances for their comfort and entertainment that waited for their touch. By implication it took in twenty-six rooms, five cars, nine robots. Morey said, with an effort, "It isn't what you're used to, is it?"

"I can't help it," Cherry said. "Morey, you know I've tried. But back home—"

"Dammit," he flared, "*this* is your home. You don't live with your father any more in that five-room cottage; you don't spend your evenings hoeing the garden or playing cards for matchsticks. You live here, with me, your husband! You knew what you were getting into. We talked all this out long before we were married—"

The words stopped, because words were useless. Cherry was crying again, but not silently.

Through her tears, she wailed: "Darling, I've tried. You don't *know* how I've tried! I've worn all those silly clothes and I've played all those silly games and I've gone out with you as much as I *possibly* could and—I've eaten all that terrible food until I'm actually getting fa-fa-*fat!* I thought I could stand it. But I just can't go on like this; I'm not used to it. I—I love you, Morey, but I'm going crazy, living like this. I can't help it, Morey—*I'm tired of being poor!*"

Eventually the tears dried up, and the quarrel healed, and the lovers kissed and made up. But Morey lay awake that night, listening to his wife's gentle breathing from the suite next to his own, staring into the darkness as tragically as any pauper before him had ever done.

Blessed are the poor, for they shall inherit the Earth.

Blessed Morey, heir to more worldly goods than he could possibly consume.

Morey Fry, steeped in grinding poverty, had never gone hungry a day in his life, never lacked for anything his heart could desire in the way of food, or clothing, or a place to sleep. In Morey's world, no one lacked for these things; no one could.

Malthus was right—for a civilization without machines, automatic factories, hydroponics and food synthesis, nuclear breeder plants, ocean-mining for metals and minerals . . .

And a vastly increasing supply of labor . . .

And architecture that rose high in the air and dug deep in the ground and floated far out on the water on piers and pontoons . . . architecture that could be poured one day and lived in the next . . .

And robots.

Above all, robots . . . robots to burrow and haul and smelt and fabricate, to build and farm and weave and sew.

What the land lacked in wealth, the sea was made to yield and the laboratory invented the rest . . . and the factories became a pipeline of plenty, churning out enough to feed and clothe and house a dozen worlds.

Limitless discovery, infinite power in the atom, tireless labor of humanity and robots, mechanization that drove jungle and swamp and ice off the Earth, and put up office buildings and manufacturing centers and rocket ports in their place . . .

The pipeline of production spewed out riches that no king in the time of Malthus could have known.

But a pipeline has two ends. The invention and power and labor pouring in at one end must somehow be drained out at the other . . .

Lucky Morey, blessed economic-consuming unit, drowning in the pipeline's flood, striving manfully to eat and drink and wear and wear out his share of the ceaseless tide of wealth.

Morey felt far from blessed, for the blessings of the poor are always best appreciated from afar.

Quotas worried his sleep until he awoke at eight o'clock the next morning, red-eyed and haggard, but inwardly resolved. He had reached a decision. He was starting a new life.

There was trouble in the morning mail. Under the letterhead of the National Ration Board, it said:

"We regret to advise you that the following items returned by you in connection with your August quotas as used and no longer serviceable have been inspected and found insufficiently worn." The list followed—a long one,

Morey saw to his sick disappointment. "Credit is hereby disallowed for these and you are therefore given an additional consuming quota for the current month in the amount of 435 points, at least 350 points of which must be in the textile and home-furnishing categories."

Morey dashed the letter to the floor. The valet picked it up emotionlessly, creased it and set it on his desk.

It wasn't fair! All right, maybe the bathing trunks and beach umbrellas hadn't been *really* used very much—though how the devil, he asked himself bitterly, did you go about using up swimming gear when you didn't have time for such leisurely pursuits as swimming? But certainly the hiking slacks were used! He'd worn them for three whole days and part of a fourth; what did they expect him to do, go around in *rags?*

Morey looked belligerently at the coffee and toast that the valet-robot had brought in with the mail, and then steeled his resolve. Unfair or not, he had to play the game according to the rules. It was for Cherry, more than for himself, and the way to begin a new way of life was to begin it.

Morey was going to consume for two.

He told the valet-robot, "Take that stuff back. I want cream and sugar with the coffee—*lots* of cream and sugar. And besides the toast, scrambled eggs, fried potatoes, orange juice—no, make it half a grapefruit. *And* orange juice, come to think of it."

"Right away, sir," said the valet. "You won't be having breakfast at nine then, will you, sir?"

"I certainly will," said Morey virtuously. "Double portions!" As the robot was closing the door, he called after it, "Butter and marmalade with the toast!"

He went to the bath; he had a full schedule and no time to waste. In the shower, he carefully sprayed himself with lather three times. When he had rinsed the soap off, he went through the whole assortment of taps in order: three lotions, plain talcum, scented talcum and thirty seconds of ultra-violet. Then he lathered and rinsed again, and dried himself with a towel instead of using the hot-air drying jet. Most of the miscellaneous scents went down the drain with the rinse water, but if the Ration Board accused him of waste, he could claim he was experimenting. The effect, as a matter of fact, wasn't bad at all.

He stepped out, full of exuberance. Cherry was awake, staring in dismay at the tray the valet had brought. "Good morning, dear," she said faintly. "Ugh."

Morey kissed her and patted her hand. "Well!" he said, looking at the tray with a big, hollow smile. "Food!"

"Isn't that a *lot* for just the two of us?"

"Two of us?" repeated Morey masterfully. "Nonsense, my dear, I'm going to eat it all by myself!"

"Oh, Morey!" gasped Cherry, and the adoring look she gave him was enough to pay for a dozen such meals.

Which, he thought as he finished his morning exercises with the sparring-robot and sat down to his *real* breakfast, it just about had to be, day in and day out, for a long, long time.

Still, Morey had made up his mind. As he worked his way through the kippered herring, tea and crumpets, he ran over his plans with Henry. He swallowed a mouthful and said, "I want you to line up some appointments for me right away. Three hours a week in an exercise gym—pick one with lots of reducing equipment, Henry. I think I'm going to need it. And fittings for some new clothes—I've had these for weeks. And, let's see, doctor, dentist—say, Henry, don't I have a psychiatrist's date coming up?"

"Indeed you do, sir!" it said warmly. "This morning, in fact. I've already instructed the chauffeur and notified your office."

"Fine! Well, get started on the other things, Henry."

"Yes, sir," said Henry, and assumed the curious absent look of a robot talking on its TBR circuits—the "Talk Between Robots" radio—as it arranged the appointments for its master.

Morey finished his breakfast in silence, pleased with his own virtue, at peace with the world. It wasn't so hard to be a proper, industrious consumer if you *worked* at it, he reflected. It was only the malcontents, the ne'er-do-wells and the incompetents who simply could not adjust to the world around them. Well, he thought with distant pity, someone had to suffer; you couldn't break eggs without making an omelet. And his proper duty was not to be some sort of wild-eyed crank, challenging the social order and beating his breast about injustice, but to take care of his wife and his home.

It was too bad he couldn't really get right down to work on consuming today. But this was his one day a week to hold a *job*—four of the other six days were devoted to solid consuming—and, besides, he had a group therapy session scheduled as well. His analysis, Morey told himself, would certainly take a sharp turn for the better, now that he had faced up to his problems.

Morey was immersed in a glow of self-righteousness as he kissed Cherry good-by (she had finally got up, all in a confusion of delight at the new regime) and walked out the door to his car. He hardly noticed the little man in enormous floppy hat and garishly ruffled trousers who was standing almost hidden in the shrubs.

"Hey, Mac." The man's voice was almost a whisper.

"Huh? Oh—what is it?"

The man looked around furtively. "Listen, friend," he said rapidly, "you look like an intelligent man who could use a little help. Times are tough; you help me, I'll help you. Want to make a deal on ration stamps? Six for one. One of yours for six of mine, the best deal you'll get anywhere in town. Naturally, my stamps aren't exactly the real McCoy, but they'll pass, friend, they'll pass—"

Morey blinked at him. "No!" he said violently, and pushed the man aside. Now it's racketeers, he thought bitterly. Slums and endless sordid preoccupation with rations weren't enough to inflict on Cherry; now the neighborhood was becoming a hangout for people on the shady side of the law. It was not, of course, the first time he had ever been approached by a counterfeit ration-stamp hoodlum, but never at his own front door!

Morey thought briefly, as he climbed into his car, of calling the police. But certainly the man would be gone before they could get there; and, after all, he had handled it pretty well as it was.

Of course, it would be nice to get six stamps for one.

But very far from nice if he got caught.

"Good morning, Mr. Fry," tinkled the robot receptionist. "Won't you go right in?" With a steel-tipped finger, it pointed to the door marked GROUP THERAPY.

Someday, Morey vowed to himself as he nodded and complied, he would be in a position to afford a private analyst of his own. Group therapy helped relieve the infinite stresses of modern living, and without it he might find himself as badly off as the hysterical mobs in the ration riots, or as dangerously anti-social as the counterfeiters. But it lacked the personal touch. It was, he thought, too public a performance of what should be a private affair, like trying to live a happy married life with an interfering, ever-present crowd of robots in the house—

Morey brought himself up in panic. How had *that* thought crept in? He was shaken visibly as he entered the room and greeted the group to which he was assigned.

There were eleven of them: four Freudians, two Reichians, two Jungians, a Gestalter, a shock therapist and the elderly and rather quiet Sullivanite. Even the members of the majority groups had their own individual differences in technique and creed, but, despite four years with this particular group of analysts, Morey hadn't quite been able to keep them separate in his mind. Their names, though, he knew well enough.

"Morning, Doctors," he said. "What is it today?"

"Morning," said Semmelweiss morosely. "Today you come into the room for the first time looking as if something is really bothering you, and yet the schedule calls for psychodrama. Dr. Fairless," he appealed, "can't we change the schedule a little bit? Fry here is obviously under a strain; *that's* the time to start digging and see what he can find. We can do your psychodrama next time, can't we?"

Fairless shook his gracefully bald old head. "Sorry, Doctor. If it were up to me, of course—but you know the rules."

"Rules, rules," jeered Semmelweiss. "Ah, what's the use? Here's a patient in an acute anxiety state if I ever saw one—and believe me, I saw plenty—and we ignore it because the *rules* say ignore it. Is that professional? Is that how to cure a patient?"

Little Blaine said frostily, "If I may say so, Dr. Semmelweiss, there have been a great many cures made without the necessity of departing from the rules. I myself, in fact—"

"You yourself!" mimicked Semmelweiss. "You yourself never handled a patient alone in your life. When you going to get out of a group, Blaine?"

Blaine said furiously, "Dr. Fairless, I don't think I have to stand for this sort of personal attack. Just because Semmelweiss has seniority and a couple of private patients one day a week, he thinks—"

"Gentlemen," said Fairless mildly. "Please, let's get on with the work. Mr. Fry has come to us for help, not to listen to us losing our tempers."

"Sorry," said Semmelweiss curtly. "All the same, I appeal from the arbitrary and mechanistic ruling of the chair."

Fairless inclined his head. "All in favor of the ruling of the chair? Nine, I count. That leaves only you opposed, Dr. Semmelweiss. We'll proceed with the psychodrama, if the recorder will read us the notes and comments of the last session."

The recorder, a pudgy, low-ranking youngster named Sprogue, flipped back the pages of his notebook and read in a chanting voice, "Session of twenty-fourth May, subject, Morey Fry; in attendance, Doctors Fairless, Bileck, Semmelweiss, Carrado, Weber—"

Fairless interrupted kindly, "Just the last page, if you please, Dr. Sprogue."

"Um—oh, yes. After a ten-minute recess for additional Rorschachs and an electro-encephalogram, the group convened and conducted rapid-fire word association. Results were tabulated and compared with standard deviation patterns, and it was determined that subject's major traumas derived from, respectively—"

Morey found his attention waning. Therapy was *good;* everybody knew that, but every once in a while he found it a little dull. If it weren't for therapy, though, there was no telling what might happen. Certainly, Morey told himself, he had been helped considerably—at least he hadn't set fire to his house and shrieked at the fire-robots, like Newell down the block when his eldest daughter divorced her husband and came back to live with him, bringing her ration quota along, of course. Morey hadn't even been *tempted* to do anything as outrageously, frighteningly immoral as *destroy* things or *waste* them—well, he admitted to himself honestly, perhaps a little tempted, once in a great while. But never anything important enough to worry about; he was sound, perfectly sound.

He looked up, startled. All the doctors were staring at him. "Mr. Fry," Fairless repeated, "will you take your place?"

"Certainly," Morey said hastily. "Uh—where?"

Semmelweiss guffawed. *"Told* you. Never mind, Morey; you didn't miss much. We're going to run through one of the big scenes in your life, the one you told us about last time. Remember? You were fourteen years old, you said. Christmas time. Your mother had made you a promise."

Morey swallowed. "I remember," he said unhappily. "Well, all right. Where do I stand?"

"Right here," said Fairless. "You're you, Carrado is your mother, I'm your father. Will the doctors not participating mind moving back? Fine. Now, Morey, here we are on Christmas morning. Merry Christmas, Morey!"

"Merry Christmas," Morey said half-heartedly. "Uh—Father dear, where's my—uh—my puppy that Mother promised me?"

"Puppy!" said Fairless heartily. "Your mother and I have something much better than a puppy for you. Just take a look under the tree there—it's a *robot!* Yes, Morey, your very own robot—a full-size thirty-eight-tube fully automatic companion robot for you! Go ahead, Morey, go right up and speak to it. Its name is Henry. Go on, boy."

Morey felt a sudden, incomprehensible tingle inside the bridge of his nose. He said shakily, "But I—I didn't *want* a robot."

"Of course you want a robot," Carrado interrupted. "Go on, child, play with your nice robot."

Morey said violently, "I *hate* robots!" He looked around him at the doctors, at the gray-paneled consulting room. He added defiantly, "You hear me, all of you? I *still* hate robots!"

There was a second's pause; then the questions began. It was half an hour before the receptionist came in and announced that time was up.

In that half hour, Morey had got over his trembling and lost his wild, momentary passion, but he had remembered what for thirteen years he had forgotten.

He hated robots.

The surprising thing was not that young Morey had hated robots. It was that the Robot Riots, the ultimate violent outbreak of flesh against metal, the battle to the death between mankind and its machine heirs . . . never happened. A little boy hated robots, but the man he became worked with them hand in hand.

And yet, always and always before, the new worker, the competitor for the job, was at once and inevitably outside the law. The waves swelled in—the Irish, the Negroes, the Jews, the Italians. They were squeezed into their ghettoes, where they encysted, seethed and struck out, until the burgeoning generations became indistinguishable.

For the robots, that genetic relief was not in sight. And still the conflict never came. The feed-back circuits aimed the anti-aircraft guns and, reshaped and newly planned, found a place in a new sort of machine—together with a miraculous trail of cams and levers, an indestructible and potent power source and a hundred thousand parts and sub-assemblies.

And the first robot clanked off the bench.

Its mission was its own destruction; but from the scavenged wreck of its pilot body, a hundred better robots drew their inspiration. And the hundred went to work, and hundreds more, until there were millions upon untold millions.

And still the riots never happened.

For the robots came bearing a gift and the name of it was "Plenty."

And by the time the gift had shown its own unguessed ills, the time for a Robot Riot was past. Plenty is a habit-forming drug. You do not cut the dosage down. You kick it if you can; you stop the dose entirely. But the convulsions that follow may wreck the body once and for all.

The addict craves the grainy white powder; he doesn't hate it, or the runner who sells it to him. And if Morey as a little boy could hate the robot that had deprived him of his pup, Morey the man was perfectly aware that the robots were his servants and his friends.

But the little Morey inside the man—*he* had never been convinced.

Morey ordinarily looked forward to his work. The one day a week at which he *did* anything was a wonderful change from the dreary consume, consume, consume grind. He entered the bright-lit drafting room of the Bradmoor Amusements Company with a feeling of uplift.

But as he was changing from street garb to his drafting smock, Howland from Procurement came over with a knowing look. "Wainwright's been looking for you," Howland whispered. "Better get right in there."

Morey nervously thanked him and got. Wainwright's office was the size of a phone booth and as bare as Antarctic ice. Every time Morey saw it, he felt his insides churn with envy. Think of a desk with nothing on it but work surface—no calendar-clock, no twelve-color pen rack, no dictating machines!

He squeezed himself in and sat down while Wainwright finished a phone call. He mentally reviewed the possible reasons why Wainwright would want to talk to him in person instead of over the phone, or by dropping a word to him as he passed through the drafting room.

Very few of them were good.

Wainwright put down the phone and Morey straightened up. "You sent for me?" he asked.

Wainwright in a chubby world was aristocratically lean. As General Superintendent of the Design & Development Section of the Bradmoor Amusements Company, he ranked high in the upper section of the well-to-do. He rasped, "I certainly did. Fry, just what the hell do you think you're up to now?"

"I don't know what you m-mean, Mr. Wainwright,"

Morey stammered, crossing off the list of possible reasons for the interview all of the good ones.

Wainwright snorted. "I guess you don't. Not because you weren't told, but because you don't want to know. Think back a whole week. What did I have you on the carpet for then?"

Morey said sickly, "My ration book. Look, Mr. Wainwright, I know I'm running a little bit behind, but—"

"But nothing! How do you think it looks to the Committee, Fry? They got a complaint from the Ration Board about you. Naturally they passed it on to me. And naturally I'm going to pass it right along to you. The question is, what are you going to do about it? Good God, man, look at these figures—textiles, fifty-one per cent; food, sixty-seven per cent; amusements and entertainment, *thirty* per cent! You haven't come up to your ration in anything for months!"

Morey stared at the card miserably. "We—that is, my wife and I—just had a long talk about that last night, Mr. Wainwright. And, believe me, we're going to do better. We're going to buckle right down and get to work and—uh—do better," he finished weakly.

Wainwright nodded, and for the first time there was a note of sympathy in his voice. "Your wife. Judge Elon's daughter, isn't she? Good family. I've met the Judge many times." Then, gruffly, "Well, nevertheless, Fry, I'm warning you. I don't care how you straighten this out, but *don't let the Committee mention this to me again.*"

"No, sir."

"All right. Finished with the schematics on the new K-50?"

Morey brightened. "Just about, sir! I'm putting the first section on tape today. I'm very pleased with it, Mr. Wainwright, honestly I am. I've got more than eighteen thousand moving parts in it now, and that's without—"

"Good. Good." Wainwright glanced down at his desk. "Get back to it. And straighten out this other thing. You can do it, Fry. Consuming is everybody's duty. Just keep that in mind."

Howland followed Morey out of the drafting room, down to the spotless shops. "Bad time?" he inquired solicitously. Morey grunted. It was none of Howland's business.

Howland looked over his shoulder as he was setting up the programing panel. Morey studied the matrices silently, then got busy reading the summary tapes, checking them back against the schematics, setting up the instructions on the programing board. Howland kept quiet as Morey completed the setup and ran off a test tape. It checked perfectly; Morey stepped back to light a cigarette in celebration before pushing the *start* button.

Howland said, "Go on, run it. I can't go until you put it in the works."

Morey grinned and pushed the button. The board lighted up; within it, a tiny metronomic beep began to pulse. That was all. At the other end of the quarter-mile shed, Morey knew, the automatic sorters and conveyers were fingering through the copper reels and steel ingots, measuring hoppers of plastic powder and colors, setting up an intricate weaving path for the thousands of individual components that would make up Bradmoor's new K-50 Spin-a-Game. But from where they stood, in the elaborately muraled programing room, nothing showed. Bradmoor was an ultra-modernized plant; in the manufacturing end, even robots had been dispensed with in favor of machines that guided themselves.

Morey glanced at his watch and logged in the starting time while Howland quickly counter-checked Morey's raw-material flow program.

"Checks out," Howland said solemnly, slapping him on the back. "Calls for a celebration. Anyway, it's your first design, isn't it?"

"Yes. First all by myself, at any rate."

Howland was already fishing in his private locker for the bottle he kept against emergency needs. He poured with a flourish. "To Morey Fry," he said, "our most favorite designer, in whom we are much pleased."

Morey drank. It went down easily enough. Morey had conscientiously used his liquor rations for years, but he had never gone beyond the minimum, so that although liquor was no new experience to him, the single drink immediately warmed him. It warmed his mouth, his throat, the hollows of his chest; and it settled down with a warm glow inside him. Howland, exerting himself to be nice, complimented Morey fatuously on the design and poured another drink. Morey didn't utter any protest at all.

Howland drained his glass. "You may wonder," he said formally, "why I am so pleased with you, Morey Fry. I will tell you why this is."

Morey grinned. "Please do."

Howland nodded. "I will. It's because I am pleased with the world, Morey. My wife left me last night."

Morey was as shocked as only a recent bridegroom can be by the news of a crumbling marriage. "That's too ba— I mean is that a fact?"

"Yes, she left my beds and board and five robots, and I'm happy to see her go." He poured another drink for both of them. "Women. Can't live with them and can't live without them. First you sigh and pant and chase after 'em—you like poetry?" he demanded suddenly.

Morey said cautiously, "Some poetry."

Howland quoted: " 'How long, my love, shall I behold this wall between our gardens—yours the rose, and mine the swooning lily.' Like it? I wrote it for Jocelyn—that's my wife—when we were first going together."

"It's beautiful," said Morey.

"She wouldn't talk to me for two days." Howland drained his drink. "Lots of spirit, that girl. Anyway, I hunted her like a tiger. And then I caught her. *Wow!*"

Morey took a deep drink from his own glass. "What do you mean, *wow?*" he asked.

"*Wow.*" Howland pointed his finger at Morey. "*Wow,* that's what I mean. We got married and I took her home to the dive I was living in, and *wow* we had a kid, and *wow* I got in a little trouble with the Ration Board— nothing serious, of course, but there was a mixup—and *wow* fights.

"Everything was a fight," he explained. "She'd start with a little nagging, and naturally I'd say something or other back, and *bang* we were off. Budget, budget, budget; I hope to die if I ever hear the word 'budget' again. Morey, you're a married man; you know what it's like. Tell me the truth, weren't you just about ready to blow your top the first time you caught your wife cheating on the budget?"

"Cheating on the budget?" Morey was startled. "Cheating how?"

"Oh, lots of ways. Making your portions bigger than hers. Sneaking extra shirts for you on her clothing ration. You know."

"Damn it, I do *not* know!" cried Morey. "Cherry wouldn't do anything like that!"

Howland looked at him opaquely for a long second. "Of course not," he said at last. "Let's have another drink."

Ruffled, Morey held out his glass. Cherry wasn't the type of girl to *cheat*. Of course she wasn't. A fine, loving girl like her—a pretty girl, of a good family; she wouldn't know how to begin.

Howland was saying, in a sort of chant, "No more budget. No more fights. No more 'Daddy never treated me like this.' No more nagging. No more extra rations for household allowance. No more—Morey, what do you say we go out and have a few drinks? I know a place where—"

"Sorry, Howland," Morey said. "I've got to get back to the office, you know."

Howland guffawed. He held out his wristwatch. As Morey, a little unsteadily, bent over it, it tinkled out the hour. It was a matter of minutes before the office closed for the day.

"Oh," said Morey. "I didn't realize—Well, anyway, Howland, thanks, but I can't. My wife will be expecting me."

"She certainly will," Howland sniggered. "Won't catch *her* eating up your rations and hers tonight."

Morey said tightly, "Howland!"

"Oh, sorry, sorry." Howland waved an arm. "Don't mean to say anything against *your* wife, of course. Guess maybe Jocelyn soured me on women. But honest, Morey, you'd like this place. Name of Uncle Piggotty's, down in the Old Town. Crazy bunch hangs out there. You'd like them. Couple nights last week they had—I mean, you understand, Morey, I don't go there as often as all that, but I just happened to drop in and—"

Morey interrupted firmly. "Thank you, Howland. Must go home. Wife expects it. Decent of you to offer. Good night. Be seeing you."

He walked out, turned at the door to bow politely, and in turning back cracked the side of his face against the door jamb. A sort of pleasant numbness had taken possession of his entire skin surface, though, and it wasn't until he perceived Henry chattering at him sympathetically that he noticed a trickle of blood running down the side of his face.

"Mere flesh wound," he said with dignity. "Nothing to cause you *least* conshter—consternation, Henry. Now kindly shut your ugly face. Want to think."

And he slept in the car all the way home.

It was worse than a hangover. The name is "holdover." You've had some drinks; you've started to sober up by catching a little sleep. Then you are required to be awake and to function. The consequent state has the worst features of hangover and intoxication; your head thumps and your mouth tastes like the floor of a bear-pit, but you are nowhere near sober.

There is one cure. Morey said thickly, "Let's have a cocktail, dear."

Cherry was delighted to share a cocktail with him before dinner. Cherry, Morey thought lovingly, was a wonderful, wonderful, wonderful—

He found his head nodding in time to his thoughts and the motion made him wince.

Cherry flew to his side and touched his temple. "Is it bothering you, darling?" she asked solicitously. "Where you ran into the door, I mean?"

Morey looked at her sharply, but her expression was open and adoring. He said bravely, "Just a little. Nothing to it, really."

The butler brought the cocktails and retired. Cherry lifted her glass. Morey raised his, caught a whiff of the liquor and nearly dropped it. He bit down hard on his churning insides and forced himself to swallow.

He was surprised but grateful: It stayed down. In a moment, the curious phenomenon of warmth began to repeat itself. He swallowed the rest of the drink and held out his glass for a refill. He even tried a smile. Oddly enough, his face didn't fall off.

One more drink did it. Morey felt happy and relaxed, but by no means drunk. They went in to dinner in fine spirits. They chatted cheerfully with each other and Henry, and Morey found time to feel sentimentally sorry for poor Howland, who couldn't make a go of his marriage, when marriage was obviously such an easy relationship, so beneficial to both sides, so warm and relaxing . . .

Startled, he said, "What?"

Cherry repeated, "It's the cleverest scheme I ever heard of. Such a funny little man, dear. All kind of *nervous,* if you know what I mean. He kept looking at the door as if he was expecting someone, but of course that was silly. None of his friends would have come to *our* house to see him."

Morey said tensely, "Cherry, *please!* What was that you said about ration stamps?"

"But I told you, darling! It was just after you left this morning. This funny little man came to the door; the butler said he wouldn't give any name. Anyway, I talked to him. I thought he might be a neighbor and I certainly would *never* be rude to any neighbor who might come to call, even if the neighborhood was—"

"The ration stamps!" Morey begged. "Did I hear you say he was peddling phony ration stamps?"

Cherry said uncertainly, "Well, I suppose that in a *way* they're phony. The way he explained it, they weren't the regular official kind. But it was four for one, dear—four of his stamps for one of ours. So I just took out our household book and steamed off a couple of weeks' stamps and—"

"How many?" Morey bellowed.

Cherry blinked. "About—about two weeks' quota," she said faintly. "Was that wrong, dear?"

Morey closed his eyes dizzily. "A couple of weeks' stamps," he repeated. "Four for one—you didn't even get the regular rate."

Cherry wailed, "How was I supposed to know? I never had anything like this when I was *home!* We didn't have food riots and slums and all these horrible robots and filthy little revolting men coming to the door!"

Morey stared at her woodenly. She was crying again, but it made no impression on the case-hardened armor that was suddenly thrown around his heart.

Henry made a tentative sound that, in a human, would have been a preparatory cough, but Morey froze him with a white-eyed look.

Morey said in a dreary monotone that barely penetrated the sound of Cherry's tears, "Let me tell you just what it was you did. Assuming, at best, that these stamps you got are at least average good counterfeits, and not so bad that the best thing to do with them is throw them away before we get caught with them in our possession, you have approximately a two-month supply of funny stamps. In case you didn't know it, those ration books are not merely ornamental. They have to be turned in every month to prove that we have completed our consuming quota for the month.

"When they are turned in, they are spot-checked. Every book is at least glanced at. A big chunk of them are gone over very carefully by the inspectors, and a certain percentage are tested by ultra-violet, infra-red, X-ray, radio-isotopes, bleaches, fumes, paper chromatography and every other damned test known to Man." His voice was rising to an uneven crescendo. *"If* we are lucky enough to get away with using any of these stamps at all, we daren't—we simply *dare* not—use more than one or two counterfeits to every dozen or more real stamps.

"That means, Cherry, that what you bought is not a two-month supply, but maybe a two-*year* supply—and since, as you no doubt have never noticed, the things have expiration dates on them, there is probably no chance in the world that we can ever hope to use more than half of them." He was bellowing by the time he pushed back his chair and towered over her. "Moreover," he went on, "right *now*, right as of this *minute*, we have to make up the stamps you gave away, which means that at the very best we are going to be on double rations for two weeks or so.

"And that says nothing about the one feature of this whole grisly mess that you seem to have thought of least, namely that counterfeit stamps are against the *law!* I'm poor, Cherry; I live in a slum, and I know it; I've got a long way to go before I'm as rich or respected or powerful as your father, about whom I am beginning to get considerably tired of hearing. But poor as I may be, I can tell you *this* for sure: Up until now, at any rate, I have been *honest.*"

Cherry's tears had stopped entirely and she was bowed white-faced and dry-eyed by the time Morey had finished. He had spent himself; there was no violence left in him.

He stared dismally at Cherry for a moment, then turned wordlessly and stamped out of the house.

*Marriage!* he thought as he left.

He walked for hours, blind to where he was going.

What brought him back to awareness was a sensation he had not felt in a dozen years. It was not, Morey abruptly realized, the dying traces of his hangover that made his stomach feel so queer. He was hungry—actually hungry.

He looked about him. He was in the Old Town, miles from home, jostled by crowds of lower-class people. The block he was on was as atrocious a slum as Morey had ever seen—Chinese pagodas stood next to rococo imitations of the chapels around Versailles; gingerbread marred every facade; no building was without its brilliant signs and flarelights.

He saw a blindingly overdecorated eating establishment called Billie's Budget Busy Bee and crossed the street toward it, dodging through the unending streams of traffic. It was a miserable excuse for a restaurant, but Morey was in no mood to care. He found a seat under a potted palm, as far from the tinkling fountains and robot string ensemble as he could manage, and ordered recklessly, paying no attention to the ration prices. As the waiter was gliding noiselessly away, Morey had a sickening realization: He'd come out without his ration book. He groaned out loud; it was too late to leave without causing a disturbance. But then, he thought rebelliously, what difference did one more unrationed meal make, anyhow?

Food made him feel a little better. He finished the last of his *profiterole au chocolate,* not even leaving on the plate the uneaten one-third that tradition permitted, and paid his check. The robot cashier reached automatically for his ration book. Morey had a moment of grandeur as he said simply, "No ration stamps."

Robot cashiers are not equipped to display surprise, but this one tried. The man behind Morey in line audibly caught his breath, and less audibly mumbled something about *slummers.* Morey took it as a compliment and strode outside feeling almost in good humor.

Good enough to go home to Cherry? Morey thought seriously of it for a second; but he wasn't going to pretend he was wrong and certainly Cherry wasn't going to be willing to admit that *she* was at fault.

Besides, Morey told himself grimly, she was undoubtedly asleep. That was an annoying thing about Cherry at best: she never had any trouble getting to sleep. Didn't even use her quota of sleeping tablets, though Morey had spoken to her about it more than once. Of course, he reminded himself, he had been so polite and tactful about it, as befits a newlywed, that very likely she hadn't even understood that it was a complaint. Well, *that* would stop!

Man's man Morey Fry, wearing no collar ruff but his own, strode determinedly down the streets of the Old Town.

"Hey, Joe, want a good time?"

Morey took one unbelieving look. "You again!" he roared.

The little man stared at him in genuine surprise. Then a faint glimmer of recognition crossed his face. "Oh, yeah," he said. "This morning, huh?" He clucked commiseratingly. "Too bad you wouldn't deal with me. Your wife was a lot smarter. Of course, you got me a little sore, Jack, so naturally I had to raise the price a little bit."

"You skunk, you cheated my poor wife blind! You and I are going to the local station house and talk this over."

The little man pursed his lips. "We are, huh?"

Morey nodded vigorously. "Damn right! And let me tell you—" He stopped in the middle of a threat as a large hand cupped around his shoulder.

The equally large man who owned the hand said, in a mild and cultured voice, "Is this gentleman disturbing you, Sam?"

"Not so far," the little man conceded. "He might want to, though, so don't go away."

Morey wrenched his shoulder away. "Don't think you can strongarm me. I'm taking you to the police."

Sam shook his head unbelievingly. "You mean you're going to call the law in on this?"

"I certainly am!"

Sam sighed regretfully. "What do you think of that, Walter? Treating his wife like that. Such a nice lady, too."

"What are you talking about?" Morey demanded, stung on a peculiarly sensitive spot.

"I'm talking about your wife," Sam explained. "Of course, I'm not married myself. But it seems to me that if I was, I wouldn't call the police when my wife was engaged in some kind of criminal activity or other. No, sir, I'd try to settle it myself. Tell you what," he advised, "why don't you talk this over with her? Make her see the error of—"

"Wait a minute," Morey interrupted. "You mean you'd involve my wife in this thing?"

The man spread his hands helplessly. "It's not me that would involve her, Buster," he said. "She already involved her own self. It takes two to make a crime, you know. I sell, maybe; I won't deny it. But after all, I can't sell unless somebody buys, can I?"

Morey stared at him glumly. He glanced in quick speculation at the large-sized Walter; but Walter was just as big as he'd remembered, so that took care of that. Violence was out; the police were out; that left no really attractive way of capitalizing on the good luck of running into the man again.

Sam said, "Well, I'm glad to see that's off your mind. Now, returning to my original question, Mac, how would you like a good time? You look like a smart fellow to me;

you look like you'd be kind of interested in a place I happen to know of down the block."

Morey said bitterly, "So you're a dive-steerer, too. A real talented man."

"I admit it," Sam agreed. "Stamp business is slow at night, in my experience. People have their minds more on a good time. And, believe me, a good time is what I can show 'em. Take this place I'm talking about, Uncle Piggotty's is the name of it, it's what I would call an unusual kind of place. Wouldn't you say so, Walter?"

"Oh, I agree with you entirely," Walter rumbled.

But Morey was hardly listening. He said, "Uncle Piggotty's, you say?"

"That's right," said Sam.

Morey frowned for a moment, digesting an idea. Uncle Piggotty's sounded like the place Howland had been talking about back at the plant; it might be interesting, at that.

While he was making up his mind, Sam slipped an arm through his on one side and Walter amiably wrapped a big hand around the other. Morey found himself walking.

"You'll like it," Sam promised comfortably. "No hard feelings about this morning, sport? Of course not. Once you get a look at Piggotty's, you'll get over your mad, anyhow. It's something special. I swear, on what they pay me for bringing in customers, I wouldn't do it unless I *believed* in it."

"Dance, Jack?" the hostess yelled over the noise at the bar. She stepped back, lifted her flounced skirts to ankle height and executed a tricky nine-step.

"My name is Morey," Morey yelled back. "And I don't want to dance, thanks."

The hostess shrugged, frowned meaningfully at Sam and danced away.

Sam flagged the bartender. "First round's on us," he explained to Morey. "Then we won't bother you any more. Unless you want us to, of course. Like the place?" Morey hesitated, but Sam didn't wait. "Fine place," he yelled, and picked up the drink the bartender left him. "See you around."

He and the big man were gone. Morey stared after them uncertainly, then gave it up. He was here, anyhow;

might as well at least have a drink. He ordered and looked around.

Uncle Piggotty's was a third-rate dive disguised to look, in parts of it at least, like one of the exclusive upper-class country clubs. The bar, for instance, was treated to resemble the clean lines of nailed wood; but underneath the surface treatment, Morey could detect the intricate laminations of plyplastic. What at first glance appeared to be burlap hangings were in actuality elaborately textured synthetics. And all through the bar the motif was carried out.

A floor show of sorts was going on, but nobody seemed to be paying much attention to it. Morey, straining briefly to hear the master of ceremonies, gathered that the wit was on a more than mildly vulgar level. There was a dispirited string of chorus beauties in long ruffled pantaloons and diaphanous tops; one of them, Morey was almost sure, was the hostess who had talked to him just a few moments before.

Next to him a man was declaiming to a middle-aged woman:

*Smote I the monstrous rock, yahoo!*
*Smote I the turgid tube, Bully Boy!*
*Smote I the cankered hill—*

"Why, Morey!" he interrupted himself. "What are you doing here?"

He turned farther around and Morey recognized him. "Hello, Howland," he said. "I—uh—I happened to be free tonight, so I thought—"

Howland sniggered. "Well, guess your wife is more liberal than mine was. Order a drink, boy."

"Thanks, I've got one," said Morey.

The woman, with a tigerish look at Morey, said, "Don't stop, Everett. That was one of your most beautiful things."

"Oh, Morey's heard my poetry," Howland said. "Morey, I'd like you to meet a very lovely and talented young lady, Tanaquil Bigelow. Morey works in the office with me, Tan."

"Obviously," said Tanaquil Bigelow in a frozen voice,

and Morey hastily withdrew the hand he had begun to put out.

The conversation stuck there, impaled, the woman cold, Howland relaxed and abstracted, Morey wondering if, after all, this had been such a good idea. He caught the eye-cell of the robot bartender and ordered a round of drinks for the three of them, politely putting them on Howland's ration book. By the time the drinks had come and Morey had just got around to deciding that it wasn't a very good idea, the woman had all of a sudden become thawed.

She said abruptly, "You look like the kind of man who *thinks*, Morey, and I like to talk to that kind of man. Frankly, Morey, I just don't have any patience at all with the stupid, stodgy men who just work in their offices all day and eat all their dinners every night, and gad about and consume like mad and where does it all get them, anyhow? That's right, I can see you understand. Just one crazy rush of consume, consume from the day you're born *plop* to the day you're buried *pop!* And who's to blame if not the robots?"

Faintly, a tinge of worry began to appear on the surface of Howland's relaxed calm. "Tan," he chided, "Morey may not be very interested in politics."

Politics, Morey thought; well, at least that was a clue. He'd had the dizzying feeling, while the woman was talking, that he himself was the ball in the games machine he had designed for the shop earlier that day. Following the woman's conversation might, at that, give his next design some valuable pointers in swoops, curves and obstacles.

He said, with more than half truth, "No, please go on, Miss Bigelow. I'm very much interested."

She smiled; then abruptly her face changed to a frightening scowl. Morey flinched, but evidently the scowl wasn't meant for him. "Robots!" she hissed. "Supposed to work for us, aren't they? Hah! We're their slaves, slaves for every moment of every miserable day of our lives. Slaves! Wouldn't you like to join us and be free, Morey?"

Morey took cover in his drink. He made an expressive gesture with his free hand—expressive of exactly what, he didn't truly know, for he was lost. But it seemed to satisfy the woman.

She said accusingly, "Did you know that more than three-quarters of the people in this country have had a nervous breakdown in the past five years and four months? That more than half of them are under the constant care of psychiatrists for psychosis—not just plain ordinary neurosis like my husband's got and Howland here has got and you've got, but psychosis. Like I've got. Did you know that? Did you know that forty per cent of the population are essentially manic depressive, thirty-one per cent are schizoid, thirty-eight per cent have an assortment of other unfixed psychogenic disturbances and twenty-four—"

"Hold it a minute, Tan," Howland interrupted critically. "You've got too many per cents there. Start over again."

"Oh, the hell with it," the woman said moodily. "I wish my husband were here. He expresses it so much better than I do." She swallowed her drink. "Since you've wriggled off the hook," she said nastily to Morey, "how about setting up another round—on my ration book this time?"

Morey did; it was the simplest thing to do in his confusion. When that was gone, they had another on Howland's book.

As near as he could figure out, the woman, her husband and quite possibly Howland as well belonged to some kind of anti-robot group. Morey had heard of such things; they had a quasi-legal status, neither approved nor prohibited, but he had never come into contact with them before. Remembering the hatred he had so painfully relived at the psychodrama session, he thought anxiously that perhaps he belonged with them. But, question them though he might, he couldn't seem to get the principles of the organization firmly in mind.

The woman finally gave up trying to explain it, and went off to find her husband while Morey and Howland had another drink and listened to two drunks squabble over who bought the next round. They were at the Alphonse-Gaston stage of inebriation; they would regret it in the morning; for each was bending over backward to permit the other to pay the ration points. Morey wondered uneasily about his own points; Howland was certainly getting credit for a lot of Morey's drinking tonight. Served him right for forgetting his book, of course.

When the woman came back, it was with the large man Morey had encountered in the company of Sam, the counterfeiter, steerer and general man about Old Town.

"A remarkably small world, isn't it?" boomed Walter Bigelow, only slightly crushing Morey's hand in his. "Well, sir, my wife has told me how interested you are in the basic philosophical drives behind our movement, and I should like to discuss them further with you. To begin with, sir, have you considered the principle of Twoness?"

Morey said, "Why—"

"Very good," said Bigelow courteously. He cleared his throat and declaimed:

*Han-headed Cathay saw it first,*
*Bright as brightest solar burst;*
*Whipped it into boy and girl,*
*The blinding spiral-sliced swirl:*
*Yang*
*And Yin.*

He shrugged deprecatingly. "Just the first stanza," he said. "I don't know if you got much out of it."

"Well, no," Morey admitted.

"Second stanza," Bigelow said firmly:

*Hegal saw it, saw it clear;*
*Jackal Marx drew near, drew near:*
*O'er his shoulder saw it plain,*
*Turned it upside down again:*
*Yang*
*And Yin.*

There was an expectant pause. Morey said, "I—uh—"

"Wraps it all up, doesn't it?" Bigelow's wife demanded. "Oh, if only others could see it as clearly as you do! The robot peril *and* the robot savior. Starvation *and* surfeit. Always twoness, always!"

Bigelow patted Morey's shoulder. "The next stanza makes it even clearer," he said. "It's really very clever—

I shouldn't say it, of course, but it's Howland's as much as it's mine. He helped me with the verses." Morey darted a glance at Howland, but Howland was carefully looking away. "Third stanza," said Bigelow. "This is a hard one, because it's long, so pay attention."

*Justice, tip your sightless scales;*
*One pan rises, one pan falls.*

"Howland," he interrupted himself, "are you *sure* about that rhyme? I always trip over it. Well, anyway:

*Add to A and B grows less;*
*A's B's partner, nonetheless.*
*Next, the Twoness that there be*
*In even electricity.*
*Chart the current as it's found:*
*Sine the hot lead, line the ground.*
*The wild sine dances, soars and falls,*
*But only to figures the zero calls.*
*Sine wave, scales, all things that be*
*Share a reciprocity.*
*Male and female, light and dark:*
*Name the numbers of Noah's Ark!*
*Yang*
*And Yin!*

"Dearest!" shrieked Bigelow's wife. "You've never done it better!" There was a spatter of applause, and Morey realized for the first time that half the bar had stopped its noisy revel to listen to them. Bigelow was evidently quite a well-known figure here.

Morey said weakly, "I've never heard anything like it."

He turned hesitantly to Howland, who promptly said, "Drink! What we all need right now is a drink."

They had a drink on Bigelow's book.

Morey got Howland aside and asked him, "Look, level with me. Are these people nuts?"

Howland showed pique. "No. Certainly not."

"Does that poem mean anything? Does this whole business of twoness mean anything?"

Howland shrugged. "If it means something to them, it means something. They're philosophers, Morey. They see deep into things. You don't know what a privilege it is for me to be allowed to associate with them."

They had another drink. On Howland's book, of course.

Morey eased Walter Bigelow over to a quiet spot. He said, "Leaving twoness out of it for the moment, what's this about the robots?"

Bigelow looked at him round-eyed. "Didn't you understand the poem?"

"Of course I did. But diagram it for me in simple terms so I can tell my wife."

Bigelow beamed. "It's about the dichotomy of robots," he explained. "Like the little salt mill that the boy wished for: it ground out salt and ground out salt and ground out salt. He had to have salt, but not *that* much salt. Whitehead explains it clearly—"

They had another drink on Bigelow's book.

Morey wavered over Tanaquil Bigelow. He said fuzzily, "Listen. Mrs. Walter Tanaquil Strongarm Bigelow. Listen."

She grinned smugly at him. "Brown hair," she said dreamily.

Morey shook his head vigorously. "Never mind hair," he ordered. "Never mind poem. Listen. In *pre-cise* and el-e-*men*-ta-ry terms, explain to me what is wrong with the world today."

"Not enough brown hair," she said promptly.

"Never mind hair!"

"All right," she said agreeably. "Too many robots. Too many robots make too much of everything."

"Ha! Got it!" Morey exclaimed triumphantly. "Get rid of robots!"

"Oh, no. No! No! No. We wouldn't eat. Everything is mechanized. Can't get rid of them, can't slow down production—slowing down is dying, stopping is quicker dying. Principle of twoness is the concept that clarifies all these—"

"No!" Morey said violently. "What should we *do?*"

"Do? I'll tell you what we should do, if that's what you want. I can tell you."

"Then tell me."

"What we should do is—" Tanaquil hiccupped with a look of refined consternation—"have another drink."

They had another drink. He gallantly let her pay, of course. She ungallantly argued with the bartender about the ration points due her.

Though not a two-fisted drinker, Morey tried. He really worked at it.

He paid the price, too. For some little time before his limbs stopped moving, his mind stopped functioning. Blackout. Almost a blackout, at any rate, for all he retained of the late evening was a kaleidoscope of people and places and things. Howland was there, drunk as a skunk, disgracefully drunk, Morey remembered thinking as he stared up at Howland from the floor. The Bigelows were there. His wife, Cherry, solicitous and amused, was there. And oddly enough, Henry was there.

It was very, very hard to reconstruct. Morey devoted a whole morning's hangover to the effort. It was *important* to reconstruct it, for some reason. But Morey couldn't even remember what the reason was; and finally he dismissed it, guessing that he had either solved the secret of twoness or whether Tanaquil Bigelow's remarkable figure was natural.

He did, however, know that the next morning he had waked in his own bed, with no recollection of getting there. No recollection of anything much, at least not of anything that fit into the proper chronological order or seemed to mesh with anything else, after the dozenth drink when he and Howland, arms around each other's shoulders, composed a new verse on twoness and, plagiarizing an old marching tune, howled it across the boisterous barroom:

*A twoness on the scene much later*
*Rests in your refrigerator.*
*Heat your house and insulate it.*
*Next your food: Refrigerate it.*
*Frost will damp your Freon coils,*
*So flux in Nichrome till it boils.*

*See the picture? Heat in cold*
*In heat in cold, the story's told!*
*Giant-writ the sacred scrawl:*
*Oh, the twoness of it all!*
*Yang*
*And Yin!*

It had, at any rate, seemed to mean something at the time.

If alcohol opened Morey's eyes to the fact that there *was* a twoness, perhaps alcohol was what he needed. For there was.

Call it a dichotomy, if the word seems more couth. A kind of two-pronged struggle, the struggle of two unwearying runners in an immortal race. There is the refrigerator inside the house. The cold air, the bubble of heated air that is the house, the bubble of cooled air that is the refrigerator, the momentary bubble of heated air that defrosts it. Call the heat Yang, if you will. Call the cold Yin. Yang overtakes Yin. Then Yin passes Yang. Then Yang passes Yin. Then—

Give them other names. Call Yin a mouth; call Yang a hand.

If the hand rests, the mouth will starve. If the mouth stops, the hand will die. The hand, Yang, moves faster.

Yin may not lag behind.

Then call Yang a robot.

And remember that a pipeline has two ends.

Like any once-in-a-lifetime lush, Morey braced himself for the consequences—and found startledly that there were none.

Cherry was a surprise to him. "You were so funny," she giggled. "And, honestly, so *romantic.*"

He shakily swallowed his breakfast coffee.

The office staff roared and slapped him on the back. "Howland tells us you're living high, boy!" they bellowed more or less in the same words. "Hey, listen to what Morey did—went on the town for the night of a lifetime *and didn't even bring his ration book along to cash in!*"

They thought it was a wonderful joke.

But, then, everything was going well. Cherry, it seemed, had reformed out of recognition. True, she still hated to go out in the evening and Morey never saw her forcing herself to gorge on unwanted food or play undesired games. But, moping into the pantry one afternoon, he found to his incredulous delight that they were well ahead of their ration quotas. In some items, in fact, they were *out*—a month's supply and more was gone ahead of schedule!

Nor was it the counterfeit stamps, for he had found them tucked behind a bain-marie and quietly burned them. He cast about for ways of complimenting her, but caution prevailed. She was sensitive on the subject; leave it be.

And virtue had its reward.

Wainwright called him in, all smiles. "Morey, great news! We've all appreciated your work here and we've been able to show it in some more tangible way than compliments. I didn't want to say anything till it was definite, but—your status has been reviewed by Classification and the Ration Board. You're out of Class Four Minor, Morey!"

Morey said tremulously, hardly daring to hope, "I'm a full Class Four?"

"Class Five, Morey. *Class Five!* When we do something, we do it right. We asked for a special waiver and got it— you've skipped a whole class." He added honestly, "Not that it was just our backing that did it, of course. Your own recent splendid record of consumption helped a lot. I told you you could do it!"

Morey had to sit down. He missed the rest of what Wainwright had to say, but it couldn't have mattered. He escaped from the office, sidestepped the knot of fellow-employees waiting to congratulate him, and got to a phone.

Cherry was as ecstatic and inarticulate as he. "Oh, darling!" was all she could say.

"And I couldn't have done it without you," he babbled. "Wainwright as much as said so himself. Said if it wasn't for the way we—well, *you* have been keeping up with the rations, it never would have got by the Board. I've been meaning to say something to you about that, dear, but I just haven't known how. But I do appreciate it. I—

Hello?" There was a curious silence at the other end of the phone. "Hello?" he repeated worriedly.

Cherry's voice was intense and low. "Morey Fry, I think you're mean. I wish you hadn't spoiled the good news." And she hung up.

Morey stared slack-jawed at the phone.

Howland appeared behind him, chuckling. "Women," he said. "Never try to figure them. Anyway, congratulations, Morey."

"Thanks," Morey mumbled.

Howland coughed and said, "Uh—by the way, Morey, now that you're one of the big shots, so to speak, you won't—uh—feel obliged to—well, say anything to Wainwright, for instance, about anything I may have said while we—"

"Excuse me," Morey said, unhearing, and pushed past him. He thought wildly of calling Cherry back, of racing home to see just what he'd said that was wrong. Not that there was much doubt, of course. He'd touched her on her sore point.

Anyhow, his wristwatch was chiming a reminder of the fact that his psychiatric appointment for the week was coming up.

Morey sighed. The day gives and the day takes away. Blessed is the day that gives only good things.

If any.

The session went badly. Many of the sessions had been going badly, Morey decided; there had been more and more whispering in knots of doctors from which he was excluded, poking and probing in the dark instead of the precise psychic surgery he was used to. Something was wrong, he thought.

Something was. Semmelweiss confirmed it when he adjourned the group session. After the other doctor had left, he sat Morey down for a private talk. On his own time, too—he didn't ask for his usual ration fee. That told Morey how important the problem was.

"Morey," said Semmelweiss, "you're holding back."

"I don't mean to, Doctor," Morey said earnestly.

"Who knows what you 'mean' to do? Part of you

'means' to. We've dug pretty deep and we've found some important things. Now there's something I can't put my finger on. Exploring the mind, Morey, is like sending scouts through cannibal territory. You can't see the cannibals—until it's too late. But if you send a scout through the jungle and he doesn't show up on the other side, it's a fair assumption that something obstructed his way. In that case, we would label the obstruction 'cannibals.' In the case of the human mind, we label the obstruction a 'trauma.' What the trauma is, or what its effects on behavior will be, we have to find out, once we know that it's there."

Morey nodded. All of this was familiar; he couldn't see what Semmelweiss was driving at.

Semmelweiss sighed. "The trouble with healing traumas and penetrating psychic blocks and releasing inhibitions— the trouble with everything we psychiatrists do, in fact, is that we can't afford to do it too well. An inhibited man is under a strain. We try to relieve the strain. But if we succeed completely, leaving him with no inhibitions at all, we have an outlaw, Morey. Inhibitions are often socially necessary. Suppose, for instance, that an average man were not inhibited against blatant waste. It could happen, you know. Suppose that instead of consuming his ration quota in an orderly and responsible way, he did such things as set fire to his house and everything in it or dumped his food allotment in the river.

"When only a few individuals are doing it, we treat the individuals. But if it were done on a mass scale, Morey, it would be the end of society as we know it. Think of the whole collection of anti-social actions that you see in every paper. Man beats wife; wife turns into a harpy; junior smashes up windows; husband starts a black-market stamp racket. And every one of them traces to a basic weakness in the mind's defenses against the most important single anti-social phenomenon—failure to consume."

Morey flared, "That's not fair, Doctor! That was weeks ago! We've certainly been on the ball lately. I was just commended by the Board, in fact—"

The doctor said mildly, "Why so violent, Morey? I only made a general remark."

"It's just natural to resent being accused."

The doctor shrugged. "First, foremost and above all, we do *not* accuse patients of things. We try to help you find things out." He lit his end-of-session cigarette. "Think about it, please. I'll see you next week."

Cherry was composed and unapproachable. She kissed him remotely when he came in. She said, "I called Mother and told her the good news. She and Dad promised to come over here to celebrate."

"Yeah," said Morey. "Darling, what did I say wrong on the phone?"

"They'll be here about six."

"Sure. But what did I say? Was it about the rations? If you're sensitive, I swear I'll never mention them again."

"I *am* sensitive, Morey."

He said despairingly, "I'm sorry. I just—"

He had a better idea. He kissed her.

Cherry was passive at first, but not for long. When he had finished kissing her, she pushed him away and actually giggled. "Let me get dressed for dinner."

"Certainly. Anyhow, I was just—"

She laid a finger on his lips.

He let her escape and, feeling much less tense, drifted into the library. The afternoon papers were waiting for him. Virtuously, he sat down and began going through them in order. Midway through the *World-Telegram-Sun-Post-and-News,* he rang for Henry.

Morey had read clear through to the drama section of the *Times-Herald-Tribune-Mirror* before the robot appeared. "Good evening," it said politely.

"What took you so long?" Morey demanded. "Where are all the robots?"

Robots do not stammer, but there was a distinct pause before Henry said, "Belowstairs, sir. Did you want them for something?"

"Well, no. I just haven't seen them around. Get me a drink."

It hesitated. "Scotch, sir?"

"*Before* dinner? Get me a Manhattan."

"We're all out of Vermouth, sir."

"All out? Would you mind telling me how?"

"It's all used up, sir."

"Now that's just ridiculous," Morey snapped. "We have never run out of liquor in our whole lives and you know it. Good heavens, we just got our allotment in the other day and I certainly—"

He checked himself. There was a sudden flicker of horror in his eyes as he stared at Henry.

"You certainly what, sir?" the robot prompted.

Morey swallowed. "Henry, did I—did I do something I shouldn't have?"

"I'm sure I wouldn't know, sir. It isn't up to me to say what you should and shouldn't do."

"Of course not," Morey agreed grayly.

He sat rigid, staring hopelessly into space, remembering. What he remembered was no pleasure to him at all.

"Henry," he said. "Come along, we're going belowstairs. Right now!"

It had been Tanaquil Bigelow's remark about the robots. *Too many robots—make too much of everything.*

That had implanted the idea; it germinated in Morey's home. More than a little drunk, less than ordinarily inhibited, he had found the problem clear and the answer obvious.

He stared around him in dismal worry. His own robots, following his own orders, given weeks before . . .

Henry said, "It's just what you *told* us to do, sir."

Morey groaned. He was watching a scene of unparalleled activity, and it sent shivers up and down his spine.

There was the butler-robot, hard at work, his copper face expressionless. Dressed in Morey's own sports knickers and golfing shoes, the robot solemnly hit a ball against the wall, picked it up and teed it, hit it again, over and again, with Morey's own clubs. Until the ball wore ragged and was replaced; and the shafts of the clubs leaned out of true; and the close-stitched seams in the clothing began to stretch and abrade.

"My God!" said Morey hollowly.

There were the maid-robots, exquisitely dressed in Cherry's best, walking up and down in the delicate, slim shoes, sitting and rising and bending and turning. The cook-robots and the serving-robots were preparing dionysian meals.

Morey swallowed. "You—you've been doing this right along," he said to Henry. "That's why the quotas have been filled."

"Oh, yes, sir. Just as you told us."

Morey had to sit down. One of the serving-robots politely scurried over with a chair, brought from upstairs for their new chores.

Waste.

Morey tasted the word between his lips.

Waste.

You never wasted things. You *used* them. If necessary, you drove yourself to the edge of breakdown to use them; you made every breath a burden and every hour a torment to use them, until through diligent consuming and/or occupational merit, you were promoted to the next higher class, and were allowed to consume less frantically. But you didn't wantonly destroy or throw out. You *consumed*.

Morey thought fearfully: When the Board finds out about this . . .

Still, he reminded himself, the Board hadn't found out. It might take some time before they did, for humans, after all, never entered robot quarters. There was no law against it, not even a sacrosanct custom. But there was no reason to. When breaks occurred, which was infrequently, maintenance robots or repair squads came in and put them back in order. Usually the humans involved didn't even know it had happened, because the robots used their own TBR radio circuits and the process was next thing to automatic.

Morey said reprovingly, "Henry, you should have told—well, I mean reminded me about this."

"But, sir!" Henry protested. " 'Don't tell a living soul,' you said. You made it a direct order."

"Umph. Well, keep it that way. I—uh—I have to go back upstairs. Better get the rest of the robots started on dinner."

Morey left, not comfortably.

The dinner to celebrate Morey's promotion was difficult. Morey liked Cherry's parents. Old Elon, after the pre-marriage inquisition that father must inevitably give to daughter's suitor, had buckled right down to the job of adjustment. The old folks were good about not interfering, good about keeping their superior social status to themselves, good about helping out on the budget—at least once a week, they could be relied on to come over for a hearty meal, and Mrs. Elon had more than once remade some of Cherry's new dresses to fit herself, even to the extent of wearing all the high-point ornamentation.

And they had been wonderful about the wedding gifts, when Morey and their daughter got married. The most any member of Morey's family had been willing to take was a silver set or a few crystal table pieces. The Elons had come through with a dazzling promise to accept a car, a bird-bath for their garden and a complete set of living-room furniture! Of course, they could afford it—they had to consume so little that it wasn't much strain for them even to take gifts of that magnitude. But without their help, Morey knew, the first few months of matrimony would have been even tougher consuming than they were.

But on this particular night it was hard for Morey to like anyone. He responded with monosyllables; he barely grunted when Elon proposed a toast to his promotion and his brilliant future. He was preoccupied.

Rightly so. Morey, in his deepest, bravest searching, could find no clue in his memory as to just what the punishment might be for what he had done. But he had a sick certainty that trouble lay ahead.

Morey went over his problem so many times that an anesthesia set in. By the time dinner was ended and he and his father-in-law were in the den with their brandy, he was more or less functioning again.

Elon, for the first time since Morey had known him, offered him one of *his* cigars. "You're Grade Five—can afford to smoke somebody else's now, hey?"

"Yeah," Morey said glumly.

There was a moment of silence. Then Elon, as punctilious as any companion-robot, coughed and tried again. "Remember being peaked till I hit Grade Five," he reminisced meaningfully. "Consuming keeps a man on the go, all right. Things piled up at the law office, couldn't be taken care of while ration points piled up, too. And consuming comes first, of course—that's a citizen's prime duty. Mother and I had our share of grief over that, but a couple that wants to make a go of marriage and citizenship just pitches in and does the job, hey?"

Morey repressed a shudder and managed to nod.

"Best thing about upgrading," Elon went on, as if he had elicited a satisfactory answer, "don't have to spend so much time consuming, give more attention to work. Greatest luxury in the world, work. Wish I had as much stamina as you young fellows. Five days a week in court are about all I can manage. Hit six for a while, relaxed first time in my life, but my doctor made me cut down. Said we can't overdo pleasures. You'll be working two days a week now, hey?"

Morey produced another nod.

Elon drew deeply on his cigar, his eyes bright as they watched Morey. He was visibly puzzled, and Morey, even in his half-daze, could recognize the exact moment at which Elon drew the wrong inference. "Ah, everything okay with you and Cherry?" he asked diplomatically.

"Fine!" Morey exclaimed. "Couldn't be better!"

"Good, Good." Elon changed the subject with almost an audible wrench. "Speaking of court, had an interesting case the other day. Young fellow—year or two younger than you, I guess—came in with a Section Ninety-seven on him. Know what that is? Breaking and entering!"

"Breaking and entering," Morey repeated wonderingly, interested in spite of himself. "Breaking and entering what?"

"Houses. Old term; law's full of them. Originally applied to stealing things. Still does, I discovered."

"You mean he *stole* something?" Morey asked in bewilderment.

"Exactly! He *stole*. Strangest thing I ever came across. Talked it over with one of his bunch of lawyers later; new one on him, too. Seems this kid had a girl friend, nice kid but a little, you know, plump. She got interested in art."

"There's nothing wrong with that," Morey said.

"Nothing wrong with her, either. She didn't do anything. She didn't like him too much, though. Wouldn't marry him. Kid got to thinking about how he could get her to change her mind and—well, you know that big Mondrian in the Museum?"

"I've never been there," Morey said, somewhat embarrassed.

"Um. Ought to try it some day, boy. Anyway, comes closing time at the Museum the other day, this kid sneaks in. He steals the painting. That's right—*steals* it. Takes it to give to the girl."

Morey shook his head blankly. "I never heard of anything like that in my life."

"Not many have. Girl wouldn't take it, by the way. Got scared when he brought it to her. She must've tipped off the police, I guess. Somebody did. Took 'em three hours to find it, even when they knew it was hanging on a wall. Pretty poor kid. Forty-two room house."

"And there was a *law* against it?" Morey asked. "I mean it's like making a law against breathing."

"Certainly was. Old law, of course. Kid got set back two grades. Would have been more but, my God, he was only a Grade Three as it was."

"Yeah," said Morey, wetting his lips. "Say, Dad—"

"Um?"

Morey cleared his throat. "Uh—I wonder—I mean what's the penalty, for instance, for things like—well, misusing rations or anything like that?"

Elon's eyebrows went high. "Misusing rations?"

"Say you had a liquor ration, it might be, and instead of drinking it, you—well, flushed it down the drain or something . . ."

His voice trailed off. Elon was frowning. He said, "Funny thing, seems I'm not as broadminded as I thought I was. For some reason, I don't find that amusing."

"Sorry," Morey croaked.

And he certainly was.

It might be dishonest, but it was doing him a lot of good, for days went by and no one seemed to have penetrated his secret. Cherry was happy. Wainwright found occasion after occasion to pat Morey's back. The wages of sin were turning out to be prosperity and happiness.

There was a bad moment when Morey came home to find Cherry in the middle of supervising a team of packing-robots; the new house, suitable to his higher grade, was ready, and they were expected to move in the next day. But Cherry hadn't been belowstairs, and Morey had his household robots clean up the evidences of what they had been doing before the packers got that far.

The new house was, by Morey's standards, pure luxury.

It was only fifteen rooms. Morey had shrewdly retained one more robot than was required for a Class Five, and had been allowed a compensating deduction in the size of his house.

The robot quarters were less secluded than in the old house, though, and that was a disadvantage. More than once Cherry had snuggled up to him in the delightful intimacy of their one bed in their single bedroom and said, with faint curiosity, "I wish they'd stop that noise." And Morey had promised to speak to Henry about it in the morning. But there was nothing he could say to Henry, of course, unless he ordered Henry to stop the tireless consuming through each of the day's twenty-four hours that kept them always ahead, but never quite far enough ahead, of the inexorable weekly increment of ration quotas.

But, though Cherry might once in a while have a moment's curiosity about what the robots were doing, she was not likely to be able to guess at the facts. Her upbringing was, for once, on Morey's side—she knew so little of the grind, grind, grind of consuming that was the lot of the lower classes that she scarcely noticed that there was less of it.

Morey almost, sometimes, relaxed.

He thought of many ingenious chores for robots, and the robots politely and emotionlessly obeyed.

Morey was a success.

It wasn't all gravy. There was a nervous moment for Morey when the quarterly survey report came in the mail. As the day for the Ration Board to check over the degree of wear on the turned-in discards came due, Morey began to sweat. The clothing and furniture and household goods the robots had consumed for him were very nearly in shreds. It had to look plausible, that was the big thing—no normal person would wear a hole completely through the knee of a pair of pants, as Henry had done with his dress suit before Morey stopped him. Would the Board question it?

Worse, was there something about the *way* the robots consumed the stuff that would give the whole show away? Some special wear point in the robot anatomy, for instance, that would rub a hole where no human's body could, or stretch a seam that should normally be under no strain at all?

It was worrisome. But the worry was needless. When the report of survey came, Morey let out a long-held breath. *Not a single item disallowed!*

Morey was a success—and so was his scheme!

To the successful man come the rewards of success. Morey arrived home one evening after a hard day's work at the office and was alarmed to find another car parked in his drive. It was a tiny two-seater, the sort affected by top officials and the very well-to-do.

Right then and there Morey learned the first half of the embezzler's lesson: Anything different is dangerous. He came uneasily into his own home, fearful that some high officer of the Ration Board had come to ask questions.

But Cherry was glowing. "Mr. Porfirio is a newspaper feature writer and he wants to write you up for their 'Consumers of Distinction' page! Morey, I *couldn't* be more proud!"

"Thanks," said Morey glumly. "Hello."

Mr. Porfirio shook Morey's hand warmly. "I'm not exactly from a newspaper," he corrected. "Trans-video Press is what it is, actually. We're a news wire service; we supply forty-seven hundred papers with news and feature material. Every one of them," he added complacently, "on the required consumption list of Grades One through Six inclusive. We have a Sunday supplement self-help feature on consuming problems and we like to—well, give credit where credit is due. You've established an enviable record, Mr. Fry. We'd like to tell our readers about it."

"Um," said Morey. "Let's go in the drawing room."

"Oh, no!" Cherry said firmly. "I want to hear this. He's so modest, Mr. Porfirio, you'd really never know what kind of a man he is just to listen to him talk. Why, my goodness, I'm his wife and I swear *I* don't know how he does all the consuming he does. He simply——"

"Have a drink, Mr. Porfirio," Morey said, against all etiquette. "Rye? Scotch? Bourbon? Gin-and-tonic? Brandy Alexander? Dry Manha—I mean what would you like?" He became conscious that he was babbling like a fool.

"Anything," said the newsman. "Rye is fine. Now, Mr. Fry, I notice you've fixed up your place very attractively here and your wife says that your country home is just as nice. As soon as I came in, I said to myself, 'Beautiful home. Hardly a stick of furniture that isn't absolutely necessary. Might be a Grade Six or Seven.' And Mrs. Fry says the other place is even barer."

"She does, does she?" Morey challenged sharply. "Well, let me tell you, Mr. Porfirio, that every last scrap of my furniture allowance is accounted for! I don't know what you're getting at, but——"

"Oh, I certainly didn't mean to imply anything like *that!* I just want to get some information from you that I can pass on to our readers. You know, to sort of help them do as well as yourself. How *do* you do it?"

Morey swallowed. "We—uh—well, we just keep after it. Hard work, that's all."

Porfirio nodded admiringly. "Hard work," he repeated, and fished a triple-folded sheet of paper out of his pocket to make notes on. "Would you say," he went on, "that anyone could do as well as you simply by devoting himself to it—setting a regular schedule, for example, and keeping to it very strictly?"

"Oh, yes," said Morey.

"In other words, it's only a matter of doing what you have to do every day?"

"That's it exactly. I handle the budget in my house—more experience than my wife, you see—but no reason a woman can't do it."

"Budgeting," Porfirio recorded approvingly. "That's our policy, too."

The interview was not the terror it had seemed, not even when Porfirio tactfully called attention to Cherry's slim waistline ("So many housewives, Mrs. Fry, find it difficult to keep from being—well, a little plump") and Morey had to invent endless hours on the exercise machines, while Cherry looked faintly perplexed, but did not interrupt.

From the interview, however, Morey learned the second half of the embezzler's lesson. After Porfirio had gone, he leaped in and spoke more than a little firmly to Cherry. "That business of exercise, dear. We really have to start doing it. I don't know if you've noticed it, but you *are* beginning to get just a trifle heavier and we don't want that to happen, do we?"

In the following grim and unnecessary sessions on the mechanical horses, Morey had plenty of time to reflect on the lesson. Stolen treasures are less sweet than one would like, when one dare not enjoy them in the open.

But some of Morey's treasures were fairly earned.

The new Bradmoor K-50 Spin-a-Game, for instance, was his very own. His job was design and creation, and he was a fortunate man in that his efforts were permitted to be expended along the line of greatest social utility—namely, to increase consumption.

The Spin-a-Game was a well-nigh perfect machine for the purpose. "Brilliant," said Wainwright, beaming, when the pilot machine had been put through its first tests. "Guess they don't call me the Talent-picker for nothing. I knew you could do it, boy!"

Even Howland was lavish in his praise. He sat munching on a plate of petits-fours (he was still only a Grade Three) while the tests were going on, and when they were over, he said enthusiastically, "It's a beauty, Morey. That series-corrupter—sensational! Never saw a prettier piece of machinery."

Morey flushed gratefully.

Wainwright left, exuding praise, and Morey patted his pilot model affectionately and admired its polychrome gleam. The looks of the machine, as Wainwright had lectured many a time, were as important as its function:

"You have to make them *want* to play it, boy! They won't play it if they don't *see* it!" And consequently the whole K series was distinguished by flashing rainbows of light, provocative strains of music, haunting scents that drifted into the nostrils of the passerby with compelling effect.

Morey had drawn heavily on all the old masterpieces of design—the one-arm bandit, the pinball machine, the juke box. You put your ration book in the hopper. You spun the wheels until you selected the game you wanted to play against the machine. You punched buttons or spun dials or, in any of 325 different ways, you pitted your human skill against the magnetic-taped skills of the machine.

And you lost. You had a chance to win, but the inexorable statistics of the machine's setting made sure that if you played long enough, you had to lose.

That is to say, if you risked a ten-point ration stamp—showing, perhaps, that you had consumed three six-course meals—your statistic return was eight points. You might hit the jackpot and get a thousand points back, and thus be exempt from a whole freezerful of steaks and joints and prepared vegetables; but it seldom happened. Most likely you lost and got nothing.

Got nothing, that is, in the way of your hazarded ration stamps. But the beauty of the machine, which was Morey's main contribution, was that, win or lose, you *always* found a pellet of vitamin-drenched, sugar-coated antibiotic hormone gum in the hopper. You played your game, won or lost your stake, popped your hormone gum into your mouth and played another. By the time that game was ended, the gum was used up, the coating dissolved; you discarded it and started another.

"That's what the man from the NRB liked," Howland told Morey confidentially. "He took a set of schematics back with him; they might install it on *all* new machines. Oh, you're the fair-haired boy, all right!"

It was the first Morey had heard about a man from the National Ration Board. It was good news. He excused himself and hurried to phone Cherry the story of his latest successes. He reached her at her mother's, where she was spending the evening, and she was properly impressed and affectionate. He came back to Howland in a glowing humor.

"Drink?" said Howland diffidently.

"Sure," said Morey. He could afford, he thought, to drink as much of Howland's liquor as he liked; poor guy, sunk in the consuming quicksands of Class Three. Only fair for somebody a little more successful to give him a hand once in a while.

And when Howland, learning that Cherry had left Morey a bachelor for the evening, proposed Uncle Piggotty's again, Morey hardly hesitated at all.

The Bigelows were delighted to see him. Morey wondered briefly if they *had* a home; certainly they didn't seem to spend much time in it.

It turned out they did, because when Morey indicated virtuously that he'd only stopped in at Piggotty's for a single drink before dinner, and Howland revealed that he was free for the evening, they captured Morey and bore him off to their house.

Tanaquil Bigelow was haughtily apologetic. "I don't suppose this is the kind of place Mr. Fry is used to," she observed to her husband, right across Morey, who was standing between them. "Still, we call it home."

Morey made an appropriately polite remark. Actually, the place nearly turned his stomach. It was an enormous glaringly new mansion, bigger even than Morey's former house, stuffed to bursting with bulging sofas and pianos and massive mahogany chairs and tri-D sets and bedrooms and drawing rooms and breakfast rooms and nurseries.

The nurseries were a shock to Morey; it had never occured to him that the Bigelows had children. But they did and, though the children were only five and eight, they were still up, under the care of a brace of robot nursemaids, doggedly playing with their overstuffed animals and miniature trains.

"You don't know what a comfort Tony and Dick are," Tanaquil Bigelow told Morey. "They consume *so* much more than their rations. Walter says that every family ought to have at least two or three children to, you know, help out. Walter's so intelligent about these things, it's a pleasure to hear him talk. Have you heard his poem, Morey? The one he calls *The Twoness of—*"

Morey hastily admitted that he had. He reconciled himself to a glum evening. The Bigelows had been eccentric but fun back at Uncle Piggotty's. On their own ground, they seemed just as eccentric, but painfully dull.

They had a round of cocktails, and another, and then the Bigelows no longer seemed so dull. Dinner was ghastly, of course; Morey was nouveau-riche enough to be a snob about his relatively Spartan table. But he minded his manners and sampled, with grim concentration, each successive course of chunky protein and rich marinades. With the help of the endless succession of table wines and liqueurs, dinner ended without destroying his evening or his strained digestive system.

And afterward, they were a pleasant company in the Bigelow's ornate drawing room. Tanaquil Bigelow, in consultation with the children, checked over their ration books and came up with the announcement that they would have a brief recital by a pair of robot dancers, followed by string music by a robot quartet. Morey prepared himself for the worst, but found before the dancers were through that he was enjoying himself. Strange lesson for Morey: When you didn't *have* to watch them, the robot entertainers were fun!

"Good night, dears," Tanaquil Bigelow said firmly to the children when the dancers were done. The boys rebelled, naturally, but they went. It was only a matter of minutes, though, before one of them was back, clutching at Morey's sleeve with a pudgy hand.

Morey looked at the boy uneasily, having little experience with children. He said, "Uh—what is it, Tony?"

"Dick, you mean," the boy said. "Gimme your autograph." He poked an engraved pad and a vulgarly jeweled pencil at Morey.

Morey dazedly signed and the child ran off, Morey staring after him. Tanaquil Bigelow laughed and explained, "He saw your name in Porfirio's column. Dick *loves* Porfirio, reads him every day. He's such an intellectual kid, really. He'd always have his nose in a book if I didn't keep after him to play with his trains and watch tri-D."

"That was quite a nice write-up," Walter Bigelow commented—a little enviously, Morey thought. "Bet you make Consumer of the Year. I wish," he sighed, "that we could get a little ahead on the quotas the way you did. But it just never seems to work out. We eat and play and consume like crazy, and somehow at the end of the month we're always a little behind in something—everything keeps piling up—and then the Board sends us a warning, and they call me down and, first thing you know, I've got a couple of hundred added penalty points and we're worse off than before."

"Never you mind," Tanaquil replied staunchly. "Consuming isn't everything in life. You have your work."

Bigelow nodded judiciously and offered Morey another drink. Another drink, however, was not what Morey needed. He was sitting in a rosy glow, less of alcohol than of sheer contentment with the world.

He said suddenly, "Listen."

Bigelow looked up from his own drink. "Eh?"

"If I tell you something that's a *secret,* will you keep it that way?"

Bigelow rumbled, "Why, I guess so, Morey."

But his wife cut in sharply, "Certainly we will, Morey. Of course! What is it?" There was a gleam in her eye, Morey noticed. It puzzled him, but he decided to ignore it.

He said, "About that write-up. I—I'm not such a hot-shot consumer, really, you know. In fact—" All of a sudden, everyone's eyes seemed to be on him. For a tortured moment, Morey wondered if he was doing the right thing. A secret that two people know is compromised, and a secret known to three people is no secret. Still—

"It's like this," he said firmly. "You remember what we were talking about at Uncle Piggotty's that night? Well, when I went home I went down to the robot quarters, and I—"

He went on from there.

Tanaquil Bigelow said triumphantly, "I *knew* it!"

Walter Bigelow gave his wife a mild, reproving look. He declared soberly. "You've done a big thing, Morey. A mighty big thing. God willing, you've pronounced the death sentence on our society as we know it. Future generations will revere the name of Morey Fry." He solemnly shook Morey's hand.

Morey said dazedly, "I *what?*"

Walter nodded. It was a valedictory. He turned to his wife. "Tanaquil, we'll have to call an emergency meeting."

"Of course, Walter," she said devotedly.

"And Morey will have to be there. Yes, you'll have to, Morey; no excuses. We want the Brotherhood to meet you. Right, Howland?"

Howland coughed uneasily. He nodded noncommittally and took another drink.

Morey demanded desperately, "What are you talking about? Howland, you tell me!"

Howland fiddled with his drink. "Well," he said, "it's like Tan was telling you that night. A few of us, well, politically mature persons have formed a little group. We—"

"*Little* group!" Tanaquil Bigelow said scornfully. "Howland, sometimes I wonder if you really catch the spirit of the thing at all! It's everybody, Morey, everybody in the world. Why, there are eighteen of us right here in Old Town! There are *scores more* all over the world! I knew you were up to something like this, Morey. I told Walter so the morning after we met you. I said, 'Walter, mark my words, that man Morey is up to something.' But I must say," she admitted worshipfully, "I didn't know it would have the *scope* of what you're proposing now! Imagine—a whole world of consumers, rising as one man, shouting the name of Morey Fry, fighting the Ration Board with the Board's own weapon—the robots. What poetic justice!"

Bigelow nodded enthusiastically. "Call Uncle Piggotty's, dear," he ordered. "See if you can round up a quorum right now! Meanwhile, Morey and I are going belowstairs. Let's go, Morey—let's get the new world started!"

Morey sat there open-mouthed. He closed it with a snap. "Bigelow," he whispered, "do you mean to say that you're going to spread this idea around through some kind of subversive organization?"

"Subversive?" Bigelow repeated stiffly. "My dear man, *all* creative minds are subversive, whether they operate singly or in such a group as the Brotherhood of Freemen. I scarcely like——"

"Never mind what you like," Morey insisted. "You're going to call a meeting of this Brotherhood and you want *me* to tell them what I just told you. Is that right?"

"Well—yes."

Morey got up. "I wish I could say it's been nice, but it hasn't. Good night!"

And he stormed out before they could stop him.

Out on the street, though, his resolution deserted him. He hailed a robot cab and ordered the driver to take him on the traditional time-killing ride through the park while he made up his mind.

The fact that he had left, of course, was not going to keep Bigelow from going through with his announced intention. Morey remembered, now, fragments of conversation from Bigelow and his wife at Uncle Piggotty's, and cursed himself. They had, it was perfectly true, said and hinted enough about politics and purposes to put him on his guard. All that nonsense about twoness had diverted him from what should have been perfectly clear: They were subversives indeed.

He glanced at his watch. Late, but not too late; Cherry would still be at her parents' home.

He leaned forward and gave the driver their address. It was like beginning the first of a hundred-shot series of injections: you know it's going to cure you, but it hurts just the same.

Morey said manfully: "And that's it, sir. I know I've been a fool. I'm willing to take the consequences."

Old Elon rubbed his jaw thoughtfully. "Um," he said.

Cherry and her mother had long passed the point where they could say anything at all; they were seated side by side on a couch across the room, listening with expressions of strain and incredulity.

Elon said abruptly, "Excuse me. Phone call to make." He left the room to make a brief call and returned. He said over his shoulder to his wife, "Coffee. We'll need it. Got a problem here."

Morey said, "Do you think—I mean what should I do?"

Elon shrugged, then, surprisingly, grinned. "What can you do?" he demanded cheerfully. "Done plenty already, I'd say. Drink some coffee. Call I made," he explained, "was to Jim, my law clerk. He'll be here in a minute. Get some dope from Jim, then we'll know better."

Cherry came over to Morey and sat beside him. All she said was, "Don't worry," but to Morey it conveyed all the meaning in the world. He returned the pressure of her hand with a feeling of deepest relief. Hell, he said to himself, why *should* I worry? Worst they can do to me is drop me a couple of grades and what's so bad about that?

He grimaced involuntarily. He had remembered his own early struggles as a Class One and what *was* so bad about that.

The law clerk arrived, a smallish robot with a battered stainless-steel hide and dull coppery features. Elon took the robot aside for a terse conversation before he came back to Morey.

"As I thought," he said in satisfaction. "No precedent. No laws prohibiting. Therefore no crime."

"Thank heaven!" Morey said in ecstatic relief.

Elon shook his head. "They'll probably give you a reconditioning and you can't expect to keep your Grade Five. Probably call it anti-social behavior. Is, isn't it?"

Dashed, Morey said, "Oh." He frowned briefly, then looked up. "All right, Dad, if I've got it coming to me, I'll take my medicine."

"Way to talk," Elon said approvingly. "Now go home. Get a good night's sleep. First thing in the morning, go to the Ration Board. Tell 'em the whole story, beginning to end. They'll be easy on you." Elon hesitated. "Well, fairly easy," he amended. "I hope."

The condemned man ate a hearty breakfast.

He had to. That morning, as Morey awoke, he had the sick certainty that he was going to be consuming triple rations for a long, long time to come.

He kissed Cherry good-by and took the long ride to the Ration Board in silence. He even left Henry behind.

At the Board, he stammered at a series of receptionist

robots and was finally brought into the presence of a mildly supercilious young man named Hachette.

"My name," he started, "is Morey Fry. I—I've come to—talk over something I've been doing with—"

"Certainly, Mr. Fry," said Hachette. "I'll take you in to Mr. Newman right away."

"Don't you want to know what I did?" demanded Morey.

Hachette smiled. "What makes you think we don't know?" he said, and left.

That was Surprise Number One.

Newman explained it. He grinned at Morey and ruefully shook his head. "All the time we get this," he complained. "People just don't take the trouble to learn anything about the world around them. Son," he demanded, "what do you think a robot is?"

Morey said, "Huh?"

"I mean how do you think it operates? Do you think it's just a kind of a man with a tin skin and wire nerves?"

"Why, no. It's a machine, of course. It isn't *human*."

Newman beamed. "Fine!" he said. "It's a machine. It hasn't got flesh or blood or intestines—or a brain. Oh—" he held up a hand—"robots are *smart* enough. I don't mean that. But an electronic thinking machine, Mr. Fry, takes about as much space as the house you're living in. It has to. Robots don't carry brains around with them; brains are too heavy and much too bulky."

"Then how do they think?"

"With their brains, of course."

"But you just said—"

"I said they didn't *carry* them. Each robot is in constant radio communication with the Master Control on its TBR circuit—the 'Talk Between Robots' radio. Master Control gives the answer, the robot acts."

"I see," said Morey. "Well, that's very interesting, but—"

"But you still don't see," said Newman. "Figure it out. If the robot gets information from Master Control, do you see that Master Control in return necessarily gets information from the robot?"

"Oh," said Morey. Then, louder, "Oh! You mean that all my robots have been—" The words wouldn't come.

Newman nodded in satisfaction. "Every bit of information of that sort comes to us as a matter of course. Why, Mr. Fry, if you hadn't come in today, we would have been sending for you within a very short time."

That was the second surprise. Morey bore up under it bravely. After all, it changed nothing, he reminded himself.

He said, "Well, be that as it may, sir, here I am. I came in of my own free will. I've been using my robots to consume my ration quotas—"

"Indeed you have," said Newman.

"—and I'm willing to sign a statement to that effect any time you like. I don't know what the penalty is, but I'll take it. I'm guilty; I admit my guilt."

Newman's eyes were wide. "Guilty?" he repeated. "Penalty?"

Morey was startled. "Why, yes," he said. "I'm not denying anything."

"Penalties," repeated Newman musingly. Then he began to laugh. He laughed, Morey thought, to considerable excess; Morey saw nothing he could laugh at, himself, in the situation. But the situation, Morey was forced to admit, was rapidly getting completely incomprehensible.

"Sorry," said Newman at last, wiping his eyes, "but I couldn't help it. Penalties! Well, Mr. Fry, let me set your mind at rest. I wouldn't worry about the penalties if I were you. As soon as the reports began coming through on what you had done with your robots, we naturally assigned a special team to keep observing you, and we forwarded a report to the national headquarters. We made certain—ah—recommendations in it and—well, to make a long story short, the answers came back yesterday.

"Mr. Fry, the National Ration Board is delighted to know of your contribution toward improving our distribution problem. Pending a further study, a tentative program has been adopted for setting up consuming-robot units all over the country based on your scheme. Penalties? Mr. Fry, you're a *hero!*"

A hero has responsibilities. Morey's were quickly made clear to him. He was allowed time for a brief reassuring visit to Cherry, a triumphal tour of his old office, and then he was rushed off to Washington to be quizzed. He found the National Ration Board in a frenzy of work.

"The most important job we've ever done," one of the high officers told him. "I wouldn't be surprised if it's the last one we ever have! Yes, sir, we're trying to put ourselves out of business for good and we don't want a single thing to go wrong."

"Anything I can do to help—" Morey began diffidently.

"You've done fine, Mr. Fry. Gave us just the push we've been needing. It was there all the time for us to see, but we were too close to the forest to see the trees, if you get what I mean. Look, I'm not much on rhetoric and this is the biggest step mankind has taken in centuries and I can't put it into words. Let me show you what we've been doing."

He and a delegation of other officials of the Ration Board and men whose names Morey had repeatedly seen in the newspapers took Morey on an inspection tour of the entire plant.

"It's a closed cycle, you see," he was told, as they looked over a chamber of industriously plodding consumer-robots working off a shipment of shoes. "Nothing is permanently lost. If you want a car, you get one of the newest and best. If not, your car gets driven by a robot until it's ready to be turned in and a new one gets built for next year. We don't lose the metals—they can be salvaged. All we lose is a little power and labor. And the Sun and the atom give us all the power we need, and the robots give us more labor than we can use. Same thing applies, of course, to all products."

"But what's in it for the robots?" Morey asked.

"I beg your pardon?" one of the biggest men in the country said uncomprehendingly.

Morey had a difficult moment. His analysis had conditioned him against waste and this decidedly was sheer destruction of goods, no matter how scientific the jargon might be.

"If the consumer is just using up things for the sake of

using them up," he said doggedly, realizing the danger he was inviting, "we could use wear-and-tear machines instead of robots. After all why waste *them?*"

They looked at each other worriedly.

"But that's what *you* were doing," one pointed out with a faint note of threat.

"Oh, no!" Morey quickly objected. "I built in satisfaction circuits—my training in design, you know. Adjustable circuits, of course."

"Satisfaction circuits?" he was asked. "Adjustable?"

"Well, sure. If the robot gets no satisfaction out of using up things—"

"Don't talk nonsense," growled the Ration Board official. "Robots aren't human. How do you make them feel satisfaction? And adjustable satisfaction at that!"

Morey explained. It was a highly technical explanation, involving the use of great sheets of paper and elaborate diagrams. But there were trained men in the group and they became even more excited than before.

"Beautiful!" one cried in scientific rapture. "Why, it takes care of every possible moral, legal and psychological argument!"

"What does?" the Ration Board official demanded. "How?"

"You tell him, Mr. Fry."

Morey tried and couldn't. But he could *show* how his principle operated. The Ration Board lab was turned over to him, complete with more assistants than he knew how to give orders to, and they built satisfaction circuits for a squad of robots working in a hat factory.

Then Morey gave his demonstration. The robots manufactured hats of all sorts. He adjusted the circuits at the end of the day and the robots began trying on the hats, squabbling over them, each coming away triumphantly with a huge and diverse selection. Their metallic features were incapable of showing pride or pleasure, but both were evident in the way they wore their hats, their fierce possessiveness . . . and their faster, neater, more intensive, more *dedicated* work to produce a still greater quantity of hats . . . which they also were allowed to own.

"You see?" an engineer exclaimed delightedly. "They

can be adjusted to *want* hats, to wear them lovingly, to wear the hats to pieces. And not just for the sake of wearing them out—the hats are an incentive for them!"

"But how can we go on producing just hats and more hats?" the Ration Board man asked puzzledly. "Civilization does not live by hats alone."

"That," said Morey modestly, "is the beauty of it. Look."

He set the adjustment of the satisfaction circuit as porter robots brought in skids of gloves. The hat-manufacturing robots fought over the gloves with the same mechanical passion as they had for hats.

"And that can apply to anything we — or the robots — produce," Morey added. "Everything from pins to yachts. But the point is that they get satisfaction from possession, and the craving can be regulated according to the glut in various industries, and the robots show their appreciation by working harder." He hesitated. "That's what I did for my servant-robots. It's a feedback, you see. Satisfaction leads to more work—and *better* work—and that means more goods, which they can be made to want, which means incentive to work, and so on, all around."

"Closed cycle," whispered the Ration Board man in awe. "A *real* closed cycle this time!"

And so the inexorable laws of supply and demand were irrevocably repealed. No longer was mankind hampered by inadequate supply or drowned by overproduction. What mankind needed was there. What the race did not require passed into the insatiable—and adjustable—robot maw. Nothing was wasted.

For a pipeline has two ends.

Morey was thanked, complimented, rewarded, given a ticker-tape parade through the city, and put on a plane back home. By that time, the Ration Board had liquidated itself.

Cherry met him at the airport. They jabbered excitedly at each other all the way to the house.

In their own living room, they finished the kiss they had greeted each other with. At last Cherry broke away, laughing.

Morey said, "Did I tell you I'm through with Bradmoor? From now on I work for the Board as civilian consultant. *And,*" he added impressively, "starting right away, I'm a Class Eight!"

"My!" gasped Cherry, so worshipfully that Morey felt a twinge of conscience.

He said honestly, "Of course, if what they were saying in Washington is so, the classes aren't going to mean much pretty soon. Still, it's quite an honor."

"It certainly is," Cherry said staunchly. "Why, Dad's only a Class Eight himself and he's been a judge for I don't know *how* many years."

Morey pursed his lips. "We can't all be fortunate," he said generously. "Of course, the classes still will count for *something*—that is, a Class One will have so much to consume in a year, a Class Two will have a little less, and so on. But each person in each class will have robot help, you see, to do the actual consuming. The way it's going to be, special facsimile robots will—"

Cherry flagged him down. "I know, dear. Each family gets a robot duplicate of every person in the family."

"Oh," said Morey, slightly annoyed. "How did you know?"

"Ours came yesterday," she explained. "The man from the Board said we were the first in the area—because it was your idea, of course. They haven't even been activated yet. I've still got them in the Green Room. Want to see them?"

"Sure," said Morey buoyantly. He dashed ahead of Cherry to inspect the results of his own brainstorm. There they were, standing statue-still against the wall, waiting to be energized to begin their endless tasks.

"Yours is real pretty," Morey said gallantly. "But—say, is that thing supposed to look like me?" He inspected the chromium face of the man-robot disapprovingly.

"Only roughly, the man said." Cherry was right behind him. "Notice anything else?"

Morey leaned closer, inspecting the features of the facsimile robot at a close range. "Well, no," he said. "It's got a kind of a squint that I don't like, but—Oh, you mean *that!*" He bent over to examine a smaller robot, half hidden between the other pair. It was less than two feet high, big-headed, pudgy-limbed, thick-bellied. In fact, Morey thought wonderingly, it looked almost like—

"My God!" Morey spun around, staring wide-eyed at his wife. "You mean—"

"I mean," said Cherry, blushing slightly.

Morey reached out to grab her in his arms.

"Darling!" he cried. "Why didn't you *tell* me?"

# EQUALITY
## A POLITICAL ROMANCE

James Reynolds

# EQUALITY—A POLITICAL ROMANCE.

In those regions lately discovered by political philosophers. there is an island, the singularity of whose government and manners, deserve the attention of the curious, and the particular notice of those who would wish to make discoveries in those latitudes in time coming.

Having been engaged in exploring those seas where lie the countries of Utopia, Brobdignag, Lilliput, &c. and touching to take in fresh water at an island, which I afterwards found to be called Lithconia, I was so struck with the order and regularity with which every thing was conducted, that I was resolved to stay some time amongst them, to observe whether there was any thing in their constitution or form of government, worthy of being recorded for the instruction of our modern politicians.

For that purpose I prevailed upon the master of the vessel to permit me to remain on the island, and call for me on his homeward passage. This he readily agreed to. being equally curious with myself to know some further particulars respecting a people so apparently happy. As soon as I packed up what necessaries I supposed would be wanting, the boat was ordered to carry the captain and myself on shore, he being willing to see what reception I should meet with from the natives, upon their being acquainted with my intention of staying among them. It was about four o'clock P. M. A great number of the people came down to meet us on the beach : I was surprised that there should be more this time than ever I had seen before, at any of our former landings : but I afterwards found that it was past their hour of labour, and that they were then beginning to their sports and pastimes, as is their custom, every day in fine weather, after the hour of four o'clock.

We immediately informed them of my intention, upon which I was conducted to a man, who seemed to be past the prime of life, but active, healthy and robust. His first enquiry was, how I intended to employ myself during my residence on the island ? I informed him, that I wished to travel, and visit the principal towns and villages, in order to make such observations on the manners, customs, and laws of the people, as my time or abilities would permit.—When the elder understood this, he let me know the impracticability of my scheme, by reason of my not being furnished with those marks or signs, by which alone I could obtain provisions on my journey. These signs I immediately supposed to be money ; upon which I drew out my purse and shewed him an hundred guineas, which I imagined would be a sufficient passport to every town in the island, at least, for the short time I had to stay. He smiled at my simplicity ; and, at the same time, gave me to understand, that such pieces of metal would be of no service to me in the country of Lithconia. But the good man, when he saw my disappointment and embarraſſment, bid me have comfort, for that I ſurely would be willing, as he ſaw I was able, to perform ſome labour, at the appointed times, which alone could obtain for me the privilege of travelling. By making further enquiries I found, that there is no money in the country, that the lands are in common, and that labour is a duty required of every citizen, till a certain age, and that duty being performed, the remainder of his time is his own. I therefore agreed to take my ſhare of labour, being convinced I ſhould have ſufficient time to ſpare both for excurſion and obſervation.

Four hours each day is ſet aſide for work ; this I could eaſily accompliſh, and walk a moderate day's journey afterwards— and this is the manner in which I ſpent my time, during a three month's reſidence on the iſland : in the forenoon I performed my work, which was ſometimes in the field, and often in the *work-ſhops*, where ſhoes are made, of which trade I had ſome knowledge, having ſerved part of an apprenticeſhip to it before I went to ſea.

Having obtained my certificate and dined, I would walk 16 or 20 miles along the beſt roads in the world, before ſupper, to obtain which I had nothing to do, but preſent my certificate to the *Menardon*, or director of labour, who, immediately, ſhewed me where I might ſup, ſleep, and what I ſhould employ myſelf in next day. Sometimes I ſtaid ſeveral days in one place, and at other times I would travel ſeveral days ſucceſſively ; but when I had an intention of doing the latter, I uſed to perform two days labour in one, for as many days as I intended to travel ; this being noted in my certificate, gained me permiſſion to travel on, without any interruption of labour.

There is the ſame regulations for the natives. No man is permitted to do another's work, though he may anticipate his own—the practice of ſuffering the work allotted to one man to be performed by his neighbour, was formerly, ſay the Lithconians, the beginning of barter, and barter introduced money, which was the root of all evil. Therefore, if a man were to perform three days labour in one, he cannot beſtow it upon any individual, ſuppoſing it a thing which might be ſeparated from other labour ; for induſtry is a duty which every man owes the ſtate, and which he is not required to perform, unleſs he be able. There is, therefore, no occaſion to perform it by proxy.

Nothing but fame or love of country, can induce a Lithconian to extra labour, but theſe two paſſions frequently produce great exertions. All the ornamental part of the country, whether it be the decorations of buildings, or ſtatues and paintings, are all produced by theſe principles—for the regulations of the ſtate require only the uſeful.

A clock-maker made a curious clock at leiſure hours : the metal, the wood and tools. were all the property of the community—he could not purchaſe them. By making the materials into a clock, he had only improved the goods of the community, and, as he could not, in juſtice, beſtow the clock upon any perſon, it became the property of the ſtate, and no people being more fond of public ornament than the Lithconians, it was put up in the great work-shop for workers in metal, adorned with some elegant mason work, and a handsome copy of verses engraved underneath, celebrating the genius of the artists, and transmitting their names to posterity, together with that of the poet. The whole was the extra labour of young men, stimulated by no other motives than the passions above-mentioned.

There are no towns or markets in all the island of Lithconia—the whole is only one large city upon a grand scale ; for the roads, from one end of the island to the other, have houses (with a small opening betwixt each house) on both sides all the way, and there are fifty such roads from north to south, the length of the island, and upwards of 200 from east to west.

The houses are all built upon one plan, two stories high, which contain nine sleeping apartments, a kitchen and public hall, with offices behind : no houses are built on the back ground, except for cattle ; so that there is no such thing as a cluster of houses that may be called a town. At the crossings a square of 100 yards is left vacant, without any houses, adjoining to which the public buildings, such as granaries, work-shops, &c. are regularly erected.

I found in the history of the country, that there were formerly large towns, as in Europe ; but the evils, natural and moral, which are the concomitant of great cities, made them think of abandoning them, and building in the manner above described —but what finally determined them, was, an earthquake, which destroyed 1000 houses, a fire which burnt 3000 in the principal city, and the plague which swept away 500,000 inhabitants, from the different cities of the empire. But since the people have spread themselves over the country, no such calamities have afflicted them.

As to markets, there are three large stores in each district ; one for provisions of every kind, one for clothing, and a third for household utensils and furniture. The keepers of provisions, whose stores are supplied from the field, send round, twice a week, in covered carts, to each house, every necessary for the consumption of a family. Clothing is distributed once a year, and household utensils as they are wanted ; so that no idle people are seen lounging behind the counters, anxiously expecting customers, whom they may impose upon. Two men will distribute as much provisions, as half the hucksters, grocers, bakers, and butchers, in Philadelphia ; and two more can distribute as much clothing in one month as all the quakers in Pennsylvania will sell in a year.——Hence that host of shop keepers which seem so necessary in barbarous countries, are here unknown.

The agriculturist and manufacturer has only to deposit his commodities in the public stores ; he has nothing to do with the knavery of merchandize, and the words, " a good market," if such a term were in use here, could only have one idea, viz. *a plentiful supply* ; whereas it is well known, that what is a good market for the seller, is a bad one to the buyer in all the disjointed countries in Europe and America.

Every person above the age of fifteen, has a separate apartment—from five to fifteen two sleep together, and children under five sleep in the mother's chamber. They are distributed in the houses as chance, passion or accident direct, male and female promiscuously.

Marriage, formerly, I understand, was held as sacred here as in other countries; but when property became in common, it fell gradually into disuse—for children being the property of the state, educated and brought up at the public expence, and as women could live as well single as united. young people were seldom at the trouble to make such a contract. Children were born, and no man thought it his business or interest to enquire who was the father. But a thousand inconveniences arose out of this legislative negligence, which, for the sake of order, and to make love a blessing to society, it was necessary to correct.—The great evil that called for legislative interference was, the frequent quarrels that took place between rival lovers.

Weak women were too often unable to determine betwixt two admirers, which should have the preference, and it was necessary, for the good of society, that she should decide. To accomplish this, it was decreed, that all the young women of each district, who had arrived at a certain age, should on the first day of the year after, inscribe the name of her lover in the matrimonial register of the district—Next day, all the young men, unengaged, go to examine this register, and as many as are satisfied with the girls who have chosen them, signify their assent to the recorder. After which it would be a crime, punishable by imprisonment, and sometimes flagelation, if either of the parties should be found to admit, or give encouragement to another lover.

This kind of marriage, however, occasions no separation of property from the stock of the community, nor any of the property of the parties,—They continue to live in separate apartments, and never sleep together only every seventh night.—— Whether this last regulation is a positive law, or only a political custom, I could never learn: but it certainly has the happiest effects. It seems to be an institution or custom, calculated to make the most of love, the only solace of mankind, and to make it last to the longest possible period of our existence. Nevertheless, it sometimes happens that lovers thus united, become dissatisfied with each other, and that for the happiness of one or both of the parties, a separation is necessary.———In that case the party aggrieved announces his or her intention of erasing the opposite party's name from the matrimonial register—four weeks is then given for further deliberation, and if at the end of that time the same resolution is persisted in the process of separation is recorded, and the parties are at liberty to inscribe other names on the register.

When a young woman is within three months of her time, she announces the same to the senior, who has the immediate direction of her work, who exempts her from attendance, and a nurse is allowed, if necessary, and every thing else convenient to accommodate her; and if she have a safe delivery, there is always rejoicings, entertainments and mirth among the neighbours.

Here are no parents repining at the increase of a family, from the fear of being unable to support them.

Here the laws do not make the trembling female swear to the father of her child ; for no man can have any reason to deny or confess his offspring—and child murder, a crime so frequent in barbarous nations—a crime which the happier females of Lithconia would shudder at the idea of, is totally unknown.

Here there is no occasion for asylums for the wretched and outcast female. because none are wretched or outcast.

Here also there is no seduction, except it be on the part of the women—they are the only seducers : their bewitching manners had nearly seduced my unwary heart ;——unaccustomed to see nature unveiled, I was insensibly allured by their native and artless simplicity, how much more charming than the studied coyness of our English fair : and I must say, that the freedom and gaiety of their manners made me regret, more than any thing else, my departure from the country. Every where the female character is superior to the male, but here, women are transformed to angels.

Every evening the chief of my entertainment proceeded from them. They would invite me to dance on the green, an amusement which was practised every fine evening, and they seemed to take a pleasure in shewing me the beauties of nature and the decorations of the public buildings, such as work-shops, &c. At supper they vied with each other in helping me to the most delicate morsels ; and I was often charmed with the soft music of their fine voices ; some singing in their own apartments, and others in the hall or public room ; for in each house there is a hall for public recreation free to all. But no person presumes to enter, or even make advances, towards the private chamber of another, without being asked. These are sacred to retirement, to love and friendship.

In short, the duties of hospitality in this country seemed to be given up to the women, and they are not backward in performing it ; yet when I made this observation to a Lithconian, he remarked, that the men were equally attentive to women who were strangers, and so I found afterwards.

Friendship I found to be more frequent and durable here than in any other country. For, if we consider that it is the equality of men's conditions and the similarity of their pursuits, that unite men in the bonds of friendship, we shall not be suprised to find attachments more lasting in this country, where all men are equal. What is it that produces false and inconstant friends in barbarous nations, but the sickleness of fortune (occasioned by a want of government) which is for ever altering men's conditions and changing their pursuits. It is well known that a rich and poor man, not having the same views, nor the same objects to pursue, are never united in the intimate bonds of friendship : but in this country, where there are no rich or poor, and where the terms are even unknown, friendships are as durable as the existence of the parties. Hence I heard no complaints of false and deceitful friends in all my travels through this island, a theme so frequent in every other country.

And so much are their institutions favorable to friendship, that if two persons of congenial spirits meet, and find a pleasure in the company and conversation of each other, they have the liberty of dwelling in the same house if they please ;—for a person may remove to any part of the island, or to any house where there is a vacancy: nothing can hinder him but the want of a certificate that he has performed the accustomed labour ; having done *that* he is at perfect liberty ; nor has the seniors the power (if it could be supposed they were willing) to refuse a certificate. Hence the houses are in general occupied by nine or ten persons, whom love or friendship has drawn together. If any difference arises (which is but seldom) one of the parties retires to another house, where he thinks of meeting with people more congenial to his temper and disposition.

Every year at the end of harvest, all the men and women above 50 years, assemble together in their respective districts ; the oldest presides and the youngest is the secretary: those above 60 may attend or not as they please.

Those who have the superintendence of the work-shops, the care of the warehouses and granaries, and the distribution of every necessary, being all above fifty years, and necessarily present in the assembly, give in their accounts of the produce of the fields, of the workshops, of the consumption, and of what remains in stock. Likewise what has been received from and delivered to other districts ; all which is laid before the meeting The secretary makes out a general return, which is carried, with other matters, to the grand assembly of the ancients, in the centre of the island, by the oldest man of each district, who chuses to go, above 60, and if all above 60 decline, which they have the privilege of doing, then he or she that is nearest that age is obliged to go. It therefore happens that all the public business of every kind generally falls upon those betwixt 50 and 60.

Here is no election, and consequently no intriguing for places. Every man or woman, if they live long enough, will succeed in their turn to the duties of administration. None can be excepted but those who are suffering the punishments due to crimes.

Elections for the purpose of chusing men of great abilities, or men best acquainted with the interests of nations, or who are most conversant in the constitution and laws of the state ; or, those who have much at stake in the country, and are supposed on that account to have the greatest interest in its prosperity and grandeur—is quite unnecessary here. Every man's stake in the country is equal. The laws are not contained in huge volumes—they are written in the hearts of the Lithconians. Every child of five years can repeat, without book, the whole code ; and the abilities required of those whose duty it is to attend the grand assembly, is not so great as the ordinary duties of superintending workshops, instructing youth, adjusting differences, &c. require. Besides, those who have a right to attend the grand assembly never thing of making new laws—they assemble to fulfil the laws already made, which says, " Let thy neighbours partake of thy abundance, that thou mayest partake of theirs."

In this meeting the accounts from every district are read over, and the wants of one directed to be supplied out of the abundance of another. It is also settled, what quantity of each article of necessity should be produced, or manufactured, in the districts for the ensuing year, and likewise, what quantity may be exported or imported.

These matters being arranged, every one retires to his home, and communicates the result to a meeting of the seniors in his district, who make the necessary regulations for the reception of such articles as they may want, and for the conveyance of the superfluities to the districts requiring them.

This whole country has the appearance of one vast manufactory, conducted by one mind; and although it was some time before I could understand the motions of this immense machine, it being so new, and what I had no previous conception of; yet after I had got a perfect comprehension of all its parts it appeared much more simple than any other form of government in the world.

Labour is performed by every citizen equally—The exceptions are—

1st. Infants under five years.

2d. Women in the last three months of their time, and nine months afterwards, if they have a happy delivery.

3d. All sick persons whatever.

4th. Every man and woman above 50 years, who have in right of their age, the direction of labour; the instruction of youth; the distribution of goods; and the exercise of the judicial powers.

As to what in other countries is called the legislature, there is no such thing, unless we call the district meetings, which have been already noticed, a legislative body, or the grand assembly of ancients; but both these bodies have more the appearance of an executive deliberating upon the best mode of carrying the principles of justice into execution, than a legislature.

By the fundamental laws, or constitution of Lithconia, crimes are divided into two classes—personal and public. Personal comprehending every thing which may be done to injure the person of another—such as murder, maiming, striking, abusive language, and want of respect or attention. Public crimes are such things as injure the community; as idleness, waste and negligence, or disobedience to the command of the seniors.

In personal crimes (except murder) he who receives the offence must be the accuser: but for murder or public crimes, any of the elders may, and it is their duty, to accuse. The punishment for murder is death—every other crime is punished at the discretion of the jurors. For personal crimes the party offended may forgive—but for crimes against the society or public, there is no pardon.

In every district there is a person who is called the serastedor or recorder, whose business it is to keep a list of the jurors, and the record of the trials.

Every man and woman in the diſtrict, above 50, are ranged alphabetically in the liſt of jurors : on each trial fifteen are taken as they ſtand on the liſt—every ſucceeding trial has five ſtruck off and five added, which makes every juryman ſtand three trials. In pronouncing a man guilty, they muſt be unanimous—but in affixing the puniſhment, the majority is ſufficient. There is no other judge. The recorder has no further buſineſs but to record, minutely, the proceedings, and receive the verdict. The oldeſt man of the jury pronounces the ſentence.

As there is no ſuch thing as debtor and creditor, ſo there is no property to contend for, conſequently no lawyers.

As every trial commences immediately after the accuſation, and as no perſon can poſſibly eſcape from juſtice, ſo there is no jails, which, are the nurſeries of vice, in barbarous nations.— To give inſtruction and advice being the duty of the ſeniors, there is no occaſion for prieſts or phyſicians, and it being every man's duty to defend his country, there can be no ſoldiers by profeſſion.

The period of the life of *one* man is employed nearly in the ſame manner as any other. To give the hiſtory then, of one Lithconian, is to deſcribe the manners of the nation.

Children, as has been already obſerved, until five years old, remain with the mother. From their earlieſt age they are inſtructed in the principles of equal rights—No ſuch words as *mine* and *thine* are ever heard. Ours and yours are words which are made uſe of, only when ſpeaking of diſtricts, and even that phraſeology is diſcouraged ; and. conſequently, not reckoned ſo polite as to mention the name of the diſtrict.

Children are alſo taught to repeat by memory, the ſhort ſentences which are the principles of their government—their politics and moral—upon which the verdicts of juries are founded, and which ſerve them for a conſtitution and laws. For the Lithconians are not a people that are progreſſing from a ſtate of nature, to what is vulgarly called, civilization ; on the contrary, they are progreſſing from civil ſociety to a ſtate of nature, if they have not already arrived at that ſtate : for in the hiſtory of the country, many and ſurpriſing revolutions are recorded.

But previous to the revolution which ſettled the preſent ſyſtem of things, there was a wonderful propenſity or deſire, in the men of thoſe times, to form conſtitutions, or fundamental laws, which *ſhould*, like the laws of the Medes and Perſians, be unalterable and eternal.

Hiſtory records no leſs than ten infallible conſtitutions, all declared to be founded on the rights of man, in the ſhort period of forty years ; each of which, in its turn, gave way to its ſucceſſor, and was buried in oblivion. After the failure of the firſt ten, the idea of infallibility was abandoned, and the period of their exiſtence was then limited to a certain number of years, when a reviſal was to take place. This ſcheme alſo failing, it was at laſt diſcovered, that the will of the people was paramount to every ſyſtem of laws ; and the only good thing produced by this fermentation of opinion and changes of government, was, that of getting the people into the habit of peaceably expressing their will, and of having it accurately known—this was indeed one great point gained, as it was the first step to every subsequent improvement.

But quitting this digression, let us proceed in shewing how the life of a Lithconian is spent. At five he begins to be under the direction of one of the seniors, who instructs him *gradually* in all the duties of a citizen. His first task is to work at some easy employment one hour a day. and one hour more is employed in learning to read ; the rest of his time is spent in play in the open air. These are the duties of the sixth year.

The seventh year, half an hour per day is added to the time required for work ; and so on, half an hour every year, till it comes to four per day,—which has been found, upon experience. to be sufficient for all the labour of the state.

All labour is performed either in the public work shops or in the fields. At my different stages I made a point of going thro' as many of the work-shops as my time would allow. there being always in them something curious to be seen, if it were nothing but the order and regularity with which every thing was conducted—here was always industry, without bustle, hurry, or confusion.

Instead of workshops being mean, cold and inconvenient, as in other countries, I found them elegant, well finished, and furnished with every convenience. The first I entered was the joiners' shop of the district ; one hundred benches was ranged on each side of the lower apartment: on the second storey were as many lathes and benches for turning. Adjoining was a large hall for placing the work when finished. and previous to its distribution.—The company of so many young active men at work together, makes labour rather a recreation than otherwise —and the senior who has the superintendence of the shop feels delighted, at the alacrity and promptness with which his orders are obeyed—no bad debts sour his mind—he rejoices in the ease, independence and superiority, which crowns his old age.

But the spinning and weaving far surpassed my conception— both which are performed by the power of water. Cotton, woolen and linen, are all spun by machinery, but in different districts. In the south part of the island, where cotton grows, there it is spun and wove. In the middle of the country, where there are the best sheep, *there* wool is manufactured into cloth ; and towards the north, where the land is suitable for flax, linen, is the staple commodity.

The looms are also moved by the force of water, in which cloth is wove ten yards wide. A great deal of time, attention and labour is saved in all their manufactories, by not having any necessity for weighing the materials, upon delivery to the workmen, and entering the same in books—Hence there are no clerks employed, as in other countries, merely to keep men honest : indeed the temptation to steal, or embezzle the materials, or finished work of the manufactories, is reduced to nothing, since no man can appropriate any thing to his own use, or conceal it from the public eye:

From the age of 15, he begins to be taught the nicer branches of the arts: at 18 he is generally confidered a finifhed adept in his profeffion—he amufes himfelf with the ufe of arms : is fond of all kinds of exercife and diverfion; attachments take place with fome favorite female ; and in this manner his life is fpent betwixt love, friendfhip, amufements, and the arts, till he arrives at fifty years, when he undertakes the direction and management of fome portion of the national induftry, or affifts in the inftruction of youth, and the diftribution of juftice. At 60, no focial duties are any longer required, though they are not forbidden him ; and peace, ferenity, and independence, accompany him through the remainder of his days.

Such is the life of the Lithconians.

Poverty and riches, as may be eafily conceived, are words not to be found in the language. There are no diftinctions, but what are founded in nature ; no artificial inequalities. When a perfon's rank in fociety is mentioned, it is only by the natural diftinctions of infancy, youth, manhood, and feniority--Hence the fource of the malevolent paffions are dried up. No man looks upon his neighbours' riches with envy, nor with contempt upon another's poverty. The only pride or ambition is, in that of excelling in the mechanic arts, or handling with dexterity the tools of a man's profeffion.

Family pride has been long extinct in this ifland ; there being only one great family which comprehends all the Lithconians. Even national pride is unknown, a they have never been at war for many ages. So their feniors have not had occafion to deceive them by a falfe eftimation of themfelves, or degradation of their neighbours. They have no *natural enemies*, as is frequent with barbarous nations. The people of the neighbouring iflands, or the more remote inhabitants of the continent, are all naturally *friends* (without being allies) of Lithconia, however they may difagree and quarrel among themfelves.

Variety of drefs and equipage is alfo unknown. Every citizen having a certain quantity of cloths diftributed to him at ftated periods, the whole country appears almoft in uniform — The only difference that I could perceive was, that fome people, better economifts than others, had their clothes frefh and clean, confequently had a better appearance. But the women, without exception, are remarkable for economy and neatnefs in drefs.— In their head drefs I remarked a fanciful variety, which I found to be decorations of their own invention—this being the only part of their drefs which is fubject to fafhion or fancy.

The whole ifland may be compared to a city fpread over a large garden : not a fpot can be feen but what is in a high ftate of cultivation. Every diftrict is divided into as many fields as is thought convenient and advantageous for culture, and numbered from one upwards : each field is entered in a book—on one page the crops and management, and on the other the produce. The management for each fucceeding year is determined at the annual meeting of each diftrict ; a matter which is eafily fettled, as the approved routine of crops is always preferred, ex-

cept in a certain limitted number of fields, referved for experiments.

The old men who have the fuperintendence of thefe fields,
may, if neceffary, demand from the workfhops, as many hands
over and above the ordinary agriculturifts, as will execute the
intended labour.

Any man who finds out a method of making the foil produce
more abundantly, may, if he pleafes, be exempt from work.—
He who invents a machine, to facilitate or expedite labour, has
the fame reward. Here are no idle difputes about the propriety
of introducing machines into practice : no vain fears of depriving the poor of work, and of the means of fubfiftence. Every
man is convinced, that he who can make ufeful labour more eafy
and expeditious, or who makes three grains of wheat to grow
where there was only two, augments the number of the enjoyments of every Lithconian, and deferves the applaufe of his
country. Therefore, no country in the world has fuch excellent tools, or perfect machinery, as are to be found here. Nothing excites ridicule fo much as a man labouring with a bad in-
ftrument, or machine out of repair. On the other hand, nothing feems to give a Lithconian fo much pleafure, as the fight
of a dextrous workman, ufing an excellent machine.

The genius of this people has been difplayed in nothing fo
much as in their aqueducts, public baths, canals, and roads,
which excel every thing of the kind I ever faw : befides, they
have a kind of road peculiar to this country, for the tranfporta-
tion of heavy commodities in thofe places where a level may be,
without much difficulty, obtained, yet not fufficient water for the
fupply of a canal. Thefe are firft made upon a perfect level,
by means of bridges, mounds of earth, or cutting a little from
the tops of hills—then a tract of caft iron is laid for each wheel,
which is concave, and rifes above the road about a foot ; the
carriages having their wheels made convex to fit the tract, fo
that the carriage runs upon a fmooth furface, on level ground,
and by this means one horfe can draw as much as four on the
ordinary roads. One horfe carriages are in moft ufe here ; but
one man will conduct five or fix along thefe roads, at thofe
feafons of the year, when the interchange of commodities takes
place between the diftricts : at other times the roads are
not much occupied, except in leading to and from the fields,
or on the *feventh* day, which, as in other countries,
is a day of ceffation from labour—and, confequently, devoted
to pleafure and recreation. It is on thofe days that they mount
their wicker coach, which is impelled forward, not by the power
of horfes, but by the force of the perfons within, who, turning
a crank, gives motion to the axle-tree and wheels fixed thereon.
Along the roads above defcribed, thefe carriages move with in-
credible fwiftnefs, and are turned at pleafure, by the action of a
fet of reins, upon the fore wheels which are made, as in other
four-wheel'd carriages.

Thefe roads, though they require a great induftry to perfect
them at firft, are eafily kept in repair. I have been told, that
one of them extends above 500 miles, befides the fmaller

branches which run into it.

Here are no idle people employed to collect tolls, nor annui-
tants living in splendid idleness upon the profits of these tolls :
indeed it would be endless to recount the many institutions
which are found necessary in barbarous countries, to patch up a
bad government ; but which are not wanting, because unnecessary, in the perfect government of Lithconia. For example—
of what use would an infirmary be here, where not only the
sick, but those in health, are all maintained from the public stock
—or an insurance company from fire, where no loss can fall
upon an individual—Or banks, where there are no bills to dis-
count—Or hospitals for poor, where there are no poor—Or for
orphans, where there are no orphans—Or Magdalens, where
there are no prostitutes to reform. In a word, there is no charitable institutions of any kind. In this country charity remains
where nature placed it—in the heart.

Although they are not destitute of religion, I could perceive
neither an order of men, nor a place, dedicated to divine worship. That part of the duty of the priesthood, which consists
in teaching morality, is chiefly practised by the old men, who
have made eloquence their favourite pursuit.

The principal theme of their declamation, is the evil of idleness, and waste of the public stores—from whence (say they)
proceeds the judgment of famine, upon the whole land. Indeed
their morality is so intimately interwoven with their constitution
and laws, that a stranger would find it a hard matter to distinguish whether their discourses belonged properly to law or religion—whether it was a priest, or lawyer, that spoke—when it
was neither one nor the other. Their religion is the love of
order and harmony, their constitution and laws, is that order
and harmony systemized.

As to the mysterious rites of their religion, which I did not
understand. I shall say nothing, only that they appeared to consist chiefly of vocal and instrumental music and dancing, in which
every person joined, and was always performed in the open air.
Every instrument was also equally sacred. The organ has no
peculiar privileges here. String'd instruments have the preference of wind instruments, in general, because the performer
can play and sing at the same time ; for without a vocal accom-
panyment, instrumental, in the opinion of the Lithconians, is
only half music. When they play in concert, which they sometimes do, with a thousand voices and instruments ; it is always
some studied piece adapted to the occasion—the grandeur and
harmony of which would astonish an inhabitant of the barbarous
nations of Europe, unaccustomed as they are, to such concerts.
But when an individual performs it is always an extempore
piece, except when they are either learning to play, or practi-
sing for the public festivals ; for it would be deemed puerile to
amuse themselves with the lessons even of the greatest masters.
The subject of these extempore pieces is always love, or religion,
or more properly devotion ; for they seem to have no idea of
any other subject being adapted for music ; and therefore they
have no hunting, historical, drinking or war songs ; nevertheless
beautiful descriptions of nature are not wanting in their songs of

love. Mufic may be confidered here as a principal branch of liberal education. If the word *liberal* be a proper expreffion where a thing is rather *taken* than *beftowed*.

Education, or inftruction, is beftowed or held out, to every member of the community alike ; but fome, as in every other country, not having fo great a genius, talent or capacity, for knowledge, as others, will not imbibe fo great a quantity.

Painting, and the lovers of that fublime art, are held in high eftimation. All the workfhops are ornamented with the labors of young men and women, whofe genius has led them to ftudy that noble art.

There are alfo few young men or women, of bright parts, but who are taught the art of printing—there being one printing-prefs to each diftrict, with a fufficient number of types of various founts. Every perfon is at liberty to ufe them under the direction of a fenior, and to throw off a limited number of fheets. at fpare hours, of any piece of his own production ; but if the work be judged of fufficient importance, by the grand affembly, and time can be fpared from the neceffary labours of the ftate, it is then ordered that a certain number of copies be printed in the ordinary time of labour, and diftributed to the diftricts.

It has been already obferved, that there are in Lithconia, no foldiers by profeffion ; but it muft alfo be obferved, that every man is a defender of his country, and obliged to learn the art of acting in the field together, as foldiers in other countries ; for under the old government, and during the infancy of the new, they had been fo frequently attacked by their ambitious neighbours, that it was found neceffary to continue the ufe of arms.

Every male is furnifhed with a compleat fet of arms and accoutrements, as foon as he arrives at the age of 18 : for two years he is confidered as in a ftate of pupilage After twenty years every man is claffed in different requifitions—The firft from 20 to 25 ; the fecond from 25 to 30; the third from 30 to 35 ; and the fourth from 35 to 40—and the laft clafs includes all the healthy male citizens above forty.

When the firft requifition is called out, they are officered by the oldeft men of the fecond, and when the fecond are called out, they are in like manner officered by the oldeft men of the third and fo on—but when the nation rifes in mafs, all the officers are taken from the fenior clafs, or men above 50—And at all times the commander of any expedition, confifting of 1000 men, is taken from the clafs of feniors. Nothing can be fo eafy as to raife and organize an army upon this plan.

Upon the firft fuppofition of an invafion, the firft requifition are ordered to be in readinefs, to march towards that quarter, from whence the attack is expected, together with all thofe in their 30th year—thefe are all officers, and the whole is divided into as many fmall divifions as there are officers: Every thoufand is then put under the command of a fenior, who organizes his regiment in the following manner : The right wing, confifting of 500 men, is commanded by the oldeft man among the clafs of officers, and the left wing by the next eldeft—he next divides each wing into two grand divisions, giving the command of these to the four next eldest—He then proceeds to divide each grand division into two divisions, and gives the command of these to the eight next eldest, and so on, continually dividing till there are no officers left. All of whom are armed with long pikes.

Formerly, when an invasion had actually taken place, the men of the second requisition were generally called on, and they were either marshaled into separate regiments, or mixed with the first requisition, as was deemed most advantageous for defence or annoyance ; but, in general, they were kept separate. I was not informed of their having any cavalry, for the purpose of fighting, but the troops at a distance from the scene of action, were often transported thither on horseback.

Though they have not had occasion to marshall an army of late years, their young men still learn the art of war. They are taught to fire six times in a minute, and to perform various evolutions—to advance or retreat with either a more extended or more contracted front—to wheel upon the right or left flank, or upon the centre, in order to change their position—all which is performed without any word of command or beat of drum. A standard. with two crosses, is lifted up in the centre, to which all the officers eyes are directed. The first is the signal of attention, which shews the crosses in their natural position—they are then moved by pullies and strings, which pass down the side of the shaft of the standard, and being pulled by the operator at the order of the commander, throws the crosses into various figures, expressive of the movement he means should be performed. Each officer has small crosses upon his pike, with which he repeats the signals to his division. All which can be easily done amidst the greatest confusion and noise of musquetry, cannon, or the cries and groans of the dying. They have signals performed by lights for the night also.

While the island had foreign possessions during the old form of government, they kept up a powerful fleet at an amazing expence, and it was at that time deemed the only sure defence of the island ; but one of their wise reformers, in a small pamphlet, ridiculed the folly of going out to fight their enemies upon the ocean, when they had no longer distant possessions to maintain, with so much success, and demonstrated the wisdom of waiting till their invaders should actually land, when they might be so easily driven into the sea, that the Lithconians agreed to burn the whole fleet, which they actually put in force. Since which they have never thought of fighting upon an element, which has, in its own nature, evils and dangers sufficient, without adding that moral evil, *war*, to the catalogue.

This political philosopher demonstrated, that no nation. who has not distant foreign possessions, have any occasion for ships of war, even if the sea-coast was ever so extensive—and that it would be cheaper, and more certain, to defend the country on shore, than at sea—And in answer to those who objected, that commerce could not be so well defended, it was observed, that commerce was not, particularly, for the benefit of one nation ; but for the reciprocal advantage of all ; and that no individual nation could expect to monopolize the trade of intelligent nations, by warfare, although ignorant countries have been, in former times, deluded and over reached by a superior naval force. Such an instance was never more to be expected in the enlightened state in which nations are at this day—as the juggler hath no more power when his tricks are known. While there were wild and barbarous nations to discover, conquer, and keep in awe, a navy might be of use; but since the world has been discovered, and considerably enlightened, those nations who have a large navy, may, as it is said of Alexander, sit down and weep, that there are no more worlds to conquer; for upon such enterprises their navies depend, as well as formerly did his conquering army.

Such were the subject of the arguments adduced by this political reformer, enforced with such a vein of irony and wit as did not fail, (bursting from the bonds of prejudice as they were) to convince the Lithconians.

———

# HISTORY

## OF THE

## *LITHCONIANS.*

That strange propensity in all nations, of tracing their history to the remotest antiquity, is also to be found in Lithconia.— Like the Jews, they commence the history of their nation, with a fabulous account of the creation. Their first chapter runs so much in the style of the first of Genesis, that if there had so lowed an account of the fall of man, and the flood, we should have been led to think, that the one had been taken from the other—but of these events no mention is made, neither have they any account of a race of giants, or of the sons of God being smitten with the fairness of the daughters of men, so that we must conclude, notwithstanding the similarity, that the first historians of Lithconia were totally unacquainted with the writings of Moses.

Although I only intend to give an abridgement of the histories I have read, and that from memory only, I cannot resist the desire I have of giving the world a few verses of the first chapter as I read it myself—it is in these words.

When the gods began to create the planetary system, this world was only a round globe of liquid matter, of a diameter four times larger than the earth is, moving in the immensity of space, void of inhabitants, and darkness was upon the face of the deep.

And God said, " let there be light," and the spirit of God, exerting itself, on the surface of the waters, produced light, and the revolution from darkness to light was the first epocha.

And God said, let there be a light in the middle of the system, to divide the day from the night, and let it be for seasons, and for days and years.

At this period God made two great lights; the greater light to rule the day, and the reflected light to rule the night:

he made the stars also ; and it was so. This is the second epocha.

And God said, let there be firm land, in the midst of the waters, and let it percolate the fresh from the salt waters.

And God said, let the salt waters be gathered together into one place, and let the dry land appear, and it was so. This is the third epocha.

And God said, let the waters bring forth abundantly the moving creature that hath life ; and God created great whales, and every living creature that moveth, which the waters brought forth abundantly after their kind. This is the fourth epocha.

And God said, let the earth bring forth grafs, the herb yielding seed, and the fruit tree yielding fruit, and it was so. This is the fifth epocha.

And God said, let the earth bring forth the living creature after his kind, cattle and creeping thing, and man to govern and subdue the earth, and all that is therein, and to direct nature to the best end, and it was so. This is the sixth epocha.

After this the historians proceed to relate, that God delegated to man a certain power of directing the principal operations of nature on this globe of the earth.

And the earth teemed with man and beast, and fruits, and herbs, and flowers, which an eternal spring continued in gay succession. And God said unto the men whom he had created, Behold, I have given you the whole earth to inhabit, and have stored it with every thing necessary for use and for enjoyment. I have also given you the means of knowledge, whereby you may discover the road to happiness ; and for your good I have strewed a few difficulties in your paths, to spur you to enquiry, and to exercise the means of knowledge. Consider yourselves as one great family, cherish and comfort each other ; but beware of dividing your patrimony.

So, we never hear of the agency of superior powers, every thing is ascribed to natural causes, or men directing these causes.

Ten millions of years (according to the historians) rolled away in plenty, innocence and peace, without affording matter for the historian, who only delights to record great and terrible events—but abundance for the peaceful muse, whose pleasure is the beauties and the charms of nature. This is called the age of innocence.

While men contented themselves with fruits and herbs, they lived in harmony with the brute creation ; and while their lands were undivided, and the whole stock continued in common, they cultivated peace and friendship with each other. But, in process of time, several causes co-operated to destroy this state of felicity.

The liquid element, or salt sea, was continually diminishing, from two natural causes constantly operating—one was, the immense beds of shell-fish, which being formed from the liquid, but never returning to that element, raised strata of limestone at the bottom of the deep ;—and, secondly, that immense body of water annually converted into vegetable and animal substances, but which never return to water again, caused, in time, new islands to rise above the surface of the ocean, and the old continents to extend further into the clouds. This caused a great inequality, and changed the climates from temperate to a greater degree of heat and cold. Summers became intense, and winters severe. During the age of innocence men multiplied prodigiously on the earth; and therefore a greater foresight was necessary to provide against future contingencies. The necessities of man increased faster than his knowledge—instead of making experiments and inquiring into the operations of nature, in times of plenty and peace; the days were suffered to pass away in pleasure and enjoyment—this lost time has never been recovered in any country, except in Lithconia. They only have improved their situation, by a knowledge of their errors, and made industry and experience get the start of their wants.

The face of the earth changing, by the mountains increasing in height—marshes being formed by the retiring of the waters, rendered the face of the globe more unhealthy, diseases began to appear before man had a knowledge of their cure—the heats of summer caused droughts and a scarcity of herbs, before the use of irrigation was known: thus, a change of climate, an increase of population, and, above all, ignorance—all contributed to bring to a period the age of innocence, and to usher in the age of iron, so called, from men beginning to prey on the inferior animals, and by seeking, in the bowels of the earth, the materials for sharp instruments of destruction. Then began men to be dreaded by his fellow animals, and these, to seek refuge in caverns, rocks, and impenetrable forests, to hide themselves from his view. From this period, for 20 millions of years, nothing is to be found in the history of man worthy of recording, or, if recorded, would give any pleasure to the philanthropic mind. Famine, pestilence, and war, had nearly extinguished the human race—and those who survived, were little superior to the beasts of the forests. Their wants, and the passions those wants created, made man a savage and an hostile animal—so much had they departed from their native innocence, that some have asserted, that man is only a superior species of monkey, capable of improvement, which the common monkies are not.

How deplorable and unsatisfactory would this history have been, if we had not seen, in the foregoing pages, the redemption of man in the country of Lithconia. And from thence the pleasing inference may be drawn, that such will be the case all over the globe. Let it not damp the spirits, or obliterate the hope of the chosen few, that the day of regeneration is slow in its approaches; or that ten millions of years was the short period of the age of innocence, while thirty millions have elapsed, and man has not renewed his nature in any other country but in that small island—But good example is like a grain of mustard-seed.

---

## *Equality* — A Political Romance.

Man had not long commenced a warfare upon the brutes, than they divided themselves into separate hunting parties, for the better securing the prey—and very few generations had elapsed, before these separate hunting parties, forgetting their original, considered themselves as distinct nations,—and, on the slightest offence, cherished the most implacable hatred, rivalship and animosity ; and waged against each other, fell and bloody wars : peace was only brought about, by necessity, and from a fear of being mutually exterminated. Such was the lot of human nature, (with only now and then an effort in some great minds to elevate man to his native dignity) for more than 20 millions of years.

What a number of circumstances must combine before any effort can be successful in favour of human nature ! Time ; place ; the dispositions of the people to receive instruction ; and above all, the powers, or capacity of the instructor to give it— If one of these fail, the process is incomplete, and the condition of our species is thrown back, at least a million of years.

Happily for mankind, the same causes which had put an end to the age of innocence, contributed, in some degree, to put an end to the age of iron, which had made the globe almost a desert, and assisted in putting in train another era, which, though not in itself much preferable to the age of iron, yet tended. in its effects, to bring about the regeneration of the human race : and when we applaud the subsequent revolutions that have taken place in the affairs of mankind, it is not so much on their intrinsic merit as that they are harbingers of that glorious era, when the reign of equality shall be universally established all over the world, and the age of innocence be renewed.

Islands rising above the surface of the ocean-—mountains towering to the clouds—having been the cause of the decline of the age innocence, are now shewn to be the cause of the age of brass.

In a small island, a few leagues from the continent of Europe, a number of people had taken up their hunting quarters, thinking themselves safe from the intrusions of that fiercer enemy, man, on the continent.—But what happened ? In a few years the island was destitute of prey—almost all the quadrupeds were destroyed ; so that those islanders were in the greatest distress imaginable, at a season too when it was hazardous to sail to the continent. In this extremity a council was called, of those reputed the wisest men of the nation, in which it was determined, that the few cattle and sheep remaining, should be caught alive preserved, and domesticated for a breed, to supply the wants of the island. Such a proposition, when first made, was treated with sovereign contempt by the great body of the people, and considered as a thing totally impracticable. The trouble of rearing, and tending of herds and flocks, was deemed too great to be compensated by any profits that could arise from it : however, the necessity of the case, and a conviction of some of the wisest men, made the resolution to be followed.— Patience and perseverance, for a few years, and hope, which every day was growing into certainty, convinced the most sceptical of the propriety of the measure. Now, we may fancy we see the country spread over with herds and flocks—and success in one undertaking always having the effect to stimulate the mind to fresh pursuits, the arts of making cheese and butter, followed almost as a matter of course: it could not fail to strike these men, that every part of the animal might be rendered more useful and commodious, than they had hitherto seen it—hence tanning of hides, and spinning and weaving of wool, were arts which followed each other in quick succession.

These people, living in peace, and at a distance from their turbulent neighbours, increased in population and wealth; and the first evil that presented itself to these otherwise happy people, was a claim that some discontented minds set up to a few choice and particular cattle, which they had paid more attention to in breeding and rearing, than the rest. These contentions and claims growing frequent, and likely to embroil the whole community, it was resolved to divide the flocks, into equal parts among each family; and soon after, by reason of other contentions, a division of the land took place.

Little did those islanders think, that a trifling regulation, made to remedy a great evil, should, in its consequences, disturb the felicity of mankind, and put back the regeneration of the human race for at least ten millions of years.

If we were to enumerate all the evils that have sprung out of this system of separate property, it would fill a volume, and divert us from the main subject of this history. It was from this small island that the larger one of Lithconia was afterwards peopled, and hither they brought their principles of government, founded on the system of separate property. As yet the ground had not been tilled—they lived on milk, some fruit, and the flesh of animals. The first dawn of the pastoral life had many charms, in a country with few inhabitants: the range for their cattle being almost unbounded, they had abundance of leisure to contemplate the beauties and grandeur of nature—hence astronomy, and music, were cultivated, and characters were invented in that age. The poets still sing of the enjoyments of shepherds, and their scenes are laid at that period of time.

Indeed the pastoral life was infinitely superior to the life of a hunter, which preceded it, or to the more stormy scenes which followed after—during the life of a hunter one man was sufficient for every square mile, but during the pastoral life 20 might be maintained on the same spot.

A greater increase of population in either of these stages, brought on poverty contentions and war—in a few hundred years that event took place—the population became too numerous for their manner of life, and they were also liable to frequent invasions, for the sake of plunder, from their neighbours. The first evil that shewed itself, springing from the system of separate property, was, that the people in the interior not being liable to be plundered, would not march to assist their brethren on the coast. Neither would those on the one coast move to the affistance of thofe on the other. As long as a man's own property was fafe, he gave himfelf no cares about his neighbors. In the mean while population increafed—poverty and want was the confequence. While thefe things were going forward, a fortunate event took place, which fhould be recorded as a remarkable zra in the hiftory of man. A few invaders from the continent, had taken poffeffion of a corner of the ifland, both as a fhelter from the iflanders and the ravagers from the main; but being deftitute of herds or flocks, and well knowing that if they attempted to fupply themfelves by depredations, the confequence would be a certain extermination—they therefore attempted to multiply. by art, the fruits and herbs which the peninfula fpontaneoufly produced—their fuccefs furpaffed their moft fanguine expectation, infomuch. that the Lithconians, who had not yet turned up the glebe, and who were confequently in want of fuch articles, made the generous and noble propofal of exchanging the fkins of animals for the fruits and herbage of the peninfulians. What a pity that the name of thefe inhabitants of the peninfula was not tranfmitted to after times—but it is probable they had no name as a diftinct people, but retained that of their anceftors on the continent, until they mixed with the Lithconians. which it is probable they very foon did. Thofe events. which have produced the greateft revolutions in the affairs of mankind, and have fhewn man under a variety of afpects, which have funk his character fometimes below the brutes, and at other times elevated him above the angels, (if there are fuch beings)—having been confidered of little moment at the time they happened, the actors have been fuffered to fink into oblivion, and future hiftorians have paffed them over in filence. Thus we have to lament our ignorance of the people and time when thofe two important events occurred, the firft ploughing of the earth, and the introduction of barter.

The prefent age will hardly believe, that upwards of thirty millions of years had paffed away. before tillage or barter could be introduced among men, though they had frequently been fuggefted and recommended for experiment, by wife men in different ages, feveral millions of years before neceffity. fituation and peculiar circumftances, brought them into ufe.

The hiftorians then proceed to fhew the happinefs and flourifhing ftate of Lithconia, and the increafe of population: as alfo the evils that were averted from that country by the introduction of barter and tillage, and the union of the agricultural and paftoral life. Still they have to lament and defcribe other evils fpringing up out of the fyftem of feparate property and the filly means that were taken, from time to time, to patch up that fyftem. It was too common for children to fall out about the lands and other property of their deceafed parents; and it is equally curious to obferve the various cuftoms that were adopted, and grew up, in different parts of the ifland. At firft, the females were heirs to all the property of the deceafed, and the youngeft fon was heir to the homefted, or dwelling houfe—becaufe it was thought that the females and the youngeft fon would generally be incapable of acquiring property, whereas the eldest, while there was land uncultivated, might easily acquire by their greater experience and strength, new acquisitions —and this plan succeeded very well while there was land capable of improvement, and in cases where the females or youngest son had arrived at the age of maturity, and were capable of managing the property ; but where that was not the case, and the elder sons obliged to take care of the property for the helpless younger branches of a family, they generally embezzled or gave a very bad account to their wards.

Innumerable were the laws and regulations made, from time to time, respecting the rights of individuals to separate property, insomuch that no man knew his own right. From hence a new order of beings sprung up, who, under the pretence of explaining their rights, acquired an authority over the lives and property of their fellow men, which nearly deprived them of all right. In those days the acquisition of property was every thing, and the cunningest knave was the best man.

Such was the progress of evil which arose out of the system of separate property, that nine-tenths of mankind groaned under the most oppressive tyranny, labouring from morning till night for a poor and scanty diet, and hardly clothes to protect them from the inclemency of the seasons, while the other tenth enjoyed every luxury, and rioted in waste and profusion.

But as wealth and property was the object of every man's pursuit, it was, sometimes, hardly gained before it was snatched away by another more dextrous knave; so that it was no unfrequent thing to see the man of affluence reduced to poverty, and the poor man elevated above the necessity of labour, which begat an habit of idleness, which begat disease. The wise man was the slave of a fool, and an idiot commanded the man of talents. All these evils were ascribed to fortune, or to the gods ; and no man dreamt of its being the effects of the system of separate property, agreed to at first by fools, and continued by knaves. However, if the system had been compleat in all its parts, the evils resulting from it would not have been so terrible. This will be better understood by the following explanation.

When nations enjoyed their property in common, during the age of innocence, and while they continued to be hunters, they were then merely numerical societies without any local boundaries—their divisions were into tribes, families and individuals ; and the duties of each were prescribed, without any regard to place ; but when the division of land and separate property commenced. each nation lost its numerical character, or boundary, and assumed a local one. The divisions and subdivisions were also of necessity local, but the misfortune was, that they retained the family division, which is a numerical one.— This ought not to have been done. In a local society or government, there should be no numerical division—nor in a numerical society should there be any local section.

By this inadvertency in their first institutions, nine-tenths of the families were excluded from any local inheritance, and the whole country was in possession of the other tenth.

When tribes was the division under the numerical government, all the children born in the tribe was maintained and educated out of the public stock of the tribe : but when local governments took place by the division of the land then families were left to shift for themselves, and children remained a heavy burthen on parental affection. Nature has, indeed, made that affection very powerful ; but sometimes it has sunk under the weight imposed on it, by this abominable institution. It is fine talking of a social compact, where a pair, who have eight or ten children, are obliged to provide for them all ; and where the society, local or numerical, to which that family is said to belong, takes no share in their burthen. As far as it respects them, it is a dissolution of the social compact, and they would have been justified before God, if they had committed depredations upon such an ill organized society.

After a long term of years and infinite wretchedness, the loud cry of nature was, in some degree, attended to, and a partial return to reason took place, in certain districts, and the extreme of misery was, in a small degree. relieved by private and public institutions. The poor contributed to the support of the poorest, but the rich, who governed every thing, made a great shew of charity, without doing any real good—the bread was by them snatched from the mouth of the indigent, that part of it might be returned in ostentatious alms.

This misery and distress of families, prevented prudent people from entering into the state of matrimony, and by this means half the women were thrown into a state of prostitution, disease and infamy—Which, however distressing such a life must be, it was often preferred to the still more miserable condition of being obliged to support a large family of children.

In those miserable times, when men saw the innumerable evils with which they were surrounded, they could not help enquiring sometimes into the cause of it ; and it astonishes the Lithconians that their ancestors were so stupid as not to discover, with a very little reflection, that those evils sprung out of the division of property. But their wonder ought to cease when it is known, that the rich actually paid and maintained an order of men to teach the people, that all the evils which afflict the generations of men were appointed by God the Supreme Ruler,—that a little good, mixt with a great deal of evil, had always been, and always would be, the lot of humanity ; so that it was of no use to repine, or study how to avoid that which was unavoidable. To make this matter more feasible to the wretched poor, these hired deceivers told them, that the possession of wealth was the cause of still more misery—that the poor had many enjoyments, whereas with riches it was impossible to be happy ; and to crown all, they pretended to receive these hellish doctrines from God himself.

That such a state of things was permitted for a time, by the Almighty. is not to be denied : but since we have seen, that the happiness of man. in society, altogether depends upon their own wisdom in organizing their communities, and forming their institutions, and that God has provided no other means but the united wisdom and reason of men to work out their happiness on earth, it must be highly criminal in those who obstruct its operation and prevent the full exercise of reason and enquiry.

However, to shew that this state of things was not useless, and that although mind was fettered in one way, it had free scope in others. This was the age in which the genius and powers of the mind were displayed more than in any other—— It might be very properly termed, the age of invention—So many thousands of families without any inheritance were continually striving to make the most of their ingenuity and wit, and it would fill a volume itself to describe the various means by which men of genius converted every thing to their use—the wealth of the rich and the labour of the industrious.

It is certain that the Lithconians, with all their system of equality, are indebted for the principal part of their enjoyments, and even their art of government, to the state of things we are now speaking of. It was evidently a link in that great chain of events, which is certainly drawing mankind to a state of happiness on earth. It had been a dogma of the schools, that God created the world out of nothing, by the word of his power, and for this reason they have complained against their Maker, because all his operations are not performed in the same manner, because in many cases, especially in that of the perfection of the social system, he has employed the agency of finite beings; because his purposes are to be accomplished by wisdom, acquired by experience, which necessarily supposes time. Nature is a wonderful machine, put in motion by immense power, and all its operations are consequently precognizable by that wisdom which contrived it. But they would change this admirable order, and have a nature which, like an instrument in the hands of power, might be used to correct the general principles of being.————The Lithconians are contented to use the means which God hath appointed to accomplish human happiness, namely, the united reason of man; and, finding that sufficient, smile at their forefathers for expecting any immediate interference of the Gods.

But what gave me the most entertainment in this part of the history, while it made me blush at the folly of the times, was, the absurdity, not to say criminality of some of their laws.

It was difficult for me to conceive the design of some of them; but I could easily discover that the greater part were framed for the purpose of keeping the power in the hands of those who governed, and seldom with any view to the public happiness.

It was strictly forbidden for any person to scratch, however he might itch, without permission; and it was held infamous to perform the necessary evacuations before a certain hour in the day. In some places no person was admitted to eat flesh till they arrive at a certain age, and whatever kind of meat was chosen at the first time, must be the person's food for life, however it might disagree with the appetite—This meat was also chosen without tasting, and frequently without seeing it. It is not difficult to conceive the innumerable evils that must follow

from such an obvious opposition to the principles of nature—
But what appeared worst of all, was, that few of their laws extended to every member of the community, and notwithstanding there were laws prohibiting murder, robbery, larceny, swindling, cheating, extortioning and idleness, yet there were various classes of men who were licensed to commit these crimes—
For example, there was a class of privileged murderers, who were held in high estimation and honour—another class of avowed robbers, equally respected. The class of swindlers were very numerous, and lived in great pomp. The cheats were looked up to with the most profound reverence and holy fear. And the extortioners, as they were only licensed from year to year, though they were not considered so honorable as the other classes, yet held a considerable rank in the country, and as it was a lucrative trade, and raised the envy of the other classes, the journeymen murderers were frequently quartered upon them ; to keep the one down, and raise the spirits of the others ; for murder was but a lean trade, though it was, of all others, the most honourable, and was also a proof of honour—for if a murderer's honor was called in question, he had only to appoint a time, when he would, before witnesses, murder or be murdered, to prove how very honorable he was.

To support, and do greater honor to these classes of men, severe punishment were inflicted upon those, who, in any manner, degraded, dishonored, or opposed their interest. For example, when the class of murderers was required to be filled up, if a man refused to join them he was put in prison, and otherwise severely handled, till at last he was forced to comply ; and if afterwards any qualms of conscience should happen to seize him, and he was induced to run away from a scene of iniquity which would have harrowed up the soul of a reasonable being, he was, for the first offence, flogged most severely, and shot for a coward for the second.

As an encouragement to the licensed extortioners who dealt in the necessary article of drink, other people who were contented with a reasonable profit, were prohibited from selling it in small quantities to the poor, under severe penalties, which ruined many an industrious honest man.

As the deceivers could only be detected by the free use of reason and investigation, this faculty was cried down as dangerous to civil society ; and, *doubt*, that state of the mind which calls forth the exercise of reason, was threatened with eternal punishment. In short, every person was deterred by temporal or eternal punishments, either by the laws of fools or the prejudices created by knaves, from using the faculties given him by the God of nature, to discover the tricks of the class of deceivers. As for the public robbers, that class of privileged thieves, pretending as they did, to rob by rule, and steal under the sanction of law, having also the whole class of murderers at their nod, it was in vain to resist them.

There must have been a wonderful sympathy between those classes—they cherished and protected each other with a zeal which astonishes ; and as all the officers of government and legislators were generally in one or other of these classes, we need not be surprized that their laws were numerous, and all calculated for the benefit and protection of themselves.

But the idlers, the most powerful and influential class in the state, because they possessed all the land, was, perhaps, of all others, the most pernicious and destructive—they were the canker worms which preyed upon the vitals of the people—they were protected in the high privilege of doing nothing, by a variety of statutes, denominated poor laws, and laws against vagabonds. It was highly criminal in any person not of this class to turn vagabond. They were right in one respect, for no state can maintain many of these.

In those days, men were so ignorant as to believe, that this class had no right to work, or any social duties to perform, and when any of them yielded to this dictate of nature, it was considered as an extraordinary act of virtue and uncommon merit.

We shall now hasten to that part of the history which gives an account of the revolutions which led them to the genuine system of property. It appears, as has been already observed, that for many thousands of years there had been always men of superior talents, who considered all the evils, with which they saw themselves surrounded, had certainly their origin in the folly of human institutions ; and, that the remedy was within the power of human reason, if it could only be exerted to that end. But these men were continually watched, and persecuted, by the privileged classes above mentioned ; and, particularly, by the class of deceivers, who were urged on by the robbers, and abetted by the swindlers, &c.

Notwithstanding the intelligent class saw the pernicious tendency of the others, their artillery was directed only against the deceivers, by this means the other classes, not seeing themselves attacked, either stood neutral, or joined the intelligent class. The deceivers, thus abandoned, soon lost their influence, and the lies by which they had imposed upon mankind, were every day detected. No sooner was the power of the deceivers abridged and investigation laid open, in some measure, to the people, than they began to suspect the class of public robbers ; and the men of intelligence, seeing the people on their side, took courage, called in question their right of plunder ; and, what was fortunate for them was, that the murderers took part against the robbers, and their power was also very much curtailed, though the class still had an existence, and continued to commit great depredations on the community.

The intelligent class now become so formidable, and were so much respected by the people, as to create a considerable alarm in the minds of the privileged orders, but it was too late ; reason could not be made to take a retrograde movement, but she unfortunately became stationary, for a considerable time.

It appeared then, even to the most intelligent, that every thing depended on the form of government. One form, namely monarchy, was universally condemned ; but it was not so clearly seen what would produce the happiest result, and lead the human race to a state of felicity, suitable to their nature. Long after it was acknowledged, that men had the right of self-government, the privileged claffes (which ftill continued to exift, though not to be fo formidable) were afraid of trufting men with that power, to its full extent.

Certain fundamental principles of government, or what was then called conftitutions, were not to be touched or altered, but at certain periods by felect individuals, and much formality.—whatever might be the general op'nion concerning them ; and, as we have mentioned in the firft part of this work, notwith-ftanding they confidered thefe conftitutions, or forms of government, as the foundation of human happinefs, it was not eafy to pleafe the privileged claffes in this particular ; and, therefore, we find them often changed, without ever producing any confiderable alteration on the fum of human happinefs.—Public plunder was ftill carried on—The murderers indeed were not fo often employed, but they were ftill a feparate clafs, and treated with refpect. The fwindlers did more bufinefs than ever, living on the contentions naturally bred out of the fyftem of feparate property. The idlers were ftill as numerous, fo that the on y benefit that accrued, for a long time, was the humiliation of the deceivers, and the elevation of the mortal enemies of all the claffes, the intelligent beings.

After having experienced the truth of thefe lines of a cele-brated poet,

*For forms of government let fools conteft—*
*Whatever is beft adminiftered is beft.*

The world feemed to be fatisfied, that election and reprefenta-tion, and a total annihilation of the clafs of deceivers, if not the beft poffible form, would ultimately lead to it.——Accord-ingly, men of intelligence having feen this point gained, were determined to try the ftrength of reafon, and to mark its ef-fects, in changing the condition of human fociety. It was foon difcovered, that a great portion of the evils of which mankind complain, lurked under the laws, unperceived, and unqueftion-ed, by reafon of the facred character they had affumed. Rea-fon would have nothing facred, fhe now entered boldly into the fanctuary of the law, as fhe had before done into the fanctuary of the deceivers. Every law which militated againft the eter-nal principles of juftice and reafon was profcribed, and it was thought better to have no rule of conduct than one which ad-mitted uncertainty or doubt ; and it was founded upon this principle, that where there is no law there is no tranfgreffion.—Jurors began to give in their verdict, in thefe words,—" *The law is filent*"—or when the firft lawyers of the country dif-covered a diverfity of opinion, by long harangues, and nume-rous quotations, the jury was fure to bring in a verdict of, *The law is obfcure*, from which verdict no judge could pafs a fentence of punifhment. Such conduct frequently occurring, among ra-tional jurors, had two good effects ; firft, to make legiflators more attentive and correct ; and fecond, to banifh from the bar, that hoft of fwindlers who had been fo long fanning the flames of difcord, and living on the contentions of their fellow citi-zens. It was not long after the clafs of fwindlers had been swept from the courts of justice, and the legislators had simplified the laws, before the inutility of the judges themselves was apparent, and jurors, as has been mentioned in the first part of this work, were found adequate to all the purposes of distributive justice.

In those days it seemed to be the first object in the attention of intelligent men, to endeavor, with all their might, to bring law and justice into union ; and the genuine system of property began to be spoken of, as no visionary phantom, but as a *good*, which might be realized. Philosophers mentioned it in terms of approbation, and the people listened with attention : but the class of idlers, which was the only formidable class that remained, was its bitter and avowed enemies.

Every man of reflection, saw that a revolution in the system of property of such magnitude, could not be accomplished without great difficulty, and hazarding the peace of society, and the wisest were puzzled to find an opening that would admit an entering wedge. But when men are zealous in a cause, and never lose sight of the darling object, occasions will present themselves which would otherwise be overlooked, and which the attentive and intelligent observer, seizes with avidity.———— When by the force of the elective principle the people had placed men of intelligence, their steady friends, into the legislature, it became a maxim, that as long as moral evil existed, a government could not be called the best possible, it was presumable that there was still occasion for the exertion of his faculties, and that it was folly to look beyond the moon, for remedies which, if infinite wisdom rules on high, must be placed within his grasp.

The evils which called forth the attention of the men of these times, and produced considerable agitation, was the care society as such, ought to take of the aged, the lunatic, the widow, orphan, illegitimate children and their mothers, and finally, to put an end to prostitution, and the diseases which accompany it. It was proposed that an adequate provision should be made, by law, for people reduced to the above circumstances ; and the idlers, fearing that the burden should principally fall on this class, wished to have no alteration or innovation upon the ancient practice, or if any thing was done, it should be by a tax that should operate equally upon the citizens ; and as for the mothers of illegitimate children and their offspring, and the whole host of prostitutes and their encouragers, nothing but the severest punishment, said they, could put a stop to the growing evil, which, it is true, had encreased to an alarming degree, ever since the threatenings of eternal punishment had ceased with the class of deceivers.

On the contrary it was insisted on, by the intelligent, that society were bound to relieve every kind of distress, brought on by the operations of nature—That getting children was an irresistible dictate of nature, and ought not to be held as a crime, or subject to punishment ; that prostitution was an excrescence from a bad law, which would perish when the law which gave it being, ceased to exist : and in order to find a stepping stone by which the river might be croffed, it was propofed, inftead of a tax, that the laws of defcent fhould be altered, and the benefits arifing therefrom, extended to thofe objects of, what was then called, charity. In a word, the law of defcent was confined to the defcendant in a right line ; and thofe of a collateral branch were cut off from the fucceffion.

It was therefore enacted, that all real and perfonal eftates which had no heirs in a right line fhould be vefted in the nation for the benefit of that defcription of people above enumerated, whom the ancient inftitutions had abandoned to chance, to infamy, or at beft, to a miferable and fcanty fubfiftence.

The natural operation of this law, in a fhort time, made an ample provifion for thofe who had before been the outcafts of fociety. It had alfo that effect, which was forefeen by the promoters of it, namely, to prevent young women of no fortune from entering into the ftate of matrimony,—they faw that themfelves and their offspring would be treated with more care and attention, from that fund, than they poffibly could be, by the induftry of the beft man that ever exifted—from that moment there were few marriages, except among the rich—fo that while the funds were increafing, the objects which it were deftined to funport were increafing alfo.

At the commencement of this inftitution, thefe baftards were put apprentices to mechanical arts, at the age of 15 ; at 21 a handfome fum was beftowed on them to begin the world ; but, as it frequently happened, that thefe young people faw their children educated under the fame inftitution, and whatever fortunes they might gain in life naturally, or rather lawfully defcended to the fame fund—they procured a law by which they were permitted to remain attached to the inftitution from this period. that part of the community who poffeffed feparate property, were every year diminifhing in number, and they faw themfelves fubjected to a thoufand cares and anxieties from which thofe who lived in common were totally exempt ; while at the fame time all the riches and property of the nation was running with a rapid current into the aggregate fund.

This ftate of fociety is defcribed by the hiftorians as being very ftormy and factious ; when the two parties became nearly balanced, the feparate property-men who ftill had the government in their hands. and being preffed for money, as all fuch governments are, propofed to feize upon the aggregate property. and fell it, as they faid, for the benefit of the nation. but the equal right men who had laboured indefatigably to render the aggregate fund beneficial to thofe, whom the law had placed under its protection, were convinced that it would be better for mankind, and produce a greater fum of happinefs, if all the property in the community were under like regulations, and many men of intelligence, though poffeffed of great fortunes, thought it to their advantage, to fink it in the aggregate fund, rather than expofe their children to the caprice of fortune. Thefe contentions continued for many years—in the mean while the families poffeffing feparate property were grow-

ing fewer in number: they saw themselves loaded with a thousand anxieties, from which those who lived under the genuine
system of property were totally exempt. Pride, however, for
a long time, prevented them from joining the institution, and
the same pride pushed on the society to take every step which
should render the members of it comfortable and happy.

To give retirement and peace to the aged, every person after
the age of 60, was exempted from duty: and to give wisdom
and experience to their councils, the principle of election was
laid aside for that of seniority, which had an effect, not at first
foreseen, that of producing almost perfect unanimity.

---

# THE COUP D'ÉTAT OF 1961

Henry Dwight Sedgwick

# THE COUP D'ÉTAT OF 1961

Now that a generation has passed since the disturbed events of which I write, and that most of the actors therein have died, it is possible to sketch, with an impartiality that would have been well-nigh impossible heretofore, the circumstances under which the present Imperial Dynasty mounted the throne of the Americas. Some men still regard the final acts of the drama as so many parricidal thrusts, whereas others heap praises on praises upon the great protagonist. My purpose is to give a brief account of the facts as accurately as I can, not extenuating, not exaggerating, not setting down anything with political bias.

In the ten years from 1950 to 1960 the social and political changes in the United States presaged great events. Scientific discovery was the apparent root of the good or evil. Mr. Phillips and Professor Czerny in their laboratory discovered the marvelous effects produced by radio-electric discharges upon the chemical constituents of the soil. Their most ingenious subsoil batteries by some

method, not yet fully understood, affected
the properties of sand and gravel to such a
degree that they were converted into pseudo-
vegetable mold, and with very slight expense
land which had been a desert became productive to an extraordinary extent. The desert lands of Arizona, New Mexico, and Utah
brought forth crops that the banks of the
Nile could not rival. The application of these
wonderful scientific discoveries was due entirely to the will and energy of the man who
at that time was plain Robert Campbell.

Campbell was born in Ohio, of Scotch-Irish
parentage. He was educated at the public
schools, and when a lad of fourteen was employed by Mr. Phillips in his laboratory as an
assistant. The boy learned far more quickly
than his master the value of the discoveries.
He left the laboratory, returned at the end
of three years with a few thousand dollars,
bought the apparently valueless patents, and
put them to use in some land in Arizona
bought at fifty cents an acre. The history of
the next ten years of his life is the story of
the development of the arid regions in the
southwestern part of the country. The desert
bloomed like a rose. Immigrants swarmed

from every country in Europe. The population of Arizona increased a million a year. Men who had earned twenty cents a day found themselves rich. Wheat, corn, rice, and potatoes grew as if by magic in an abundance sufficient to feed the world. Citizenship was granted within a month after declaration of an intention to renounce the old allegiance, and a vast number of immigrants were admitted to the franchise without any knowledge of republican institutions or any interest in them. Mr. Campbell acquired fabulous wealth. Wherever land was barren, there he was besought to bring his healing touch, and in payment of fruitfulness he always took a mortgage upon the land. In seven states his political power was despotic; he controlled conventions; he selected members of Congress; he named the senators. He was the idol of the small proprietors, their savior from the oppression of the great eastern capitalists; he had found them degenerate and on the way to becoming peasants, he raised them to the most compact and important class in the country.

It was about this time that our war with England broke out. President Schmidt hated the English, and did all in his power to provoke war: he persuaded Congress to make discrimination in the tariff to the injury of England and in favor of Germany; and with no color of excuse he closed the Panama Canal to all vessels flying the British flag; he violated the rules of neutrality in the revolt of South Africa, known as the Second Boer War, and insulted the British Ambassador at a reception in the White House. It is supposed that Schmidt provoked the war for the aggrandizement of himself and his family. Our ships, it was officially said, excelled the British in every particular, and outnumbered them three to two; but the successful termination of the war was due, not to our naval victories, — for by some mischance we were vanquished in the two engagements off Long Island, — but to the fact that England was put on starving rations the day war was declared. This country, with its marvelous development under the Campbell-Czerny patents, had become England's butcher and greengrocer; and the moment supplies were stopped the price of food there went up sixty-fold. The result of the war was that Great Britain ceded to us her Chinese provinces, while we, on our part, agreed not to discriminate against her either in the tariff or in regard to the Panama Canal. These Chinese provinces, added to our own, made an empire of four hundred millions of people, and as the President, under decisions of the Supreme Court, had, by virtue of the authority appertaining to him as *Pater Patriæ*, complete control, he appointed Campbell, then believed to be in his interest, governor-general. It seemed that China had always affected Campbell's imagination, and he wished very much to go there. From his memoirs, however, we know that he believed that China would be the battlefield in the great international struggle for the domination of the world, and therefore he wished to study the country himself. He went there in 1958, and remained nearly two years. As usual, the country where he went bourgeoned and bloomed. His administration was admirable, — efficiency was established, dishonesty stopped; he ruled despotically, but with absolute justice. The Chinese revenues doubled in the first year. Campbell's personal popularity was immense, and rumor accused him of an ambition to become Emperor of China.

At this time, however, matters were going

ill in America. At the end of ten years the
wonderful richness imparted to the soil by the
radio-electric treatment departed as mysteri-
ously as it had begun. The great fabric of
prosperity fell with its foundation. Half the
farmers in the country, and all those in the
so-called Campbell states, became bankrupt.
Distress spread from the farmers to the
manufacturing interests. Railroads fell off in
their dividends, factories closed, failure succeeded failure. Of the great cities San Francisco suffered most, as it was the port of
shipment for all the grain exported to Asia;
but Chicago and New York shared in the
losses. The trouble was increased by the fact
that, after the war with England, all Europe
succeeded in making treaties establishing a
common tariff against the United States.
The respective European governments at last
understood that it was a struggle between
continents; their mutual jealousies were laid
aside, and a commercial compact was made
between them. In spite of these mishaps the
country did not lose confidence in Campbell.

The financial crisis in the United States
was reached in October, 1960, shortly before
the presidential election. There was division

in the ranks of the Republican party because, while President Schmidt, who had served two terms, desired to serve a third term or else have his son, Hugo Schmidt, nominated, several powerful senators had their own ambitions, and were rigorously opposed, as they declared, to permitting the president's office to become hereditary in the Schmidt family. The Democratic and Socialist parties, though small and broken into petty groups, having dwindled to almost nothing during the ten fat years, began to show their heads. New England had a party of its own, and hinted at secession. The House of Representatives, consisting, of course, solely of nominees of the senators, divided in the same way as the Senate; but as the House had long ceased, except in theory, to be a coördinate branch of the legislature, its actions were of slight importance. The Republican convention had been held in the beginning of October. In the last century it used to be held in June or July, but since the time when the election of the president became determined by the action of the Republican convention, there had been no need for a long political campaign. There was a great struggle between the Schmidts and their adversaries ; but the President had used his patronage lavishly, and Wall Street, fearing that a change in the government might add to the business difficulties, spent money with unexampled daring, and Hugo Schmidt was nominated by the convention.

The country had for some thirty years been governed by an oligarchy represented by the Senate. Almost every great combination of capital had its senator; in fact, it had become the custom for a retiring president of a billionaire corporation to enter the Senate, and continue to watch over its interests. Had it not been for the singular concatenation of events that produced the great panic, the system might have lasted indefinitely. Property was gradually settling in strata ; the capitalists coalesced into a natural aristocracy, the professions constituted an upper middle class, the tradespeople a lower middle class, and as soon as the agricultural interests had been properly handled, the actual farmers would gradually have developed into an American equivalent for a peasantry. But that was not to be. No sooner was Hugo Schmidt nominated than disaffection appeared. Senator Mason of Massachu-

setts refused to be bound by the action
of the convention, and New England acted
with him; Senators Brown of Washington,
Petersen of Minnesota, and Elkinhorn of Alabama followed his example. The Campbell
states held a convention by themselves
and declared for Campbell. The Schmidts
acted with their usual vigor: they offered
Campbell the office either of Secretary of
State or of Vice-Suzerain of South America;
they took all possible measures to secure
election officers favorable to their interest
throughout the United States; they issued
a proclamation depriving Chile of all legal
rights, as punishment for its late revolt,
and offered its land as public property to all
loyal citizens who should receive the proper
certificates from Washington. The President
sent a mandate to the members of the Supreme Court, then away for the summer
recess, to convene in Washington, and ordered various regiments to the chief cities
of his opponents. His adversaries were not
idle. In New England members of the Republican convention who had supported
Schmidt were indicted for high treason on
the charge of attempting to make the office

of president hereditary, and bills were filed
in the United States Courts to restrain
election officers from printing the name of
Schmidt's electors on the official ballots.
Campbell sailed at once from Hong Kong,
and arrived in San Francisco on October 9,
after a voyage of four days. There he met
his supporters, and issued a proclamation to
the effect that the action of the Republican
convention was illegal and void for bribery
and corruption; that the convention which
had nominated him was regular and valid;
that he was the only legal candidate in the
field, and that he would support and maintain the Constitution, cost him what it might.
Possession of the vast machinery of the
government in all its parts, and the custom
of the voters apathetically to vote the Republican ticket, were likely to give the
Schmidts victory, but Campbell was fertile
in resources.

It so happened that on October 13 there
was a panic in every stock exchange in the
country; railroad bonds fell off twenty to
forty points; industrial stocks went up and
down like feathers in the wind; but the
great blows fell upon government bonds.

The issues for the extravagant undertakings of the administration in the years of prosperity, especially for the construction of automobile roads and for the maintenance of our garrisons in South America and in China, had been enormous. The country had played the prodigal; it was said that every tradesman had a country house, and every gentleman kept his yacht; and now the balloon had burst and everybody was bruised. Government bonds fell on October 13 from 130 to 110, on the 14th to 95, on the 15th to 60. People thought that the country was ruined forever; men lost their heads, and acted as if crazed; America, the envy of the world, seemed to fall like Lucifer. On the morning of the 16th Robert Campbell entered the clubrooms of the New York Stock Exchange. He was dressed in his undress uniform as governor of the Chinese provinces,—loose white trousers with a purple sash and a loose white silk shirt with a gold collar, and over it a light purple cloak with a border of peacock feathers. His rugged face, cold and calm, with bushy eyebrows, and deep wrinkles around the mouth, looked like bronze. It was one minute before eleven o'clock, the hour of opening the Exchange, and the brokers were all gathered together. Everybody was there, eleven senators and two hundred and forty representatives, who were accustomed to make the New York Stock Exchange their headquarters when Congress was not in session, also many distinguished citizens. Campbell's entrance was the signal for great excitement; reporters crowded about, hindering the senators in their attempts to greet him. "What will he do, what will he do?" buzzed through the hall. Campbell, who always had a touch of the theatrical in his temperament, motioned the reporters aside, and, bowing somewhat coldly to the senators, asked for his broker. Sonnenschein rushed up and began to whisper. "There is no need for whispers, Mr. Sonnenschein," said Campbell, in a voice loud enough to be heard through the hall; "Robert Campbell is ready to sacrifice his private fortune for his country. You will buy government bonds till my last dollar shall be spent." A cheer went up; the reporters rushed off to telegraph the news over the world; the clock struck eleven, and Sonnenschein's firm bought government bonds as fast as they could buy. The price rose to 70, to 90, to 110; Campbell bought and bought for immediate delivery; the great bank, known as the " Senate's Own," honored his checks for millions of dollars. The news spread abroad; crowds besieged the Exchange; everybody tried to buy government bonds, and the whole market rallied and rose; bonds and stocks got up like sick men from their beds; the scene outdoes description; merchants who were ready for bankruptcy became rich men again; savings banks which had closed the day before opened their doors, paying and receiving thousands of deposits. At the close of business hours the whole country smiled, like a withered land after a rain. How Campbell was able to pay for the vast amounts of bonds which he had purchased, whether he had used the Chinese funds, as his enemies said, whether he bought and then sold again to himself as the market rose, or whether he and his friends had managed to put their money together for this great political stroke, are questions that everybody asked and Campbell never publicly answered. However it was, the panic had ended, and Robert Campbell

had won the reputation of being the ablest
and most patriotic man in the land.

The next day the public learned that he
was closeted with the governor and the district attorney for New York County. These
men belonged to the Schmidt faction, but
rumor said that Campbell had saved them
both from beggary, for they were specula-
tors. The day after, a special court of Oyer
and Terminer was held, a special grand jury
summoned, and that same night the two
senators of New York, the two of Pennsylvania, and one of Connecticut, together with
the president and half the board of direc-
tors of the New York Stock Exchange (all
of Schmidt's party), were indicted for con-
spiracy with the intent fraudulently to injure and destroy certain railroad properties,
largely affected by the late panic. Excitement was raised to fever point when the
judge refused bail and the alleged conspirators were locked up in the city prison. The
Schmidt partisans were very angry. They
obtained a decree from the United States
Circuit Court quashing the indictments, but
the state courts refused to acknowledge its
authority. Then they applied to the governor,

who answered that the law must take its course. The President instructed the United States Marshal to release the prisoners; the Marshal took a posse, but the city police prevented them from approaching the jail; the Marshal telegraphed to the President for soldiers, and the President ordered five regiments to the city. The governor called out the militia; there was every prospect of civil war; the country turned instinctively to Campbell. The next day news was radiographed from the Atlantic to the Pacific that Campbell had gone to the state court and offered himself as bail for the prisoners; his bail was accepted, and they were released.

Election day drew near, attended by excitement without parallel. Campbell went all over the country, showering money in gifts to persons whom he was pleased to call his " indigent fellow citizens," as a slight endeavor on his part to repair the great wrongs done to them and the country by the " New York conspirators." The election was at last held on November 6; there were riots in all the great cities, many voting machines were smashed, and thousands of voters deprived of their votes, but the automatic official count

returned Schmidt first, Campbell second, and
Elkinhorn of Alabama third. The newspapers resounded with cries of fraud; Elkinhorn mustered out the militia in the Gulf
states to support his claim; but Campbell
announced that, though he had been deprived of the high office by gross fraud, he
would seek no redress, in the fear lest his
country might suffer. To the general surprise
he returned to China. Those friends who were
not in his inner counsels could not understand
his action except on the ground of true patriotism, and his popularity with them became
almost a passion. Campbell's course made
Elkinhorn's movement ridiculous; the militia
disbanded, Elkinhorn was arrested on the
charge of high treason, but was soon released,
as the country plainly showed its desire to
avoid internal troubles and return to business,
for industry everywhere felt the disastrous
effects of the panic.

Affairs remained in this condition till the
end of February, when preparations for the
inauguration of Hugo Schmidt (Schmidt the
Second, as his enemies called him) were being
made. Campbell was invited to be present,
and accepted; he landed in San Francisco on

February 24, and proceeded to Washington. His friends hailed him as a hero returned from exile, and he spoke at every town on the road, briefly alleging that the first duty of an American was to obey the law, that only in this way would the country be enabled to fulfill its great duties toward God and civilization in the manner in which it had so gloriously done theretofore. On the morning of the 2d of March, a beautiful sunny day, everything seemed as placid as a village Sabbath. That morning the newspapers announced decrees by the United States Circuit Courts in the first, second, fifth, seventh, and thirteenth districts, according to the redistricting of 1952, annulling the presidential election on the grounds of bribery and fraud. There was further news of equal importance: indictments had been found in some forty courts all over the country, state and national, against thirty-three senators and three hundred and forty-seven representatives, all of the Schmidt faction. Besides this the so-called " New York conspirators " had been rearrested, as their bail suddenly declined further responsibility, and had been carried forcibly and secretly to New York. The commotion was immense; the President tried to summon soldiers to the capital, but the railroad companies in most cases refused to let their cars be used, and ran their locomotives out of reach of seizure. On the next day it was announced that the United States Circuit Court in Arizona had tried and convicted Hugo Schmidt, President-elect, for a violation of the election laws. His notices of the charge and summons to attend his trial had come by radiograph at eight o'clock the night before, and of course he had not paid any heed to them. The Schmidts, on their side, hurried on preparations for the inauguration. They had provided for great ecclesiastical processions, as part of their strength lay in their religious pose, and they evidently relied on the presence of the clergy to help maintain order. Large forces of the President's guard, as the National Constabulary was called, were under arms day and night. On the morning of the 4th of March Washington was crowded; never had the city worn such a gala aspect. Blue and red, the Schmidt colors, floated under the stars and stripes from every flagpole, and the troops of constables and the uniformed bands of employees of the great trusts all displayed blue

and red. Among the ladies, however, green
and white, the Campbell colors, were as frequent as the blue and red, and the contrast
made a very gay and splendid sight as the
carriages moved slowly down the new boule-
vard. Down to the 100-yard vertical line the
air was full of dirigibles, brave in flags and
pennants. It was remarked that several regiments from Arizona had secured positions
near the Capitol, and that the uniformed
bands of the Copper Syndicate, of the Great
Central Railroad, of the Farmers' Union, of
the Coal Trust, of the Compressed Air Trust,
and of the Combined Radiograph Company,
the most powerful corporations in the world,
all largely owned by the capitalists of the
Campbell faction, occupied the approaches to
the Capitol; they, however, all showed the
blue and red colors. Afterwards it was learned
that they had taken their stations at midnight. By half-past eleven the President-elect
and his party came to the steps of the Capitol
amid tumultuous cheering. Campbell and a
group of senators were close behind him, so
that it was difficult to say whether the cheers
were all meant for the President or not. The
great bells of the New Belfry rang out; the

vast crowd became wonderfully still, it seemed to have fallen asleep. The Chief Justice of the Supreme Court, in his robes, stepped out bareheaded into the vacant space at the top of the steps, and, picking up a copy of the Constitution from the gold table, in a clear, ringing voice bade the President-elect step forward and take the official oath. Hugo Schmidt stepped forth, but one of the Campbell senators pushed by, and, pressing to the Chief Justice, handed him a sealed document. The crowd was as still as death; the breaking of the seal was distinctly heard fifty yards away. The Chief Justice glanced at the document, read it over carefully, and then said deliberately, in his most resonant tones: "The ceremony cannot proceed. I am enjoined by the Circuit Court of this district from administering the oath, on the ground that Hugo Schmidt, alleged President-elect, procured his alleged election by fraud and bribery." The elder Schmidt, turning to Campbell, cried out: "This is your dirty trick!" Then, facing the Chief Justice, he said: "As President of the United States I command you to administer the oath to my successor." The Chief Justice replied: "In

this country not even the President is above
the law. I am enjoined. I cannot administer
the oath." A great cheer burst forth from
every side, and green and white cockades
suddenly replaced blue and red down all the
lines of uniformed bands and of the Arizona
regiments. The elder Schmidt glanced over
the multitude, and whispered to his son: " If
there is no election, the choice of President
falls on Congress under the law of 1936."
" Ay," answered Campbell, " Congress must
elect." Cries of " Congress ! " and " To the
House ! To the Senate Chamber ! " rose on
all sides. There was great confusion. Senators
and representatives tried to force their way
into the Capitol ; slowly, one by one, pushing,
shoving, shouting, and swearing, they reached
the chambers, only to find them filled with
armed men, who called themselves special
constables, and would let no man enter without proof satisfactory to themselves that he
was a duly authorized member of Congress.
Outside the crowds knew nothing of what
was going on ; it was impossible to move, the
crush was so dense ; men talked and shouted
and cheered ; women chattered and giggled
and fainted; the uniformed bands and the

Arizona regiments stood firm under arms and let nobody pass except upon a countersign. Hours went by; the multitude became hungry; the crowding became more dangerous; many men were knocked down and injured by exploding automobiles; people flocked in from everywhere, lured by the extraordinary rumors. Accidents became frequent; the constables and soldiers tried to disperse the newcomers and relieve the pressure, but with no success. Five thousand and eighty people were killed or seriously injured. At four o'clock the great bells of the New Belfry rang out; under the stars and stripes on the Capitol a great green and white banner was displayed. The two Houses had chosen Campbell President. It appeared that there was a majority of the two Houses present, but, owing to the previous arrests of some supporters of the administration, and the inability of others to prove their identity to the guardians of the two chambers, the Campbell men outnumbered their opponents more than two to one. The election was certified to the Chief Justice, who proceeded to administer the oath to Campbell. There was then a rush for the steps by the blue and red constabulary, but they were in a small minority, and after twenty minutes of a rough and tough fight, peace was sufficiently restored to allow the ceremony to proceed. The streets were then cleared by the Arizona regiments, the two Schmidts were arrested on the charge of levying war against their country, and a proclamation issued that the proceedings had of necessity been somewhat unusual, if not, strictly speaking, irregular, but that every question would be submitted to the courts, and that the newly elected President would spare not even his life in the preservation of the Constitution.

The next few weeks were comparatively calm, except in New York, where the only acts of violence were committed. Nothing has astonished foreigners more than that these great political events took place, not only without civil war, but practically without any bloodshed. The truth is that Americans have always had an immense love of law and order, and are immensely proud of their Constitution, which has been a guide and stay in all troublous times, and yet has proved itself sufficiently elastic to suit the empire as well as the republic. This elasticity of the Constitution is mainly due, not to the forefathers who framed it, but to those greater interpreters of the last century who have realized that law is founded upon policy, and that policy must keep watchful eye upon the material prosperity of the citizens of this noble country, the freest, the most just, the most spiritual, the most beautiful fabric of civilization ever known.

In New York the governor was shot from a window as he was driving down the street; the lieutenant-governor who succeeded him was a Schmidt man, and immediately reversed his predecessor's policy. He released the "New York conspirators," ordered out the militia, refused to acknowledge Campbell's election, attempted to draw Connecticut, New Jersey, and Pennsylvania into a league for the recovery of state rights; but the country showed such plain signs of acquiescence in Campbell's election that the revolt smouldered and died out. Business revived; everybody believed in the Midas touch of that remarkable man; he immediately made friendly overtures to the European nations, dispatched special envoys to every South American state, asking it to make known any grievances and promising immediate redress. He courted property owners by holding levees open to all whose incomes exceeded a million dollars a year; he offered state aid to multitudinous corporations; he repressed an extensive strike among the laborers of the Combined Radiograph Company on the ground that it interfered with the public utilities of transportation and light, and more and more strengthened the rights of property against the proletariat. He pardoned the Schmidts, who were found guilty of high treason, and rewarded his enemies as well as his friends with positions in high places; it was remarked afterwards that most of his enemies were not confirmed by the Senate, but the nominations helped to break down all immediate opposition.

The next steps were, to reduce meetings of the House from a session every year to one every third year, then every fifth year, while the Senate sat permanently; to regulate the calendar of the Supreme Court in such a way that no causes should be heard except on permission received from the Secretary of the Interior; to limit by law the

right of election to the Senate to persons
who should produce a certificate signed by
the chairman of the Republican National
Committee. Each of these measures was
approved by a judgment of the Supreme
Court. The last step was begun by the
Attorney-General, who filed a bill in the
Supreme Court temporarily to enjoin the
meeting of both Houses; the case was elaborately argued, and the President invited all
bar associations throughout the country to
file briefs on either side. The Court decided
that the President's obligation "to preserve,
support, and defend the Constitution of the
United States" was, in the intention of the
contracting states, paramount to all other
provisions, and that if in his judgment it
became necessary to act alone in order to
fulfill that duty laid upon him, then it became his duty to certify that fact to his
attorney-general, who in his turn should
file a bill setting forth that fact, and there-
upon the Court had no choice but to enforce
the Constitution and enjoin the Senate and
House, not only from taking any action, but
even from meeting.

Since then, however, both Senate and

House have met regularly. They have authorized stock transactions in each chamber, and the principal business of the country is now transacted there. The President has assumed the titles of Lord Suzerain of South America, High Protector of China, Chief Ruler of the Pacific Archipelago, and has established the Orders of George, of Abraham, of Ulysses, and of William, in honor of Washington, Lincoln, Grant, and McKinley; the members are appointed by him after an examination and sworn inventory of their private fortunes. President Campbell was renominated and reëlected every four years; and since his death his son has succeeded to the party nomination. "The Constitution," as some famous lawyer says, "is like the skin of a great animal, that stretches, expands, and grows with its growth."

# THE CURIOUS REPUBLIC OF GONDOUR

[ Mark Twain ]

## THE CURIOUS REPUBLIC OF GONDOUR.

As soon as I had learned to speak the language a little, I became greatly interested in the people and the system of government.

I found that the nation had at first tried universal suffrage pure and simple, but had thrown that form aside because the result was not satisfactory. It had seemed to deliver all power into the hands of the ignorant and non-taxpaying classes; and of a necessity the responsible offices were filled from these classes also.

A remedy was sought. The people believed they had found it; not in the destruction of universal suffrage, but in the enlargement of it. It was an odd idea, and ingenious. You must understand, the constitution gave every man a vote; therefore that vote was a vested right, and could not be taken away. But the constitution did not say that certain individuals might not be given two votes, or ten! So an amendatory clause was inserted in a quiet way; a clause which authorized the enlargement of the suffrage in certain cases to be specified by statute. To offer to " limit " the suffrage might have made instant trouble; the offer to " enlarge " it had a pleasant aspect. But of course the newspapers soon began to suspect; and then out they came! It was found, however, that for once, — and for the first time in the history of the republic, — property, character, and intellect were able to wield a political influence; for once, money, virtue, and intelligence took a vital and a united interest in a political question. For once these powers went to the " primaries " in strong force; for once the best men in the nation were put forward as candidates for that parliament whose business it should be to enlarge the suffrage. The weightiest half of the press quickly joined forces with the new movement, and left the other half to rail about the proposed " destruction of the liberties " of the bottom layer of society, the hitherto governing class of the community.

The victory was complete. The new law was framed and passed. Under it every citizen, howsoever poor or ignorant, possessed one vote, so universal suffrage still reigned; but if a man possessed a good common-school education and no money, he had two votes; a high-school education gave him four; if he had property likewise, to the value of three thousand *sacos*, he wielded one more vote; for every fifty thousand sacos a man added to his property, he was entitled to another vote; a university education entitled a man to nine votes, even though he owned no property. Therefore, learning being more prevalent and more easily acquired than riches, educated men became a wholesome check upon wealthy men, since they could outvote them. Learning goes usually with uprightness, broad views, and humanity; so the learned voters, possessing the balance of power, became the vigilant and efficient protectors of the great lower rank of society.

And now a curious thing developed itself — a sort of emulation, whose object was voting-power! Whereas formerly a man was honored only according to the amount of money he possessed, his grandeur was measured now by the number of votes he wielded. A man with only one vote was conspicuously respectful to his neighbor who possessed three. And if he was a man above the commonplace, he was as conspicuously energetic in his determination to acquire three for himself. This spirit of emulation invaded all ranks. Votes based upon capital were commonly called " mortal " votes, because they could be lost; those based upon learning were called " immortal," because they were permanent, and because of their customarily imperishable character they were naturally more valued than the other sort. I say " customarily " for the reason that these votes were not absolutely imperishable, since insanity could suspend them.

Under this system, gambling and speculation almost ceased in the republic. A man honored as the possessor of great voting-power could not afford to risk the loss of it upon a doubtful chance.

It was curious to observe the manners and customs which the enlargement plan produced. Walking the street with a friend one day, he delivered a careless bow to a passer-by, and then remarked that that person possessed only one vote and would probably never earn another; he was more respectful to the next acquaintance he met; he explained that this salute was a four-vote bow. I tried to "average" the importance of the people he accosted after that, by the nature of his bows, but my success was only partial, because of the somewhat greater homage paid to the immortals than to the mortals. My friend explained. He said there was no law to regulate this thing, except that most powerful of all laws, custom. Custom had created these varying bows, and in time they had become easy and natural. At this moment he delivered himself of a very profound salute, and then said, "Now there's a man who began life as a shoemaker's apprentice, and without education; now he swings twenty-two mortal votes and two immortal ones; he expects to pass a high-school examination this year and climb a couple of votes higher among the immortals; mighty valuable citizen."

By and by my friend met a venerable personage, and not only made him a most elaborate bow, but also took off his hat. I took off mine, too, with a mysterious awe. I was beginning to be infected.

"What grandee is that?"

"That is our most illustrious astronomer. He has n't any money, but is fearfully learned. Nine immortals is *his* political weight! He would swing a hundred and fifty votes if our system were perfect."

"Is there any altitude of mere moneyed grandeur that you take off your hat to?"

"No. Nine immortal votes is the only power we uncover for — that is, in civil life. Very great officials receive that mark of homage, of course."

It was common to hear people admiringly mention men who had begun life on the lower levels and in time achieved great voting-power. It was also common to hear youths planning a future of ever so many votes for themselves. I heard shrewd mammas speak of certain young men as good "catches" because they possessed such-and-such a number of votes. I knew of more than one case where an heiress was married to a youngster who had but one vote; the argument being that he was gifted with such excellent parts that in time he would acquire a good voting strength, and perhaps in the long run be able to outvote his wife, if he had luck.

Competitive examinations were the rule in all official grades. I remarked that the questions asked the candidates were wild, intricate, and often required a sort of knowledge not needed in the office sought.

"Can a fool or an ignoramus answer them?" asked the person I was talking with.

"Certainly not."

"Well, you will not find any fools or ignoramuses among our officials."

I felt rather cornered, but made shift to say, —

"But these questions cover a good deal more ground than is necessary."

"No matter; if candidates can answer these it is tolerably fair evidence that they can answer nearly any other question you choose to ask them."

There were some things in Gondour which one could not shut his eyes to. One was, that ignorance and incompetence had no place in the government. Brains and property managed the state. A candidate for office must have marked ability, education, and high character, or he stood no sort of chance of election. If a hod-carrier possessed these, he could succeed; but the mere fact that he was a hod-carrier could not elect him, as in previous times.

It was now a very great honor to be in

the parliament or in office; under the old system such distinction had only brought suspicion upon a man and made him a helpless mark for newspaper contempt and scurrility. Officials did not need to steal now, their salaries being vast in comparison with the pittances paid in the days when parliaments were created by hod-carriers, who viewed official salaries from a hod-carrying point of view and compelled that view to be respected by their obsequious servants. Justice was wisely and rigidly administered; for a judge, after once reaching his place through the specified line of promotions, was a permanency during good behavior. He was not obliged to modify his judgments according to the effect they might have upon the temper of a reigning political party.

The country was mainly governed by a ministry which went out with the administration that created it. This was also the case with the chiefs of the great departments. Minor officials ascended to their several positions through well-earned promotions, and not by a jump from gin-mills or the needy families and friends of members of parliament. Good behavior measured their terms of office.

The head of the government, the Grand Caliph, was elected for a term of twenty years. I questioned the wisdom of this. I was answered that he could do no harm, since the ministry and the parliament governed the land, and he was liable to impeachment for misconduct. This great office had twice been ably filled by women, women as aptly fitted for it as some of the sceptred queens of history. Members of the cabinet, under many administrations, had been women.

I found that the pardoning power was lodged in a court of pardons, consisting of several great judges. Under the old *régime*, this important power was vested in a single official, and he usually took care to have a general jail delivery in time for the next election.

I inquired about public schools. There were plenty of them, and of free colleges too. I inquired about compulsory education. This was received with a smile, and the remark, —

" When a man's child is able to make himself powerful and honored according to the amount of education he acquires, don't you suppose that that parent will apply the compulsion himself? Our free schools and free colleges require no law to fill them."

There was a loving pride of country about this person's way of speaking which annoyed me. I had long been unused to the sound of it in my own. The Gondour national airs were forever dinning in my ears; therefore I was glad to leave that country and come back to my dear native land, where one never hears that sort of music.

# Utopian Literature

AN ARNO PRESS/NEW YORK TIMES COLLECTION

Adams, Frederick Upham.
**President John Smith;** The Story of a Peaceful Revolution.
1897.

Bird, Arthur.
**Looking Forward:** A Dream of the United States of the
Americas in 1999. 1899.

[Blanchard, Calvin.]
**The Art of Real Pleasure.** 1864.

Brinsmade, Herman Hine.
**Utopia Achieved:** A Novel of the Future. 1912.

Caryl, Charles W.
**New Era.** 1897.

Chavannes, Albert.
**The Future Commonwealth.** 1892.

Child, William Stanley.
**The Legal Revolution of 1902.** 1898.

Collens, T. Wharton.
**Eden of Labor;** or, The Christian Utopia. 1876.

Cowan, James.
**Daybreak.** A Romance of an Old World. 1896. 2nd ed.

Craig, Alexander.
**Ionia;** Land of Wise Men and Fair Women. 1898.

Daniel, Charles S.
**AI: A Social Vision.** 1892.

Devinne, Paul.
**The Day of Prosperity:** A Vision of the Century to Come.
1902.

Edson, Milan C.
**Solaris Farm.** 1900.

Fuller, Alvarado M.
**A. D. 2000.** 1890.

Geissler, Ludwig A.
**Looking Beyond.** 1891.

Hale, Edward Everett.
**How They Lived in Hampton.** 1888.

Hale, Edward Everett.
**Sybaris and Other Homes.** 1869.

Harris, W. S.
**Life in a Thousand Worlds.** 1905.

Henry, W. O.
**Equitania.** 1914.

Hicks, Granville, with Richard M. Bennett.
**The First to Awaken.** 1940.

Lewis, Arthur O., editor
**American Utopias:** Selected Short Fiction. 1790–1954.

McGrady, Thomas.
**Beyond the Black Ocean.** 1901.

Mendes H. Pereira.
**Looking Ahead.** 1899.

Michaelis, Richard.
**Looking Further Forward.** An Answer to
  *Looking Backward* by Edward Bellamy. 1890.

Moore, David A.
**The Age of Progress.** 1856.

Noto, Cosimo.
**The Ideal City.** 1903.

Olerich, Henry.
**A Cityless and Countryless World.** 1893.

Parry, David M.
**The Scarlet Empire.** 1906.

Peck, Bradford.
**The World a Department Store.** 1900.

Reitmeister, Louis Aaron.
**If Tomorrow Comes.** 1934.

Roberts, J. W.
**Looking Within.** 1893.

Rosewater, Frank.
**'96; A Romance of Utopia.** 1894.

Satterlee, W. W.
**Looking Backward and What I Saw.** 2nd ed. 1890.

Schindler, Solomon.
**Young West;** A Sequel to Edward Bellamy's Celebrated
   Novel "Looking Backward." 1894.

Smith, Titus K.
**Altruria.** 1895.

Steere, C. A.
**When Things Were Doing.** 1908.

Taylor, William Alexander.
**Intermere.** 1901.

Thiusen, Ismar.
**The Diothas,** or, A Far Look Ahead. 1883.

Vinton, Arthur Dudley.
**Looking Further Backward.** 1890.

Wooldridge, C. W.
**Perfecting the Earth.** 1902.

Wright, Austin Tappan.
**Islandia.** 1942.